THREADS OF DESTINY

THE VEILGUARD SAGA

1

TRAVIS STARNES

Threads of Destiny

The Veilguard Saga, Book I

ISBN 978-1-960747-12-9

Maps available at

https://tstarnes.com/book-series/shattered-lands/

Signup to get free previews of upcoming books before they're released at

http://tstarnes.com/preview-notification-newsletter/

Table of Contents

The Secrets of the Forest

"Osric? Osric! Damn you, boy, answer me!"

Osric hurried out from the small back room, nearly tripping over his own feet in his haste.

"Sorry, Master Ironhand," he said, skidding to a halt by the forge.

The burly blacksmith turned from the anvil he had been hammering at and scowled at his young apprentice. Though not an unusually tall man, Ironhand had a presence that could fill up a room. His powerful frame spoke of decades spent shaping metal. For all his size, Osric knew him to be an incredibly gentle and caring man, underneath the gruff exterior.

"Sleeping on the job again?" Ironhand rumbled, wiping sweat from his brow with the back of one meaty hand. "I told you I needed that new stove casing shaped by lunchtime. Edar is expecting his new stove this afternoon, and I'll be damned if it isn't ready."

"No, not sleeping, Master Ironhand. Just fetching some materials from the storeroom. I must have lost track of time."

"See that it doesn't happen again. A blacksmith without discipline is no better than a drunken fool."

Osric ducked his head, abashed. "Yes, Master Ironhand."

As he picked up the tongs and began working the first iron strip into shape over the forge's glowing coals, Osric could feel Ironhand's eyes still lingering on him for a few moments before the blacksmith turned back to his own task.

Truth be told, while he had gone to the storeroom for supplies, he'd taken longer than was really needed.

It was the height of summer, and this close to the forge there were times it felt like his skin might boil off. The small storeroom, which doubled as Osric's sleeping quarters, might not be all that much cooler, but as the sun started to climb in the sky, he'd take it over the forge.

Besides, it wasn't like it mattered. Yes, Edar needed the new stove, but Osric knew for a fact he ate at the tavern half the time anyway, and it wasn't like he needed it for warmth. A few hours here or there wasn't going to kill anyone. Nothing around here was worth getting that excited about.

Life in Eldham was so uneventfully mundane. Day after day, it was the same routine, which for Osric was, wake up at dawn, stoke the forge's fires, and spend the daylight hours pounding out horseshoes, stove parts, and farm tools.

Osric sighed loudly in spite of himself, prompting Master Ironhand to glance over.

"Something on your mind, boy?" the gruff black-smith asked.

"I was just thinking," Osric said as he brought the hammer down again. "Doesn't it grow tedious just making the same types of things, day in and day out? Horseshoes, stove parts, axes; it's always the same. I saw that sword you made for that Greenwood Ranger last year. If you went to Wolfsridge, you could be one of the greatest smiths in the Crownlands. People would travel for leagues to get one of your fabled blades."

Osric lifted up his tongs and jabbed with it a few times, as if it were a sword he could use to vanquish unseen opponents.

Master Ironhand turned to fully face Osric, his brow furrowed. "Glory and excitement? Is that what you're after? Let me tell you, boy, those things are fleeting. What we do here may not seem glorious, but it's honest work that keeps this village going. A knight's pretty mail won't plow the fields or keep a family warm come winter. Don't underestimate the value of mundane things."

"I know, it's just that … I want more. To test myself against true challenges, to see the wider world beyond the forest. I know, I'm an ingrate who doesn't appreciate how good I have it here."

"No, lad," he said, his expression softening. "Those feelings are only natural for a young man like you. I'll admit to a longing or two when I was your age as well. You know I trained in Wolfsridge."

"You trained in the capital? I didn't know that," Osric said, lowering his tong-shaped sword.

"Aye, I spent nigh on five years there as a young lad," he said, getting a faraway look. "My father sent me to apprentice under the master smith, Enthnor."

"What was it like?" Osric asked eagerly.

Master Ironhand hardly ever talked about his past. As far as Osric knew, he was born with a hammer in one hand, yelling at his mother for taking too long!

"Noisy, crowded, smelly, everything you'd expect of a big city. The capital has ten times the people of Eldham in one of its markets alone. Everyone's in a hurry to get somewhere or to sell you something. You have to keep one hand on your coin purse at all times," he said. "But I'll admit the sights were something. The sprawling markets, the towering castle, the nonstop activity day and night. As a wide-eyed farm boy, it was like another world opened up."

Osric tried to imagine it, a bustling city packed with exotic wares, grand buildings, and opportunity. It sounded like the polar opposite of sleepy little Eldham.

"Is that where you learned to forge a sword like you made for the ranger?" he asked.

Master Ironhand snorted, leaning a hand against the anvil. "No. Swordsmithing is a whole 'nother skill. But I did pick up plenty working under Enthnor. How to shape a sturdy plow or smooth out buckles. The fundamentals."

"Why'd you leave?" Osric blurted out. "If the capital was so amazing, why come to somewhere like Eldham? Why not set up a smithy there?"

"Because cities have a way of swallowing your soul, boy. All that rushing about leaves no time to catch your breath. No stillness, no peace. Out here, we've got clean air, open skies, and good, honest folk."

"Boring folk," Osric muttered under his breath.

"Enough of your grumbling, boy. If you crave adventure so desperately, I'll send you on one. We're almost out of limestone dust. Grab the sack and head into the forest to collect as much as you can. Maybe when you get back, you'll be able to focus on your job and stop daydreaming about adventuring. We're nearly out, and I'll not have a useless grindstone in my smithy. Take your pickaxe and fetch enough to fill a sack. And you better not take your time getting back, or it'll be your hide."

"Yes, Master Ironhand. Right away," Osric said, setting his tongs down and hurrying into the back room.

He gathered his tools and a large empty sack before hurrying out the door, not wanting to further provoke the blacksmith's ire. Walking down the path to the forest, Osric kicked an errant rock. As adventures go, this wasn't exactly what he had in mind. He went to the forest all the time for supplies, or really whenever he annoyed Master Ironhand a little too much.

"And don't stop to talk to Talia," Ironhand called out as Osric left.

Talia Penrose was the assistant and apprentice, of sorts, to Elder Miriam, although what a village elder apprentices someone for, Osric never quite knew. She was also a lot like Osric, in that they'd both been given over by their guardians to be apprenticed. The difference was Osric had lived with his aunt, who shuffled him off to have one less mouth to feed, while

Talia's parents had died in a fire when she was little, and Elder Miriam had taken her in.

Osric liked Talia. She was kind, clever, and maybe one of the nicest people he knew. He enjoyed spending time with her when neither of them had duties, although that was also because there were only a handful of others in their age range that lived in the village proper, and not out in one of the far-flung scratch farms or forest cabins where a lot of the population in this area actually lived. The villagers themselves tended to be much older, closer to Master Ironhand's age, so as two of the few young adults, they had been kind of thrown together out of circumstance as much as anything else.

Osric hadn't been intending to sneak off to see her, though. For one, she had her own duties, and she was much more conscientious about doing those than Osric was about doing his, and because he recognized when Master Ironhand was in a mood, he had no intention of setting him off again.

As he entered the cool shadows of the forest, Osric returned to the story he'd been telling himself, imagining himself as a hero on a quest rather than a lowly apprentice on a chore. His pickaxe became a sword, and the rabbit that ran by a fearsome beast, out for blood.

His adventure only lasted as long as it took to get far enough into the forest to find the special limestone rock that Master Ironhand had shown him, which was part of his secret to making good, strong iron. Then, it was the backbreaking work of prying it out of the ground and smashing it into small enough pieces to fit inside his sack.

One time, he'd asked why they didn't just buy it like they did the iron they bought from the mine, which they had to make a day-long ride to in Tom Sorral's wagon once every month or two. Master Ironhand had told him that this stone, which they crushed and melted into the slag, wasn't found in the mines. As far as his master knew, their forest was the only place to find it. It was also why Master Ironhand's wares were some of the best around.

Setting the nearly full bag down by a stream, Osric knelt down and splashed cool water on his face.

"Some adventure this is," he muttered to himself.

After a few more moments of brooding, Osric stood and picked up his tools. It didn't take long to locate another decent chunk of limestone to chip away at.

Osric wedged his pickaxe into a crevice in the limestone and pushed down with all his weight. The rock slowly shifted and cracked, with a few pieces breaking loose. He crouched down and brushed away the debris, then inserted the bar again for another attempt. As he strained against the unyielding stone, his mind wandered once more.

What would it be like to be one of those adventurers from the tales, boldly venturing into the unknown? Slaying vile monsters, rescuing fair maidens, uncovering treasures beyond imagination? Osric was jolted out of his daydream as the rock suddenly gave way and lurched to the side.

"Finally," he muttered, bending down to inspect the now-exposed cavity.

He froze as his eyes fell upon something within the crevice that glinted in the dappled sunlight. Gingerly reaching in, Osric extracted an intricately engraved metal ring, stunned by its craftsmanship. It somehow looked old. Ancient, even. Yet, it was polished to an almost bright finish. A delicate and highly detailed image sat in the middle, where a gem would otherwise go, depicting some kind of bird in flight, a sword in its talons, and a wreath or halo on its head. Osric wasn't an expert, but the workmanship was exquisite. He knew what this was, or at least, what it might be.

He'd seen the scribe who sometimes came through town with the tax collectors with a ring something like this. A ring with a pattern, in that case that of the king, set in the middle. Osric had once watched as he talked to Master Ironhand, and when they finished, the scribe wrote out a long document for him. Although Osric knew his letters, he hadn't paid much attention to the document. He had, however, noticed when the scribe rolled up the document and poured some wax into the seam to seal it, and then pressed that ring into the wax, leaving behind an impression of the symbol of the king. It had struck Osric then because it had seemed important, formal.

This ring was similar to the scribe's ring, but ... more. The detail on this ring put the scribe's to shame, but it looked as if the purpose was the same. The head of the ring wasn't all that was fancy and impressive. The scribe's had been smooth metal aside from the king's symbol on the top, but this one was detailed across the band of the ring as well, including four tiny blood-red gems just down from the symbol in the middle. Low enough that they would not leave their impression, or at least not obscure the impression of the bird, if it was pressed into wax, but still surrounding it.

Osric reached to pick the small piece of jewelry up and thought for a moment that the gems around the face of the ring almost glowed as his fingers touched it, giving an almost pulsing sensation. It lasted for an instant before the feeling was gone, but Osric knew what he felt. Magic.

He didn't really understand magic, although he knew that it was used by mages and sorcerers featured in many of the stories he'd heard or read. He didn't know why, but it was the first thing Osric thought of as he touched the ring and saw that pulse. It felt … otherworldly, and special.

After a moment's hesitation, Osric carefully picked the ring up. Holding it flat in his palm, he examined it closely, slowly turning the cool metal over in his hand. Although it was clearly very old, it showed no sign of corrosion. Looking into those small gems, they still seemed to have an ethereal glow. As he gazed upon it, Osric felt an inexplicable connection to the artifact. It felt like more than just a ring. It felt ... important.

It was both exhilarating and like the treasure he'd been dreaming of, only it was real. Looking around, as if someone was going to yell at him any moment to put it back or call him a thief, Osric slid the ring into his pocket. The forest was quiet. He hadn't been paying that much attention before, but Osric thought maybe it was quieter than it had been before. Not eerily silent, there were still far-off noises, but ... it didn't feel as peaceful as before.

Osric checked his bag. He'd collected enough stone for Master Ironhand. Maybe not as much as he'd originally intended; but enough, all the same. What he knew was that he didn't want to stay in the forest any longer. He could feel the ring in his pocket, unnaturally heavy, weighing him down.

He didn't want to be out here on his own anymore, but he also didn't want to put the ring back.

Besides, he wanted to know more about it, and he knew who to ask. Returning to the village, Osric stopped by the forge to drop off the stone he had collected. Thankfully, Master Ironhand wasn't anywhere to be seen. It was already late in the day, which meant Master Ironhand had most likely gone to the inn, as he normally did. Collecting the stones had been Osric's only real duty for the day, so he unloaded his limestone, and hurried away. Yes, his life might be easier tomorrow if he started work on the new order of brackets for Farmer Dolan's new wagon, but he had a mission now, and he wasn't going to be deterred.

Leaving the smithy, Osric headed to the center of the village, toward the longhouse that sat at its heart. It was the place where the villagers met and partied, where their elders governed and people were married; it was the business part of Eldham. The elders had their own homes, but at this time of day, he knew that Elder Miriam would be there. She was always sitting outside on a small bench, a book in her lap, alternating between reading and watching the people go about their day.

Osric had always been amazed by Elder Miriam. She seemed to have an infinite store of knowledge, and she was as kind as she was wise. She'd always been nice to Osric when he was small, and he still felt a warm place in his heart when he thought of her. Of course, she was nice to everyone, but Osric liked to think that maybe she was a little extra nice to him.

She was, indeed, sitting on her bench, reading, when Osric got to the longhouse. Her silver hair was tucked tight against the back of her neck, as always, probably to keep it from getting in the way of her reading, Osric thought. She seemed to sense him approaching and looked up as he did. Although he'd come to talk to her many times in the past, she somehow realized today was different the moment her gaze hit him. He could see it in her eyes, the way the corners crinkled as they narrowed, like a hawk considering a mouse.

"You had a busy day in the forest?" she asked.

While it wasn't unusual for Osric to make trips into the forest to collect things for Master Ironhand, he was surprised that she knew that's where he had been all the same.

"I found something," Osric said in almost a whisper, leaning closer to her, concerned that someone else might overhear about his unusual treasure.

Elder Miriam raised her eyebrows, the lines on her face deepening with curiosity. Closing her book, she beckoned Osric to sit beside her.

"The forest often holds secrets, Osric, but they're not often shared lightly," she said, her voice a soft blend of intrigue and compassion. "Show me what it has given to you."

As Osric sat down, he hesitantly reached into his pocket. His hand trembled slightly as he carefully drew the ring out, presenting it to her on his outstretched palm. Here, in the sun, the ring's detailed craftsmanship stood out even more than it had in the shade of the forest. Elder Miriam's eyes widened slightly as she saw the ring, a mixture of recognition and surprise flickering over her face. She extended a delicate, aged hand towards the artifact, her fingers hovering over it, stopping as if sensing the energy it radiated.

"This is no ordinary trinket, Osric," she murmured, her voice barely above a whisper. "There is an aura around it, an energy that feels ancient, arcane. Where did you find this?"

Osric didn't answer right away. A farmer, someone he had known for years, started to walk past, causing Osric to close his fingers around the ring, hiding it from view. Elder Miriam looked around for the first time since the ring appeared, seeming to notice that there were people around them going about their business on the warm summer afternoon.

"Yes," she said, almost to herself as well as to Osric. "Yes. Come, let's discuss this further in my cottage, away from curious ears."

She stood up from the bench, a steadying hand on Osric's shoulder, and began to walk towards her residence. It wasn't far, barely a stone's throw from the longhouse, as befit her status as a village elder. Even with her importance, Eldham was still a very small village, and her cottage mirrored that fact. A quaint two-room structure with a nice garden outside, although Osric knew her neighbors and friends tended to that more than Miriam did these days. At her age, spending time kneeling in the dirt, tending to it, was a bit more than her frail body could handle.

As they walked the village's everyday sounds faded into a hushed backdrop. He was focused on the ring in his hand, which felt heavier than anything so small had a right to be. He felt as if everyone around them could see it, no matter how tightly he clenched his fist around the metal. It felt as if they could sense its presence, the foreignness of it. He was glad to follow her into her cottage and shut the rest of the world out, away from them. Elder Miriam's cottage felt like a safe haven, a place free from the prying eyes of the village.

As Miriam opened the door, Talia, who was tidying up books and scrolls when they walked in, looked up suddenly, a surprised expression on her face as Osric walked in behind Miriam. She had probably not expected Miriam home so soon, since she usually stayed by the longhouse until near dark, and almost certainly didn't expect Osric, who'd normally still be at Master Ironhand's shop.

Closing the door behind them, Elder Miriam gestured for Osric to take a seat at the small table.

"Osric! What brings you here at this hour?" Talia asked, smiling in a way that made Osric temporarily forget why he had come.

"I found something ..." Osric started.

"Talia, would you be a dear and put on some tea?" Miriam interjected, cutting Osric off.

"Yes, Elder," Talia said, setting about preparing the tea while Miriam cleared space on the table.

Osric opened his hand and carefully set the ring on the table. As she brought the tea, Osric could see Talia trying to peek at what he and Elder Miriam were looking at, clearly interested.

"This craftsmanship is ancient, and these markings," she said, pointing to the detailed bird with the sword and halo, "they are not any I've seen before. I have a faint memory… no, I can't recall, but I know this symbol is old. I can *feel* the energy rolling off it. There is powerful magic here. Powerful."

Shaking a thought away, she pointed at one of the open chairs and said, "Talia, come assist me."

Talia didn't bother to sit, moving quickly to stand beside Miriam, looking down at the ring before the elder could even finish her sentence. Sitting back,

Elder Miriam's hands began to move with purpose above the ring. Her fingers traced through the air, forming complex gestures as she began to weave her magic. The ring responded to her motions, emitting a soft blue glow that intensified with each pass of her hands.

After a moment, much to Osric's surprise, Talia began the same motions, mimicking the Elder, but maybe in reverse. It was hard to tell as he looked from their hands, to their concentrating faces, and back to the ring. It was too much for Osric to take in all at once.

Suddenly, a thin tendril of blue magic extended from the ring, reaching towards Osric and lightly brushing against him.

"This ring," Miriam said, her voice filled with a mixture of awe and seriousness, "is not just old and powerful; it is connected to you. There's a bond present such as I've never seen before. This is far outside of my understanding or anything I've read about."

Osric, taken aback, could only stare in stunned silence. Everyone knew how wise and knowledgeable Elder Miriam was, so it shouldn't have come as a shock to learn that she could weave magic. And Talia too! Miriam didn't even tell her what to do. She just watched what the Elder did with her hands and knew what to do, their combined motions, or power, or whatever, causing the sudden light to appear.

Talia caught Osric staring at her open-mouthed and blushed a little but remained completely focused on her motions, her delicate fingers never stopping their fluid contortions.

His moment of wonder was marred by what the elder had said. Why was it tied to him, and how could someone as wise as Elder Miriam not only not know what it was but say it was outside of her experience? The words filled Osric with dread and gave him far more questions than answers.

Miriam stopped her motions, with Talia following suit a moment later. The blue tendril dissipated as the glow from the ring slowly faded. The Elder looked at Osric, her expression a mix of concern and fascination.

"You must be careful, Osric. A bond like this is rare and can attract unwelcome attention. This ring holds secrets, perhaps even dangers, that we don't yet understand."

Osric nodded, resisting the urge to swallow hard, and asked, "What should I do with it?"

For a moment, she didn't reply, only leaned back in her chair, watching him through the flickering candlelight.

"For now, keep it safe and hidden," she advised solemnly. "There are people who would do terrible things to possess an artifact as old and powerful as this. We must learn more about this ring and its origins. Until we do, and can figure out a way to disconnect it from you, I'm not sure how much danger getting rid of it or losing it might cause you.

These kinds of connections can be powerful and could potentially cause you great harm.”

“So I just... keep it?” Osric asked, a little panicked at what she meant by ‘great harm.’

“Talia and I will research in my books. There may be something in the histories that can tell us what this is. But until we know more, you must tread carefully, Osric. Such items can change the course of lives, and not always for the better.”

Stunned by all of this, Osric carefully picked up the ring, feeling the cool metal against his skin. He could almost sense the pulsing energy that Elder Miriam had mentioned and feel that tendril still reaching out to him. Slipping the ring back into his pocket, he stood up and bowed awkwardly toward her.

“I ... um ... thank you, Elder Miriam.”

“No, thank you, Osric. Life is so quiet here that sometimes I forget how exciting the world can be, with ...” she said, trailing off, not finishing the thought. "Never mind. You go. I'm sure Master Iron-hand will have much for you to do in the morning."

Osric nodded, still feeling shaken by everything that had just happened, and headed for the door. As he stepped outside, Talia gently caught his arm, stopping him in the doorway.

"Osric, wait," she said softly, looking left and right to see if they were alone as he turned to face her.

"Try not to worry," Talia said. "Elder Miriam is the wisest person I know. If anyone can uncover the secrets of that ring, she can."

Osric gave her a small, grateful smile. "I know. It's just ... a lot to take in."

He wanted to ask her about her knowing magic, about what just happened and what she did, but he didn't dare. Not out here in the open knowing that both she and Elder Miriam had kept their abilities secret. Besides, he'd had about enough revelations for one night. He didn't think he could take any more. Talia stepped closer and squeezed his arm reassuringly. He could feel the heat of her body as she brushed against him.

"We'll figure this out," she said. "I promise. I won't let anything happen to you."

Her words sent a rush of warmth through Osric. He reached up and briefly clasped her hand with his own.

"Thank you, Talia," he said quietly. "Good night."

CHAPTER 2

A Stranger's Interest

After the excitement of finding the ring and his discussion with Elder Miriam, life returned more or less to normal. It had been nearly a month since he found the ring in the forest, and yet it was as if his life hadn't changed at all. He was still here, working the forge, occasionally missing a step and getting yelled at by Master Ironhand, and he still slept in the small storage room behind the forge.

And yet, in other ways, it had changed completely. He was more distracted, for sure. Master Ironhand was forced to correct him much more regularly, to the point where he even contemplated sending him to a nearby village that had a healer, fearing Osric had somehow fallen ill. Osric had convinced his master that wasn't the case, but it had been a close thing.

He knew why he was having so much trouble focusing, of course. He could feel the reason lying heavy under his shirt. Each evening, when work was done, Osric would hurry to Elder Miriam's cottage, asking if she'd found anything, and every evening, he'd been sent away, disappointed. Last week, she'd told him she'd all but exhausted her own materials, but that that wasn't the end. She'd reached out to friends in Wolfsridge, the baronial capital, asking for their help in the search. Those assurances had also come with not-too-subtle hints that perhaps Osric should stop checking every night. She promised to let him know the very moment she heard anything.

He hadn't been back since then. Not that he distrusted her, he just found the wait unbearable, and desperately wanted answers. Absently, Osric's fingers clasped the ring that hung from a chain beneath his tunic. Its etched band was warm against his skin. Over the passing weeks, he swore he'd felt it stir subtly ... but decided it was just his imagination, fueled by his restlessness.

Osric barely saw Master Ironhand in time to refocus on his work. Ironhand stopped and inspected the glowing shoe Osric had on the anvil in front of him.

"Well struck, lad. See, if you just focus on your work, you do fine," he must have seen the look on Osric's face, because he paused and said, "Go on then, get going. Try to relax; shake off whatever has you so preoccupied. I want you back in the morning, focused and ready to do an honest day's work."

"Yes, Master Ironhand. Thank you," Osric said, ducking his head in appreciation as he cleaned up his work area.

In ten minutes, he had everything put away and the forge cooling for the night. Like he had all week, he stepped out of Master Ironhand's shop and stopped in the doorway, looking one way toward the center of town and Elder Miriam, and then the other toward the tavern where he would find dinner and a cold drink before returning to sleep on his pallet in the storage room.

He looked back toward the city center, thinking hard. It wasn't just finding out about the ring, although that was certainly part of the pull toward the town center. He also wanted to talk to Talia. Ever since that night, the Elder had kept her apprentice Talia close at hand.

He wanted to ask her about the magic he'd seen that night. Not only what they had done to make the light appear, but how she even knew magic. They had talked so many times and not once did she let it slip. He couldn't imagine keeping something like that a secret.

Or maybe he could, he thought, his hand going again to the ring hanging around his neck. It wasn't really an option, though. The Elder was keeping her locked away, limited to quick trips here or there to retrieve things, on purpose, and she'd made it clear she wanted fewer visits from Osric.

Sighing, he turned towards the tavern. As with every night, the tavern was a hive of activity as people came and went, drinking with friends or getting something to eat that they didn't have to make themselves. You could hear the laughter and noise even before you stepped through the door.

Osric entered the familiar warmth of the tavern and nodded greetings to the regulars as he pushed his way through the crowded room, finding an open table. They were a small community, so every face was a familiar face. Some he saw regularly, like the stable master, who always seemed in need of a horseshoe, while others he saw only on rare occasions, like Osbert, who lived far north of town.

He'd just taken his seat and waved for Lily to bring him a drink when he caught the briefest snippet of conversation. It was one of those moments when the sound dies down just enough that a word or phrase can be picked out of a conversation from a nearby table. While that wasn't uncommon, what was said was. He heard the words 'unusual,' 'found,' and 'recently.' Separately, they might not mean much to others, but they sent a shiver down Osric's spine. Turning as subtly as he could, he looked over his shoulder to see who had said the words. The man had a hood pulled up over his head, covering most of his face, making it impossible to see what he looked like. That was also strange. It was warm outside and warmer still in the tavern. Much too warm to have a cloak on, let alone with the hood pulled up. He was talking to three men that Osric knew, none of whom seemed much interested in the stranger.

Osric felt his blood run cold as he stared at the hooded stranger. He knew with sudden, absolute certainty that this man was looking for the ring. How could he have found out about it already? Elder Miriam said she had told no one other than her friend in the capital.

Osric slowly turned back around, his mind racing. The man was making his way from table to table, talking to different groups around the tavern. Finally, he got close enough that Osric caught snippets of his questions.

"Have you ... unusual discovery ...?"

When the villagers shook their heads no, he moved on to the next table, and then the next. Each time, the man was met with confused responses or casual dismissals. As the hooded stranger stood up and moved toward the next table, his hood fell slightly back, revealing a face marked by an impressive scar trailing down one cheek. A face unfamiliar to Osric. The stranger's demeanor seemed urgent, frantic even.

Osric knew he couldn't stay there. The man was getting closer, and would soon be on him, asking him questions. Osric wasn't a strong liar; it just wasn't a skill he'd ever had. If the man asked him questions about the ring, Osric didn't know if he could make him believe he didn't have it.

As Lily came over and set his drink down, Osric set a copper piece on the table and stood up, leaving his drink untouched.

"Don't you want this?" she asked, a confused look on her face.

Osric looked at the man, worried her question would draw attention to him, but the man was still several tables away and didn't seem to be paying attention.

"Uhh, no. I just realized I forgot something. I'll be right back," Osric said, and turned to hurry out of the tavern.

His first steps took him toward home, toward the blacksmith shop, then he thought better of it. The man might ask who the fellow who ran out was. They all knew Osric, knew where he slept. Finding him would be simple. He thought about Elder Miriam, but he couldn't bring this kind of danger to her or Talia.

He settled on a side road that would take him out of town toward the hut where Fergus lived. Fergus was little more than a laborer, hired to do this or that simple job, which was fine for Fergus, who was equally simple. He was also as large as a house and Osric's friend. If anyone could protect him, it was Fergus.

He'd just turned the corner when a figure stepped out from the shadows, blocking his path. It was the hooded stranger from the tavern, his scar seemingly more pronounced in the dim light, his eyes fixed on Osric with serious intent.

"What do you want?" Osric asked, his voice cracking slightly from nerves as he took a small step back, putting some room between him and the stranger.

"I'm looking for something ... unique," he said, his voice low and menacing. "Something recently found in this area. You wouldn't happen to know anything about that, would you?"

Osric could feel the weight of the ring against his chest.

"N... No. I haven't seen anything. Have you asked in the tavern?" Osric said, gesturing vaguely back toward the tavern.

"You're not a very good liar, lad," he said with a cold, almost menacing chuckle. "Now, you can give me what I want, or I can kill you and take it afterward."

To make his point, the man reached down and gripped the hilt of his sword, sliding it an fraction out of its scabbard, allowing the steel to reflect the moonlight and the light from the flickering torches near the much-too-far-away tavern.

Osric lunged forward. His movements, fueled by adrenaline, were more instinctual than skill. He grabbed the man's arms, pinning them to his sides, preventing him from drawing his weapon.

The stranger growled in surprise and anger, wrestling to break free of Osric's grip as they stumbled back against the wall of a nearby hut. Osric gritted his teeth, holding firm despite the man's furious struggles. Terrified, not knowing what to do, but knowing that if the man got loose, he would kill him, Osric reared his head back and then slammed it brutally into the man's face.

There was a sickening crunch as the man's nose broke, blood streaming down his face. He cried out in pain, sagging in Osric's grip. Seizing the moment, Osric released the man and stepped back, unsure what to do next. The man staggered, then steadied himself, his face contorted in fury. Blood dripping from his mangled nose, he reached again for his sword.

Osric had lost. He knew he was a dead man. Unthinking, he reached up and grabbed the ring through his shirt, regret filling him for all the things he hadn't done. As the man drew his sword free, the ring began to glow, an intense crimson light emanating from beneath Osric's tunic. Suddenly, a swirling tongue of magical energy lashed out, engulfing the stranger. He had only a moment for his eyes to go wide in shock before his entire body disintegrated into ash.

Osric stood there, stunned, staring at the pile of ash and the man's fallen sword as the glowing light dimmed and then vanished. Hands shaking, Osric reached down, grabbed the sword, and fled.

He ran through the dark streets, his breath coming in panicked gasps, clutching the ring beneath his tunic. He had killed a man. The stranger had threatened him, reached for his blade with clear, lethal intent, but still ... Osric had taken a life. Was it self-defense when he used the ring's power? He didn't even understand what had happened, only that an intense light had erupted from the ring and engulfed the man.

He couldn't think. Elder Miriam would know what to do. She always had answers.

Osric stumbled to a halt outside her door, chest heaving. He raised a shaking hand to pound on the wood.

"Osric, I'm sorry, but Talia is away on an errand. She doesn't have ..." she said, and then stopped, taking in his panicked state. "Child, what's happened?"

His words tumbled out in a jumbled rush, "A man ... he attacked ... wanted the ring ... there was a light and ... and he turned to ash ..."

"Slow down, slow down," she soothed, guiding him into the cottage and easing him into a seat. "Start from the beginning."

"A man ... he attacked me," Osric said, nearing the verge of panic. "He said he was looking for something unique, an artifact, and he knew I had it. I tried to lie, tell him I didn't, but he knew. He drew his sword and attacked me. We struggled, and I touched the ring and it glowed. It ... I don't know ... it turned him into ash. Just burned him away in the blink of an eye. Right there."

"What you describe, it's a kind of magic I've only ever read about. This is powerful magic. Powerful. And you say the man knew you had it?"

"Yes. I don't know how, but he knew."

"This is dangerous, Osric. If the ring can do what you say, then it is far more dangerous than I thought. Not just to others, but to you as well."

"I know," Osric all but shouted. "What do I do? Do I get rid of it? Throw it away?"

"No, that would be a mistake. If it has truly bonded to you, and someone else finds it, someone who knows how to work its secrets, or even is just talented in the arts of magic, they could use it to find you or even potentially harm you. No, it's much too dangerous to get rid of."

"Then what am I to do?" Osric practically begged.

"I don't know, but things are moving much too fast. Over the last several days, I've heard about unfamiliar faces in town. Strangers. If they are like the man you met, then you are in great danger if you remain here. You must leave Eldham, at least for now. Hide in the forest. Hopefully, in time, the strangers will lose interest."

"But ... this is my home."

Elder Miriam placed a gnarled hand on his shoulder. "I know, child. And it pains me to send you away, but it's for your own safety. Your life is at risk. I can pass the word; have our friends tell anyone who asks that you traveled the road north. These are strangers to our forest, and they don't know the woods like we do. Our forest is large, and it's easy for a person to get lost in it, but you've spent many hours over the years in it, collecting stone for Master Ironhand. You know it as well as most of us. You should be able to go deep into the forest and hide from them. I will give you some food. Stay there for two weeks, and then come back cautiously. Find either myself or Master Ironhand. I will let him know what's happening, and we will keep an eye out for the strangers. If they've left, we will let you know it's safe to return."

Elder Miriam rose stiffly, shuffling to a shelf lined with leather-bound books and curious artifacts. She retrieved a small pouch and continued around her cottage, quickly gathering essential supplies. She added some food and a flask of water to the pouch, and picked up a cloak for warmth before returning to press them into Osric's hands.

The reality of his situation sank in. He had to leave Eldham, the only home he'd ever known.

Osric, clutching the items, looked around the cottage. It was small, but even someone with her status had little, at least not enough to be giving it away to a scared young man.

"Thank you. You've been very kind to me. I know I'm putting you in danger, and I'm sorry."

She waved the words away as if they were an annoyance and said, "Nonsense. I have looked over this village since before you were born and watched you grow from a small child. You are as much my responsibility as you were your parents; may the fates watch over their spirits."

Stepping closer to him, she placed both hands on his shoulders, and her voice turned more serious. "Be vigilant, Osric. Trust your instincts and stay hidden. I will send word if I learn anything."

"I will. Thank you again."

With a final, lingering look at the safety of the Elder's cottage, Osric stepped out into the cool night air. He wrapped the cloak around the sword to further hide it and hurried through the darkened streets, his head swiveling constantly. As he made his way to the forest's edge, the darkness seemed to envelop him, which he hoped was a good thing. With one last look back at his village, his home, Osric stepped into the underbrush.

Chapter 3

Into the Forest

Osric plunged deeper into the forest, pushing himself as fast as he could without breaking his neck by stumbling over a root or a stone. He was still in the section of the forest familiar to him. He'd wandered through this section many times over the years, but that had always been in daylight. Things looked very different when it was pitch-black. Maybe if he had a torch or lantern to guide him, he would recognize his landmarks, but he dared not light anything. Not with those men out there, searching for him.

The darkness only amplified his fears. Every snap of a branch or rustle of a leaf sent his pulse racing, afraid that they'd found him. Osric slowed as more moonlight shone through the tree canopy. He wasn't a woodsman by any stretch of the imagination, but he'd spent enough time in the forest to know that it meant he was coming up to a road.

Moments later, he stepped through the thick underbrush onto one of the roads that crisscrossed through the forest, leading from small village to small village. He looked in both directions. Seeing no one, he quickly crossed and headed toward the thick underbrush on the far side. He had gone no more than a thirty meters when he nearly collided with a cloaked figure suddenly emerging from behind a wide oak.

Osric stumbled back, hand flying to the hilt of his sword. The figure let out a startled gasp and dropped the bundle they had been carrying. As the bundle spilled open, the flickering light of a small lantern in the person's hand illuminated a familiar face framed by wild red curls.

"Talia!" Osric said, breathing out in surprise and relief.

"Osric?" Talia whispered back. "What are you doing out here?"

"I'm sorry. I didn't mean to frighten you," he said.

Instead of replying, she stepped back, looking him up and down, taking in his disheveled appearance. "You look like you've seen a ghost. Has something happened?"

"It's ... it's a long story."

Talia kneeled to gather up the spilled herbs and roots she had dropped, packing them back into her basket.

"Right. We shouldn't stay out for long. Miriam gets angry if I'm on the road too late, but I was delayed, and ... it doesn't matter. Do you want to walk with me back to the village?"

Osric hesitated, his eyes darting back to the trees. "I can't go back to the village, Talia. Elder Miriam told me to flee into the woods and hide. She said it wasn't safe."

"What? Why would she say that? Did something happen?"

"It's … complicated. I ran into some trouble. A strange man was in the village, asking about someone finding something old, special, maybe in the forest. I tried to go back to Master Ironhand's, but he followed me, demanding I hand the 'artifact' over. When I refused, he tried to take the ring by force. We struggled, and in desperation, I grabbed the ring. It … it unleashed some kind of magical energy. There was a blinding glow, and when it faded, the man had been reduced to ash."

Osric and Talia both spun around at the sound of snapping twigs behind them. Two dark shapes emerged from the brush on the other side of the road. As they stepped into the faint glow of Talia's lantern, Osric's gut twisted with dread.

"Bandits," she said under her breath in surprise.

Osric knew they weren't bandits. He recognized the heavy black cloaks, tall boots, and swords at the men's waists. They were dressed like the stranger from the village.

"Thought you could run from us," one of the men said with a high-pitched sneer.

"I wasn't ... we're just travelers. Please, I just want to continue on my way," Osric said.

"Aww, you hear that, Kaelen? He wants to continue on his way," the first man said.

"You aren't going anywhere, boy," the larger bandit, presumably Kaelen, said. "We heard what you said and we know what you're carrying, and you're going to hand it over or we're going to take it off your corpse."

"Run," he said to Talia. "Tell Elder Miriam ..."

"Oh, she's not going anywhere," the smaller man said, pulling his sword. "Neither of you are."

Osric's hand clenched around the hilt of his sword. He'd only been in one fight, and that hadn't gone well for anyone. Pulling the sword, he stepped away from Talia, in front of her, in the vain hope he could somehow protect her. He braced himself, sword held out before him with both hands, like Master Ironhand had shown him.

The smaller man moved in first, a cruel grin on his face. He lunged forward, slashing high with his sword. Osric parried, metal clanging off metal, as he stepped back to avoid the blow. The man pressed on, raining down quick strikes that Osric struggled to block.

Out of the corner of his eye, Osric saw the larger man, the one who'd been called Kaelen, moving to get around him. Osric shoved back hard, pushing his opponent off balance before spinning to face the new threat. Kaelen's sword came sweeping low. Osric jumped back, the tip just missing his stomach.

Regaining his footing, the smaller man renewed his attack. Osric found himself driven back, a blade cutting across his stomach, not deep, but leaving a red line in its wake and pain searing through him.

"No!" Talia screamed.

Dropping her basket, she began moving her hands in an intricate pattern; her left hand held up with three fingers splayed. Her right hand moved in a quick circle in front of the outstretched fingers, tracing a glowing path in the air. As the circling hand completed its rotation, Talia thrust it forward. Three glowing bolts of light sprang from her outstretched palm, shooting forth in a straight trajectory toward Kaelen.

The bolts flew in rapid succession, trailing comet-like tails as they raced through the air. Kaelen had no time to react before the missiles slammed into his chest one after another, sending him flying backward, slamming into a tree before collapsing, unmoving, to the forest floor.

Osric stared at Talia in disbelief as the magic bolts flew from her hand, felling the large attacker.

Distracted, he was a moment too slow in raising his sword as the smaller man lunged forward, driving his sword deep into Osric's chest. Pain exploded through him as the blade pierced his body. Osric cried out, the sword falling from his suddenly numb fingers. He sank to his knees as the man yanked the blade free in a spray of crimson.

Clutching the gushing wound, Osric fell back, dimly aware of Talia rushing to his side. She caught him, lowering him gently as his lifeblood spilled out onto the forest floor. Osric's vision tunneled, the pain receding as shock set in.

Above him, the man who had run him through stood grinning wickedly, blade poised for a final blow. With the last of his fading strength, Osric's fingers closed around the ring in his hand. He didn't know what he was doing, only acting on instinct.

The ring flared, bathing the forest in blinding radiance. The man screamed as he was engulfed, flesh and bone disintegrating until only a scattering of ash remained, just as the man in Eldham had been. This time, however, something else happened. The light turned on Osric, tendrils of energy lancing into his wound. He convulsed in Talia's arms as the mystical force knit torn flesh and restored spilled blood. Just as suddenly as it had begun, it ended. Osric gasped, strength flooding back into his limbs. The pain was gone, the mortal wound sealed as if it had never been.

Osric stared down at his blood-soaked tunic in disbelief.

"It ... it healed me," he stammered. "I don't understand. How is this possible?"

He looked up at Talia. She was pale, her eyes wide with shock. Slowly, she took a shaky step back from him.

"Talia, it's okay," Osric said gently. He got to his feet, holding his hands out in a gesture of reassurance.

Talia stepped away from his reaching hands, eyes darting between the pile of ash that had been the assassin, the crumpled form of the other across the road, and back to Osric.

"You ... we killed them," she whispered, her hands covering her mouth. "Oh my God. I killed that man. Elder ... she said never to use my knowledge to harm, but they were attacking you, and I got so scared. Oh my God, what have I done?"

"You saved my life, Talia," Osric said. "If you hadn't done that spell, I'd be dead right now."

"You were dead," she said, her voice quavering as she wrapped her arms around herself, looking small and lost. "He stabbed straight through you. I saw the blade come out the other side. You were dying. I could see it. Then the light, it ... I don't understand how that happened."

"I don't understand either," Osric said. "It doesn't ..."

He stopped, turning his head towards the trees. The sound of voices, distant but drawing nearer, echoed through the forest.

"We have to go, now," Osric said urgently, grabbing his sword from the ground and reaching out his hand to her.

Talia hesitated only a moment before taking it, allowing Osric to pull her into the underbrush, away from the road. They ran through the dark forest, branches whipping against them. For hours, they ran, both pushing as fast as they could. Talia had dropped her lantern when she'd gone to him as he fell, and left it behind when they ran. Several times, they almost collided with a tree, seeing it at the last possible moment, but both were too scared to slow down, even for safety's sake.

Finally, exhaustion overtook them, and they were forced to stop, collapsing against the thick trunk of an ancient oak tree. Gasping for breath, they leaned against the rough bark. Osric's legs shook with fatigue, and his chest burned from exertion. Talia was pale, her wild red curls sticking to her sweat-dampened face.

"I think ... I think we lost them," Osric panted, peering back through the dense trees.

Talia wrapped her arms around herself, shivering despite the warm night air. Her wide eyes kept darting to Osric's bloodstained tunic.

"You should have died back there," she said, her voice barely above a whisper. "That sword went right through you. I saw the blood, so much blood ..."

Her words trailed off as a shudder ran through her slender frame. Osric's hand went reflexively to his chest, where the fatal blow had landed. Through the rent in the fabric, the skin beneath was smooth and unmarked.

"It was the ring," he said.

Talia shifted uneasily away from him. "That ring ... Elder Miriam warned that it was dangerous magic. Now it's slain two men and brought one back from the dead. Be careful with it."

"I know. I just ... I don't know how any of this works. I wish I'd never picked it up. All I know is Elder Miriam said it's bound to me now, which means maybe I can't ever get rid of it. Maybe it would be safer if we split up. They're not after you, only me and this cursed ring."

"I can't. We ran for so long ... I'm lost. I don't know how to get back to Eldham from here. And we're not alone. They're out there somewhere still looking for you, maybe both of us. I dropped my things. They'll find them. Know I was with you."

Osric wasn't sure that was right. A lantern and a basket of herbs weren't much to go on, but he knew of hunters who could track a single animal for days through forest and stream, so it was possible they'd realize there were now two of them.

"You're probably right," he said. "Maybe things will look different in the morning. More familiar."

He tried to sound more confident than he felt. Talia managed a weak smile, though her arms remained wrapped tightly around herself. Osric noticed her shivering had gotten worse as the sweat from their panicked flight cooled on her skin. He removed his cloak and draped it around her slender shoulders. She clutched the edges, pulling it close.

"Thank you," she said through still chattering teeth. "Sorry, I just feel so cold all of a sudden. We probably shouldn't start a fire, though. They might see the light."

They sat in silence for a time, the quiet sounds of the forest night around them. An owl hooted in the distance. Somewhere nearby, a stream gurgled over rocks and roots. The gentle noises blended into a soothing backdrop, lulling him to sleep. Osric felt his eyes become heavy, his head lolling to the side, causing him to jerk himself back upright. He needed to stay awake in case more men showed up.

Talia's head dropped against his shoulder, a few loose curls brushing against his neck. Her shivering had subsided, and her breathing had become steady and soft. The warmth of Talia's body and the weight against him, combined with the exhaustion from the day's events, allowed sleep to creep through Osric's body. His eyelids grew heavier until they finally drifted shut.

Osric's eyes snapped open as he felt a gentle yet firm nudge on his shoulder, jolting him from his nightmare. He'd been running endlessly through darkness, an evil crimson glow pursuing him, turning everyone he encountered to ash.

His memory of the dream vanished in an instant when he saw the large, intensely focused eyes and broad grey muzzle of an enormous wolf centimeters from his face, its hot breath tickling his skin. Talia's hand clutched his shoulder painfully hard, her nails digging into his flesh.

Its gaze was intense, with deep yellowish-brown eyes staring directly at Osric. He could see his own reflection in its dark pupils.

The wolf regarded him for a long moment before slowly taking two steps back, putting a bit of distance between itself and the humans, but never looking away. Osric instinctively reached out with his left hand, slowly moving it toward the sword lying in the leaves beside him. His movement was cautious, but the wolf ignored it, continuing to stare at him.

"We need to run, now!" Talia whispered urgently.

Osric's eyes remained locked on the wolf in front of him, its amber eyes staring back unwaveringly. It wasn't making any move to attack, but it was still incredibly close to them, near enough for Osric to see every detail of its shaggy grey pelt. There was no way for them to get up and run before the beast could be on them. Still, he continued to let his hand drift toward the sword with excruciating slowness so as not to alert or anger the wolf. Talia's fingers dug deeper into his shoulder, her rapid breaths loud and warm against his ear.

Just as Osric's hand finally wrapped around the leather-bound hilt of his blade, the wolf stepped forward again, stretching its neck toward him. Osric froze, expecting to be ripped apart at any moment.

Except, it didn't attack. Instead, it brushed its snout against the ring under Osric's shirt. An odd tingling sensation went through his body like a wave, crackling along his arms and down his legs. The wolf did it again, more insistently this time, its nose cold even through the fabric. Osric exchanged an astonished look with Talia, whose face had gone from pure terrified pallor to shocked curiosity, her green eyes wide.

He hadn't imagined it.

"I ... I don't think he means us any harm."

"What ... how did you do that?" she asked.

"I didn't do anything. You saw it. He did it on his own."

"Did the ring call the wolf?"

"You know more about magic than I do," he pointed out.

She didn't reply. Instead, she watched as Osric slowly let go of the sword and extended his trembling hand toward the animal. It showed no signs of aggression, simply watching Osric's movements. When his hand was halfway extended, the wolf stepped forward again and pressed its head up beneath Osric's palm.

Osric gently ran his hand over the wolf's thick, coarse fur, feeling an odd, deep resonance as the wolf made a low, rumbling noise that vibrated through Osric's hand. It wasn't a growl, however. He'd never heard anything like it. Talia watched wide-eyed, then tentatively reached her own hand out. To both their surprise, the wolf stepped back abruptly, regarding her now with wariness, almost suspicion. It didn't attack, but it didn't offer its head to her the way it had to him. She pulled her hand back quickly, looking puzzled.

"So only you, then?" she said.

"I ... I guess. I don't know. It's so strange."

The wolf turned and made a sharp, yipping sound, causing the two of them to freeze again. As if in response, more wolves began to emerge from the shadows between the trees around them. There were at least six in total, moving to surround Osric and Talia. These wolves were all smaller than the large one, and kept their distance, but didn't seem any more hostile than the large one was.

The lead wolf stepped away from them, turning and taking a few steps away from the tree that they'd been leaning against. When Osric and Talia didn't move, it returned, nudged Osric's hand firmly with its cold, wet nose, then walked away again, pausing to look back at them expectantly.

"Does he want us to follow?" Talia asked.

"Maybe? I don't know. This is the first time I've actually been this close to a wolf and I don't think anyone's had one act like this before."

"I don't think so either," she said. "But I think he definitely wants us to follow him."

The wolf was looking from him to her and back again as they spoke. Osric stood up, picked up his sword, securing it to his belt, and took a step toward the animal. The wolf walked forward a few more steps before turning and looking at them again.

"I guess we follow," Osric said.

Osric took a tentative step forward and then another, following the wolf as he turned and padded softly into the trees. Talia fell in beside him, her head swiveling as she tried to watch the smaller wolves as they disappeared and reappeared through the thick underbrush to their left and right, shadowing them.

It was hard to keep track of time, this deep in the trees, but it felt like they followed the wolf for several hours, plodding forward one step after another. Osric wanted to sit and rest, but the wolf seemed to be immune to exhaustion, continually looking back to make sure they were following. As they walked, Osric shared with Talia some of the small amount of food Elder Miriam had given him. She had dropped everything, including the food she'd had with her, when they ran. So this was all they'd have for a while. They ate sparingly, saving as much as they could.

After a while, Osric noticed the trees beginning to thin ahead. The wolf quickened his pace, leading them out of the close-knit woods into a small, sunny clearing. Osric froze as his eyes fell upon two men standing in the middle of the clearing, working on what looked like a trap, perhaps. His hand instinctively went to the hilt of his sword as he exchanged an anxious glance with Talia.

The wolf turned toward the right, moving along the outline of the clearing but never stepping out of the trees. Osric tapped Talia's arm and motioned for her to follow the wolf, not wanting to make extra noise that might alert the men.

He was less successful than he'd hoped.

"Hello, there," the larger of the two men said. "Who's out there?"

Osric cursed under his breath. Both men were armed, but not like the strangers. Even from here, Osric could tell they wore older and less used weapons. Weapons he'd seen on hunters and trappers, kept for protection only.

Still, Osric rested his hand on the hilt of his sword as they stepped cautiously into view. The wolf had disappeared into the brush again.

"Apologies for disturbing you," Osric said in what he hoped was a polite tone. "We were just passing through and didn't mean to intrude."

The men both looked at Osric wearily, and then at each other.

"You two are a long way from any villages," said the larger man with the bushy black beard. "What brings you out this deep into the forest?"

Osric hesitated. They may not be after them, but the strangers had asked everyone around about Osric, or at least what Osric carried, and the two men on the road seemed to know who Osric was. If they came across these hunters and told them about the young man and his red-haired friend from Eldham, it would be the same as if they just gave the men their names and told them they were being chased.

"We're from Norham, a village west of here," he lied, picking a random name. "She was sent on an errand to another village, and I came along to make sure she arrives safely. As you say, we're deep in the forest."

"The girl doesn't speak for herself?" the smaller of the two men said. "Seems foolish to send a slip of a girl into the woods, even with someone like you to mind her."

"I can," Talia bristled.

Osric gave what he hoped was a disarming smile. "Oh, don't let looks deceive you. She may be small but she can take care of herself. I saw her brain a drunk with a piece of firewood. Laid him out cold. I'm mostly here to carry any game she snares along the way."

The pockmarked man looked incredulous, but the bearded one chuckled.

"I've known a few tiny ladies who could put a man on his ass. Best not to underestimate them," he said to his friend before turning back to Osric. "Still, the woods have been more dangerous of late. Strange men about. Attacked a few trappers I know, so we've been wary. Best you get where you're going quick as you can."

Osric nodded gravely. "We appreciate the warning. We'll be on our way swiftly."

He and Talia moved to leave the clearing. As they reached the tree line, Osric risked a glance back and was relieved to see the wolf had not emerged.

Hopefully, it had sensed his desire for it to remain hidden.

They walked until the clearing was out of sight before slowing their pace again. Moments later, the wolf appeared beside them as if it had been patiently waiting just ahead. Talia jumped a little when it materialized from the bushes.

"You're pretty smart, you know that?" Osric said appreciatively.

The wolf just stared back for a moment before turning to begin walking deeper into the forest.

"Do you really think it understands you?" Talia asked.

Osric shook his head. "I've no idea, but it circled all the way around, just like I said."

Talia nodded, looking after the wolf, who'd stopped to watch them again when they didn't immediately follow.

"Come on," Osric said.

They followed the wolf on and on, for hours more, as the sun slowly began to drop in the sky, turning the trees into long shadows. That wasn't the only change in the forest, though. As they walked, Osric started to notice the woods themselves beginning to change. The trees grew larger, ancient, gnarled trunks covered in places with gray-green moss. The undergrowth thinned out save for tall ferns and bushes with vibrant red berries. It felt older here, wilder, with the trees slowly becoming more sparse as they got larger, until they saw another clearing ahead.

Osric slowed, worried they might encounter more men, or expose themselves by stepping into the clearing. Through the trees was a large open field, tall grass swaying gently in the breeze. At its center stood a large stone structure.

Even in its current dilapidated state, Osric could tell that it had once been an impressive structure. The keep's once-proud walls were cracked and eroded, all but the central structures reclaimed by the relentless tides of nature. Empty windows gazed sightlessly across a courtyard overgrown with weeds and brambles. The outer towers had collapsed completely, reduced to little more than piles of stone.

Yet at the courtyard's heart, the great hall still stood, though much diminished. Entire sections of its roof had rotted through or caved in over the centuries, leaving gaping holes open to the elements. Any doors that might have stood in the large stone doorway had long ago decayed into dust. All that remained were crumbling remnants around an empty, darkened doorway.

Beside him, Talia whispered in awe, "Can you believe this place? It must be ancient."

Ahead of them, the wolf waited, partway to the keep, looking at them, still expecting them to follow. The rest of the pack seemed to have scattered, and Osric wondered what could have happened to them. Were they out there, just beyond the tree line, or had they left them?

"It wants us to go in there?" Talia asked.

"I think so," Osric said, taking her hand and leading her toward the ancient building as the wolf disappeared inside the darkened doorway.

CHAPTER 4

The Ruined Keep

The inside of the crumbling structure was both amazing and sad, its once fine craftsmanship and splendor now torn down by the relentless passage of time. It was impossible not to marvel at the grandeur of the space, even in its current ruined state. Shafts of light streamed in from gaps in the partially intact roof, illuminating swirling motes of dust that danced through the air.

Across from them, the far wall had completely collapsed into a mound of rubble, opening into what must have been a great hall of some kind in its heyday, based on the soaring broken columns that reached toward the high ceilings. Several of the columns had crumpled under the weight of the now missing roof, leaving them leaning at precarious angles. The open ceiling had let in decades of wind, rain, and snow, accelerating the decay inside. Piles of stone and debris lay here and there where what might have once been an upper balcony or second level had succumbed to gravity and collapsed down into the hall below. Vines crept up the remaining stone walls, which were cracked and eroded. It seemed like some kind of painting might have been on the far wall, although it was more an impression of there having been art, than any semblance of it remaining.

Or maybe that was only in Osric's mind, filling in the space with how he thought a keep should look.

Ahead of them, the wolf paused by the room's only fully intact wall, which surprisingly held an open doorway with stairs descending into darkness. The creature glanced back at Osric and Talia, with its piercing yellow eyes, before turning and descending slowly down the crumbling steps into the void.

Osric felt Talia shudder next to him.

"It wants us to go down there?" she asked nervously.

"I think so," Osric replied, squinting futilely, trying to see what lay ahead.

Pulling his sword, he led Talia toward the stairwell. The temperature dropped noticeably as they descended into the shadows, and the air grew damp and heavy. The stairway walls and ceiling were intact, although gnarled roots had forced their way through the cracks, and Osric had to duck under them in places as they descended further from the fading light above them.

"I wish we had a torch," he said. The ambient light was fading fast now that they had left the brighter upper hall.

Talia stopped partway down the stairs and pulled her hand free from his. For a moment, Osric thought she might have lost her nerve and wanted to go back up the stairs. What he didn't expect was for her to pull her sleeves back and hold the tips of her thumbs and index fingers together in front of her to form an upward-pointing triangle. He watched as she slowly separated her hands while still keeping the triangle shape with her fingers. Suddenly, a glowing orb of light materialized, small at first, lighting her palms as if she were holding fire. She slowly increased the spacing between her hands, keeping her fingers in the same position, causing the orb to grow as she increased the amount of space.

When it reached the size of a small melon, she stopped expanding the triangle and opened her fingers evenly, out away from the others, like how a flower might open its petals, causing the glowing orb to gently drift up and away from her palms. It floated to about shoulder height and stopped, its eerie white light falling on everything around them. Not as bright as a torch, perhaps, but the light seemed more solid and to reach further out.

"How did you do that?" Osric whispered, again amazed at the powers she'd been hiding all this time.

Talia smiled softly and said, "Just a simple light spell, one of the first ones Elder Miriam taught me to weave."

Osric shook his head in wonder. Magic never ceased to astonish him. Between the power stored in his mysterious ring and Talia's own innate talents, he realized how little he knew of the world, working at Master Ironhand's forge.

"Well, at some point, you're going to have to explain how you know to do everything you do," he said.

"I can try," she said, but she looked doubtful.

Osric didn't blame her. She and Elder Miriam were the smartest people he knew. If that is what it took to learn magical powers, he was almost certainly not cut out for it.

They made their way down the remaining stairs, Talia's glowing orb lighting their path. The basement was in as rough shape as the levels above, perhaps worse, since it lacked any natural light. Rotted wooden beams littered the floor amidst piles of rubble and debris. Many of the walls had collapsed into mounds of stone blocks and shattered mortar.

Despite the decay, Osric could see shapes of stone around the room that might be signs that this was some kind of kitchen. He thought he could make out the outline of a large brick oven built into one wall, now crumbling and choked with tangled roots. A massive stone basin against another wall held a layer of fetid rainwater and leaves.

The wolf stood in the middle of the debris-strewn chamber, eyes fixed on the far wall where part of the mortar between the large foundation stones had crumbled away. Tree roots thick as a man's arm wriggled through the gaps.

"Is there something behind there?" Talia asked, staring at him.

"Maybe," Osric said. "He seems pretty focused."

Giving each other a look, they carefully made their way across the debris-strewn floor toward the wolf. The orb of light floated just ahead of them, casting an eerie light around the room, shards of broken pottery, rusted metal fragments, and other rubble creating shadows that bent and moved as they passed.

They were halfway to the wolf when Talia suddenly cried out. Osric turned just in time to see the section of floor she was standing on start to collapse. Without hesitation, he lunged forward, grabbing her arm and yanking her away from the crumbling stones an instant before they gave way completely. Talia stumbled into him with a gasp as several flagstones dropped into a dark pit that opened up where she had just been standing.

One arm wrapped firmly around Talia, Osric peered past her down into the hole. Jagged chunks of stone lined the edges where part of the floor had fallen away. He couldn't see the bottom in the dim light—it descended into inky blackness.

"Thank you," Talia said shakily, clutching at Osric as she, too, stared wide-eyed into the pit.

If he hadn't pulled her clear in time ... Osric shook the thought away.

On the opposite side of the hole, the wolf stared back at them, yellow eyes glowing in Talia's summoned light. It turned and paced farther into the chamber, still fixated on the crumbling section of wall.

"I guess we need to find a way over there," Osric said.

"Look, part of that beam is still intact. We might be able to lay it across the hole and use it as a bridge," Talia said, pointing at part of the wall to their left, where the ceiling above had only partially collapsed.

Osric looked where she'd indicated and saw a long wooden roof beam. It looked half-rotted through, but as he made his way over to it, poking at it, the core seemed still intact. Sheathing his sword, he gripped the intact end, dragging it over and levering it across the gap. It only just reached, sagging slightly in the middle.

"I'll go first, test it out," he said.

Talia opened her mouth to object, but Osric was already edging out onto the precarious plank bridge. The aged wooden plank creaked and groaned under his weight, and he held his arms out for balance, concentrating on finding secure footing. With careful steps, he slowly made his way across, the bridge lurching and swaying beneath him.

When he reached the other side, he let out a breath he hadn't realized he'd been holding. Turning back, he extended a hand towards Talia, beckoning for her to follow. She hesitated.

"If it held me, it'll hold you," he said.

"Maybe," she said, eyeing the beam skeptically.

Taking a deep breath, she stepped out onto it, taking small, shuffling steps. As she hit the middle, she began to sway, teetering back and forth slightly. Osric was just about to step out to her to help her across, when she recovered and managed one large step. Reaching out, he grabbed her hand and pulled her the rest of the way over.

"That's about the last scare I'm going to be able to stand," she said.

"No problem. I'm sure the pitch black, ancient, crumbling basement is perfectly fine from here on out," Osric said, giving her a grin that was much more calm and playful than he felt.

She gave him a look that told him she was aware he was putting on a front for her benefit, but she still gave a weak smile and said, "Shut it."

Osric gave her shoulder a pat and carefully made his way toward the wolf, prepared in case the ground gave way again. As he neared the animal, it stepped aside but kept its intense gaze fixed on the cracks in the mortar.

Osric placed his hands on the wall, trying to feel what had it so enthralled, and stopped suddenly. As his hand passed a section, he could feel a slight breeze on his palm. He moved his hand away and then back over the cracked and missing mortar, feeling the air again. Kneeling down, he examined the spot. It was a small crack, maybe a little larger than some of the others, but still too small to see through. But apparently, not small enough to be airtight.

"There's something here," Osric said. "I can feel … air coming through the wall."

Talia moved next to him, sliding her hand over the same spot as he stood and stepped aside. He could see the expression on her face change as she found the spot he had discovered.

"There's something on the other side," she said.

"Air, at the very least," he said, running his hand over the wall, feeling it out, trying to get a sense of what was back there.

She did the same on the opposite side, her hands moving over the rough and worn stone. She paused as her hand reached the edge of a large stone, not more than a hand span from the opposite wall. Peering over, he saw her nails had caught on an almost invisible seam cut in the rock. She looked at him, and then dug her fingernails in and pulled. With a faint grinding noise, the block shifted inward slightly on concealed hinges, revealing a dark cavity behind it.

"A hidden door!" she exclaimed.

Placing his hands on that section of wall, Osric pushed with all his might. At first, it seemed like it might have been a fluke, or some small deformation, but then the wall shifted, slowly at first and then faster until it swung in on its protesting hinges, emitting a low scraping sound.

As soon as it was opened, the wolf stepped through the door, leaving them little choice but to follow, ducking their heads as they entered the low passageway. As Osric reached out to steady himself, his hand brushed one of the hinges, stopping as he realized something felt off.

Leaning forward, he brushed away a thin layer of dirt to reveal dull metal underneath. Dull, but not rusted.

"These hinges can't be more than a few years old," he murmured.

"Do you mean someone's been down here? And why would they build a hidden room off an ancient keep's basement?"

"I don't think they built this room," Osric said, pointing at the passage on the other side of the doorway. "Look at all that. The stone here looks as old as the stone out there. Hell, even the door looks old … weathered. Only the hinges are new."

"So someone repaired it? Why?"

"I have no idea," Osric said. "Come on."

Osric led the way, walking cautiously through the short, narrow stone passageway. The walls and floors were rough-hewn, with jagged edges that snagged at Talia's cloak as she followed along behind him. The passage opened up into a chamber perhaps five meters across with small slits carved into the opposite wall, pointing back toward the passage they had just come through. Between the slits was a doorway leading off into more darkness.

Osric stepped up to it, reaching high to grab something from the lintel above the doorway. He tugged hard and a shower of rust flakes drifted down. Turning, he held his hand out, palm up, to Talia. In his hand was a ragged chunk of discolored metal, one side was pitted and blackened as if burned long ago.

"See, this door hinge is as old as the castle. Look how brittle the metal is. I think maybe the door here was wood, but it rotted through a long time ago," he said, looking around the room and at the slits in the wall. "I think this might have originally been a trap. Master Ironhand told me about a trip he took to the Baron's castle, where there was something like this at the front entrance. The room was meant to funnel people into the path of these slits, where, I think, archers or crossbowmen could fire through."

He waved her through the doorway, which led into yet another room, this one nearly six meters across. Some of the stone had collapsed on one side of the room, blocking off most of the space, but Osric thought he noticed something and went to pull it free, coming away with a rather thin, twisted piece of metal sheeting.

"Armor ... I think. If that room was for funneling intruders, then perhaps this was a guard room of some type. To keep anyone who discovered the room from getting further," he said, gesturing at yet another open doorway opposite them.

"I don't know," she said doubtfully. "I've never seen nor read about anything like this before in the histories. This place feels ... wrong somehow."

"Yeah. Are you okay to keep going?"

She bit her lip nervously but nodded. Osric took her free hand, and they stepped through the doorway, which opened into a large chamber, the ceilings vaulting above them. Talia lifted her slender arms, sending the glowing orb higher into the air, illuminating a vast expanse that extended into the shadows.

Maybe four meters ahead stood what Osric thought might have been a large statue, from the wide stance of the legs. It was impossible to tell, however, since the rest of the figure was missing. The area where its torso would have met the stone legs had a melted, almost liquefied appearance.

Talia's curiosity must have overpowered her fear because she approached the remaining fragment of the statue and ran her fingers along the rippled, melted stone. She peered upward, squinting to see if she could imagine what must have once stood there.

"I've never seen anything that could melt stone like this," she said.

"Me either, and we've had the forge hot enough to slag iron and soften steel."

"What is this place?" She asked yet again.

He still had no answer. Each discovery only brought new questions.

"Look," he said, pointing to doorways on either side of the chamber. "Should we keep going straight, or see where those lead?"

She looked back and forth between the rooms. It seemed as if, now that her curiosity was engaged, the fear that had plagued her since their battle in the forest had started to fade, and she was back to the confident, headstrong Talia he remembered from the village.

"I think we should see where these other doorways lead first, before going deeper in," she said decisively. "If this place was meant to guard something important, there could be clues in these side areas about what lies ahead."

"Okay, which one first," he asked.

Since they'd stepped into the area, the wolf had stopped being a guide, and was looking back and forth between them as they talked, or otherwise sniffing around this new area. It was as curious as they were.

Talia considered a moment before pointing to the left passage. "That way."

They walked cautiously, Osric going first, checking for any more surprises like the trap from before, as they entered through the dark stone doorway on the left. Beyond lay a strange rectangular room. Along one wall was a row of cramped stone cubicles, each sealed off from the rest by a grid of rusty metal bars thick with grime.

With a flick of her wrist, Talia sent her glowing orb gliding ahead, bathing the room in pale light. Squinting through the rusted partitions, Osric could make out a layer of dust and ancient bones littering the grimy floors of the cages. Bones that looked too small to be from a person.

"Some kind of kennel, maybe?" Osric mused aloud. "An odd place for it, buried away behind a secret door and guarded room. This old fortress must have held animals of some kind, but why keep them caged up and hidden down here?"

A low, rumbling growl drew Osric's attention. He turned to see the wolf stalking along the cubicles, its nose twitching as it sniffed and snarled at one of the small enclosures. The wolf's hackles raised as it backed out of the room.

"I don't blame him," Talia said. "This place gives me the creeps."

Osric nodded slowly, glancing around. "It's okay. I don't think there's anything helpful in here. Let's check out the other side."

They crossed through the center chamber again, passing the melted statue, and stepped through the doorway on the other side. Osric wouldn't have thought it possible, but this room was even more unusual than the kennel they had found.

The room's walls were lined with smashed workbenches, the metal frames showing where wood must have once been. Scattered tools lay strewn across the dusty stone floor, having fallen as the wood rotted away into nothing with the passing of time.

"What are these?" Osric asked, bending down to examine one of the tools closely.

He'd spent the last almost ten years under Master Ironhand's tutelage, learning the art of smithing. In that time, Osric had seen and helped craft tools of all kinds - farming implements, woodworking tools, sculpting equipment. But never before had he laid eyes on tools such as these.

"I've seen something akin to these in a book Elder Miriam once showed me," Talia said. "It was a tome on enchantments, I believe. They would use tools like these to … pull, for lack of a better word, the magic into the item being enchanted. And this to connect and seal the magic into the item."

Talia ran her fingers along the length of the rod. "I believe implements like these are only ever employed by the mages of the Ascended Conclave."

They spent several minutes edging along the room, looking through the tools and benches, but anything that wasn't metal had long ago turned to dust, leaving little behind for them to examine.

"There's another door," Osric said, pointing across from the entry to a door opposite it.

They'd both seen it when they'd entered the room, of course, but Osric felt that they'd looked through this room enough. While interesting, this room held no more answers than the kennel had. To Talia, this had become a curiosity, something academic to explore, but Osric could still feel the ring hanging around his neck, a weight, pushing him to find answers.

Osric stepped through the doorway, Talia and the wolf close behind him. This room was larger than the others, with a few more sturdy workbenches and shelves carved into the rock walls along the side closest to the door. Strange glass vials, metal tools, and crystals were scattered across the tables' surfaces.

The thing that was most interesting, however, was the large form in the center of the room, holding what might have been a large ring or something else, although it was impossible to tell. As with the statue, it was partially melted, leaving only the bottom third of the ring and the brackets holding it to the floor. Scattered around the ring on the dusty floor were hundreds of tiny shards of what looked like some kind of crystal, too opaque and marbled to be glass.

As they moved farther into the room, the hair on the back of Osric's neck began to prickle. There was a charge in the air, a faint crackling energy he could almost taste on his tongue. Acting on instinct, his hand went to the ring hanging beneath his tunic. As soon as he made contact with it, it began to glow again, except not the red light it had previously emitted. This time, the light pulsed a vibrant blue-white, growing and diminishing in intensity in a steady rhythm.

Talia looked at him, but Osric only shook his head. He didn't know why the ring did anything that it did, but this was new and even more unexpected.

Without warning, the ring flared brilliantly. Osric cried out as a tremendous force slammed into his chest, hurtling him backward. He crashed painfully to the stone floor several meters away, the wind knocked from his lungs. Gasping, he looked up to see Talia rushing over, her face creased with concern.

"Osric! Are you all right?" She helped pull him to his feet, supporting him as he swayed unsteadily.

"I'm fine," he wheezed, still struggling to regain his breath. "The ring … it was like running full force into a …"

Whatever Osric was going to say died in his throat as an immense tearing sound echoed around the stone room, drawing their attention toward the platform. The air pulsated with energy before them, distorting as if seen through intense heat. Then, before their astonished eyes, the fabric of reality itself seemed to tear apart right in the center of the platform, where the melted ring would have rested. A jagged rift split open in midair, roughly four meters across and three meters high. Its edges glowed and pulsed weirdly.

Osric and Talia stumbled back in shock. On the other side of the shimmering portal hovered an impossible sight - the same chamber they currently occupied, but superimposed, as if layered over their surroundings. Everything he could see in the room on the other side of the platform was the same, but cleaner. Newer. The same workbenches lined the walls, free of dust and decay. In place of the broken shards and rubble littering their surfaces stood strange instruments and bubbling vials, glowing with colorful liquids and unknowable purposes.

The floor beyond the portal was smooth and un-marred, without the rubble and debris.

Even more astounding than the pristine state of the space were its occupants. Half a dozen men dressed in flowing, deep black robes bustled about, engaged in various tasks.

"Can they see us?" Talia whispered, leaning in close to Osric.

Before he could reply, one of the robed men looked up directly at them. The man's mouth dropped open in surprise, and he took an involuntary step in their direction. Just as it seemed that the man on the other side of the portal was going to say something, there was a shout and some sort of commotion. It was coming from the room on the other side of the tear, and from the direction where they now stood, near the door leading to the outer workshop.

"You are under arrest by order of the Council!" a commanding voice bellowed from out of sight. "Sur-render yourselves now!"

The dark-robed men exchanged alarmed glances. One began weaving his hands in complex motions, sparks dancing between his fingers, coalescing into a pulsating sphere of liquid flame. With a flick of his wrist, he sent the roiling ball streaking toward the doorway where they stood.

A deafening explosion shook the chamber, causing some of the dust on their side of the room to leap into the air. The scene visible through the shimmering tear winked out abruptly, as if a thick curtain had been drawn across a window. An instant later, the rift itself collapsed with a sharp, resounding crack. Talia and Osric were left staring at a solid stone wall where, moments before, they had gazed into another world and time.

After several heartbeats of stunned silence, Osric found his voice. "What ... what was that?"

Talia just stared at the melted ring, her mouth hanging open.

"Talia?" Osric prodded.

"Sorry," she said, shaking her head and blinking a few times. "It looked like this room but ... newer. I think, maybe, we were somehow looking back in time. To the people who originally used this room."

"How?"

"I have no idea. I've never even heard about something like this happening. Do you think, with the door hidden in the kitchen, the guard room, is it possible the people who owned this keep were doing something they shouldn't have been?"

"The voice said they were under arrest, so maybe."

"It would explain the melted ring and statue. Whatever spell that man was weaving, it looked like it could do that."

"I think it could. I've never seen that spell used before, but I read about it in one of Elder Miriam's books. It could easily melt stone if the mage was powerful enough."

"Wow," Osric said, stunned.

He'd heard tales of powerful mages, but that had just been stories. Having confirmation like this made it suddenly real. Dangerous.

"But, what kind of magic is illegal?" Talia asked, her mind clearly still on the mystery they'd stumbled into.

"You're the expert. I'm more concerned about why the ring would lead us to a place that practiced illegal magic."

"I ... I don't know. I'm not sure we should keep going," Talia said. "I know you want to find out what's happening, but we already had trouble with those men in the forest. People who can melt stone? That's a kind of power neither of us is ready for."

"But you just said that was a window through time, right? They aren't here now. No one's here. Look at the layer of dust. No one's been here for a long time."

"But you said the hinges on the door were new," Talia countered.

"Yes. You're right, but that's ... I don't know, normal. People who can melt stone and open windows through time don't need to replace a hinge, do they?"

"Maybe. I'm just saying, this is dangerous."

"We knew that when we came in here. The magic brought us here and it's protected me the entire way. Either way, I have to know."

"Okay. I'm not going to leave you. I just wanted to ... I don't know."

"It's okay. I'm scared, too," Osric said.

"Good," Talia said, seeming to relax a bit. "I guess we keep going."

CHAPTER 5

Glimpses into the Past

They headed back into the crumbling hallway, still shaken by what they had witnessed. The wolf had stopped leading them. Now, it only padded along beside Osric, its head swiveling from side to side and nose twitching. Not that they needed a guide any longer.

There was only one direction left to go, and the three turned and headed deeper into the secret underground complex. They didn't have to go far. The shadows had made the room seem larger than it was, deeper. In reality, they found the back wall after going only thirty meters, with a very large arched doorway in the center of it.

He felt Talia tense beside him, and for a moment, he thought maybe something about it frightened her, except her expression was one of wonder and amazement, not fear, as she approached the doorway, stopping in front of it and staring at the intricate carvings around its arch.

Reaching out, she ran her hands over the glyphs. For a full minute, she said nothing. Just ran her hands back and forth over the symbols, tracing out the detailed patterns.

"It's some kind of barrier," she murmured. "The glyphs are for protection, to keep whatever's on the other side from crossing over to this side."

Osric glanced back the way they had come and asked, "So if we go through, we won't be able to get back?"

Talia traced a slender finger over one of the cracks spiderwebbing across the surface of the weathered glyphs.

"I don't think that is true. Elder Miriam had books that talked about glyphs like this. They are very complex and take powerful mages to construct, but one thing was clear; the integrity of the glyphs is key. These are cracked and broken in places. They no longer hold any power, or function."

"I would expect these to be for the other direction, keeping anyone from going deeper, sort of like a magic version of the guard room back there," he said, gesturing vaguely behind them. "Was this some kind of prison?"

"Your guess is as good as mine. All I can tell you is that we'll be able to return this way. Nothing about them suggests why they were put here."

Osric thought for a moment, watching Talia examine the doorway and the glyphs and, not for the first time since she first showed her ability in Elder Miriam's cottage, he wondered about how much she knew. And why she'd never told him.

"Talia, why didn't you ever tell me about this? About magic?" The words tumbled from him almost against his will.

"Is this the right time to talk about this, Osric?" she asked, her voice barely above a whisper.

She didn't even look at him, her focus still on the glyphs.

"Maybe not, and it's okay if you don't want to talk about it. It's just ... every time I think I've come to terms with it, you do something even bigger, more impressive. We were friends for so long ..."

He let his voice trail off. He wanted to let it go, just continue their search, but he couldn't. He knew she had reasons for not telling him, for keeping it secret, and he didn't want to pry, but their lives were on the line. The more he knew about her, and her amazing abilities, the safer they would be. Which is why he was surprised when she sighed and turned to face him. He'd expected anger or maybe annoyance. Instead, she looked almost sad.

"It's not because I didn't trust you, Osric. I did. There's just ... a lot you don't know about my life," she said in a soft, resigned voice, before pausing for what felt like a long time.

He could see a battle playing out on her face, as if she was at war with herself. He was about to tell her never mind, that he didn't want to pry, when she seemed to make up her mind.

"I didn't say anything because it was a secret. It had to be. Elder Miriam was teaching magic outside the Conclave. While it's not illegal or unallowed, it's certainly frowned upon. We didn't want to draw attention from them. They have strict rules about how magic should be taught and used. I'm not sure exactly what danger she would have been in from them, but she made me promise to tell no one. Ever." She paused, her expression softening. "And I didn't tell you because I didn't want to put you in danger."

Osric wanted to tell her she wouldn't, and that he would take the danger if it meant their friendship being closer, but he didn't. As she said, this was the wrong time for that and, with everything going on, it didn't feel right. Something did confuse him about the story, though.

"Why not send you to the Conclave then? If what Elder Miriam was doing was so dangerous?"

Talia shrugged, "I don't know. Elder Miriam left the Conclave over some disagreement, but she never talked about it with me. She never talked about them at all, really, beyond telling me she left and I wasn't to tell anyone what she was teaching me."

"Okay," he said.

She looked halfway between conflicted and relieved, and he didn't want to push her anymore. Besides, the rest was Elder Miriam's story to tell, although right now, it seemed unlikely that they'd ever get back home for her to tell it.

Instead, he turned and stepped through the door-way. Even though she'd said the magic carved into the doorway was long gone, he half expected to feel something, like when the ring did its magic. But he felt nothing.

It was just a normal doorway now.

A short hallway extended beyond the door before opening up into a vast, cavernous space, the ceiling soaring up into darkness. Talia made a series of motions with her hands, sending the glowing orb of light flying up and around the chamber, showing them just how large and deep the space really was: a rectangle stretching at least a hundred meters ahead of them toward another rough, stone wall and an arched doorway.

The sheer size of the room was impressive, but even more amazing were the objects it contained. Arrayed along the perimeter were a dozen stone pedestals, six lining each long side of the chamber. Perched atop each pedestal was a large, upright stone ring, reminiscent of the one they had seen the rift appear in earlier; except these were completely unbroken and intact. The rings stood tall enough for a person to step through, if only there had been an opening on the other side. Instead, the back of each ring was smooth, flat stone. Steps led up the side of each pedestal, providing access to the solid rings, though they served no discernible purpose.

"What are these?" Osric murmured.

Talia drifted towards the nearest stone, scrutinizing the intricate symbols and patterns etched around its circumference. She reached out a hand, her fingers hovering just over the weathered engravings without touching them, as if the ancient carvings were something fragile to be handled with care.

"Some kind of portal … or they were meant to be, I think," she said. "The markings look similar to teleportation circles I read about in one of Elder Miriam's books, they only exist within the Conclave's major towers. Something about the unpredictable nature and dangers that can come from their use.

The books were never clear on what those dangers were."

"Could they have opened rifts like the one we saw earlier?"

"I'm not sure. Like I said, I only read about them in books. Elder Miriam never mentioned anything like this in her actual teachings. I think the magic required ... it's beyond anything I've encountered."

Osric joined her beside the stone ring. This close, he could make out individual glyphs and symbols etched into the surface. They seemed crisp, untouched by time. He reached out a hand but paused before making contact.

"Should I touch it?"

"I don't know. I don't think they have any magic left in them, at least I don't feel any. But that other ring was all but melted, and we saw what that did when your ring came in contact with it."

"Then … maybe I shouldn't," Osric said, backing away from it, choosing instead to stare around the room in open-mouthed wonder.

"Probably not," Talia said. "I'm not sure there's much more to see. This is ruins, just like the rest of this place."

"Yeah," Osric said, still staring around the room. "I'd love to know what this was all about."

"I know, but unless you have some way of asking the people who lived here …" she said, letting the words trail off. "Besides, we have other things to worry about. Like why we're here, what your ring is, and what we're going to do about it."

"Yeah, I guess we keep going," Osric said, taking one last look around before continuing to the open doorway at the end of the rectangular room.

To Osric's surprise, when they reached it, they found another set of stairs going down even deeper into the earth. They looked at each other for a moment before Osric took the lead, walking down the steps.

The stairwell deposited them in another magnificent room. Though much of the room's contents had long ago turned to dust, the soaring architecture still conveyed a sense of importance and grandeur.

The chamber had a high, arched ceiling, not quite as high as the room with the rings, but still very tall and impressive. Spaced evenly along the curving walls were something that looked like alcoves. The walls themselves looked like they might have once held some kind of mural or painting, although it was all so faded by time that it was impossible to tell what the images had been.

The two most notable, and intact, things in the room were a large stone table in the center of the room and a dark metal door at the far end, opposite where the stairwell dropped them off.

For a moment, Osric didn't move, once again caught up by his wonder, just staring at another in what was turning out to be a long line of incredible sights. Talia wasn't so enamored, pushing past him and starting to walk the circumference of the room, forcing Osric to hurry after her.

He caught up as she paused to examine one of the recessed alcoves along the curving wall. Fragments of cracked pottery, what might have once been leather book covers, and shards of glass were heaped haphazardly amidst the rubble. She delicately shifted some pieces with her foot, squinting at them, but as far as Osric could see, it was all destroyed beyond recognition.

With a sigh, she pushed past him again, heading toward the large circular stone table. It was intricately carved from a single slab of black marble, with clawed feet and symbols etched around the rim. The surface was covered in some kind of engraving, but it was so worn down by time that, at first, Osric couldn't make out what the markings were.

"It's a map of the world," Talia said, seeing his expression.

Osric tilted his head, trying to see it from a different vantage point. After a moment, he thought he could make out the outline of Peridia, although he didn't know the shape that well. He'd seen it a few times in a shop he and Master Ironhand had gone to with finished orders, but studying in books and looking at maps had never held much interest for him.

"Are you sure?"

"I think so. I can sort of make out the mountains and the great forest. The shape is right," she said, and then ran her hand over one side of it. "This is odd, though."

"What?" he said, trying to make out what she was looking at.

"Here. This must have been important, since it's the only symbol large enough that it is still showing. It's in the wrong place, though. These are the Shadowfell

Marshes. There's nothing here now and no one ever goes there."

"I've heard of that, I think," Osric said, trying to remember where he heard it mentioned.

"It's in the far northwest between the Dun River and the Craigshire Mountains. According to all the histories I've read, it's a horrible place filled with monsters, exiled things and the occasional bandit on the run from justice. It's not a place anyone would ever want to go to, at least not if they want to survive, which is why having something marked in the middle of it makes no sense."

"As opposed to the rest of this place?" Osric pointed out.

"I suppose that's true," she said, running her hand over the map once more.

He knew she'd stay and stare at the tableau for the rest of the day if he let her. Mission or no, something this old and interesting was like sweets to an infant for her. For him, there was something more practical and much more interesting drawing his attention.

Now that they were in the center of the room, Osric had a better look at the door on the opposite end of the room, and it was obvious that it was quite a bit newer than everything else in this room.

Stepping away from Talia, he approached the door, running his hand over it. The metal wasn't new exactly, but it wasn't ancient, either. Rusted and pitted in places, it might have been ten or fifteen years old, but probably not older than that. It also looked very sturdy. It was impossible to tell with it closed, but the way it hung, he had to guess it was very heavy, which meant thick. It swung inward, putting the hinges inside the room, which was smart.

Some might argue that it would be better to have it swing out, put the pressure on the wall and closed hinge, in addition to the door, but that exposes the hinges to the people on this side, and they are almost always weaker than the door itself. If it had been that way, Osric could have potentially found a way to remove the door from its hinges. As it was, if the door was barred in any way from the other side, it would be all but impossible to budge.

"I can open it, I think," Talia said from behind him, causing Osric to almost jump in the air. "Sorry."

"It's okay. You just move too damn quietly."

"You can open this? With magic?"

"Yes. Unless it's enchanted, the spell isn't that hard to weave."

"Be my guest," Osric said, stepping back and bowing, both arms extended toward the door in an exaggerated posture.

Shaking her head but otherwise ignoring him, Talia took a step closer.

Talia took a deep breath and closed her eyes, stepping apart slightly as if bracing herself. As Osric watched, she lifted her hands up in front of her chest, palms facing each other as if cradling an invisible sphere. Slowly, she interlaced her fingers, joining her thumbs together and pointing them upwards to form an oval shape. Keeping her fingers interlocked, she rotated her hands outward, pivoting her thumbs downwards.

Once her palms faced outward, she pulled her hands apart, stretching the invisible space between them. She moved her hands to shoulder width, palms still facing forward. With her right hand, Talia reached upward, while her left hand pointed down, both perpendicular to the door.

Finally, she slammed her palms together, striking them in the space before the door. As her hands connected, the metal door clicked and swung inward.

In any other instance, Osric would have stood there, mouth agape at the amazing feat of magic his friend once again completed. This time, however, he didn't have the luxury. As soon as the door swung open, they found themselves face to face with two men dressed very similarly to their previous attackers.

Both men's eyes went wide with surprise, mirroring the shock on Osric and Talia's faces. For a heartbeat, both pairs stared at each other, frozen at the sudden appearance of the other.

Osric reacted first, feeling anger and fury at seeing more of the men who'd hounded him and tried to kill him. Lunging forward, he sliced at the man on the left, his blade biting deep into the man's shoulder, eliciting a guttural cry as he stumbled back.

Talia, however, was not as fortunate. The man to her right reacted more quickly; he pulled a dagger and lunged forward. The blade slashed through the muscle in Talia's arm. She screamed, clutching at the injury.

Anger surged through Osric at the sight of her being wounded. He started to move toward her attacker but was forced back. Bringing up his sword just in time, he blocked a blow from the man on the left, who tried to pay Osric back for wounding him earlier.

Out of the corner of his eye, Osric saw Talia lift her hands to chest level, palms facing each other, close but not touching. In a sudden, swift motion, she clenched both hands into fists and then snapped her right hand open, pressing it flat against the other man's chest.

Crackling blue electricity erupted around her hand and coursed into the man's body. He convulsed wildly, smoke rising from his clothes as electricity coursed through him. With a strangled cry, he collapsed to the ground, twitching uncontrollably.

There wasn't time for Osric to react to that, as his man continued to press the attack. Osric, clearly not as well trained, could barely block the blows. Several of them got perilously close when suddenly, a dark gray blur shot past him. The wolf slammed into the wounded man, jaws clamping down on his sword arm. The man screamed as fangs shredded flesh, forcing him to drop his blade.

Seizing the opportunity, Osric lunged forward and drove his sword deep into the man's chest. A look of shock crossed the man's face before it went slack, his body sliding off Osric's blade and falling lifelessly to the floor.

A pained shout made Osric whirl around. The second man had regained his feet and now had Talia by the neck, his dagger pressed to her throat.

"Drop the sword or she dies!" he spat.

Osric hesitated briefly before reluctantly lowering his blade to the floor. The man grinned wickedly.

"Good, now kick it ov..." the man began to say before Talia went wild when his blade moved slightly away from her neck, clawing at his face, gasping for breath, eyes wide with fear.

The man acted on instinct, hands going to protect his face, giving her the opportunity to push away from him, backing up several steps. As Osric began to reach down for his sword, a furious Talia brought her hands up in front of her chest, rubbing her palms together rapidly. After a few quick circles, she pulled them apart and a flickering orange flame burst forth, hovering above her palms.

Before the man could react, she slammed her hands forward. A cone of roaring flames erupted, splashing across his chest, setting part of his hair on fire and melting leather into skin.

The man dropped his blade entirely, trying to pat out the flames quickly moving across his head as Talia stumbled away, massaging her bruised neck. Osric retrieved his sword and started to take a step forward, but the wolf moved faster. It leaped through the dissipating flames to clamp its jaws around the man's neck, viciously tearing into the flesh. With a sickening crunch, the man fell silent, his ravaged body dropping to the floor in a smoldering heap.

"Are you all right?" Osric asked Talia, who looked equally terrified and pained.

"Here, let me see," Osric said gently, taking her arm.

Talia winced but allowed him to examine the knife wound. Blood was dripping from the wound and Osric could see sinew and muscle through the tear, showing how very deep the gash was.

Remembering the strange power the ring had shown the last time, how it had healed his own injuries before, Osric wrapped his hands around her arm and closed his eyes. Talia, maybe guessing what he was doing, muffled a cry of pain, but did not pull away.

Osric focused his mind, visualizing the ragged flesh knitting back together. At first, nothing happened, and then, as before, a soft white glow emanated from beneath his palms. After a few seconds, the light faded and he lifted his hands. The wound was completely healed, not even a trace of a scar to show her injury.

Talia flexed her arm in wonder. "That's amazing! I can't even feel any pain now."

"I still have no idea how I'm doing that, but I'm glad I could do it. Are you okay?"

"Yeah. I'm fine. Better than he is," she said, kicking the inert body of the man who'd hurt her.

"Good," Osric said, reaching out to rub her shoulder before turning to face the massive door the two men had obviously been guarding.

Osric walked up to it and pressed his palm to the surface, hoping that, since the ring, through the wolf, had brought them here, maybe it would somehow be a key. Instead, nothing happened. He concentrated hard, envisioning the door opening, but still nothing happened. No white light. No red light. Nothing. After a minute, he sighed and stepped back.

"Well, that didn't work. Can you do the thing you did last time?"

"It only works on more simple locks," Talia said, running her hand over the door, keeping them a few inches away, as if the door had an invisible coating. "I can feel … energy, coming off this. I think someone has enchanted it, to keep it from opening."

"But they were protecting it, so they had to know what was in there, right?"

"Maybe they have a key," Talia offered with a shrug.

Osric moved to check the bodies of their attackers, rifling through pouches and pockets. Aside from some coins and a dagger, he found a key and a map.

Pocketing the coins and handing the dagger and map to Talia, Osric started to walk toward the vault, trying to see where the key was supposed to go. He'd heard from Master Ironhand, who had once told him of helping forge some of the vaults for the new bank in Wolfsridge, that they would hide the keyhole, making it hard for someone who didn't know how to open the door.

He'd just found it, hidden under a movable flap that had looked like just another bracket, when Talia gasped behind him.

"This map has Eldham on it," Talia said, pointing at the map.

Osric walked back to her, looking at the map as she held it out for him. There were no names on the map, but there were markings, one of which did look like it was exactly where Eldham was.

"That makes this Silham, right?" Osric asked, pointing to another circled dot that looked to be where their neighboring village was located.

"I think so. They were searching for something. The ring, and I guess you, now. All of the circled areas are together, so they knew about where to look. It's been updated too. They knew you left Eldham, and that was only a day ago. Which means these people either just came here or were in contact with someone outside the keep."

"Let's find out what's in this thing and get out of here before more show up," Osric said, turning to and opening the vault door.

Osric led the way into the vault with Talia and the wolf close behind. The walls of the vault were metal; the glowing orb following them cast an eerie glow through the space, creating strange shapes.

As the globe moved, however, he realized it wasn't just shadows and a trick of the light. The wall wasn't flat metal. There was an intricate image stamped — no, etched — into the metal face. Talia must have seen it, too, because the globe began moving closer, sweeping around the walls, illuminating them directly.

It was all one image, wrapping all the way around the room, showing a massive battle. Armored knights wielding swords and shields clashed with hideous horned beasts. Massive giants swung spiked clubs, crushing men beneath their feet. Winged demons dove from the sky, talons extended. Fire and lightning rained down amidst the chaos.

At the center of the fray stood an enormous tower, its peak disappearing into the heavens. Above it all, next to the tower, a rip in the sky yawned open, spewing forth even more nightmarish beings.

"What is this place?" Talia whispered reverently. "What kind of magic could create something like this?"

Osric didn't answer. He was too busy staring at the pedestal in the center of the room, where what looked like half a piece of parchment rested. It was old and weathered, its edges frayed and crumbling. Osric walked to it, felt himself drawn to it as he reached out to pick the parchment up.

As Osric's fingers touched the parchment, a blinding light suddenly filled the room, seeming to come from all around them, but it was brightest around the parchment and his hand, which glowed brighter than the sun. Osric shielded his eyes against the intensity, the light seeming to push even through his eyelids.

And then, just as quickly as it began, the light vanished, leaving Osric holding the parchment, blinking away the flashing afterimage in his vision.

"What was that?" Talia asked, hurrying over to Osric's side.

"I don't know," Osric said, squinting at the parchment.

It looked unchanged, exactly as it had when he'd reached out for it. Talia stepped closer to him, bringing her hands up in front of her, palms facing outward, fingers spread apart. She slowly swept her hands out to the sides, keeping her palms outward. As her hands reached shoulder width, a light blue shimmer surrounded the area around her hands for a brief moment. As the shimmer faded, the light seemed to cling to the parchment for an extra moment, encircling it, causing it to glow.

It was amazing but seemed simple compared to some of the other things she had done over the last few days, which was why Osric was surprised when she inhaled sharply.

"What is it?" Osric asked.

"The ring," Talia said in a hushed voice. "Its magic ... it's gone. I can't sense it anymore."

Osric's stomach dropped. "What? How can that be?"

"I don't know. Before, I could feel the power radiating from it. But now ..." she waved her hand over the ring again, frowning. "There's nothing."

Osric reached up and cupped the ring dangling from around his neck in his palm, feeling the cold metal and ridges of the carvings in it.

"What does this mean?" he asked Talia urgently. "Is the magic gone for good? Was it destroyed somehow?"

"I don't know. I'm sorry, but the ring was already beyond anything Elder Miriam had encountered, and she knew much more about this kind of thing than I ever will. I didn't really even understand how your ring worked, let alone what gave it its magic. It was leading us to the parchment, which is magical somehow. Maybe it gave its magic over to the parchment? Transferred it somehow?"

Osric just nodded, looking down at the parchment in his hand. It made sense, even if it was a guess. It must have been ancient, but it looked new. Freshly made. It was covered in a strange script, the flowing, interconnected symbols were completely foreign to him. He turned and held the parchment out towards Talia.

"Can you make any sense of this?" he asked.

Talia didn't take it from him but stared at it for a long moment before slowly shaking her head.

"I've never seen writing like this before," she said. "I can read and speak several languages, but this is nothing I recognize."

Osric's shoulders slumped. After everything they had gone through to find this parchment, and now they couldn't even read it.

"But it feels old," Talia continued, tilting her head as she scrutinized the symbols. "Ancient, even. The writing, I mean."

"So what do we do now?" Osric said, frustration creeping into his voice. "This parchment was so important it was hidden away and guarded down here. But it's meaningless to us if we can't understand it. We can't just stand here. They had that map on them, which means they don't just live down here. They have contact with the outside world, at the very least. It's only a matter of time before someone else comes down here."

Talia didn't answer right away, looking around the room.

"We should go to Silham," she said after a moment. "We need to find out what's happening beyond these woods. The only people who seem to know anything are the strange men who keep attacking us. If we go to some of the places they've gone, get a hold of one of them somehow, maybe we can make them talk. Eldham was marked on the map, and they came for us there. It's only reasonable that they would have gone to Silham, too."

"That sounds dangerous," Osric said doubtfully.

"Everything that we've done since I ran into you in the woods has been dangerous. Besides, is it more dangerous than waiting around here?"

"All right, Silham it is," he conceded.

Chapter 6

A Moment's Calm

Osric and Talia crouched low in the brush, peering through the leaves at the wooden palisade surrounding Silham in the distance. They had been traveling for over a day now, making their way carefully through the woods since departing the ruined keep. It had been a near sleepless journey, both of them nervous with every step they took, on the lookout for both more of the men that had been hounding them and the more typical dangers of the forest. Thankfully, they'd encountered neither, making good time and reaching the small village well before Osric had thought they would.

Surprisingly, the wolf stayed with them the entire time. Osric had thought that now that the magic of the ring had faltered, the wolf would return to the forest, no longer under the control of the ring's magic. Instead, it had stayed with them, occasionally venturing away but always returning. While part of Osric was glad, both because the wolf had proven itself to be a good protector and because he'd grown attached to the animal after their journey into the keep, it now presented a problem, and was the reason they hid out of sight of the village.

"It can't go in the village with us," Osric said. "You know how people would have freaked out if someone brought a full-grown wolf into Eldham, especially the hunters."

Wolves were one of the dangers of the forest he and Talia had been on the lookout for. While they tended to keep their distance from humans, it was easy to accidentally stumble too close to their pups or den, forcing the animals into a territorial response. If it was winter, the danger would be worse, as the animals became more aggressive as they got hungry.

This time of year, with the forest in bloom and full of small animals, that was less of a concern.

Still, people were fearful of the wolves along with bears and a variety of other animals, less common creatures that had become, unfortunately, more common in their forests. Things like webscuttlers and bramblebeaks had become a more and more common sight, and danger, in the Great Forest.

Besides, the wolf would make them stand out, make them memorable, which was the last thing someone being hunted wanted to be.

"I suppose you're right. I'll miss ... him. Or her. I never even thought to check," Talia said, glancing at the wolf, who sat patiently a few feet away, its intelligent eyes fixed on the two humans.

"We haven't even given it a name."

"What does it matter? It's not like it's going to stick around once we leave it behind."

"I guess it doesn't, but … it feels wrong, you know? After everything we've been through together."

"Fine, what do you want to call it?"

"I was thinking maybe Cinder. Its eyes kind of look like a burning coal in a furnace, and it's got an … I don't know … intensity to it that fits."

The wolf's ears perked up, and it tilted its head, almost as if it understood.

"I think it likes it," Osric said.

"You know it can't speak or understand Aelorian, right?"

"Hmm. I think he can."

"Are you sure?"

"Pretty sure. Yep, I think we should go with Cinder."

Talia rolled her eyes and said, "All right, fine. Cinder it is. Now, we've hung around here long enough. If someone notices us out here, they'll start to wonder what we're doing."

"Fine," Osric said, and went down on a knee in front of the wolf. "Listen, buddy. You can't come with us into the village. People will be scared, and we don't need any more trouble than we've already got. Can you wait out here while we're in there? We'll come back for you. I'll even try to bring you some food, okay?"

As Osric spoke, he first pointed to the village, and then to the wolf and a spot under a bush. For a moment, Cinder didn't do anything at all. Then, to Osric's surprise, it stood and padded over to the indicated bush, settling down and laying its muzzle on top of its paws, letting out a soft, mournful whine.

"I promise we'll come back," he said with one last look at the wolf before stepping out of the brush and onto the road.

"Wow," Talia said, following him. "Maybe it does understand, at least a little."

"You should have a little more faith," Osric said, smiling at her.

The pair made their way along the narrow dirt path leading into Silham, both trying to act as nonchalant as possible. The village was small, probably no more than fifty structures clustered together behind a simple wooden palisade. Much like Eldham, except for the palisade. A few villagers glanced their way as they passed, but quickly returned to their tasks, seeming to pay them no mind.

The tavern was easy to spot, a slightly larger building near the village center with a sign depicting a frothing mug hanging above the door. Osric held the door open for Talia, allowing her to enter first. The interior was dimly lit and smelled of stale ale and smoke, along with the faint scent of something cooking. It occurred to Osric, as his stomach rumbled, that he'd had hardly anything to eat since leaving the village days ago, other than the meager rations he'd split with Talia and a few berries she'd found for them on the trail. Maybe it was the fear and adrenaline, but he hadn't noticed until that moment how ravenous he was. A few patrons sat at tables nursing drinks, while others gathered around a card game in the corner.

They found a small table in the back, positioning themselves so they could observe the room. A tired looking barmaid approached and without a word, slid two wooden mugs in front of them.

"And two bowls of whatever I can smell cooking back there," Osric said. "Do you happen to have any dried meat or something like that you could wrap up for us to take? We've still got more traveling to do and are low on supplies."

The barmaid raised an eyebrow but then nodded. "We've got some sausages, but nothing dried. They should keep for a few days, though.

"Perfect."

"I'll bring 'em out with yer stew," she said, turning and walking away before he could ask anything else.

Osric took a big gulp of the ale. It was grainy, thick and tasted like heaven. Talia took smaller sips, but he could see her sharing the feeling, both forgetting their mission and just enjoying the feel of civilization again.

"So?" Talia said after a minute, starting to look around the room.

Osric followed suit. Most of the patrons seemed to be locals, though a few might be from outside the village or travelers. There were none matching the men who'd been chasing them, however.

"Seems ... normal."

"Yeah," Talia said, and then paused as the barmaid returned with two steaming bowls of stew and some greasy sausages wrapped in a cloth.

Before she could walk away, Osric asked, "Pardon me, but have there been any other strangers come through town in the last few days? We're supposed to be meeting some friends here before continuing on towards the Wyndemer, but it seems they haven't arrived yet."

The barmaid paused, thinking. "We get a fair number of travelers, since this is the only road south of Meareham that heads to the river, but none that seemed to be looking to meet up with anyone, or who stayed for long. A couple strange fellas did pass through, two days back or so, but they didn't look like you two. Real deep city folk by the look of 'em. I would have figured them for Wolfridge or maybe Farvale. They weren't looking to meet up with anyone, but they were asking around about some boy from Eldham and an old trinket or some such. Only reason they stick out in my mind, particular like."

"I can see why. Don't see many city people this far into the forest. Of course, we come from further south, not far from the boundary, so even less go there. Still, that's a strange thing to be asking about. Sound more like rangers than just travelers."

"Weren't no rangers, but I agree. Woulda told them if I'd seen the boy, though. They had a real dangerous look to 'em, the kind you don't want to lie to. Still, the few folk from Eldham who've come through here were older, so I couldn't help 'em. They headed off to Meareham, I think. Good riddance."

"Here, here. Don't take a stranger's trouble for a friend," Osric said, raising a glass.

It was an old woods saying, and one he'd heard Master Ironhand use many times. He hadn't really thought about those words on their own before, but he'd come to understand them more in the last few days than he ever had before.

"Don't I know it," she said, rapping her knuckles on the table before walking off to another table.

For a few minutes, they both ate in silence, their hunger greater than their curiosity.

"So, do we follow them to Meareham and hope we catch up to them?" Osric asked after a few minutes, finally setting his spoon down.

"We should look at the map again," Talia said, pulling the worn parchment from her pocket.

She unfolded it and held it low, partially under the table, forcing Osric to scoot his chair around so he could see it.

"There's this point marked here, halfway between us and Meareham, and another on Meareham itself. Do you think they stopped there, or have something there like the keep that they would head too?"

"Maybe. It's worth checking out."

"Okay, then we go here next, and if no one's there, we go on to Meareham," Talia said resolutely, folding the map back up.

"Wait," Osric said, reaching out and putting his hand on hers, stopping her from putting it back in her pocket. "You should stay here. It's too dangerous for you to keep going."

"What? No, I'm coming with you."

"You've already been hurt because of me. Now that the ring's power is gone, I can't heal you like before. If something happens …" His voice trailed off as he glanced at the red stain on her torn tunic, memories of the dagger in her skin, blood flowing out, vividly returning.

"And what will you do alone against these men?" Talia countered. "I did as much as you in every fight."

"I know. I'd never argue you can't handle yourself, but I'd never forgive myself if something happened to you."

"And I can?" she demanded, a little too loudly.

A man at a nearby table glanced over with a scowl.

Osric held up his hands in a calming gesture. "I'm not trying to insult you. You've more than proven yourself both brave and capable. But this is my burden to bear. I was the one who found the ring. You got roped into this by accident."

"And then I killed a man to protect you, which makes it my burden too," Talia insisted, though more quietly. "We're in this together, like it or not."

"We have been, yes, but ... Elder Miriam has done so much for me. For both of us. If something happened to you out here, I could never face her again."

"She knows the risks of magic better than anyone. I chose this path. I could have run off after that first night, when they weren't right on our heels anymore, but I chose to stay with you, because this magic ... it's important. I can feel it. After you showed her the ring, Miriam talked about it all the time. Sometimes to me and sometimes just to herself. She knew how important it was. She would understand."

He didn't say anything right away. He was torn. Part of him wanted her to stay with him, desperately. She made everything seem less strange, gave him a sense of grounding. She also knew more about all of this than he did. He never would have gotten this far without her. But … he was afraid. Afraid of what would happen if she was hurt. Or worse.

"Please, Osric," Talia said, her green eyes imploring him. "We're so close to finding answers now. I can feel it. We have to see this through."

"I don't like it, but … fine. Please be more careful. You've put yourself in too much danger already."

"We both have," Talia said, drinking the last of her ale and scooping up the sausages.

Osric hurried to finish his food and threw down some of the coins they'd taken from the men in the keep, before rushing to catch up with her as she walked out of the tavern.

"We should be able to make it to whatever's at this point before nightfall," Talia said.

Osric didn't say anything. He knew he wasn't going to win the argument, but he certainly wasn't going to act like he condoned her sticking to this quest with him. Especially since, without the ring guiding them any longer, they were just stumbling around the forest, hoping they could figure out what was going on.

They made their way out of Silham, without anyone stopping them or saying anything, and had gone a few steps down the dirt track into the forest when Cinder popped up out of the bush, its ears up and head cocked, panting slightly.

"I told you we'd be back," Osric said.

"He really is remarkable," Talia said, unwrapping the sausages and holding them out to him.

Cinder's eyes lit up, and he gobbled down the offering in seconds. Licking his jowls, he looked expectantly at her for more.

"Sorry, that's all we got," she said. "We'll find you more in the next town."

The wolf looked at her a moment before bending down and snuffling around her feet, as though perhaps she was hiding more in her boots.

"Let's get going," Osric said.

Chapter 7

The Watchtower

Osric ducked under a low tree, almost missing it in the fading light. They'd been walking for hours since leaving Silham, the air between them strained. He'd agreed that she could still go with him, in spite of the danger, but that hadn't ended the issue, apparently.

Since they'd left the village, every time Osric tried to talk to her, she'd ended the conversation quickly, with muttering he couldn't really hear, but knew were sarcastic from her tone. He knew she was angry at him, but he couldn't help wanting to keep her safe. Their trip from the keep where they'd found the map and Silham had been harrowing and nerve-wracking in its own right, but at least there they'd been a team, working together. It had felt good, having her with him.

Now, he only felt nervous, acutely aware she was both with him and far away, all at the same time. He must have been in his own head, or maybe because it was dark, but he was surprised when she grabbed his arm, stopping him from walking any further. At first, he thought she finally wanted to talk, but instead she pointed past him. It took a moment to see in the dim light, but he was able to make out what looked like a thin, crumbling stone...tower, was the closest thing he could think of, although the top of it had been gone for a long time.

"What is that?" he asked, craning his neck to try and see it better through the trees.

"An old watch tower of some kind," Talia said. "There's one maybe a half day's walk north of Eldham. It's not on any road, but it's near an area where some wild herbs Elder Miriam sometimes had me pick. When I asked her about it, she told me these towers were built in a time long ago, when the forest used to be much smaller."

"This wasn't always forest?" Osric asked, the thought never having occurred to him that The Great Forest would be anything other than The Great Forest.

"No. The forest was once, a long time ago, much smaller than it is now. I think these might have been built near the edge of the forest, but it's hard to tell, since they were put here so long ago."

"How long does it take the forest to grow from here all the way up to the Beartooth Ridge and Wolfridge. Wolfridge is hundreds of miles away."

"Hundreds or even thousands of years. Elder Miriam said these ruins likely predate the formation of the Crownlands themselves."

Osric stared in amazement at the revelation. He knew little of history and his notion of how old the Crownlands was kind of vague. To him, they might have well have always existed. He knew, somewhere, that they hadn't. He'd been told tales of the Age of Darkness, full of dragons and demons of fire, but those were as much stories. Dragons and demons weren't real. They were something made up to scare and entertain children.

Not that he doubted Talia or Elder Miriam. They both knew more of the world than he ever would, and if they said these existed from a time before the Crownlands, then they must. The crumbling structure did look old. More a stack of stones held together by vines than a structure, at least from his limited view through the trees.

Osric was about to ask something else when Cinder's ears pricked up and he began sniffing at the air, as though catching an unusual scent. Osric and Talia exchanged a glance before peering more intently at the tower in the distance, searching for whatever set the wolf off.

Osric stared through the trees for almost a minute before he saw it, a thin wisp of smoke drifting lazily up from the other side of the structure, rising in a plume that curled and twisted in the breeze.

"There," Osric whispered, pointing a little to the left of the crumbling tower. "Smoke. Coming from the other side of the tower."

It took Talia a moment before she found it, saying, "Ohh. Someone must be camped there. Do you think?"

They exchanged a glance. This was one of the locations marked on the map, more or less, which meant it might be another one of the strange men that had been chasing him. Like the ones at the bottom of the keep guarding the map.

"We should circle around and see. Real far out so he doesn't spot us."

Talia nodded. Moving as silently as possible, they looped far out and came up slowly behind the crumbling tower. Crouching in the underbrush, they could make out a small campfire flickering beside a bedroll. A figure sat hunched near the flames, dressed in dark leathers similar to the men who had attacked them.

"He's dressed like the others," Osric whispered.

"We should capture him. He might have answers about why they're after your ring, or that page, or something."

This had been why they'd come out here. To find some way to get answers. But now that he was here, looking at another one of the men trying to kill him, he hesitated.

"Osric?" Talia prompted.

"Yeah. You're right. We'll go on my signal," Osric said, before kneeling down to look directly at Cinder. "We want him uninjured. We want to frighten him. Don't bite him unless you have to."

The wolf cocked its head at him, but otherwise did nothing.

Osric looked up at Talia who whispered back, "It worked outside Silham."

"Yeah," he said, slowly pulling his sword out of its scabbard and creeping to the edge of the forest close to the ruined watchtower, ready to charge if the man gave any indication he heard them.

"Now," Osric yelled as they got to the edge, pushing himself up and charging forward.

Cinder dashed past him, springing onto the man's back and sending him crashing sideways with a startled shout. The stranger started to move and froze as he looked up, directly into the face of a wolf looming over him, lips peeled back to reveal dripping fangs as it growled menacingly.

The man's hand started to slide sideways, to a sword just in reach, maybe hoping to not startle the wolf until he struck it down. Just as his hand got near the hilt, Osric stomped hard on the back of it, eliciting another sharp cry of pain.

The man's eyes darted from the wolf to Osric, going even wider as he found Osric's blade poking into his exposed throat. Osric pressed the blade harder, drawing a thin line of blood as the man's breathing grew shallow and his eyes bulged.

"Don't try it," he warned.

The man froze, barely breathing.

"Why have you been chasing me? What do you want?"

"I don't know what you're talking about," the man said. "I'm just a traveler."

"Just a traveler? Wearing armor like that and carrying a sword? Camp right at the spot where we expected to find one of you? I think not. Cinder, rip his throat out," Osric said, hoping Cinder wouldn't actually do it.

The wolf's growl began a snarl as it leaned closer in, saliva falling down onto the man's chin as the wolf opened its mouth.

"Alright, alright!" he cried out, his composure breaking. "We're looking for something you found, some kind of relic."

"Cinder, wait," Osric ordered, although the wolf had already stopped on its own. "What kind of relic? Why were you looking for it?"

"I don't know exactly. Something small, maybe an amulet, talisman, or ring. All we know is it's very ancient. My superiors said someone found it near the village of Eldham, but they escaped and ran into the forest. We were told to find it."

"Who ordered you? Who are your superiors?"

The man hesitated again.

"He's only had a few sausages in the last day. I guarantee you he's hungry. If you won't talk, I'm willing to let him feed."

"The Brethren!" the man blurted out. "We serve the Brethren."

"What are the Brethren?"

"We protect the world. We've done so since the reckoning, a thousand years ago. We protect it from threats and tyranny."

"What do you mean..." Osric started, but his question was cut off by another voice.

"Roland, why are you ..." a man was saying as he suddenly appeared, coming around the watchtower, only to cut off mid-sentence as well, freezing in place at the sight of Osric, Cinder, and Talia standing over what was, presumably, his friend.

For a moment, no one moved, all just looking at each other in pure shock. Then everyone started at once, including Roland, who ripped his hand out from under Osric's foot and grabbed for his sword hilt.

Cinder, however, was faster, his teeth sinking into the man's neck, which was only saved by his lunge to the side, causing Cinder's teeth to rip out a chunk of flesh on the side of the neck, instead of his throat out entirely.

Roland yelled, his eyes going wide with shock and pain, his weapon clattering back to the dirt forgotten as he pressed his hand against his neck, blood seeping from between his fingers.

Talia moved nearly as fast. Raising her left hand, fingers splayed as if to grasp the very air. Her right hand began to circle rapidly in front of her splayed fingers, tracing a glowing path. As her right hand finished its circular motion, it thrust forward sharply. Suddenly, three glowing bolts shot from her thrust palm, each finding their mark on the second man's chest. He staggered back, letting out a cry of pain as the glowing bolts penetrated through his armor and into his flesh.

Osric charged the man, swinging his sword with all his might. His opponent had stumbled back as Talia's magic had struck him, however, causing Osric's sword to swing through empty air where he once stood.

Roland, still on the ground, made a desperate attempt to defend himself. He reached for his fallen sword again, only to have Cinder release him and attack again, this time straight across his throat. Roland made a weak gurgling sound as the wolf jaws clamped down.

Seeing his friend being mauled, the injured man rallied and swung with a mighty bellow. Osric tried to block it, but his sword was still out of position, easily pushed aside as the weapon slashed across Osric's side, sending a bolt of searing pain shooting through him.

Talia, however, wasn't finished. Her hands spun in front of her, dancing through their intricate pattern, sending a cone of fire past Osric and into the man's face. Osric could feel the heat of the blast as it passed, causing him to jump back to avoid being scalded.

The man let out a scream as his skin started to melt and his hair caught on fire. Dropping his sword, he turned and ran the direction he came, his screams echoing through the trees as the glowing light receded away from them.

Cinder finally released his grip as Roland's body went limp, the life drained from him.

Osric, clutching the wound on his side closed, looked from the smoldering remains of the trees where the wounded man had fled to Talia, who stood motionless, her eyes wide with shock.

"Are you alright?" he asked her.

She gave a small nod, still looking past him into the trees, the smell of burnt flesh still hanging in the air. She gave herself a little shake and looked to him.

"You're hurt!" she exclaimed, rushing over to him and moving his hand out of the way to see the injury.

"It's not too deep, I don't think."

Reaching down, she ripped a small tear in the hem of her dress and tore it around until she had a long strip of green fabric. Pulling his shirt up, she wound it around his middle, over the cut, cinching it tight.

"This isn't great, but it should help keep it closed and slow the bleeding," she said.

"Thanks."

He looked over to the body of the man they'd been questioning, his throat a bloody mess where Cinder had ripped him apart.

"So much for that," he said, pointing at the body.

"We got something at least," Talia said. "Maybe we should check him. See if he has something like those other guys."

"Yeah," Osric said, pausing a moment before walking to the man's body and bending down, digging through his pockets.

It was a strange act. Incredibly intimate and yet horribly morbid all at the same time. The man had a few silver coins, which Osric pocketed, and a small knife, which he handed to Talia. She was clearly more powerful with her magic than she'd ever be with a weapon, but he'd feel better if she had something.

What he didn't find was a map, or a note, or anything that might be helpful to finding out more.

Suddenly, a shout sounded in the direction the burning man had run. It was far off, but still close enough for them to hear it.

"His friends?" Talia asked as all three looked in that direction.

"We can't take that chance," Osric said, grabbing her hand and pulling her in the opposite direction, to the south. "We should go."

As the three hurried away from the dead man and his smoldering fire, Osric thought he could hear the voices getting closer.

Osric and Talia crashed through the underbrush, away from the sound of the approaching voices as quickly as they could, Cinder racing ahead of them. Osric hoped they could get enough distance between themselves and the watchtower that, after stopping to check on the now dead man, the trio would be far enough away that the racket they were making couldn't be heard. Branches cut into Osric's face, scratching his arms and legs, but he didn't stop. They kept running until his lungs burned.

Finally, he could take no more, and pulled up short. Talia doubled over, silently retching, although if it was from what had happened in the fight or the physical exertion, Osric didn't know.

Osric tilted his head and listened hard, Cinder circling around, sniffing the air. He couldn't hear anything, and the wolf didn't growl or otherwise react, which hopefully meant they'd left any pursuers behind.

"We should keep going," Osric said, placing a hand gently on Talia's back, as she dry-heaved into a bush. "We might have lost them, but they'll try and find us."

Talia stood up, wiped her mouth, and nodded weakly, following along silently as Osric continued their path south.

"Are you okay?" Osric asked after a few minutes. "Did you get hurt too?"

"No. I just... I'm still... I'm not used to this much violence. The way his face melted, and he ran, screaming, on fire..."

"He was going to kill us," Osric said.

"I know. I know. I don't regret it, I don't think. I just don't know if I can keep hurting people like this."

"Yeah," Osric said, putting his hand to his side, the bandage already wet with his blood.

He was less worried about hurting people than them hurting him, which had already happened several times. She at least had her magic. He didn't have the training to fight these people. He was learning, but without the ring to teach him, these lessons would turn fatal.

"Maybe you should…"

"No," she said, predicting what he was going to say. "We went over that already. I might need time to deal with melting a man's face off, but I'm not going to leave you alone out here. Especially since we have no idea where we're going."

"I know," Osric said. "We at least know more than we did."

"Not that it helps us. We already knew this was some kind of organization and they were after the ring. We also knew how ancient it was and that it had some kind of magic attached to it. All we really learned was the name of the organization, and that they had some kind of way of learning that about the ring.

We don't know why they want it aside from some vague statement of 'protecting the world.' None of that helps us find a way out of this mess."

"Yeah," Osric said, feeling dejected. "Maybe we should turn around, go to Wolfridge. Give the ring to someone there. The Greenwood Levy or find someone from the conclave. They might want it. Just... give it away. Make it someone else's problem."

"Maybe. If it's lost its magic, I'm not sure we could convince the conclave to take it. They might be able to feel some kind of residual trace on it, but I can't. And how do we explain to the Levy about everything that's happened? We killed several of them. Wouldn't they arrest us too?"

"I don't know. If... if things had gone different at the watchtower, I was thinking to give them the ring, since it's lost all its magic. That seemed to be the reason they were after it. They'd see it was empty and might leave us alone."

"Or, they'd decide the magic transferred to you somehow and keep chasing us," Talia pointed out.

"It can do that?" Osric asked, stopping and staring at her in shock.

He hadn't even considered the magic might not have gone away, but somehow gone into him.

"Maybe. I have no idea. Don't forget we also have that ripped in half page. They'd want that too."

"Fine. I don't care. We give it to them. To the Levy. To the Conclave. Whoever'll take it."

"And if they decide the magic has gone in you and want to cut it out of you, or something?" Talia asked.

Osric just shrugged. What could he say? Of course, he didn't want that, but he had no idea what else to do. He was about to say something else when, to the north, they heard voices and the braying of hounds. Squinting, he thought he could even make out torchlight.

"Damn. They're following our trail," Osric said. "We can't just keep running through the woods."

"Across the Wyndemere?" Talia suggested. "Throw them off our trail. We could cross the Wyndemere into Brakendale, make our way to Mereham from the north side of the river."

"Assuming they don't have people in Brakendale as well. For all we know, they could be on the other side of the river, waiting for us."

"What other choice do we have? Like you said, if we go south, they'll keep tracking us."

"Fine," Osric said, turning and starting east, quickening his pace back to a jog as the sounds of pursuit got closer.

The distant baying of the hounds grew louder as they ran east, spurring Osric and Talia onward. They could now hear shouting, as the men closed the distance. Talia stumbled, and Osric grabbed her, pulling her with him.

"Just a little farther," Osric urged. "We can make it to the river."

Talia nodded weakly. He spent day after day in the forest, pounding out metal. He knew physical exertion. She spent her days reading books and collecting herbs. She wasn't made for this kind of exertion. He could feel the sweat soaking through her clothes.

As the sounds behind them got closer, the forest started to thin, and he thought he could hear, above everything, the sounds of rushing water. Hope surged within him.

Osric burst from the treeline, the roar of the river no longer muffled by the trees. Ahead of them, the ground dropped off, falling to the frothing surface churning thirty feet below. The river was crashing over branches and stones, rapids that would be deadly to any who tried to swim it.

"This way!" he called to Talia and Cinder on his heels as shouts sounded behind them.

Osric ran along the edge, heading south, stopping every minute or so to peer over the edge, squinting to make out shapes in the darkness.

"What are you doing?" Talia asked after he stopped for the third time.

Instead of answering, he grabbed her hand and pulled her after him, looking back and forth along the edge. Finally, he saw what he was looking for. Skidding to a halt, he turned and knelt down in front of Cinder, whose yellow eyes looked back at him, reflecting the moonlight.

"Cinder, listen, boy," Osric urged. "I need you to run upstream along the bank. Hide in the woods if they come. If it gets bad, just run, you hear me? Don't fight if you can help it. Come back here when it's safe."

The wolf whined, ears pinned back.

Osric clenched his friend's ruff, and said, "Please. I know you understand. Go on now. Go!"

He was breathless, his voice wavering as he tried as hard as he could to get the message across to the animal. He wanted it safe, and if it stayed with them, it would get them all killed. The animal held his gaze a moment longer, then turned and loped into the brush.

"What are we doing?" Talia demanded again.

In response, Osric took her hand and led her to the edge of the cliff, to the spot he'd located. The shouts of their pursuers, until it felt like the baying of their hounds were practically on top of them.

"Here," he said, guiding Talia to the edge. "We have to climb down."

Talia's eyes widened as she looked at the steep drop. "Are you insane? We'll fall!"

"We don't have a choice," Osric insisted. "It's this or get caught."

He swung his legs over the edge, finding footholds in the rocky face. Slowly, carefully, he lowered himself down, his fingers gripping the narrow ledge. Once he was stable, he reached up to Talia.

"Come on," he urged. "I'll help you."

Talia hesitated for a moment, then nodded. She sat on the edge, letting her legs dangle over the side. Osric grasped her hand, guiding her down. She clung to him, her breathing rapid and shallow in his ear as she clung to him, audible over the roar of the river thirty feet below them.

Osric shimmied the two of them across until they were underneath a shallow overhang. Osric pulled Talia close, holding her tightly between himself and the cliff face, pressing them into the a shadow. The ledge was narrow, barely wide enough for both of them. Osric could feel Talia trembling against him.

Above them, the sounds of pursuit grew louder. Boots crunched on the ground, voices shouting to one another.

"The trail ends here!" someone called out.

"They must have jumped," another voice responded. "To get away from the hounds."

Osric held his breath, his arms tightening around Talia. He wanted to lean back and look to see where they were, but he dare not. He knew they were somewhere above him, and all it would take was one person looking over to discover them.

"It's too dark to see anything down the river," a third voice said.

"Damn it," the first man cursed. "Zev's not going to be happy about this."

"Someone needs to go back and tell him they've gone down the river," the second man said.

"If they jumped, surely they're dead? Even in the dark, I can make out the rocks," a third voice said.

"Do you want to tell Zev that?" the first voice said again. "Go tell him what's happening. The rest of you, with me."

The was a flurry of sounds above them, boots and paws moving in what seemed like every direction. In spite of the deafening sound of rushing waves, Osric held his breath, afraid someone might hear them, frozen in place even as the noises above faded.

For a long time, they remained there, minute after minute, Osric's arms cramping as he pressed them into the cliff face.

"I think they're gone," Talia finally said, her lips nearly brushing his ear.

"Yeah, I think so too."

Osric slowly released his hold on Talia, his muscles protesting as he unclenched his fingers from the rocky ledge. He tilted his head back, trying to peek past the ledge, looking for any signs of movement or sound. The night was still, but that didn't mean someone wasn't a step or two back, outside his line of sight, laying in wait.

Still, there was nothing for it.

"I think it's safe," he whispered. "But we need to move quickly. They could come back at any moment."

Talia nodded, her face pale in the moonlight. "How do we get back up?"

On answer, he looked back and forth then reached above him with one hand and bracing himself. Turning her around, he used his one free hand to place hers in the handholds he used a moment before. Making sure she had a firm grip, he slowly, slowly, carefully, he pulled himself up, his feet scrabbling for support. It was a painstaking process, each movement deliberate and cautious. One wrong step, one loose rock, and he would plummet into the churning waters below.

After what felt like an eternity, Osric hauled himself over the edge, his chest heaving with exertion. He turned immediately, laying flat on his stomach and reaching down for Talia.

"Grab my hand," he urged, stretching as far as he could.

Talia reached up, her fingers brushing against his. Osric strained, his shoulder screaming in protest, until finally, he grasped her wrist. With a grunt of effort, he pulled, bringing her up and over the edge.

They lay there for a moment, catching their breath, the solid ground a welcome respite from the precarious climb.

"We can't stay here," Osric said, pushing himself to his feet and offering a hand to Talia.

Talia glanced back at the river, then nodded. "Lead the way."

They set off at a jog, Osric in the lead, Talia close behind. The forest enveloped them once more, the branches reaching out for them. Just as they crested a small rise, a rustle in the underbrush made Osric freeze. He threw out an arm, stopping Talia in her tracks. They stood there, hardly daring to breathe, as the rustling grew louder.

And then, out of the darkness, a familiar shape emerged.

"Cinder!" Osric exclaimed.

The wolf bounded up to them, his tail wagging. Osric dropped to his knees, wrapping his arms around Cinder's neck, burying his face in the thick fur.

"Thank goodness," he mumbled. "I was so worried."

Cinder licked his face, as if to say, 'I'm here, I'm okay.'

Osric pulled back, ruffling the wolf's ears. "Good boy. You did exactly as I asked."

Standing, he said, "Okay, let's get moving."

CHAPTER 8

Fleeing South

Osric was exhausted. An hour had passed since they'd fled the cliffside, the hounds picking them up almost as soon as they started their run south. Without any tricks left, all they could do was run, barely staying ahead of the braying of the dogs and the flickering orange glow of torchlight in the woods behind them.

Talia looked as tired as he felt, and he knew they couldn't keep this up much longer. Even Cinder looked tired.

"Talia," Osric panted, "we need ... to find ... somewhere to hide. Can't ... run ... forever."

Talia nodded, too winded to speak. Her face was flushed and she clutched a stitch in her side.

The problem was that there was nowhere to run to. Nowhere to hide. Ahead, the tree line thinned and broke, and Osric hoped ... prayed, that they were coming to some kind of road or way to civilization, and maybe even help.

It wasn't to be. As they broke through the trees, they found themselves in a large clearing. They couldn't stop, the sounds still coming from behind him. They sprinted across the open ground and Osric thought they might make it across and back into the trees before their pursuers came through the forest behind them.

It wasn't until they were halfway across that he realized this was a trap. They hadn't been chased. They'd been herded.

A group of figures emerged from the shadows of the trees ahead of them. Men in dark cloaks, swords in their hands, stood between the trio and the forest. Osric skidded to a halt, Talia nearly colliding with him. He spun around, only to see more men stepping out from the woods behind them, cutting off their escape, angry hounds following behind them.

"Looks like the hunt is over, boy," one of the men said.

Osric gripped his sword hilt, mind racing. There were too many to fight. Talia knew it too, her eyes wide with fear.

"Look, you can have this cursed ring!" Osric shouted, holding up his hand, the ring flat in his palm. "I don't want it anymore. Just let us go!"

The man directly ahead of him, his face obscured by a deep hood, let out a harsh laugh.

"It's far too late for that, boy. You're coming with us."

He knew they were going to say that. Osric glanced at Talia, saw the fear on her face, and then turned back to the leader. If this was the end of his flight, he wanted to at least save her.

"What about my friend? If I go with you, will you let her go? She has nothing to do with this."

"No. She's seen too much. We know she's been helping you." He jerked his chin at one of his men. "She and the beast go in the ground."

The men started closing in, coming toward them from all sides. Talia pressed up closer to him. Osric slowly reached for his sword, fingers curling around the hilt.

Leaning in close to Talia, he whispered, "When I say run, go. Get to the trees."

She shook her head vehemently. "Osric, no. There are too many. You can't ..."

"I'll hold them off as long as I can. You have to get away. Find Elder Miriam; tell her what happened."

Tears streamed down Talia's face but she nodded. Cinder pressed against Osric's leg, a low growl rumbling in his throat as he eyed the advancing men.

Osric drew his blade, shifting into the closest thing to a fighting stance he could manage.

"This should be fun," one of the men said, laughing.

Just as the men closed in, a sudden burst of light filled the clearing. A swarm of ethereal, fire-fly-like creatures emerged from the trees, their soft chime-like voices filling the air. Each one glowed with a gentle, soothing light. The men stumbled back, shielding their eyes from the sudden brightness.

As Osric squinted to see what was happening, several wolves that looked as if they were made from wood flowed into view, their eyes glowing an eerie green color. They let out haunting howls that seemed to make the very trees tremble. Humanoid figures made entirely of living wood and foliage came running out of the forest at their call. They were followed by a dozen creatures that resembled stags, but with human-like proportions, standing on two legs, that bounded into the clearing along with a group of strange, almost shadows.

For a moment, terror flooded into Osric. These were creatures he'd never even imagined in his deepest dreams or darkest nightmares, which he assumed had come to help these men kill his friends and capture him.

Or at least, that was the first thought Osric had, seeing the strange and frightening creatures. Until the ethereal fireflies swarmed some of the men, unleashing another blinding flash of light. Several of the men cried out, their hands flying to their eyes as they stumbled about, temporarily blinded. The wooden wolves were right behind the light creatures, their thorny teeth and claws tearing into the disoriented men as they stumbled about, defenseless. Screams of pain filled the air as the wolves brought down four of the pursuers, mawing them and ripping them apart.

The tree-like humanoids raised their arms, and the grass and vines of the clearing surged to life, growing and ensnaring the feet of the men. They struggled against the sudden growth, but the plants held fast, rooting them in place.

Then came the stag-people, covering the distance in a few powerful leaps. They lowered their heads, their antlers slashing at the immobilized men. Three more pursuers fell, their blood staining the grass.

Seizing the opportunity, Osric charged forward, his sword flashing in the moonlight. He brought the blade down on one of the few remaining men not hindered by the strange creatures' attacks. The man fell, clutching at his chest.

Talia, not to be outdone, thrust her hands forward, her fingers splayed. Following the path her hands traced, three glowing bolts of arcane energy shot forth, striking another pursuer in the chest. He crumpled to the ground, wisps of smoke rising from his still form.

Cinder leaped at the nearest man, his powerful jaws clamping down on the pursuer's arm. With a vicious twist of his head, Cinder brought the man down, his scream cutting off abruptly as Cinder released his arm and went for his throat.

Only a handful of the men remained standing, and those few were in no condition to fight back effectively. Blinded, entangled, or confused, their attacks were wild and uncoordinated. Osric easily dodged a clumsy sword thrust, while a stag-creature contemptuously batted aside another with its antlers.

The wooden wolves and stag-folk pressed their advantage, and two more men fell beneath their onslaught. Finally, the tree-like people found new targets, attacking again, their powerful fists slamming into the remaining pursuers with the force of falling trees. Bones cracked and bodies crumpled under the assault.

In a matter of moments, only one pursuer remained, stumbling in confusion as a group of the amorphous shadows swarmed around him. He tried to flee, desperate to escape the fate of his compatriots, but there was no escape. The shadow creatures surged forward, enveloping the last man completely. His scream was muffled and cut off as the mass of shadows carried him off, disappearing into the dark embrace of the forest.

As quickly as it had begun, the battle was over. The clearing was still, save for the gentle chiming of the ethereal fireflies and the soft rustle of leaves in the wind. Osric backed up, putting his body between the creatures and Talia.

One of the stag-folk stepped forward, his movements graceful and fluid. He had a lean, muscular torso and powerful deer-like legs covered in soft brown fur. Small antlers protruded from his forehead above large, expressive amber eyes. He held up his hands in a placating gesture.

"Peace, travelers. You have nothing to fear from us," the stag-man said, his voice rich and melodic.

Osric didn't lower his sword. "Who ... what are you? Why did you help us?"

The stag-man smiled. "I am Valen of the Stag-folk. When we sensed the disturbance, we came to investigate. It seems we arrived just in time."

Talia peered around Osric's shoulder.

"I've read about creat... about you. Stag-folk, briar-wolves, shimmerlings ... But I thought you were just myths and legends."

"As you can see, we are quite real. We've been expecting you."

"Us? Why?"

"The sage of the forest told us you were coming, sent us to the border to wait for you."

"The border? The border of what?"

"Avendell, of course," Valen said, smiling.

Osric stared at the deer-man in disbelief.

"Avendell? That's impossible. No one goes there. The forest is haunted."

Valen chuckled, a warm and soothing sound. "That's not entirely true. It is not haunted, only protected. Some do come through our borders, if the Veilguard allows it."

Talia stepped out from behind Osric, her curiosity overcoming her fear.

"The Veilguard?"

"That is not for me to tell you. Suffice it to say, they protect Avendell and decide who may enter."

Talia wasn't done, however.

"Why are you taking us to Avendell? I thought spirits could only exist in the mystic forest; how can you be here? Who told you to find us? Who is this sage?" she said in rapid succession, the words tumbling on top of each other.

Valen's musical laughter filled the clearing, his amber eyes sparkling with amusement.

"So many questions, little one. Your curiosity is admirable, but your answers must wait," Valen said, and then cocked his head, staring at her as if he saw her for the first time. "Tell me, did you learn the magics you used here at the conclave?"

Talia hesitated, glancing at Osric before shaking her head.

"No, I didn't. I learned them from … from someone else. Someone who left the conclave before I met her."

Osric thought he saw a flicker of relief cross Valen's face, but it was gone so quickly he couldn't be sure. The stag-man nodded, as if this information confirmed something for him.

"We must make haste, now. There are more of these men in the forest and we cannot stay out of our lands for too long."

"I … may we have a moment?" Osric asked.

"Please hurry," Valen said, striding away from them.

"I don't know about this," Osric whispered to Talia as they stepped away from Valen and the other strange creatures. "Following a bunch of ... creatures into a haunted forest doesn't seem like the best idea."

"It's not haunted, it's just magical. Elder Miriam took me to the wall once, to see it. When you get close ... the air shimmers with energy. You can feel the magic. Besides, they saved our lives. Those men would have killed us. I think ... I think we should trust them."

"Are you sure? Maybe they just want to eat us."

"You saw what they did to those ... brethren. If they wanted us dead, there is little we could do to stop them."

"I guess," Osric said.

"You have nothing to fear, young ones," Valen said as they rejoined him and the other stag-men. "Avendell is a place of safety and wonder. You will see."

With that, the stag-man turned and began to walk south, the other creatures falling into step behind him. Osric and Talia exchanged a final glance before following, Cinder trotting at their heels.

After walking through the forest for only a short time, maybe thirty minutes or so, Valen held up a hand, bringing the procession to a halt. Osric tensed, his hand going to his sword hilt. But when he looked ahead, he saw nothing but more forest.

"Why are we stopping?" Osric asked.

"We have arrived," Valen said.

"I don't see anything."

As if in answer, one of the briarwolves stepped forward. As it did, a shimmering blue wall of crackling energy appeared in front of it. Without missing a beat, the animal made of wood and thorns stepped through the blue wall, disappearing from view. Osric blinked, sure his eyes were playing tricks on him. But then one of the stag-folk followed, and then a tree-person, each one vanishing as it stepped into the shimmering wall.

"It's beautiful," Talia said in a whisper.

"Indeed, it is. The barrier that protects our realm is a wonder to behold."

One by one, the creatures passed through the shimmering wall, disappearing from sight, until only Valen remained with Osric and Talia.

"Do not be afraid," he said, his voice gentle. "The barrier will not harm you unless you have ill intent for those on the other side. It is merely a precaution to keep our lands safe."

Osric hesitated, eyeing the crackling energy with apprehension. Talia, however, seemed eager to experience the magic firsthand. She took a step forward, but Osric caught her arm.

"Wait," he said. "Let me go first. Just in case."

Talia opened her mouth to protest, but the look in Osric's eyes made her pause. She nodded, stepping back to allow him to approach the barrier.

Osric took a deep breath, steeling himself, glanced back at Talia, offering her a reassuring smile before turning to face the barrier once more. With a final nod to Valen, Osric stepped forward, passing into the crackling energy. The moment he made contact, a rush of cool water seemed to envelop him, as if he had plunged into a clear, refreshing stream. For a moment, it felt like all of his worries washed away. Like he was at complete peace.

Then, something changed. The cool blue gave way to a bright, vibrant yellow, the energy crackling and sparking intensely. Osric felt a tingling sensation spread across his skin, like the prickle of static electricity. The yellow light then deepened, turning a rich, fiery red that seemed to pulse with an inner life of its own.

As the red light washed over him, Osric felt a sudden, searing heat engulf his body. It was as if his very skin was on fire, the pain intense and all-consuming. He wanted to cry out, but the pain was so overwhelming he couldn't get his mouth to open or air to leave his lungs. He wanted to pull away from the agony, but he found himself frozen in place, unable to move or escape the burning sensation.

And then, just as quickly as the pain had come, it vanished, the red light fading back to the original cool blue, and Osric stumbled forward, out of the barrier into trees and leaves again, his breath coming in ragged gasps. His legs gave out beneath him, and he collapsed to the ground, his body trembling from the ordeal.

For a moment, everything went dark, and it felt like he'd fallen into an internal pit, with no sense of time or place. And then the sky and tree canopy were back, and Valen was at his side, kneeling down to check on him. Talia and Cinder came through the barrier behind them, a rapturous expression on her face, until she noticed Osric on the ground with Valen kneeling over him.

In an instant, her expression changed to one of concern as she rushed over and dropped to the ground next to him.

"Osric! Are you alright? What happened?"

Osric nodded, pushing himself up to a sitting position with Talia's help.

"I think so," he said, his voice shaky.

He took a few deep breaths, trying to steady himself before attempting to stand. Talia and Valen each took an arm, helping him to his feet.

Once upright, Osric looked at Talia, his brow furrowed with concern. "Are you alright? Did anything strange happen when you passed through?"

Talia shook her head, her red curls bouncing. "No, I'm fine. It was actually quite pleasant. Like stepping into a cool, refreshing stream on a hot summer day. For a moment, I thought I could see … I don't know. What happened to you? What did you see?"

Osric frowned, trying to find the words to describe the experience. He looked to Valen, who was watching him with a mixture of curiosity and concern.

"I'm not sure. At first, it was like you said. Like stepping into a waterfall. It was cool and refreshing, and for a moment, all my worries just … washed away. But then it changed. The blue light turned yellow, and it started crackling and sparking. And then it turned red, and it … it felt like I was on fire. Like my skin was burning."

"That is very strange," Valen said. "As far as I know, that has never happened before."

Osric looked at the shimmering barrier, then back at Valen. "What does it mean?"

"I do not know. But I will have to tell the sage what happened. He may have some insight."

"You said that name before. Who is this sage?" Talia asked again.

"The sage is the highest druid in Avendell. He communicates with the Veilguard and decides what happens within the forest."

"You mentioned them before, too," Talia said, clearly frustrated.

"I know you have many questions, but I am not the right person to explain these things. I wish I could help, Talia red-hair, but we stag-folk … we do not delve into the mysteries. It really is best for the sage to explain."

"You said the sage told you about us, but why would he or this Veilguard be interested in us?" Osric asked. "We're just two strangers from a small village."

"Not just any strangers," Valen said. "The sage told us of two travelers and their companion who would come near the border of the forest. He said you were in great danger, and that it was of utmost importance for you to be brought before him."

"He knew we were coming? How?"

Valen shook his head. "The ways of the sage are not always clear, even to us. But his wisdom is unquestionable. If he says you must come, then it is so."

Osric exchanged a glance with Talia. The idea that someone they'd never met, in a place they'd only heard of in stories, not only knew they were coming but had sent help to save them was as unnerving as it was reassuring.

"Come," Valen said, gesturing further into the forest, away from the glowing wall. "We have a ways to go yet, and the sooner we get to the Grove, the sooner your questions will be answered."

Talia looked as if she might burst with the weight of all of her questions, but Osric knew they'd get no better answers, and that it would only make it take longer to find out what was happening if they continued with their questions. Besides, the sooner they got away from the shimmering blue wall, the happier he would be.

"We can wait for answers, I guess," he said, placing a hand on Talia's arm.

She gave him a look that suggested he maybe shouldn't have answered for her, but then she nodded and said, "Okay."

The stag-man nodded, smiling at the byplay, and turned, leading them onward.

As they walked, Osric couldn't help but marvel at the otherworldly beauty of Avendell. From the corner of his eyes, the trees were unlike any he'd ever seen, their trunks shimmering with an inner light, their leaves glowing in hues of gold and silver. When he stopped to look at them directly, however, they looked like normal trees. He didn't know if he was just tired or if it was some kind of magic, but he suspected the latter. Even the very air seemed to hum with energy that made the hair on his arms stand on end.

Cinder, who had been following close at Osric's heels, suddenly darted ahead, disappearing into the underbrush. Osric called to him, but the wolf did not return.

"Do not worry," Valen said, noticing Osric's concern. "No harm will come to your companion here. The creatures of Avendell know one another."

"He's been here before?" Talia asked, her voice filled with wonder.

Valen nodded. "Many times. He is a friend to the forest, and to the sage."

Did that mean the sage knew about the keep? About the document inside? Had the wolf been sent to guide them to it?

With every step they took he had more questions. All of which would, frustratingly, have to wait until they got to wherever Valen was leading them.

Chapter 9

The Sage of Avendell

Osric and Talia followed Valen deeper into the heart of Avendell. The forest grew denser, the ancient trees towering overhead, their branches intertwining to create a canopy that filtered the sunlight into a soft, emerald glow. The air hummed with a subtle energy, a palpable sense of life and magic that seemed to permeate every leaf and blade of grass.

As they walked, Osric noticed the growing presence of otherworldly creatures. Ethereal wisps darted between the trees, leaving trails of shimmering light in their wake. Briarwolves, their fur a mix of earthy browns and vibrant greens, watched from the shadows, their eyes glinting with an uncanny intelligence. Tree-like humanoids, their bark-covered bodies adorned with leaves and vines, moved silently through the undergrowth, blending seamlessly with their surroundings.

As they walked, Cinder eventually rejoined them, walking beside Osric, which was a relief. Even though he hadn't met the wolf that long ago, he'd come to really like his companion, finding his presence almost comforting. After a long time, with the number and variety of creatures surrounding them growing to a point that left Osric almost speechless, Valen led them into a clearing surrounded by evenly spaced, ancient trees. Each tree was unique, its bark bearing intricate carvings and symbols that seemed to pulse with a soft, inner light. In the center of the grove, an old man in flowing robes stood waiting, his silver-white hair cascading down his back, his hands clasped in front of him.

"Welcome to the Concordant Grove," Valen said to Osric after bowing his head respectfully to the old man. "The heart and soul of Avendell."

The old man smiled, his weathered features creasing with warmth.

"Thank you, Valen. You have done well in bringing our guests here safely."

"Happily, Rodan," Valen said, bowing once more before turning and disappearing into the forest, leaving Osric, Talia, and Cinder alone with the old man.

"I am glad you made it to Avendell unharmed, Osric Yarrow. I am Rordan Maddox, who some call the Sage of Avendell. We have much to discuss, I think."

"How do you know me?" Osric asked.

"I don't know you, not exactly. The Concordancy gifted me with knowledge of an artifact from long ago, one that has come through the veil and is important to the very survival of our world. The vision showed me a young man who found the artifact and was being chased by a group of people who wanted to claim it for themselves. Do you have the item with you?"

Osric hesitated for a moment before reaching into his pocket and pulling out the ring, holding it out in the palm of his hand.

"It's just a ring now," Osric said as the sage took the ring out of his hand. "The magic left it once we found the document you sent us for."

The sage's eyebrows rose, and he looked at Osric and Talia oddly. "I did not send you for a document."

"Cinder led us to it," Osric said, gesturing to the wolf. "Valen indicated that you knew Cinder, and I assumed that he guided us to the keep where we found the document on your orders."

"Strange. That wasn't my doing. It seems the Veil-guard must have communicated with him directly."

"He works for someone else? He can understand people? I mean, I knew he could, since he kind of does what we ask him to, but still... wow."

"Cinder is a special animal, indeed. He was found as a runt on the very boundary of Avendell, left to be nurtured by its magics. He has always been touched by the Veilguard, possessing abilities far beyond those of normal animals. Perhaps that is why they chose him to aid you in your quest," the Sage said, before kneeling down, coming eye-to-eye with the wolf. "Have your new friends given you a name? Do you like it?"

Cinder pawed at the ground, his tail wagging as he let out a soft bark of affirmation. Maddox chuckled, running a hand through the wolf's thick fur.

"Who are the Veilguard, and how can Cinder communicate with them? What is this ring, and how did it travel through time? What is the Veil? What is the Concordancy you mentioned? The document? What is all of this about?" Talia, who had been growing increasingly agitated, finally let out in a near solid stream.

The sage laughed again, much as Valen had done the last time Talia became overwhelmed with questions. She was less amused than Osric was, scrunching her face up in annoyance, which only made Osric smile more. Thankfully, her attention was on the sage and not him. He had experienced enough of her ire at people finding her amusing when she was being herself as children, he didn't want to taste it now that he knew what kind of power she wielded.

"I was told you were full of questions. I can see they were right. Curiosity is a common trait in those bearing the taint of magic."

"What... what does that mean?" Talia said, finally glancing back at Osric, concerned by his choice of words.

"A good question, but not a simple answer. I was told you did not study with the conclave. Is this correct?"

Osric couldn't help but wonder who had told the sage about that, since they had had that conversation with Valen, who hadn't relayed any of what they had talked about before leaving to rejoin his people.

"No. I studied with an elder from my village. She studied at the conclave, but left many years ago after a dispute."

"I see. Well, the simplest way to answer is by starting at the beginning. You see, Peridia is surrounded by a powerful force, call it energy or magic, if you will, that not only brought our world into being but also protects it from the rest of reality. This energy keeps us separate and protects us from those other realities, planes of ice and fire, spirit and life, death and all the other infinite realities that surround ours."

Osric couldn't help but let out a soft "wow" under his breath.

"I know it's a big idea, Osric. But it's important to understand that we are forever separated from those other realities, each protected from the other by this energy we call the veil. Tell me, Talia, where do you believe your magic comes from? The ability to weave the power you do?"

Talia hesitated for a moment before saying, "From the energies around us. Magic is everywhere, surrounding us."

"Yes, that is what the conclave teaches, but it isn't quite right. The magic you wield is a part of the veil itself. When you manipulate those energies, you are pulling at the very fabric of the veil, accessing the immense power it contains. And that," the sage said, his tone growing more serious, "is where the danger lies."

"What do you mean by danger? How can using magic be dangerous?" Talia asked.

"I know this is hard to accept, but it is because you, and the rest of the conclave, misunderstand the nature of magic itself. When you wield the energies from the veil, it is possible to remove a piece of it. A tiny thread, so small you might not even notice its absence."

He plucked a single thread dangling from the sleeve of his robe, holding it up for Osric and Talia to see.

"Individually, it matters very little. As you can see, even though I removed this, my clothes are still functional," he said, releasing the thread, letting it be carried away by a breeze. "But, over thousands of years, done by thousands of mages, those threads begin to add up. Worse is when the energies are used to imbue power into a more permanent object, such as a wand, a potion, or other enchanted items. What most enchanters probably don't even realize they are doing is taking one of those threads and putting it into the item, cutting it from the veil entirely."

"Surely the Conclave must know about this," Talia said. "They... control magic. Teach everyone to use it. They have to know what it is."

"Maybe they do, it is hard to say. All I can tell you is that no one I, or any of my predecessors, ever met from the conclave understood the true nature of magic. But... I can give you proof that what I'm telling you is true. You see, all of these together have damaged the veil between realities. It is why more...

strange things have been happening in recent years, as the veil weakens. It's where the strange creatures that wander our world, out of sync with it, have come from."

"Do you mean Valen and the rest?" Osric asked, gesturing towards the forest where the stag-folk and briarwolves had led them into the grove.

"No, the stag-folk, the briarwolves, and others that live in harmony with our world. They were created by the gods, who made the veil when they created our world and are able to access it and use it safely."

"Does that mean... should I stop using magic? To keep from damaging the veil?" Talia asked, paling a bit as she absorbed what the sage was telling her.

"No, not directly. There are ways to use magic without harming the veil, and we can teach you those methods."

"Really? I don't have to give up magic entirely?" she asked hopefully.

"Of course not. Or at least, not entirely. Some magics, yes, you will have to avoid. Summoning, enchantments, raising the dead—these require pieces of the veil to inhabit something, to turn the energies into physical form. Such acts always cause harm to the veil and should be avoided. But magics that redirect, move, and shift energies, those are more like when a thread is pulled but then snaps back into place. You are using it, without breaking it," he said, and then laughed softly to himself. "The metaphor isn't perfect, but that's the general idea."

"I think I understand. Please, I would love to learn whatever you could teach me. I want to learn how to use my abilities without causing harm."

"This is all fascinating, but I think we're getting a bit off track here," Osric said. "What about the other things? The Veilguard, the ring, the document, and most importantly, why these people are trying to kill us?"

"I can answer many of your questions, Osric, but not all of them. Some knowledge I do not have, and others are not mine to share."

"But you can tell me something?"

"Yes. The Veilguard are a group of gods who came together thousands of years ago, after an event known as the Reckoning. I should say they do not call themselves the Veilguard; that is what we call them. As I said before, they do not communicate with us directly, so we are often left to our own devices when it comes to defining the things they tell us. The Reckoning was a cataclysmic event when a single great tear in the veil destroyed the plains that have now become the Shadowfell Marshes, unleashing creatures from other realms onto our world. It threw our world into chaos where much of what was known was lost, which is why hardly anyone remembers a time before those dark times, thinking our world started there, instead of much earlier."

"Who were these other people, who existed before our current kingdoms?" Talia asked.

"There was once a great nation, caretakers of magic and the veil. They are, in fact, my ancestors. The gods that wanted to protect and save Peridia gathered together the remnants of this civilization and brought them here, to what we now call Avendell. Together, they managed to close the tear and repair the damage to the veil. Since then, the Veilguard has worked through us to ensure the veil between realities remains intact, repairing what damage they can."

"But they haven't done a great job, have they? If, as you said, there are more and more tears in the veil."

"Talia!" Osric hissed at her.

"No, it's okay, she isn't wrong. They have failed, in part because there are others who want to see the veil gone, the boundaries between realities removed. Some of their fellow gods have been helping these other groups, undermining the Veilguard's efforts."

"But why?" Osric asked. "Why would any god want to destroy the veil?"

"That is something I cannot answer with certainty. The gods do not speak to people directly. At best, they give visions, which are often hard to understand and interpret. As for the motivations of the gods who do not grant me visions, it is difficult to say what drives their actions."

"So you really do speak to them?" Talia asked in an awed voice. "Get visions from the gods themselves?"

"Some of them, yes," he said, sounding almost proud. "The gods who stand neutral or against the Veilguard do not speak to me, but I receive visions from the gods who want to protect our world, guiding me and my people to doing their bidding. It was they who planted these, creating the magic of Avendell. From here, I can commune with them and be blessed by their presence."

Osric looked at the trees with their intricate carvings. The idea that the very trees surrounding them were planted by the hands of gods was almost too much to comprehend.

"So, they sent me the ring? Through time?"

The sage looked at the ring in his hand and shook his head. "I don't think they sent it, or at least, they didn't send it to you. The gods don't act so ... directly. They nudge, they suggest, but they do not command. I don't know if they allowed the ring to go through, or one of the caretakers realized it was possible and sent it through on his own. If that is the case, then your finding it was happenstance."

"And if they assisted in sending it through."

"It was still probably chance. The gods do not pick their champions. They are sustained by those who worship them, and worship without free will offers no value. No, they will empower those who serve them, but they will not offer power in exchange for service. Not even Aracus or Parios would. There would be nothing in it for them."

Osric wasn't much into religion, although Master Ironhand kept a small altar to Forus, the god of smithers and tinkers, in the smithy, as most craftsmen did. They'd branded the symbol of Aracus in a sword once, for one of the nobles from Wolfsridge who came all the way to Eldham specifically for one of Master Ironhand's swords. He'd said he wanted the blessings of the god of war to help him send his enemies on their way. Until coming to Avendell, Osric hadn't even been sure the gods had been more than superstition, or at least, not something a small village like his ever needed to worry itself about.

"But, they sent Cinder."

"Once you had the ring, then yes, they would have become involved, in their own way. Although, it's unlikely even an animal as smart as Cinder here could have found directions in a vision, enough to take you to where you found this document. Without examining it and the ring, it's hard to say what they have to do with each other, or where exactly they came from. All I know is that the ring bears the symbol of the caretakers of the veil, before their fall. It's the symbol of the Calaphium."

Both Osric and Talia sucked in a sharp breath. Osric might not have been well-schooled in magic or the gods, but he knew who the Calaphium were. Everyone did. A name only whispered in scary stories, fiends from the time of Chaos, before the rise of humanity, who tried to destroy the world.

"Why would monsters send anything through and why would the gods be willing to help them? They're evil."

"So everyone believes, but it isn't true. The world has been led to believe that is who the Calaphium were, but it is a lie."

Talia and Osric both took steps back. What kind of person would defend them, and what were they capable of?

"Do I seem evil to you? Does this place?" The sage said softly, not moving or making any threatening gestures. "Did Valen seem evil? Does Cinder?"

"Looks can be deceiving," Talia said.

"Very true, but consider the adventure you have been on so far. Who was it who tried to stop you, to kill you? You have some magics and felt the ring. Did it feel evil to you?"

"No," Talia said hesitantly.

"How would a lie like that even work?" Osric asked. "Everyone knows who the Calaphium are. Every child grows up afraid of them."

"Stories can be twisted, especially over thousands of years. The truth is, civilization is far older than Aeloria and the tribes that came before. Before the Reckoning, the Calaphium had a great society that lasted for almost three thousand years. They were the first great empire on Peridia."

"That doesn't explain why everyone thinks they're evil," Talia said. "If they were so powerful, how does no one remember them?"

"I'm afraid I don't have all the answers," he admitted. "Much of the Calaphium's past has been lost to time and intentional distortion. However, the ancestral knowledge of the druids and the forest itself records a very different history than what the world beyond Avendell believes. According to our tradition, the Calaphium were caretakers of magic, not the monsters they are portrayed as today. Yes, they were the ruling government that controlled all of Peridia, but our memory is that it was a benevolent, peaceful society. More importantly, the Calaphium had the power and understanding to repair any damage to reality and limit what weaving could be done to prevent harm from occurring. Until they fell, that is."

Beyond his instinctual revulsion at hearing their name, Osric didn't really know what to make of all this. He was a simple man and this was all too much for him. He glanced at Talia, who'd always been smarter than him, but she seemed as confused and skeptical. He wished Elder Miriam, or even Master Ironhand, were here to tell them what to do. What to believe.

"I know this is a lot," the sage said, seeing the expression on Osric's face. "I know it's hard to have heard something your entire life and then to be told it's a lie. I don't blame you for your skepticism."

"If they were so powerful and had so much control over magic, how did this reckoning even happen?"

"Again, this is very ancient history. It's not entirely clear if they were overthrown or fell from within. What we do know is that, once they were gone, there was no one left to heal the damage caused to the veil. We also know that the last members of the Calaphium came here, to Avendell, seeking refuge." He spread his arms, indicating the forest around them. "The Great Forest was always one of the strongest points of the veil, where the energy was most potent. They were able to use the energies found here to close the tear over Shadowfell and stop the worst of the damage from the Reckoning. Then, they pulled back, made this part of the forest a refuge. Here, we have been able to limit the amount of damage occurring within our borders, living in harmony with those energies, never forcing or taking from them. That has brought us safety for a time, but that time is coming to an end. Even our forests are starting to be encroached upon as the small holes across the world become tears, some of which have even stretched through our own barrier."

"So what do we do?" Talia said. "The ring has lost all its magic, but people are still after it. Do we hide here forever? Run until they catch us?"

"I don't know yet. I know the gods are interested in you because you found the ring. You may not have been chosen, but you've been given a burden all the same."

"What about the torn paper?" Osric asked. "If the ring, or Cinder, or whoever led us to it, then it's important, right? It's part of this? I tried to look at it, but I don't know what the symbols mean."

"You are right, it is clearly important. When I brought you here, I only knew that you had found the artifact and there were people who wanted to take it from you. Until I saw the ring, I didn't know of connections to the Calaphium, your finding the document, or even that Cinder here was sent to aide you. I will need to spend some time examining both the ring and the paper, to see what I can learn from them. I know you two have been running for a long time and must be tired. If you'll allow, I will spend the evening in study while you eat and rest. We can then speak again in the morning, after you are refreshed and I have had time to study."

Osric knew Talia was still suspicious and the thing with the Calaphium was kind of terrifying, but ever since he'd been thrown into this, he'd been running without a clue as to what to do. Not even Talia knew what they should do, and she was brilliant. He wished Elder Miriam or even Master Ironhand were here to guide him, but they weren't. He desperately wanted someone, anyone to tell him what he should be doing. Where he should be going. He was ready to settle for any help they could get, and he honestly didn't care who it came from anymore.

Osric glanced at Talia, who still seemed uncertain, but he could see the exhaustion in her eyes. They had been through so much in such a short time, and the promise of a warm meal and a safe place to rest was too tempting to resist.

"I think we should accept the Sage's offer," Osric leaned over and whispered to Talia. "We need time to figure stuff out, and we can't do that if we're constantly looking over our shoulders."

"Okay," she said, looking almost as ready to give up as he was.

"We accept."

"I am glad to hear it. You will be safe here in Avendell. Go with the Stag-folk. They will show you to food and a place to sleep."

Although the Sage hadn't called out or made any kind of sign, several of the strange deerpeople came through the trees, standing patiently a few steps away. Osric started to walk to them and then stopped.

"Can ... would it be alright if Cinder stayed with us?" Osric asked, turning back to the sage. "I'd feel better if he was."

"That is not for me to decide, Osric. Cinder is a creature of Avendell, and he goes where he pleases. But it seems he has grown quite fond of you, so I suspect he will choose to remain by your side."

As if to confirm the Sage's words, Cinder let out a soft bark, his tail wagging happily. Osric grinned, scratching the wolf behind his ears. He took Talia by the hand and they walked to the Stag-folk who were waiting. He couldn't say how he knew, but he was pretty sure none of these were Valen. In fact, it seemed like two of them might be women. Their horns were different, as was the shape of their faces, although they still looked like deer.

With one last look back at the Sage, Osric, Talia, and Cinder followed them out of the ring of trees.

CHAPTER 10

A Quest Given

The trio followed the pair of stag-folk through the forest, still amazed by the mystical feeling of the place and how the air almost hummed. Even coming from a life spent in the Great Forest, Osric couldn't get over how full of life this place was.

Osric was so enamored, trying to see everything around him, that he almost walked into the gargantuan tree the stag-folk stopped in front of, jumping back a step out of fright. Its trunk was so wide that a dozen men could not have encircled it with their arms outstretched. One of the stag-folk, a woman, Osric thought, giggled at his sudden alarm at the appearance of the tree. It was an odd sound, almost a high-pitched chirp ending in kind of a snort. He didn't know how he knew it was a giggle, except that he somehow did.

Osric shook himself from the confusing line of thought as the stag-folk led them to an opening at the base of the tree, the edges worn smooth by countless years of use. Inside, the tree was hollowed out, creating a spacious chamber. Spider silk hammocks hung from the walls, shimmering in the soft light that filtered through small gaps in the wood above them, like something soft and glowing was sitting in the gaps.

A female stag-folk, with chestnut fur and kind eyes, approached carrying two wooden bowls. She handed one to Osric and the other to Talia.

"Please, eat. You must be famished after your journey."

Her voice was like Valen's. Soothing and pleasant, like when someone sings a gentle lullaby.

Osric glanced down at the bowl. A strange broth swirled within, flecked with herbs he did not recognize. He brought it to his lips and took a tentative sip. Flavors burst across his tongue - savory and rich, with a hint of sweetness. It warmed him from the inside out, soothing the aches in his tired muscles.

"This is delicious," Talia said, her words mumbled as she tried to eat and speak at the same time. "What is it?"

"Roots and herbs offered up by the forest. It is good for fueling the soul and the body. I'm told humans find it good for bringing strength to the weary and comfort to the soul."

"'ish good," Talia said around more food.

Osric smiled at his friend. For someone raised by the ever-proper Elder Miriam, she'd always been a little bit of a wild child herself. Not that Osric didn't finish his almost as fast. Setting the bowl aside, he couldn't help but feel a little better, although it was unclear if it was some mystical quality of the food or just that he had been famished. He was full after one bowl of root and herb soup, so he was willing to lean toward the mystical.

Talia set her empty bowl down beside her, leaning back against the smooth wood of the hollowed tree and looked over to Osric. "I don't even know what to think about all this. The Calaphium, the Veilguard, how magic really works … it's overwhelming."

"I know. Everything we thought we knew … or I guess what you knew."

"It's like the world's been turned upside down. I mean, the Calaphium being guardians of magic instead of evil monsters? It's … it's … I don't even know what to think."

"Makes you wonder what else might not be what it seems, or what else we were told is wrong."

"Exactly," Talia said, snapping her fingers. "You know, Elder Miriam, she never trusted the conclave. I didn't really give it much thought and she didn't talk about it a lot or really say why, but I can't help but wonder if she may have suspected the truth all along."

"You know her better than I do. To me, it seemed like she knew everything, so it wouldn't surprise me."

"Not everything, but certainly more than she let on."

"But do you really believe it? Everything the sage said? About the Calaphium, I mean."

Talia considered the question for a moment before saying, "I don't know. It's a lot to take in."

"Right. I mean, these ... things we've always heard about as existing before time, they were actually a real empire? With people living and breathing before our recorded history? Just because he says it's a thing ... is it?"

"It is hard to wrap my head around," Talia admitted. "But there's something about this place, about the sage. I can't quite put my finger on it, but I feel like we should trust him."

"Really? Even with all the crazy things he's telling us?"

"Yes, even then. This place, Avendell, it's clearly special. There's a magic here that feels ... pure, untainted. And the sage, he doesn't feel evil. Quite the opposite, actually."

"I suppose you're right."

Talia smiled and said, "Besides, Cinder trusts him. And how bad could he be?"

As if on cue, Cinder lifted his head from where he lay on the ground between their hammocks, his tail thumping softly against the earthen floor.

Osric chuckled, reaching down to scratch behind the wolf's ears. "You make a good point."

They chatted for a little while, in their tree trunk room seemingly separate from the whole world, talking about how different things were, about the amazing things they'd seen and done, and about home. Neither mentioned the danger they'd been in or how afraid they'd been, as if even talking about it would bring the evil back down on them. Inviting it.

Over time, their conversation slowed, the gaps of silence extended. As Osric's eyes drifted shut, he couldn't help but feel a sense of safety wash over him. For the first time in days, he felt like they could truly rest, protected by the mystical embrace of Avendell and the watchful eye of their newfound allies.

The gentle sway of the hammock and the soothing sounds of the forest lulled him into a deep, dreamless sleep, his mind finally quiet.

The next morning, Osric felt better than he had in a long time, even before all of the crazy events that had happened over the last week. He loved learning from Master Ironhand, but sometimes, the mat he slept on in the back room left his back feeling sore and stiff. When this was all over, he was going to ask the sage to let him take one of these hammocks to string up instead.

To Osric's surprise, shortly after they woke up, a human in deep brown robes collected them instead of a stag-folk, leading them to another large tree, larger than the one they'd been given to sleep in. A curtain was pulled across the entrance, but the man, who never spoke to them other than to ask them to follow him, pulled it aside, not knocking or anything.

Inside, the sage sat hunched over a table strewn with ancient tomes and scrolls. He had dark circles under his eyes and his silver-white hair looked more disheveled than the day before. He glanced up as they entered, giving them a weary smile.

"Ah, Osric, Talia, please come in. I apologize for the clutter. It's been a long night of study and meditation."

There were a few seats around the room, most with things on them. Osric picked up some scrolls and set them gently on the table before taking a seat.

"I have spent the night attempting to commune with the gods, seeking their guidance on these matters. As with any attempt to gain knowledge from them, the answers I received were ... difficult to understand. I was able to glean a bit more from the document itself, or at least deduce a few additional details."

Osric leaned forward to look at the page they'd carried with them from the keep. The symbols on it still meant nothing to him, although he thought the script itself was beautiful. As much art as language.

"It appears to be written in ancient Calaphium, that much I can tell you. However, with the page torn as it is, longways, a significant portion is missing, and in such a way as to destroy the context of everything on the page. I think, perhaps, that was deliberate. The page had been protected with powerful magics, I believe, to keep it intact. Whoever ripped it might have wanted to destroy it but had to settle for just tearing it in two parts. They were smart about it, though. Had they ripped it the other way, I would at least be able to tell what the top half said."

"So can you can translate it?" Talia asked.

"No. If it was torn the other way I could, but like this ... it's not possible. Their language was highly context dependent. Seeing only half of sentences, missing other sentences, I lose too much context and the words don't make a lot of sense. Without the other half, it's impossible to tell what it said. What I can tell you is that it's very old, likely dating back to the time near, or just before, the Reckoning."

Talia whistled. "That old. You said they were from ... before."

Osric knew what she was getting at. It was hard to fathom a time before Aeloria, or at least a time before the dark days before Aeloria came into being, when people lived in small tribes and struggled to survive.

"I can also tell you that this ring bears the symbol of the Calaphium," the sage said, picking it up off the table in front of him. "I believe whoever sent it knew how to manipulate the energies of the barrier, essentially tying a thread, for lack of a better word, of energy from the barrier itself to both the document and the ring, connecting them across time."

"They sent the ring into the future, so someone there could find the document," Talia said, suddenly connecting the dots.

"Precisely," he said, before turning to look at Osric. "You said you found the ring in the forest. Where exactly did you find this document?"

"We found it in a hidden chamber beneath an ancient keep, deep in the forest. The place was in ruins, but there were signs of recent activity. There was this secret door in what used to be the kitchens that had been repaired and put in place, so it would be hard to find again. There were also these stone rings. When the ring got close to one of them, one that was partially melted, a ... tear, I guess, like you described, opened, and we could see through it. It was the same room we were in, but clean and new. The stone ring was whole. Somebody yelled and a man in the other room cast a spell and the rift closed, but for a moment, one of the men looked like he could see us through the rift.

"Fascinating," the sage said.

"There were more portals," Talia added. "They were in this long room protected by powerful glyphs, although the glyphs had long since faded. It had more of these stone rings, but they were … I don't know, I guess dormant or something. They were just stone, but they looked like the other one. Nothing happened when Osric took the ring near them."

After that, we ran into more of the men who were chasing us, who I guess are called the Brethren, or at least that's what one of them told us. They were guarding an ancient vault, and that document was all that was inside of it."

"Interesting," the sage said, leaning back and thinking for a moment. "It is possible to use magic to create portals, essentially tearing the veil to travel from one place to another within our reality. However, such acts would cause significant damage to the veil itself, which is why it is not a technique that I or any of my predecessors tried to learn. As I said last night, it's possible to imbue an object with any spell if you know how to work the veil, tearing pieces off and making them part of the object being enchanted. They could have used the magics to create these portals and weaved that magic into the stone circles you found. Someone with that knowledge, who understood the intricacies of the veil and its tears, might also possess the power to send objects through time."

"Like the ring and the document."

"Precisely. It's possible that the document originated from that very keep, created by someone with a deep understanding of the veil's workings."

"What about the Brethren? You learned about the ring through visions from the gods, how could they possibly know anything about it? And why are they so intent on getting the ring? Why were they guarding the document?"

"Truthfully, I can't answer much of that. We have had some contact with them in the past, and we know they are part of a group that seems to have an interest in the veil and magic, but their true motives remain a mystery. As do how they found out about the ring or why they want it so specifically."

"If they were guarding this document," Talia said, "then they must know at least some of what's happening, or what happened way in the past."

"Perhaps, but again, I just don't know what they know or don't know. Occasionally, they have stumbled onto Avendell. But the ones we've managed to capture knew nothing about their group's true purpose. Until now, we thought them to be mere nuisances. Treasure seekers with some knowledge of the arcane. It is clear now that we underestimated them."

Osric reached down and picked the ring off the sage's table, turning it over in his hand. "Is this of any use anymore?"

"No," the sage said. "Once you found the document, the loop closed. The ring's purpose was fulfilled. While historically interesting, there is nothing else I can gain from it. It is yours."

"So I should keep it?"

"That decision is yours to make."

Osric closed his fist around the ring and said, "I think I'll hold onto it. As a reminder of everything that's happened."

"Are you sure that's wise?" Talia asked. "If someone recognizes it, it could be a problem."

"I won't wear it or anything," Osric said, pulling the strap he'd carried it on from his pocket and running it through the ring before putting it around his neck and inside his shirt. "Besides, they didn't recognize it, and neither did the sage, who seems to know more about the Calaphium than anyone else. If it's from a small sect, it can't be that recognizable. And, with everything that's happened, it just feels weird to throw it away."

"What should we do now?" Talia asked, turning to the sage. "We gave you everything we found, so that's all finished, but those people are still out there hunting us."

"Well, your task is not completely finished. There is another part of this page out there that has to be found. The magic protection made it so that all they could manage was to rip it in half, so it's doubtful it's been destroyed. If the Brethren had the first part, it means they probably had a connection to whoever ripped it, which means they probably have the other half, too. Or know who does. Storing the two halves of the document separately suggests that they didn't want anyone to have the whole document. If we could get it and put the two together, we could translate this and find out what's really going on."

"If it's so important, why don't you go find it?" Osric asked.

"I wish I could, but there are few druids left, and we must take care of the forest, doing the work to keep the boundary around our haven up. This is one of the stronger places in the world for the boundary. If it became corrupted, it might become impossible to keep the tears from expanding until our world would be consumed. As for the stag-folk and the others who live here, they would … not do well in the human world. Just sending them out to rescue the two of you was an extreme danger."

The sage stopped for a moment, looking at his hands, clearly considering his next words carefully before looking back up.

"The gods have chosen you, or you chose the gods, or fate did. However we say it, you are meant to do this. You found the first half of the page, which is a sign you are the right ones to find the other half, too."

"I don't even know where to start."

"Well, there are places just outside the borders of Avendell where the veil has already begun to thin.

If the person who sent the ring through time was indeed using these openings to travel and connect across the ages, those locations might be a good place to start your search. I'm not saying there is a way to connect to him through them, but ..." he said, pausing and holding his hands out in a 'maybe' gesture. "Aside from that, as with the Concordant Grove where I met with you last night, there are places where the connection to the gods is stronger. Actually, we've found that tears in the veil create an even stronger opening for communicating with the gods than the Grove, but of course, this place was created to make those very tears difficult, so to reach them, you have to travel beyond our borders. The gods, or at least those that are part of the Veilguard, are clearly trying to direct you in this, so it makes sense that such would be a good place to start."

"Okay, we'll go and try to make some kind of contact," Osric said.

"If you don't find anything, you can come back here and we will try to figure out another option. The barrier will now admit you freely as friends of the forest."

"I don't know if Valen mentioned it, but the last time I passed through the barrier, I was knocked unconscious. It was ... painful."

"He did mention it, and that should not happen again. The effect you experienced was likely a residual reaction between the ring and the barrier. The ring carried a touch of the world beyond the veil, and the barrier here is a piece of that same veil. The two energies reacted adversely," the sage said, before placing a hand on Osric's shoulder. "Whether you find something or not, return here when your search is complete, so we can decide the next steps to solve this mystery."

A Rip in the World

Bidding farewell to the sage, who promised to continue trying to learn more about the half of a document they'd left with him and the people chasing them, the trio followed the reappeared Valen and his friends through the forest, back toward the boundary wall.

Valen told them about living in the forest and his people as they walked. Osric found all of it fascinating and could have listened to the near-musical way his people spoke for hours, finding it incredibly soothing.

It couldn't last, however.

Soon, they reached the boundary, and Valen and his friends bid them farewell. The pass through the boundary this time, for Osric, was much closer to what Talia had described. It was like passing through a waterfall without getting wet, the energy flowing around him, seeming to wrap him in a cocoon for what felt like both seconds and an eternity.

And then he was stepping out the other side. It was the same forest he had lived in more or less his whole life, and yet, somehow, it felt less. Even when it had just been them, it never seemed to feel lonely inside the boundary, like the very forest was keeping them company. Now, the trees were just ... trees.

"Looks like we're on our own again," Talia said, voicing Osric's thoughts.

"Yeah. I guess our break's over. Time to get moving."

Cinder whined, pressing his nose into Osric's hand. Osric scratched the wolf behind the ears and then started walking northwest, in roughly the direction the sage had indicated.

They walked for almost two hours, following a small animal trail that should lead them where they needed to go. This was a far cry from the woodsman trails or paths around their home village and was not that much different from just pushing through untamed forest.

At first they were silent, listening for sounds around them, as they had the last time they'd been in the forest, being chased by the Brethren, but all they could hear were birds and animals out in the trees. After a while, they started chatting again, keeping the conversation light, neither wanting to talk about the massive responsibility they, or rather Osric in their name, agreed to take on.

While it felt good to have some kind of direction after running aimlessly for so long, it also felt daunting. This was a job meant for someone else, someone who understood how these things worked. Osric was just a blacksmith's apprentice.

It wasn't until Cinder stopped in his tracks that Osric noticed the sound of metal on metal ahead of them. At first, he thought it might be equipment or some kind of cart, although they were too deep in the forest for either of those. Then he heard a shout and realized it was the sound of weapons coming into contact.

"Osric, no," Talia warned as he started to take a step toward the sounds.

"Someone could be in trouble. That's a fight, not someone chasing us. We have to check."

A skeptical Talia nodded after a second and followed behind him as Osric pulled out his sword. The steel-on-steel sound grew louder.

Although Osric planned to stay back, observe what was happening in secret, he suddenly found himself in a clearing as he pushed through a particularly large, dense patch of foliage.

A man in a Greenwood Ranger's cloak was partially surrounded by four other men. A fifth lay on the ground a few feet away from them, an arrow sticking out of his chest. Although Osric couldn't say how he knew, he was certain these weren't Brethren. Something about them, maybe their clothes or the way they carried themselves, said they were something else. Bandits maybe. That wouldn't be so uncommon in the forest.

What was clear to Osric was that the Ranger, whose entire task was patrolling and protecting the people of the forest, was outmatched. He glanced back at Talia, who was thinking the same thing he was. The five people had all suddenly frozen in place, weapons held still as they looked to the newcomers, each probably wondering if the new arrivals were friends or enemies.

"Back away from him," Osric said in his most commanding voice, which was, admittedly, much less authoritative than he would have wanted it to be.

The men heard it too, each smiling a cruel smile. They'd decided Osric was something else, something more to their liking. Prey.

"Deal with them," one of the men, presumably the leader, said to two of the men.

Two men peeled off, dashing toward Osric and Talia. Cinder reacted instantly, shooting forward, a blur of dark fur and bared fangs, leaping at the closest attacker. The bandit swung his sword but missed as the wolf twisted mid-leap before his jaws clamped down on the man's forearm, tearing through leather and flesh. The bandit screamed, staggering back as blood poured from the wound.

Talia's hands danced, fingers tracing intricate patterns in the air. Three glowing bolts burst from her palms, streaking toward one of the bandits still facing the outnumbered Ranger. They struck him in the chest, sending him reeling, wisps of smoke curling out from the impact points. The Ranger seized the momentary distraction, stepping forward and slashing at the other man facing him, his blade sinking into an exposed thigh.

Osric charged the fourth bandit, his own sword arcing in a vicious overhead strike. For a moment, their blades met in a jarring clang of steel, but Osric had learned a lot in his last several fights and used a move one of the strange men had used on him. Twisting his blade, he sent the enemy's sword sailing away from him while his sunk into the man's shoulder, cutting through flesh and bone.

Cinder wasn't through with the man he'd attacked. Rebounding, after bouncing off the man, the wolf leaped again, this time going for the man's throat. The sudden second attack was fast, too fast for the man to react a second time or bring his sword up to defend himself as Cinder's teeth found the man's throat. Blood sprayed as the wolf wrenched his head back, tearing out the man's jugular. The bandit crumpled, hands scrabbling uselessly at the gaping wound.

Talia also wasn't done. Her hands had never stopped weaving, switching patterns as soon as her previous spell was completed. This time, she created an arch of lightning as she moved her hands before sending it slashing across the clearing, past Osric and the man he was fighting, striking the bandit leader, the air splitting with a vicious crack as electricity ripped through the air. The man convulsed as it connected, his mouth open in a soundless scream as electricity coursed through him. He collapsed, his face locked in a rictus scream, smoke rising from his blackened armor.

The Ranger and the remaining bandit traded blows, each hitting only metal or missing entirely, until the bandit, witnessing his leader go down in a frightening display of magic, tried to reverse himself, swinging wildly at the Ranger, who ducked under it easily. Seeing his opening, the Ranger struck, his sword cutting through the man's body from shoulder to hip, sending him crumpling to the ground.

Osric and Cinder converged on the final bandit. The man backed away, fear clear on his face as the odds had suddenly, in under a minute, turned completely around, leaving him one against four. Osric feinted left, then lunged right as Cinder leaped. The bandit managed a single, desperate swing. Osric's blade took him in the belly as Cinder's jaws closed on his thigh, tearing away meat and sinew. The bandit stumbled back, pulling himself free from Osric's blade and taking two weak, staggering steps, trying to find an escape, before toppling over lifeless.

Osric hurried to the Ranger's side. The man leaned heavily on his sword, blood seeping from numerous wounds.

"Hold still," Osric said. "This worked once before."

He laid his hands on the Ranger, silently imploring the Veilguard for aid. A soft white glow emanated from his palms, as it had from the ring once before, although this time, the ring remained dormant and lifeless beneath Osric's shirt. Under Osric's hands, visible through his opened fingers, they could see flesh knitting and wounds sealing as if they had never been. The Ranger let out a groan, almost reflexively, as the pain left him.

"Thank you," the Ranger said. "I thought I was done for."

The Ranger reached down and felt the newly mended skin, shaking his head once again before standing and sheathing his blade.

Extending a hand to Osric, he said, "The names Rowan Wycliff. I can't thank you enough for your help."

Osric clasped the offered hand. "Osric Yarrow. This is Talia, and the wolf is Cinder. What was this all about?"

Talia nodded in greeting as Cinder padded over, sniffing at Rowan curiously.

"These bandits have been raiding villages in the area, the last one about a day's walk north of here. They've been growing bolder with each attack, taking more and more each time. The villagers are terrified. I was passing through a village after their most recent raid, and they asked for my help, which I, of course, am duty bound to agree to. I followed their trail, which they were making little effort to hide, but there were more of them than I anticipated. I thought I could take them by surprise, but ..."

"Well, it's a good thing we showed up when we did," Talia said.

"Indeed," Rowan said, before looking the trio over curiously. "I don't mean this to sound insulting, but how is it that someone as young as you has what clearly seems to be a loyal wolf companion? Wolves are notoriously difficult to train, yet this one appears completely bonded to you."

"It's a very long story," Osric said, scratching Cinder behind the ears. "Cinder is my friend. He's been with us through a lot."

"Well, a good friend to have, I guess. The three of you make for a rather unusual group, if you don't mind me saying. You're not exactly equipped for a deep foray into the forest."

It was true. The Ranger had a pack that looked to carry supplies, was warmly dressed and in armor, while Osric and Talia were wearing the same things they had on since they ran from their village a week ago, only much dirtier and torn.

"I know. It's ... complicated."

"We were sent to retrieve something from a place in the forest about an hour or so northwest of here," Talia said.

Rowan raised an eyebrow. "That's rather cryptic."

Osric nodded, a wry smile tugging at his lips. "I know. Believe me, I wish I could explain it better. It's just ... hard to put into words."

"Well, whatever your reasons, you saved my life. I owe you a debt of gratitude. However, this area is known for more than just bandits. There have been reports of strange creatures lurking in these woods as well. We dealt with a nest of webscuttlers not far to the west of here only a few weeks ago."

Osric couldn't stop the shudder that went up his spine. He'd never seen a webscuttler in person, but he'd gone with Master Ironhand once to find some lost travelers and had come across their handiwork. Part spider, part humanoid, intelligent and evil, they hunted for large prey, and seemed to have little fear of people, although they tended to avoid settlements.

Master Ironhand had said that they hadn't existed in his childhood. That the first time he'd heard about them was maybe ten or fifteen years ago. Osric had never considered where they had come from, but thinking about it now, and about some of the things the sage said about larger tears allowing creatures through, he wondered if that was what was happening. The sage had said the tears were getting worse, which would explain why there were more of them every year.

He and Talia looked to each other, both worrying that this could be a problem. Bandits and the Brethren were one thing, but evil creatures … he wasn't sure that was something he could face.

"Listen," Rowan said, breaking the silence, "I don't know what your mission is, but I feel I owe you a debt for saving my life. Let me accompany you to your destination. I can provide added safety and guide you through the forest."

Again, Osric looked to Talia. They had been trying to keep a low profile, and adding another person to their group could complicate things. But Rowan was a Ranger, a trained fighter, and someone who knew the forest and its dangers. Talia gave a subtle nod, indicating her agreement.

"We'd be grateful for your help," Osric said, turning back to Rowan.

Rowan smiled. "Then it's settled. Lead the way, and I'll watch your backs."

With that, the newly formed quartet set off. As Osric took the lead with Cinder, he couldn't help but wonder how they would explain things when they finally got to their destination. If they found the tear, and it was what the sage had described, it seemed unlikely Rowan would continue to accept 'it's a long story' as an explanation.

Still, even with that hanging over his head, he felt better having someone else with them.

They walked for almost an hour and, thankfully, didn't encounter any of the dangers Rowan had warned them about. Near the end of the hour, Osric was starting to wonder how they were going to find the exact spot. The sage's directions were good, and got them to an area, but where he had indicated was a good ten mile or so area of fairly dense forest.

If they had to search all of it, they would be here for days trying to find the weak spot in the veil, assuming they would even know they found it when they did.

Osric was trying to find a way to bring this up with Talia, without freaking out Rowan, when his friend said, "We're getting close. I can feel the energy changing."

Considering their previous interactions with the veil, that wasn't necessarily a good thing.

"Is it dangerous?" Osric asked.

"I don't know. It's kind of like what I felt at the barrier, but different. Wilder." She paused, as if searching for the right words. "It's closer to what I felt in the keep, but more. Much more."

Rowan, who had been walking behind them, asked, "What are you two talking about?"

"It has to do with magic," Talia explained, not elaborating further.

Thankfully, the Ranger seemed to accept that answer, giving a slight nod before turning his attention back to the path ahead. Osric didn't blame him. Before he became involved in all of this, he would have reacted the same way.

"We should be careful," Osric warned.

They continued forward more slowly, their heads swiveling constantly, trying to see if anything looked weird. To Osric, everything seemed more or less the same. Just forest.

Clearly, Talia could sense something more, because after five minutes she said, "We're here."

There was something in her voice. Fear, or perhaps awe.

Osric frowned, looking around at the dense forest surrounding them. "Are you sure? I don't see anything."

Instead of answering, Talia pushed forward, quickening her pace. Osric and Rowan exchanged a glance before following. As they broke through a thick bunch of trees and foliage, Osric stopped short, his breath catching in his throat.

There, hovering about ten feet off the ground, was a shimmering, raggedly oblong opening in ... everything. It pulsed and writhed, with shifting colors and blurred motion visible within its depths.

"By Wyndra," Rowan breathed, his eyes wide with shock. "What is that?"

Osric swallowed, his mouth suddenly dry. "It's what we came to find."

Rowan turned to him, his expression one of stunned disbelief. "You came for that? It's like a ... a rip in the world."

Nodding, Osric took a step forward, his eyes never leaving the otherworldly tear.

"Stay back," he warned, holding out a hand to stop the others from approaching.

Talia started to make a move to stand beside him, saying, "Osric, I know more about magic than you do. I should be the one to ..."

"No," Osric said, shaking his head. "We don't know how this will react to you. Remember what the sage said? How magic affects the veil and the tears. I've interacted with it before and been okay. I should go first."

For a long moment, Talia just stared at him, her green eyes searching his face. Finally, she nodded, stepping back.

"Fine. But be careful."

Osric turned to Cinder and said, "Stay with Talia, okay boy?"

Cinder whined softly but didn't move to follow as Osric turned and faced Rowan once more.

"You don't have to tell me twice," Rowan said, holding up his hands in a surrender gesture as Osric looked to him.

Osric stepped into the clearing, consciously putting one foot in front of the other to keep himself moving, wanting nothing more than to run from the tear looming above him, seeming to defy all logic and reason as it pulsed. As he drew closer, he noticed thin, luminescent tendrils streaking out from the edges of the tear, undulating gently in the air like gossamer strands caught in a breeze.

Realization dawned on him. These must be the threads of magic the sage had spoke of, what Talia was manipulating whenever she cast spells. It was strange, seeing them physically manifested. Strange and a little terrifying.

The tendrils seemed to sense his presence, their movements becoming more agitated as he approached. Osric's hand trembled as he reached out, moving almost of its own volition. To his amazement, the threads responded, gravitating towards his outstretched fingers like iron filings to a lodestone.

They brushed against his skin, sending a tingling sensation racing up his arm. It wasn't painful, but strange, almost electric. The tendrils coiled around his hand, pulsing with a soft, ethereal glow.

"Osric, be careful!" Talia called out from the tree line.

He barely heard her; his attention focused solely on the magical threads encircling his hand. They felt warm, almost alive, thrumming with an energy he couldn't quite describe.

The threads pulsed brighter, their glow intensifying as the edges of the rift began to shimmer and ripple. Suddenly, the scene within the tear shifted, the blurred colors and motion coalescing into a vivid image of a battle raging around what appeared to be a temple. He could even hear their screams and curses, muted but still audible, as they clashed with sword and mace. Amidst the chaos, some wielded terrible magic, raining down fire, ice, and destruction. Parts of the temple cracked and shattered under the onslaught and men were thrown in every direction, like they weighed no more than dolls.

As the battle reached a crescendo, a mage stepped forward, his hands weaving intricate patterns in the air. The very earth beneath the temple began to tremble and shake. With a deafening roar, the ground opened up, a yawning chasm spreading like a gaping maw. The temple, along with many of the combatants, vanished into the abyss, swallowed whole by the hungry earth.

Then, the battle was gone from his sight. The image within the tear shifted; the scene of destruction fading away to reveal a small, humble hut. Inside, an older man sat hunched over a table, surrounded by a multitude of books and maps. Osric could almost make out some of the markings on the map. He focused hard, looking over the man's shoulder, until he realized he could make out some of the names scrawled across it. Aeloria, Edlemere, Greenwood ... places he knew, or at least knew of.

He wasn't sure how he knew, but he could almost feel that this was different than the battle. It had felt old. Long ago. This scene felt somehow current, like he wasn't looking through time, but rather through distance. There was something about it he couldn't describe, more than a feeling, but less than knowledge.

As if sensing his gaze, the old man looked up, his eyes meeting Osric's through the shimmering veil of the tear, a puzzled and somewhat frightened expression on his face.

The old man's eyes widened in shock, his mouth falling open. He stood abruptly, his chair toppling backward, forgotten. He took a halting step toward Osric, his hand outstretched. The man's lips moved, forming words Osric couldn't hear.

"Who are you?" Osric whispered, knowing the man couldn't hear him.

Reaching forward, Osric's hand touched his side of the veil, the man copied his movement, doing the same thing from his side. The threads pulsed brighter, as if in response to his question. They coiled tighter around his hand, their warmth turning to a searing heat. Osric gasped, trying to pull away. The tendrils tried to fight him, hold him in place, but he yanked as hard as he could until, with a final great tug, they released him.

As soon as he was free, a blinding flash of light erupted from the rift. A thunderous crack split the air; the force of it sent Osric flying backward. He hit the ground hard, the breath driven from his lungs, sending him into darkness.

Back to the Beginning

Osric's eyes fluttered open, his vision slowly coming into focus. Above him, the concerned faces of Talia and Rowan peered down, both looking worried.

"Osric! Thank the gods, you're awake," Talia said, her voice filled with relief, her hand resting on his shoulder as she knelt beside him.

"What happened?" Osric asked, his words slightly slurred as he tried to sit up.

His head was pounding, and his body felt like it had been trampled by a herd of wild horses.

Rowan reached down and helped pull him to his feet, saying, "You touched that ... whatever it was. There was this sudden burst of light, and you were thrown back. You've been unconscious for a few minutes."

Osric looked around, his eyes searching for the shimmering rift, but it was nowhere to be seen. The forest looked like a forest; there was no hint of the magic that had filled the air.

"Osric, what happened? What did you see?" Talia asked.

Osric tried to think how to explain it. The images he had seen were still vivid in his mind, like a dream that refused to fade upon waking, but it was so far outside of what he knew, it was hard to put into words.

"I saw ... I saw the tendrils the Sage talked about. The threads of magic. They were everywhere, like a vast web stretching across the world."

"Really?" Talia said in an awed voice.

"That isn't all. I saw an ancient battle between two giant armies in front of this massive temple, with mages among them using terrible spells, causing all kinds of destruction. Then, I saw a mage who was standing in the midst of the battle, his hands raised to the sky. He was chanting something, and even through the tear, I could feel the power he was gathering. It made my hair stand on end. There was a blinding flash of light, and the ground began to shake, and it was like he was splitting the world open, creating a vast chasm that swallowed everything in its path. It swallowed the entire temple whole."

"By the gods … that's … that's incredible."

"I know. That isn't all that I saw, though. Then the vision shifted to a small hut, like we have in Eldham or they have in Silham. There was a man reading these old books, and I could kind of see over his shoulder. Some of them, I think, mentioned the battle I saw, or at least had pictures that kind of looked like the battle, although not exactly the same. He also had some maps that had names of places from here and now. Farvale, Greenwood ... even Aeloria and the great city. I'm not sure, but it felt very recent, or like something that was happening now."

"We didn't see anything," Talia said. "Just a shimmering light inside the tear, and then you were thrown back and it closed all in a bright flash. Do you think it was the gods directing you?"

"I don't know, maybe. The Sage did say they'd already been guiding us and the point was to make contact. Although if it was a message, I'm not sure what it was trying to tell me."

"I'm glad you're okay," a somewhat flustered Rowan said. "But could someone tell me what's going on here? What was that thing in the air? And what are you two talking about with gods and visions?"

Osric and Talia exchanged a glance and then Osric said, "We're on a kind of ... quest."

"What do you mean, a quest?"

"It's really hard to explain, but I'll try. You deserve an explanation," Osric said. "What you saw was a tear in a magic barrier that surrounds the world, separating us from other … I don't know, realities or types of existence. I'm still not very clear on that. That barrier, which is called the Veil, prevents stuff from those other places getting into our world, but it's weakening and starting to tear, allowing stuff to come through. It's apparently where webscuttlers and some of the other monstrous things come from and why they're showing up more often. What we were told was that the more people use magic, or maybe the more they use magic in the wrong way, the more it damages the Veil, these little bits of damage adding up over time until they become huge holes."

"Osric found a ring," Talia added, picking up the explanation. "It was sent from a very long time ago, a time before even the founding of Aeloria, through one of those tears into our time, and that ring led us to this document that was apparently written way back, a long time ago. We can't read it yet, but we think it has warnings about these tears and maybe a way to fix them."

Osric looked at Talia and could see that she was purposefully avoiding mentioning the Calaphium by name, which was probably wise. They'd had a lot more time to adjust to this information and had been in the middle of a magical woodland being told by a man who'd saved their lives, and they'd both still been shocked. He couldn't imagine what this information would do to someone else.

"A message from the past? How ... how is that possible?"

"We don't know, we only know what we were told," Osric said.

"Told by whom?"

"We went into Avendell, where a druid who lives there and ... I guess is in charge, told us about everything we'd seen and what was happening, and about the Veil and the tears. He told us about the damage to the Veil and warned us if it continued, it could mean the end of our world.”

“You’re from Avendell?” Rowan said, awe and a little fear in his voice.

“No. We’re from a small village northeast of here called Eldham,” Talia said. “We ended up there after finding the ring and half of the document.”

“How is that possible? No one goes past the border of the magic forest. There’s a barrier that prevents it.”

“The druid, he’s called the Sage, sent people ... creatures to collect us and bring us to him,” Talia said. “We’re glad he did, since there were some men trying to kill us at that moment, and they saved our lives.”

“The men who tried to kill us, they wanted the ring and the document,” Osric added. “They’ve come after us several times now, trying to get their hands on both. We found the first piece of the document in a hidden vault, and those men were guarding it. It's clear they'll stop at nothing to get what we have."

"We appreciate your offer to accompany us, Rowan, we really do. But perhaps it's best if we part ways here. What we're doing, it's too dangerous to ask anyone else to be involved. I'm sorry we got you mixed up in it this far."

For a moment, Rowan didn't say anything. He only looked at them, down to Cinder, and over to where the tear in the Veil had been.

Finally, he said, "I don't fully understand all of this, I'll admit, but what I saw here today, that tear in the air, the power emanating from it … I believe you. I believe this is important. As a Ranger and a follower of Wyndra, it's my duty to protect nature and its wilds. If what you're saying is true, if the world itself is at risk, then the forests I love are in danger, too. I can't stand by and do nothing."

Osric started to protest, but Rowan held up a hand. "Besides, if these people are as dangerous as you say, and they were guarding the first piece of the document, they might be guarding the next one, too. You could use the help."

"He's got a point," Talia said. "We barely made it out of that keep alive, and that was with just two of them. If there are more …"

Osric looked at her and then back to Rowan.

"Alright. We'd be glad to have you with us, Rowan. Thank you."

"So what do we do now?" Osric said, turning to Talia. "That vision … it wasn't exactly a map or a set of instructions. I know the Sage said their messages could be cryptic, but I have no idea what to make of that."

"You said the man you saw, the one in the hut, seemed to be from our time, right? Not from the ancient battle?"

"Yes, that's the impression I got. And the hut itself, it looked more like something you'd find here in the forest, or at least more like the huts in our village than the buildings in Wolfridge. But there was nothing in the hut with him that gave any indication where it was. The Great Forest is a big place."

"If it's something connected to magic and located in the forest, I think I know who we could ask for help," Talia said.

"But is that safe? Going back to Eldham? What if the Brethren are there, waiting for us?"

"Who?" Rowan asked. "And where? You two are losing me again."

"The Brethren are the ones who've been chasing us, trying to get their hands on the ring and the document we found," Osric explained. "They're dangerous, and they seem to have eyes and ears everywhere. After I found the ring, they came to Eldham, our village, and tried to kill me and take it. It's what started this whole thing for us. There's an elder in the village who taught Talia her magic. She's wise and powerful and was once a member of the Conclave of

Magic, although I don't think she is anymore. She knows magic and has lived in the forest for a very long time. If anyone might have an idea about where to look, it's her. But going back there is very risky."

"Osric, we don't have any other leads right now," Talia said. "The only other option is to go back to Avendell, but that feels like backtracking. We need to keep moving forward, and Elder Miriam is our best chance at doing that."

Osric looked into her eyes. He didn't like it. He didn't want to put Elder Miriam or anyone else in the village in danger, but Talia was right. They had no other leads, and Elder Miriam was the only person he could think of who might know what to do.

"Alright," he said at last, his shoulders slumping in resignation. "We'll go back to Eldham and talk to Elder Miriam. But we'll need to be careful, and we can't stay long. The longer we're there, the greater the risk of being discovered."

"Good. It will be nice to go home again, if even for a little bit."

Osric didn't say anything. He agreed, but the entire idea was so risky, it worried him.

As they passed the post that Osric always thought of as being the edge of the Eldham, a strange feeling passed over him. In many ways, most ways, the village looked much the same as it always had, with the same buildings, the same smells, and the same sounds that he'd spent his entire life around.

And yet, somehow, it felt different. Smaller, almost insignificant compared to the wonders and horrors they had witnessed over the past days. Osric felt a strange combination of nostalgia and detachment, even though they'd been gone less than a week. It felt more like when they'd first walked into Silham, familiar but different, instead of the village where he'd spent his whole life.

"It's odd, isn't it?" he said. "Coming back after everything we've been through. It feels like a lifetime has passed, but here, it's as if nothing has changed at all."

"I know what you mean," Talia said. "This was my entire world. Now, it seems so ... small."

They made their way through the village, occasionally having people they knew calling out hellos, like they hadn't even realized they'd been gone. Everyone had just ... carried on with their daily routines.

Reaching Elder Miriam's cottage, Talia knocked and waited. Osric could see her gripping and releasing the sides of her skirt, something she'd done since they were kids whenever she was worried or nervous. The door opened revealing a distracted Elder Miriam, who froze in her tracks for a moment, her mouth hanging open as she realized who was in front of her.

"Talia! Osric!" she cried, pulling first Talia, then Osric, into her cottage, holding them in a tight embrace. "I've been worried sick about you both. When you didn't return, I feared the worst."

Talia returned the hug fiercely, burying her face in the old woman's shoulder as Rowan and Cinder entered behind them, the Ranger quietly shutting the door.

"I'm sorry, Miriam. I didn't mean to worry you. It's just … Osric ran into me on the road, and he was being chased by these people, and I … I had to help him," Talia said, pulling back from the elder. "I used my magic, Elder Miriam. I hurt someone. I … I killed someone. Several people. They were trying to hurt Osric … and me. I tried …"

A single tear escaped, trailing down her cheek. Elder Miriam reached up, gently wiping it away with her thumb.

"Oh, my dear child. You did what you had to do. Magic is a gift, a tool to protect those we care about.

That's why I taught you, so you could defend yourself and others."

Talia nodded, sniffling. She gestured to Rowan, who had been standing respectfully to the side.

"This is Rowan. We met him on the road. He's been helping us, protecting us on our journey."

Rowan stepped forward, bowing his head. "It's an honor to meet you, Elder Miriam. But I must confess, it is Talia and Osric who have been protecting me. They saved my life, in fact."

"Then I owe you my thanks, Ranger Rowan," Miriam said. "For being there for them, whatever the circumstances."

"There's something you should know, about magic," Talia said.

"What do you mean?"

"We've learned so much. After we left Eldham, we traveled to Avendell. Inside of it, beyond the boundary. There, we met a powerful druid known as the Sage."

Miriam's eyes widened, her hands clasping together. "You went inside Avendell? I've ... I've never heard of anyone doing that. And you met the Sage?"

"You know who he is?" Osric asked, surprised once again by how much the elder knew.

"I've heard tales of a group of druids living inside the boundary, but I thought them to be just a myth. I'm not aware of anyone getting through the boundary to actually confirm it, and wrote it off as tales mages like to tell to impress each other."

"You can get through the barrier, if the Veilguard lets you," Osric said.

"The Veilguard?"

"Let me back up," Talia said. "There's so much to tell you. The Sage told us incredible things, things about magic. He told us our world is surrounded by a barrier, created by the gods, or maybe created at the same time as the gods. He called it the Veil and he said it protects our reality from other realities, keeping our world separate and safe. He told us that when we use magic, we're actually manipulating pieces of the Veil, drawing upon its energy. The weaving is actually manipulating pieces, threads, of the Veil."

"Really?" Miriam said. "How would you prove such a thing, though ...?"

"It might be easier, and scarier, than you think," Talia said. "Not only can we manipulate the Veil, but we can damage it. The Sage explained that certain types of magic, like enchanting objects or summoning entities, actually tear pieces from the Veil. Over time, these tears have weakened the barrier, allowing creatures to slip through from other realms."

"Ohh," Miriam said.

He could see her trying to absorb everything. They were making huge proclamations with very little in the way of detail, but she didn't question the truth of it, or doubt them.

"There's more. The Sage knew about this ring. He was given a vision by the gods who protect the Veil, who he called the Veilguard, that something had appeared in our world that would be important. Something from another time. He told us it came from a different time, thrown through one of these tears in the Veil from a time before Aeloria and any of our recorded history. It's from the Calaphium."

"The Calaphium?"

"I know," Talia said. "He said they're nothing like the legends. They were people and there was an entire civilization here before the first kingdom was ever founded. They were wiped out in another tearing of the Veil, although the last of them managed to close the Veil."

"I always suspected there was more to the Calaphium than mere myths or legends," Miriam said. "When I was still in the Conclave, I came across scattered writings that referenced them, or rather referenced writings that referenced them, and the pieces I could see didn't quite fit."

"Does that mean the Conclave knew the truth about magic and the Calaphium?" Osric asked.

"I don't believe so," she said, shaking her head. "These were references found in ancient tomes, texts that my own mentors discouraged me from studying too deeply, considering them a waste of time. They said I was delving into forgotten lore with little left to tell and ignoring my studies. All of this is interesting, but it doesn't explain what happened after you left. Do you still have the ring or did you give it to the Sage for safekeeping? Did he tell you about its magic?"

"No, I still have it. After I ran away, the ring, or maybe the Veilguard, I guess, led us to an ancient keep deep in the forest. Inside, we found more of those men who were chasing us, guarding half of a magically enchanted document, which the Sage said was written in the script of the Calaphium. He couldn't translate it, though, without the other half."

"The Sage believed that the Veilguard guided Osric to find both the ring and the document, and that they're part of something to repair the Veil," Talia added. "But it's not entirely clear, since the visions from the gods are very confusing and hard to interpret."

"When we found the document, the ring suddenly lost all of its magic.

The Sage said this was probably because the ring itself only had power because the person who sent it through had tied it to the document somehow. He said to keep it hidden because the symbol on it was an obscure one used by the Calaphium, but otherwise, it was now just a historical oddity."

"I see," Miriam said. "The Veilguard you keep mentioning. Do you know which gods are part of this?"

Osric shook his head. "I didn't think to ask."

"I see. He's right; you should keep it hidden, in case any of those men keep looking for it. If it is just a trinket, with no more magic, bury it in a crate and forget about it for a few years. I'm just happy you're both back and safe."

"We can't stay," Osric said. "After looking over the document and realizing there was another half to it, the Sage asked us to find it since it could be helpful in repairing the damage to the Veil that has been causing all of the strange events and creatures to appear over the last few years. He says it is a sign that the Veil is close to breaking."

"Why ask you? I know you found the ring, but that part is done. Why should you go to find the other half for him?"

"He said he can't leave Avendell, as the boundary there is weakening along with everywhere else as the Veil becomes more torn. He said we were the right people to do it because the Veilguard had chosen us, was guiding us. I ... I think I believe him. He told us about a place further into the forest, not far from the boundary, where the Veil was very weak. Apparently, one of the side effects of the boundary being weak or having tears is that it gives the gods more access to us, allows them to communicate with us more easily. We found it and … they gave me a vision. It showed an ancient battle where a temple stood that was swallowed into the earth. Then it shifted to something more recent. An older man in a cottage a lot like this one, in the style of the forest, surrounded by all kinds of tomes, some of which were open and had pictures of the battle they showed me and the temple that was swallowed into the ground. I think that man might know how to find the document, and I think he's here in the forest."

"That's why we came back to Eldham," Talia said. "I hoped you might know who he is."

"I wish I could help, but there are no scholars or anyone else that would have that kind of collection in the forest that I know of. At least not in this part of it. Maybe in Brackendale or Eldamar, but even that seems unlikely. Most who dedicate themselves to such pursuits tend to gravitate towards the cities where the Conclave has a presence."

Osric felt his shoulders slump. He knew asking about one man in all of the Great Forest was a stretch, but he'd held out hope that if anyone would know him, it would be Miriam. Without her, he wasn't sure where they could turn for answers.

"Now, don't look like that," Elder Miriam chided gently. "I may not know him, but I can still help. It's likely this person has some kind of connection to the Conclave, to have the kind of books you mentioned. I never made it far in the Conclave, barely past novice, so I didn't learn about or meet many of the people who would have gone through there or their con-tacts. But I do know of a man who himself got high in the orders and served until he retired a few years ago. I heard he's taken up residence in Farvale, selling his services to the town in exchange for a comfortable living. If there is anyone in the forest with any kind of well-stocked library or notable ability, he would know."

"Really?" Osric said.

"Yes. I don't actually know him, mind you, just of him. But, seeing as how he does work for the people of Farvale, I can't imagine he'd turn you away. But, be careful. From what I remember of him, or of what people said of him, he was always very … covetous. Don't tell him too much of what you know, how you got the information, or show him the ring. Just tell him enough to find who you're looking for."

"We'll head to see him right away," Osric said, and then paused, looking at Talia and then Elder Miriam.

After a week of terror, with Talia looking either worried or scared the majority of the time, or sad at the things she'd been forced to do in the name of survival, it was good to see her looking … relaxed. Just being with Elder Miriam, a lot of her worry and concern had melted away, allowing her to go back to her old self, if only for a time.

"Talia, if you want to stay, I understand," Osric continued. "I don't know what we're going to face out there, but it'll be …

"Osric Yarrow," Talia said, in the same voice Master Ironhand would use to scold him when he'd been negligent at a task. "If you are about to tell me it's dangerous out there, so help me, I'll make it dangerous in here for you. We've already discussed this. I made a promise to the Sage the same as you did, agreeing to this quest. Same as you. You need me out there."

"She's right," Elder Miriam interjected before Osric could respond. "These are dangerous times, and I trained Talia with everything I know. I didn't know it at the time, but I think this is what I was preparing her for. She should go with you."

Talia shot Osric a triumphant look. A silent 'I told you so.'

Elder Miriam placed a hand on Osric's shoulder and said, "If you're dealing with the secrets of magic, Talia is the best person to help you. She's read every book I have and learned every lesson diligently. If anyone was meant to help make sense of all of this, she was."

Osric sighed, knowing when he was outnumbered. "Alright, alright. We'll go together."

"Good. Now, have you seen Master Ironhand since you returned?"

Osric blinked, surprised by the sudden change in topic. "We came straight here."

"He's been beside himself with worry since you left. I tried to comfort him, explain things, but … you should go see him. Let him know you're alright and tell him a little of what's happening."

Osric felt a pang of guilt. In all the chaos, he hadn't even thought about how his sudden disappearance might have affected his mentor.

"I will. I'll go now."

"Good." Elder Miriam nodded, then turned to Talia. "While he does that, Talia, I would like for you to stay behind for a moment. There are things we must discuss."

Rowan, who had been quietly standing to the side during all of this, stepped forward and said, "Neither of you are equipped for a long journey. I have a little money with me. I'll go see what I can buy to prepare us for the road ahead."

"Excellent idea," Elder Miriam said, shuffling over to a side table and pulling a small pouch from a container. "This should help. Get whatever they need and use the rest in your travels.

"I couldn't …" Rowan started, before Miriam gave him the look she used to give Osric and Talia whenever they tried to argue back when they were younger.

"I've raised these two since they were little. They are as good as my own, and I will not see them wanting. Do you understand me?"

"Of course," Rowan said, hiding a small smile as he bowed his head slightly, taking the pouch.

"Good. Use my name when dealing with the merchants. I'm sure most would already be favorably disposed to giving a Greenwood Ranger a good deal, but if they know I sent you, it will guarantee it."

Osric hid his own smile as he and Rowan left. A quick learner, that one. Osric had to be boxed around the ears for years before he learned to just shut up and do what she told him. With a nod to Rowan, who made his way to the center of the village, Osric turned and headed for the smithy.

The place was exactly as he left it, like it had been frozen in time. Again, Osric had to remind himself that it had only been a week since he'd left. But the familiar scent of hot metal and coal triggered an instant wave of nostalgia he couldn't fight.

In the center of the smithy, Master Ironhand stood at the anvil, his hammer frozen mid-strike as he turned to face the door. For a moment, they just stared at each other.

Then, with a speed that was hard to believe such a large man could have, Master Ironhand dropped his hammer and crossed the room in three great strides, sweeping Osric up into a massive bear hug that lifted his feet off the ground and drove the air from his lungs.

"By the gods, boy! I've been worried sick about you."

"I'm sorry," Osric wheezed, his ribs creaking under the force of the hug. "I didn't mean to frighten you. There were these men and ..."

Master Ironhand set him down and held him at arm's length, inspecting him. "Elder Miriam told me what happened. That's not important now. What matters is that you're alright and you're back."

"Master Ironhand, I ... I have to leave again."

"Again?"

"I know. I wish I could stay, but it's important. It's related to what Elder Miriam told you about. I don't know how long I'll be gone."

For a moment, his master said nothing, just stared at him hard with a considering look. It drew on long enough Osric was worried that Ironhand might be mad at him, that this quest might have caused a rift between himself and the man who, for all intents and purposes, was his father.

Instead, he said, "I always knew you were meant for more than working a forge, Osric. At least this way, you have a chance to live out some of those daydreams you were always having of glory and fame."

"I wish you could come with me."

"Boy, if I was ten years younger, I would!" he said with a deep, booming laugh. "Besides, who would look after this place if I wasn't here?"

"That's very true," Osric said, smiling.

He'd come back, when it was all done. Yes, he was secretly looking forward to the adventure and excitement, on top of the fear he had for this journey, but he also missed this.

"Now, if you're going to go out on some damnable adventure, I can't let you do it in breeches and a tunic. Hold on."

Ironhand disappeared into the back of the shop, emerging a few moments later with a bundle of metal in his arms, holding it out to Osric.

"Isn't this the armor you were working on for Sir Dauphin? I can't take this."

"Dauphin was only made a knight because his father was," Master Ironhand scoffed. "From what I've heard, he was a terrible squire. Why do you think he came all the way out here to have armor made? He can wait for me to make more."

Osric took the armor and ran his fingers over the cool metal, feeling tears prick at the corners of his eyes. "I don't know what to say. Thank you."

Master Ironhand pulled him into another hug, gentler this time. "I'm proud of you, Osric. Now, let's get you armored up."

As he put Osric in the chainmail, breastplate, arm and shoulder guards, he explained to him how to do this alone. Which straps to tighten and in what order, which piece to put on first, and how to go about taking it off again. He also lectured Osric on the proper care of the armor, in spite of having him polish finished, or nearly finished, armor for half his life.

By the time they were done, Osric felt like a different person. No longer the blacksmith's apprentice, but a warrior in his own right. It was difficult to finally leave when the moment came, as sadness washed over Osric. Master Ironhand seemed to be able to sense his hesitation, making jokes and pushing him along, not letting him dawdle.

Making his way back to the center of town, Osric spotted Talia and Rowan heading in his direction.

"Osric?" Talia asked. "Is that really you under all that metal?"

Osric grinned, spreading his arms wide. "Like it? It was a gift from Master Ironhand. Said he couldn't let me go off on an adventure without proper protection."

"That's some fine craftsmanship," Rowan said with a low whistle. "Your master does good work."

"The best," Osric agreed, then noticed the finely carved wooden staff in Talia's hand. "What's that?"

Talia lifted the staff, running her fingers along the smooth wood. "It's from Elder Miriam. She said it would help focus my magic, make it easier to control. Plus, if anyone got too close, I could whack them with it. She also gave me a bunch of her books, so I could continue to study and learn on the way."

"I'm afraid I can't compete with armor and magical staves," Rowan said, patting the packs at his feet. "But I did manage to procure some essentials. Bedrolls, rations, waterskins, and a few other supplies we'll need on the road."

"Well … it looks like we're prepared," Osric said, looking over the town one last time before turning to his friends. "On to Farvale."

Chapter 13

Farvale

The city of Farvale was a completely different world than their small village of Eldham, and not just because of the cobblestone streets and large stone buildings. The place was crawling with people everywhere they looked, and all of them moving with the same urgency as people being chased by wolves.

And the noise. It was all-consuming.

Merchants hawking their wares, saws and hammers and all other sundry tools clanging away in workshops, people in small and even large gatherings in every direction, and children laughing and darting between their legs or the small gaps between groups.

There were so many people.

"I know this is a far cry from Wolfridge," Osric said, craning his neck this way and that. "But I don't remember the capital being so … busy."

Rowan chuckled and said, "Because it isn't. Wolfridge is a larger city and has more people, but these border towns move at a pace like nowhere else. So many trade goods go through here on their way down to Everton and the four corners, especially out of the Western Forest, where it doesn't make sense to carry them all the way up to Wolfridge just to bring them back down the Great Road. So yeah, a lot of the bustle filters out by the time it gets that far. Also, the market is on the edge of town, not near the center, so that makes a big difference."

"You've been to Southwatch?" Osric asked, now staring at Rowan with as much amazement as he had looked at the town.

"Only as far as Everton, and not on Ranger business. Our purview doesn't go past our barony, but I picked up a fugitive from the crown and there's an outpost for the Knights of the Gold there where I could hand him over."

"And you met the knights?" Osric asked, even more fascinated.

He'd met a few Knights of Greenwood, who served as liegemen to the baron, when they'd come to Master Ironhand for repairs to armor or weapons. Those, however, were a far cry from Knights of the Gold, who were liegemen directly to the crown itself, which only accepted the most elite warriors.

"Some. Bunch of jumped-up bastards, if you ask me. Too good to talk to someone from out in the sticks."

Osric wasn't sure he'd call Greenwood the sticks. Sure, it was the barony furthest from the crown, well, with the exception of Easthaven, just north of Greenwood. But it sat on an intersection of the Great Road and the road to the kingdom of Brackendale, and also shared a northern border with the Caellond League, so it seemed to get more credit than Greenwood.

Osric went back to admiring the city as they continued to push through the crowds towards its center. That was made easier by Rowan and Cinder. While Greenwood Rangers might be less common in this area, he was sure one accompanied by a full-grown wolf, which they probably assumed belonged to the ranger, was something most had never seen before.

Cinder, for his part, seemed unperturbed by the attention. The street turned a sharp corner, and it became readily apparent they were close to their goal. It opened up into a vast central square, dominated by a sprawling open-air market. Stalls of every color jostled for space, their owners loudly proclaiming the quality of their goods. The air was thick with the scents of exotic spices, fresh-baked bread, and the musk of livestock.

But what caught Osric's eye was the building on the far side of the square. Rising above the surrounding structures was a grand mansion of pale stone fronted by large arched windows.

"That must be it," Talia said. "Miriam said it was the biggest damn house she'd ever seen."

"That isn't a house, it's a castle."

Rowan laughed again and said, "Far from it. Come on."

The three of them made their way up the ornate carved granite stairs to a large pair of double doors with massive golden door knockers in the shape of lion heads. Osric looked at the other two and then reached up and rapped the heavy knocker three times.

A minute passed where nothing happened. Osric was about to reach up and knock again when a thunk could be heard from the inside, followed by the door creaking open, revealing a young girl of no more than fourteen. The harried expression she had on her face shifted to one of curiosity as she took in the strange party. Osric couldn't blame her. With him now in good metal armor, a full-grown wolf at his side, accompanied by a girl with an ornate staff and a Greenwood Ranger, they were a strange collection.

"Good day, miss," Osric said, giving her what he hoped was a warm and disarming smile. "We're here to see your master. Elder Miriam from Eldham sent us."

The girl blinked, then nodded. "Please, come in. I'll see if he's available."

She stepped aside, ushering them into a grand foyer. Marble floors gleamed beneath their feet and massive tapestries adorned the walls. On pedestals here or there were small but well-crafted golden statues and delicate vases. Making sure they knew to stay there, the girl hurried off down a long hallway to their left.

Osric turned in a slow circle, trying to take it all in. "Can you believe this place?"

"I knew city folk lived well, but this ..." Rowan said. "The Rangers pay a gold a month. If I'd known working in a city paid like this, I might've considered a career change."

"There's no way this comes from a city salary," Talia said. "Even for a former member of the Conclave. This wealth is immense."

"My master will see you now. Please, follow me," the girl said, reappearing a few minutes later and giving them a curtsey.

She led them down the hallway and through a set of double doors into a study that made Elder Miriam's book collection look paltry. Shelves stretched from floor to ceiling, packed with leather-bound tomes. A massive desk dominated the center of the room, its surface covered in parchment and strange, glinting instruments.

The line of bookcases was only broken on one wall by three, amazingly carved, wooden and metal statues. The materials twisted together until it was unclear if the wood was woven, or the metal grown. The detail was so fine that Osric could even make out the faces of the statues, each with a unique look that made them stand out as much as strangers in the street would. The one thing they all shared was a sour, cruel expression.

They were beautiful and hideous all at the same time. Why someone would want these around them, Osric would never know.

Behind the desk sat an elderly man, his white hair and beard neatly trimmed. He wore robes of deep blue, embroidered with intricate silver patterns. As they entered, he looked up from the parchment he was studying, his piercing blue eyes taking in the group.

"Welcome," he said. "I am Godfrey Harrow. To what do I owe the pleasure of this visit?"

"Master Harrow, thank you for seeing us. My name is Osric Yarrow, and these are my companions, Talia, Rowan, and Cinder. We've come seeking your help. We're looking for someone, an older man who lives in the forest, or at least older than us, I should say.

We don't know his name or exact location, but we know he has a well-stocked library, including some very ancient tomes. His home is not in a large city, but rather one of the smaller woodland huts or cottages in the Great Forest."

"Interesting," Godfrey said, leaning back in his chair. "And what makes you think I might know of this individual?"

"We were sent to you by Elder Miriam of Eldham," Talia said. "She said she knew of you by reputation from her time at the Conclave."

"I do not know anyone named Miriam, but it is good to know my reputation precedes me," he said with a small, self-satisfied smile. "However, I must admit, your request is rather unusual. You know what this man's home looks like, what he looks like, but not his name or precise location?"

"I know it sounds strange, but it's what we have. The information came to us secondhand, and all Elder

Miriam was told was that there was a man in the forest who might be able to aid her," Osric said.

"And why, exactly, is this elder of yours seeking this man's assistance?"

"She is doing a search for a copy of a very old book and heard of a transcribed copy in the possession of this man, but the person who told her that only knew that he lived in the forest. Miriam is getting on in years and a search like this would be difficult for her, so we offered to take on the task instead," Osric said.

"What is this book, exactly?"

Osric exchanged a glance with Talia before responding. "We don't know, since honestly it didn't matter for what we were sent to do. We were just directed to come and ask you in person if you know who this man is. Depending on where he lives, we would then determine if Miriam could travel to him directly or if we needed to go ourselves. It honestly didn't occur to me to ask about the book itself. All I know is it's very old, about the early days of the Aeloria, before the formation of the Conclave."

"Before the formation of the Conclave? That is indeed very old. I can see why she would go to great lengths to find it. A book like that would be extremely hard to find. I, myself, am something of a collector, and I don't believe I've ever seen one from that time period."

Osric gave a shrug. They were walking a tricky line, and everything he said seemed to pique the mage's curiosity more and more. Which was something Osric absolutely wanted to avoid, if he could.

"Well, you may actually be in luck as I know a man that fits that description and does collect older works, although I wasn't aware he had anything that old. Jasper Fitzwilliam is a washed-up old cleric, a collector of relics, who lives in a cottage on the edge of the forest where it passes into Eldamar. I've never been to his place myself, mind you, and that is still a large area, but I'm sure some of the locals might know of him. Although, from what I've heard, he's something of a hermit, so perhaps not."

"Really? That is excellent news," Osric said excitedly, showing the first real emotion since they'd been escorted into the study. "Thank you, Master Harrow. This information is invaluable. We appreciate your help."

As they turned to leave, the door to the study slammed shut, all on its own, followed by the noticeable clicking sound of a heavy latch securing in place.

"Off so soon?" Godfrey asked, a small smile on his face as he pushed himself up from his desk. "I think not."

"What? Why?" Osric asked, confused.

"Do you think I don't know who you are, boy from Eldham?" Godfrey said, his voice becoming menacing. "You've been very busy, running around the forest, killing my brothers and causing havoc. I know what you're carrying too, and you're going to give it to me."

Osric's blood ran cold. They'd walked right into the hands of one of the Brethren. Delivered themselves to him.

"You have no authority here," Rowan said. "Release us or face the consequences of detaining a Greenwood Ranger."

Godfrey ignored him, keeping his attention on Osric.

"The ranger and the girl can leave, but you're coming with me."

"We're not leaving without him," Talia said, gripping her staff.

"Dead is just as good as alive." This time, the mage did look at her, ending his threat with a cold, hollow laugh.

Osric did not wait for the mage to make the first move.

"Cinder. Attack," Osric commanded as his hand reached for his sword.

Cinder didn't hesitate, leaping forward with fangs bared, to tear into the mage. Godfrey was prepared and moved faster than Osric would have thought someone his age capable of. His hands whirled around each other until he finally pressed one hand forward, fingers curled. Papers and even small objects went flying into the air, blown by an unseen blast of wind that struck the wolf, sending it tumbling sideways, smashing into one of the ornate bookshelves.

Godfrey didn't pause to see what happened to the animal, his hands continuing to weave around him, faster and faster. As he finished the next progressions of movement, the air in front of him shimmered and a leathery lizard-like creature with wings that connected to its front claws materialized in mid-air, flapping its arms in steady strokes as it floated above the floor.

Osric had never seen a wyvern before, but he'd heard about them in fairytales and stories, although he'd imagined them to be much larger.

"Osric, Talia, watch out!" Rowan said as he took several steps back, pulling his bow off his back and pointing past Osric.

The three strange statues that had lined one wall had started moving, arms outstretched, coming for them. Osric pulled his sword, and Talia took a step back. Lifting her staff, she smashed the butt end of it into the ground, causing a bluish, shimmering light to reach up from the bottom of the staff and stretch around her before fading like water on sand.

She had said the staff had abilities, but Osric had never imagined something so amazing. Not that he had a chance to dwell on it. The statues were closing in, their metal and wood fists already rising to strike. One lunged at Osric, its blow glancing off his armor with a dull clang. It was his first time being hit with the armor on, and it hurt more than he thought it would, the force pushing him back. But he didn't feel injured in any way, so it did its job.

Another had moved toward Rowan, swinging at him, but the agile ranger slipped past its swing, avoiding the hit. The third went for Talia, also swinging at her, its fist connecting near the side of her head . . . and bounced off in a shimmer of blue, the very air around her body rippling like water on a pond.

The wyvern had turned its attention to Cinder and made to attack the wolf, as it recovered from hitting the wall. Claws tore through fur and teeth through scales as the two animals grappled with one another, the blood of both hitting the wooden floor.

Rowan ignored the statue that had swung at him, an arrow already pulled back in his bow, aiming past it at the creatures' master halfway across the room. Loosing the string, the arrow ripped through the air and sank into the mage's thigh. Godfrey hissed in pain, but his eyes stayed focused on the three statues as his hands moved around him, creating a shimmering shield-like circle in front of him that vanished much as Talia's had.

Osric couldn't watch him, though. He had a statue to deal with, slashing at the thing with his sword, hoping it would have some effect on the animated wood and metal. His blade skidded across some of the finely wrought iron, breaking through it and cutting hard into the branches of the statue. The thing opened its mouth, or what Osric thought of as its mouth, and emitted a rattling animalistic screech that seemed to be the thing of nightmares.

Talia likewise jumped back from hers, her hands, one holding the staff, dancing through the air until what looked like a translucent greenish arrowhead as large as her palm, appeared in her outstretched left hand, shimmering and flowing like it was made of an emerald water. She threw her hand forward and the arrowhead shot out, smashing into the chest of the statue facing her, seeming to splash like water as the energy dissipated. Suddenly, the metal where the green arrowhead had hit began to darken, smoke and pit while the wood around it melted, the wood becoming almost a sludge that fell to the floor, eating into the very floorboards.

Cinder and the wyvern continued to tear at each other, the animals locked in a death struggle until the beast managed to slash with its razor-sharp claws, cutting deep into Cinder's flank. The wolf yelped and stumbled back.

Osric tried to disengage from the statue and help his friend, but a searing wave of fire smashed into him, streaking out of Godfrey's outstretched hands, searing the metal of his armor until it almost glowed red and scorched Osric's exposed skin. Thankfully, the fire only lasted a moment as the mage's spell was cut off when another arrow smashed into him, this time into his shoulder, knocking him back and ending the flames.

Osric fought through the pain, swinging his sword in a wide arc with every ounce of strength he possessed as he backed away from the statue. The blade sliced through its wooden and metal-laced torso, cutting it in two. He must have severed whatever piece of the Veil that had been imbued inside of it because it crumbled into a heap of loose materials as he finished cutting through it. Any semblance that it had once been a solid mass was gone.

Talia managed to block a swing from the statue that opposed her, pushing its massive fist out of the way, sending it whistling past her head instead of into it. Releasing the staff with her left hand, she made the complicated gestures he'd seen her make before, causing three glowing white darts of energy to spring from her hand and streak across the room, smashing into Godfrey's chest, sending him stumbling back a second step.

Her attention diverted, the statue facing her tried to take another swing, and then froze in place as the acid eating away at its middle cut through the same thing that Osric's had. Like the one he'd faced, hers collapsed into a pile of raw materials, its enchantment removed.

Rowan had been backing up the entire time, avoiding the third statue while he shot arrows at the mage, but he'd run out of room, bumping into one of the bookcases. Slinging his bow over his back in a single motion, the Ranger drew the short sword from his side and reversed direction, charging the statue closing in on him, plunging the sword into the wooden construct's center, pushing it back, but not collapsing it as Osric and Talia had managed.

Godfrey pulled the arrow from his shoulder and managed to get his now-weakened arm to lift. Slowly he began weaving another pattern. No longer hampered by flying arrows, he managed to finish the incantation, thrusting his hands forward, again emitting twin rays of searing flame.

One shot at Rowan, who managed to move aside, interposing the wooden statue, which absorbed some of the flame. Its back now crackling, as it became wreathed in fire.

Talia wasn't so lucky. She hefted her staff, but the flame blasted through the invisible energy around her, causing it to become visible again for a moment as it was shredded away and the flames hit her directly. She screamed as her skin blistered and seared before dropping to the floor, unconscious.

Osric's heart stopped when he saw Talia fall. He turned from the attack he had just started on the wyvern and ran to her side, sliding the last few feet on his knees and placing his hands over her still form, calling in his mind for the Veilguard to aid him again, as they had before. He begged with every fiber of his being for them to heal her.

He felt it the moment something touched him. Like water filling a bowl, he felt energy flow into his body, more powerfully than it had before, and then his hands glowed, a warm light emanating between his palms and Talia's scarred body. Slowly, the blackened skin turned back to its more natural, pale color, and her eyes fluttered open.

"Osric?" she murmured, her voice weak but filled with gratitude.

"I've got you," he reassured her, helping her to her feet. "We're not done yet."

"Demon," Godfrey yelled. "You are no cleric. How do you wield power beyond the Veil?"

"The gods favor us, Mage," Osric spat. "They won't let you and your kind continue to destroy this world."

Osric hated the Brethren, for good reasons, but it wasn't until that moment he became a believer in what the Sage had asked him to do. He agreed to this quest because of what the Sage had told them, but he saw it as an adventure. Fun. In that moment when the gods, whichever ones from the Veilguard had aided him and filled him with their energy, it had given him a glimpse, just a brief flash of what the Brethren were doing. He saw the world rip apart, planes of fire and pain on the other side as all manner of obscenities crossed from their side of the Veil to his.

He saw the world burn. Not only saw it. He felt it. He felt the pain and the horror. In that moment, he knew what this quest was really about. They weren't simply trying to help the Sage to repair the damage already done to the Veil. They were trying to stop it from being destroyed outright.

This was larger than the Sage had told them. Or maybe even knew.

"It's your kind that wants to destroy the world," Godfrey snapped back.

As Osric began a charge toward Godfrey, Rowan was still being pushed back by the statue attacking him, pressing the ranger close to the bookshelf, its hands reaching for his throat, that he couldn't extract his blade. Instead, the ranger ducked under the statue's hands and, grabbing the hilt of the sword with both hands, he spun around the construct, pulling the blade with him, causing it to rotate as he did, shredding wood or metal as it twisted.

He must have finally found the spot both Osric and Talia had, because suddenly his statue collapsed into its constituent parts, just as theirs had done.

Osric could see the mage calculating, watching his last statue fall and Cinder with his fangs now clamped down hard on the wyvern's neck, pulling it to the ground and shaking the last bits of life from it. Backing away as Osric neared the desk, the old man began weaving his hands. Osric wasn't going to give him the opportunity to complete his spell and launched off the desk, sinking his sword with both hands into the mage's chest just as his body began to shimmer and turn invisible.

A look of sheer surprise crossed Godfrey's face before the rest of Osric collided with him, knocking the now very dead mage to the floor.

Osric pulled his blade from the mage's chest, wiping it clean on the dead man's robes before sheathing it and turning to look at his friends. Rowan, his own sword still in hand, glanced around the room, taking in the destroyed statues and the lifeless forms of the wyvern and its master.

"We need to leave. Now. This man held a position of authority here, and it will be very bad for us if they find us here with him."

"What? Why?" Osric asked. "He attacked us. We were just defending ourselves."

"You think anyone in this town is going to believe that? Who knows what kinds of connections he has here, while we arrived just today and are strangers? I'm a ranger, but we aren't immune from arrest. If we're lucky, no one saw us enter."

"He's right, Osric. We can't stay here," Talia said.

"Okay, let's go."

Osric saw Cinder limping toward him, blood matting its fur as the wolf struggled to breathe. Kneeling next to his loyal companion, Osric placed his hand gently on the animal's flank, whispering a soft prayer.

Once more, he felt the divine energy flow through him, albeit much weaker than before. A faint glow emanated from his fingertips, and Cinder's wounds began to close, though not completely. The gashes remained visible, in spite of the magic.

Osric tried again, but nothing happened. Was there a limit to the gods' power? Did it determine how or who he asked for the power to be used on? There wasn't time to dwell on it, but he needed to investigate it. His ability to heal had quite literally saved their lives, but he needed to understand its use and, more importantly, its limitations. Not doing so, they might rely on it at the wrong moment, dooming them.

Talia was already at the door, her hands moving, weaving a spell. When she finished, he could hear a soft click as the door unlatched. Rowan pulled it open and stopped in his tracks.

On the other side stood the young girl who had greeted them earlier, her eyes wide with fear. She must have heard the whole thing.

"Don't run; we aren't going to hurt you," Osric said as gently as he could. "We're sorry your master is dead, but he ..."

"I'm not," the girl said, fear still evident on her face, but hardening as it shifted to almost anger. "I hated Master Harrow. He was ... mean. His friends were mean."

"Do you have somewhere to go?" Talia asked.

"No," the girl said, suddenly looking worried for the first time, as she seemed to realize her predicament. "I ... The only reason I stayed was because he was teaching me magic. Now that he's gone, I don't have anyone to learn from. The Conclave is so far away ..."

Talia stepped forward, placing a comforting hand on the girl's shoulder. "If you still wish to learn, there is a woman in the village of Eldham who can teach you.

It's a long and dangerous journey through the forest, but ..."

As she paused, trying to think of how to get this girl all the way to Eldham, Rowan reached into his pocket, producing a small wooden disk.

Pressing it into the girl's hand, he said, "Take this to the ranger station at the edge of town. Tell him that Rowan Wycliff asks that you be escorted to Eldham by the next rangers going that way."

The girl nodded, clutching the disk to her chest.

"I will. Thank you."

She cast one last look at her now-dead master and ran out.

"She could just go straight to the first guard she sees and tell them what happened, that we killed her master. That could have all been a ruse," Talia said.

"Right. Let's go," Rowan said. "The story about this Jasper person sounded at least somewhat true. We should try to find him."

They hurried from the mansion, pulling the door shut behind them and making their way out of the town. Osric was now thankful for how busy it was. No one seemed to notice them as they left.

Now they just had to search a large corner of the forest for one man in a hut.

An Unusual Blight

Even though it was mid-autumn, it was still hot, and getting hotter with each step south they took. They had made it to the border of Eldamar and for the last week had been wandering, almost aimlessly.

Villages in this corner of the forest were pretty spread out, but they were the only real option, as far as a place to start went. They'd tried two so far, and no one had ever heard of Jasper Fitzwilliam or a scholar of any type living in the woods.

"Maybe Godfrey was lying. I mean, he knew who I was the whole time, and that he was going to try and capture me, right? What if there's no cleric out here? Why would he have told us the truth?"

"Sometimes men like that think they are above any kind of repercussions, and do it to show their power," Rowan suggested. "They think that they can tell you what you want to know, but it doesn't matter since you won't be able to use it. Or maybe because the truth sounded better and he was trying to get us to tell him what we knew, or why we were looking for this guy, hoping it was connected to your ring and that document you stole."

"But we should have found something," Osric said.

"Maybe not," Talia countered. "We haven't been looking that long and it's a large area. We should keep going, at least for a little while longer."

"And why is it so damn hot? I know we're on the edge of the forest, so there's less cover, but it's only two months until winter. Shouldn't it start cooling down? I swear it didn't feel this hot in Farvale."

"I've only been this way a few times," Rowan said. "But I don't remember it being like this."

Osric sighed, adjusting his pack, and kept walking, putting one foot in front of the other. They were following a simple road, one of the many that twisted in and out of the forest, connecting villages and towns away from the Great Road. Normally, as they got close to a village, there'd be signs, farmhouses or just increased road traffic, so Osric was surprised when they walked around a bend and saw one in front of them without any kind of warning.

While that should have filled him with cheer, since with each village there was another chance that maybe someone had heard of this Jasper, Osric had a feeling this village wouldn't help them. While Osric wasn't exactly well-traveled, he'd started getting a feeling for what other villages were like as he had seen more cities and villages in the past month than he had in his entire life.

Which is why it was pretty easy to see something was wrong here. There was a stillness in the air. There weren't people milling about, which was a major warning sign, since gossip was the number one way most villagers spent their time. No work could be heard coming from the shops in the area, and there were no animals or children about. He would have thought it abandoned, except there were a handful of people, heads down, going wherever they needed to go.

Strangers in a village were a big deal, and yet no one looked at them or otherwise acknowledged their presence. Everyone seemed to go out of their way to avoid eye contact, their shoulders were slumped and their faces almost gaunt.

What should have been the main street of the village was lined with partially boarded up buildings and an abandoned cart sat in disrepair, weeds growing through the spokes.

"What happened here?" Talia whispered.

"I don't know. There's a tavern and it at least looks to be open. We should go find out," Rowan said.

The trio made their way across the near-deserted street, and into the tavern. Inside, the common room was dim and musty, thick with the scent of old ale and despair. It was mid-day, so Osric wouldn't have expected a full tavern, but there would usually be one or two people sitting about, even in small villages. Old-timers with nothing but time on their hands and a want for some company.

Not here, apparently. Except for the barman, there was no one in the room at all. Osric approached the bar, where a gaunt, haggard man stood polishing a pewter mug with a stained rag.

"Quiet in here," Osric observed, trying to sound friendly. "We've been on the road for a few days and could use something to drink and maybe a little information, if you have the time."

"Ain't got nothing to drink, I'm afraid. Barely enough water for washing, let alone brewing."

"Really? I thought I saw a pretty good stream a ways back heading in this direction, and assumed it ran into the town. You have no water here at all?"

"Stream runs through town, alright, but can't use it. It's tainted. Folk who drink it, they get sick, waste away. Same goes for the crops and the livestock. Hell, can't even bathe or play in it. Anyone who's smart stays as far from it as possible."

"Someone poisoned the water?" Rowan asked, shocked. "Wouldn't it just wash downstream? We were in a village a day or so to the north, and I would have thought it the same water. Why hasn't the poison washed down to them?"

"Don't rightly know, although I don't think it's a poison. Like you said, something in the water would have gone downstream, but their water's fine. Hell, we send someone out that way every day or two, so they can bring back enough water to drink. Not possible to bring back enough for the crops though. This harvest is gone and our stores aren't much. We sent word to Farvale, asking the baron for help, but he's a long ways from here."

"So it's just your stretch of the river that's tainted?" Talia asked. "How is that even possible?"

"No idea, just know that it is. Can't drink it, can't touch it, can't use it."

"Has anyone gone upstream to investigate the source of the trouble?" Osric asked.

The barman nodded wearily, setting down the mug. "Aye, we sent two groups of men that way. Brave men, but none of them came back. Now, no one dares try. They're all too scared. I reckon this village is done for. But still, it's good to have folks here, even if I've got nothing to sell ya. What brings you to these parts anyhow?"

Osric felt bad, bothering him with questions with everything he was dealing with, but they really did need answers.

"We're searching for an older cleric or scholar named Jasper. Heard he might have a cottage in the area somewhere. Would have a lot of books, although mostly histories and things like that."

The barman scratched his chin thoughtfully. "Can't say I know anyone like that around here."

Osric's heart sank. Another dead end.

"But," the man continued, "I might know someone who might."

"Really?" Talia asked, hopefully.

"There's this girl, Grace Thornton. Hell, thief's more like it." The barman chuckled ruefully. "Wild child, that one. Moves around constantly, or gets chased out of places constantly, more like. But she seems to know everybody in these parts. If this person lives within a week's journey in any direction, Grace would know them."

"Do you know where we can find her?" Talia asked.

"Last I heard, she was in the village of Tillsby, about a day and a half west of here. Of course, she could have moved on already, but she's kind of loud, I guess is the word for it. For someone who has as light of fingers as she has, she isn't particularly shy about people knowing where she is. Gods, if she didn't have a way with people, someone would have strung her up by now. Hell, I'm half surprised they haven't anyway."

"Thank you, my friend. You've been a great help."

The barman waved off the thanks. "Ah, don't mention it. Just be careful with that one. She's a slippery little minx."

"For the information," Rowan said, setting down a few silver on the counter.

It wasn't a lot, and Osric could see the man looked like he wanted to say no, but he just nodded and slid the coins into a pocket. Pride tended to be one of the first things to go when hunger came.

"We can't just leave them like this," Rowan said as they pushed through the tavern door and were back outside. "As a ranger, it's my duty to investigate what's poisoning their water. I have to go upstream and see if I can find the source."

Osric exchanged a glance with Talia, a silent understanding passing between them. Their mission was important, but he'd want someone to help Eldham, if it was in this kind of trouble, and he knew Talia felt the same.

"We're coming with you," Osric said. "We're all on this journey together, and you might need our help."

"Especially if this isn't just a poison," Talia added. "The way the barman described it, it sounds more like magic to me."

Rowan looked relieved. Osric had no doubt that, if they had stayed silent, he would have gone off on his own. Besides, it was the right thing to do.

The stream followed along the very edge of the forest, bumping in and out of the trees. They followed it for a few hours until the trees opened up as the stream emptied into a small-ish lake, half of which had trees along its bank and the other, western half without, as it looked out onto the plains.

At one time, this must have been good farmland, this close to the forest and a source of water, with gently sloping planting grounds. There was even a farmhouse not far away that was abandoned, but only recently so, with signs of human habitation in and around it that had started to decay, but hadn't all been carried off by animals and scavengers yet.

The other thing notable was how few animals there were. In the forest, there were normally lots of animals near ponds and lakes. Good grounds for foraging and a large source of water, it would have been ideal for them. Rowan actually confirmed as much.

"A place like this shouldn't feel so empty," he said. "No bird noises, no deer or stag. Just trees, dirt, and water. It's unnatural."

"That's not the only thing unnatural," Talia said, hugging herself in spite of the unusual heat. "I can feel … something, in the air. It feels like something that isn't there crawling on my skin."

There were other things. Old stones here or there, most buried enough that there could have been whole buildings under the sediment. The stones were rough, pitted, and cracked from years, maybe even centuries, of exposure, with all manner of moss and plants having found homes in the crevices. Something had been built here a long time ago, but time and the encroaching forest had reclaimed much of what had once stood here, giving no hint as to what it might have been.

Cinder sniffed the air and stayed well back from the water, not that they needed the warning. It was dark, almost thick-looking, but none of them were eager to put a limb in and test it. It reflected the trees and the sky like a black mirror, undisturbed by even bugs, which Osric had never seen before on any pond or lake. A faint, acrid odor clung to his skin, making him wrinkle his nose in distaste.

"Clearly, this is where the taint in the water is coming from, but I have no idea how to fix it," Rowan said. "I've never seen water like this."

Osric stepped closer to the water, picking up a stick and swishing it about. It moved like water, the mirror effect rippling and fading as the stick passed through, but settling down again into a shimmering solid after just a few ripples. Faster than Osric would have thought.

"I've never seen anything like this before."

Talia stepped behind him, looking over his shoulder. Reaching a hand out, she moved it around the stick, not quite touching it, but seeming to react to it as she hovered over it.

"It's not natural, that's for sure. There's something almost ... other, about it. Like it doesn't belong here."

"Of course it doesn't belong here," Rowan said. "Water doesn't smell or look like this."

"I don't mean here in this lake, I mean in our world."

"You think it's from the other side of the Veil? From one of the other realities?" Osric asked.

"The Sage said it was getting worse, that the Veil was weakening enough to let things through. What if it let something through, into the water?

Osric looked back at her, over his shoulder. "Like what?"

Before she could answer, there was a massive splash as a creature burst from the depths of the water. It was a nightmare made flesh - a twisted amalgamation of sea creature and monstrosity. Its body was a bulbous sac, pulsing with a sickly light. Underneath, a cluster of jointed appendages twitched and grasped, reminiscent of the legs of some great aquatic insect. But most horrifying of all was the gaping maw atop its body, ringed by seven writhing, suction-cupped tentacles. It let out a screech that shook the trees, its eyes burning with a feral rage.

Osric scrambled back, struggling to get to his feet in the slick mud. Before Osric was even upright, Rowan had pulled his bow and loosed his first arrow, the shaft burying itself in the creature's hide. The beast barely seemed to notice, its attention fixed on Osric.

It lunged forward, its tentacles lashing out. Osric dodged to the side, getting his sword out and slashing at the grasping appendages. One of the tentacles wrapped around his leg, trying to pull him towards the creature's waiting maw. Behind him, Talia's hands weaved a spell, sending bolts of white energy slamming into the beast's appendage. This, the monster did react to, loosening its grip on Osric and pulling its tentacle back into the water.

Osric was ready as the next tentacle launched out of the water at him, bringing his sword down on it as it neared him, severing the tip of it, black ichor spraying from the wound. The beast retaliated, its remaining tentacles whipping about in a frenzy. One caught Rowan across the chest, sending him flying. He landed hard, the breath knocked from his lungs.

Talia wove another spell, a stream of electricity arcing from her fingertips, striking the creature and rippling across its slick skin, leaving blackened, charred scales in its wake.

Osric dashed back to check on Rowan, who was pulling himself up, only to stop, his weight still on his arms, as he looked past Osric.

"Talia, stop," he called out as her hands moved through the air in preparation for another spell.

"What?" she said, her hands freezing in place, as she looked over her shoulder at him.

"Look at it," he said, pointing at the creature. "Really look at it. It's not moving up onto the land. It's even pulled back from the shore a little bit. I think this

... animal, is just defending itself, not attacking us outright."

Osric looked at the creature. Although he lived in the forest, he wasn't like the Ranger, versed in the nature and ways of its inhabitants. He'd spent his time around people and metal. Still, even he could see what the Ranger meant. The creature's movements were erratic, almost pained, hugging its injured tentacle.

Rowan lowered his bow, stepping forward slowly. He raised his hands in a gesture of peace.

"Easy now," he murmured. "We mean you no harm."

The creature slapped the ground in front of him with a tentacle. It could have grabbed him, but it didn't. To Osric, that looked more like a warning than an attack.

Rowan started muttering to himself, his hand going to the symbol of Wyndra he wore around his neck. As far as Osric knew, most Rangers worshiped the Wild

One, goddess of wildlands and beasts. As he chanted, the symbol in his closed fist began to emanate a soft, green glow. As it did, the beast stopped thrashing around, settling, its tentacles going almost limp. It let out an eerie, low whine.

"What was that?" Osric asked.

"I asked Wyndra to intercede. To calm this creature. It may not be one of hers, but here, in our place, I hoped she still had some power over it, which it seems she does."

"Can you communicate with it?" Osric asked.

"No. I don't even know what it is, but most animals … they don't communicate the way we do."

"Look at its eyes though. It's following us. Watching us," Talia said, moving side to side, the animal's eyes tracking her, to prove her point. "I think it's intelligent."

"Which doesn't mean we can speak its language," Rowan said. "Or even that it has a language."

"Maybe not," Talia said, and then reached around into her satchel, pulling a small book out of it that Osric recognized as one of Elder Miriam's.

She flipped through the worn pages, finger tracing the lines of text. Finding what she sought, she went over it several times before replacing the book and bringing her hands up, beginning a new dance of movements. As she did, the air shimmered between them.

When she finished, the air returned to normal, all trace of the magic gone, but she said, "That should do it."

"Do what?" Osric asked, still not sure what she'd just done.

"Elder Miriam gave me books to study as we traveled. It's what I've been reading. Spells she said that I wasn't ready for before, but am now. Or at least that we might need. This one allows me to communicate with ... I don't know, anyone. As long as they have language. It doesn't last long, though, so we must hurry."

"Why did you attack us?" Osric asked, glancing at Talia to make sure he was doing the right thing.

He didn't need the answer, as the creature responded, not in words, but in a series of haunting, screeching sounds that somehow came out as words in Osric's mind, even though he could hear the meaningless sounds the creature was making.

"You hurt me. Why?" it said, followed by a feeling of confusion and pain.

"I can ... feel what it's feeling," Osric said, looking to Talia again.

"It's how the spell works. Not all communication is words. It must use ... I don't know, body language or something in its speech. The spell says some creatures communicate on multiple levels."

Osric nodded and said to the creature, "It was unintentional. We were trying to find out why the water had turned poisonous. You surprised and scared us. Why are you here?"

The creature's tentacles writhed in agitation.

"I do not know. This is not my home. I live in ... a deep place. The water here is too shallow. There is no food. I starve."

"What about animals. From the shore?" Rowan asked.

"Sickness. Pain. Their flesh burns me."

"This must be one of the beings the Sage talked about," Talia said. "Pulled from another reality into ours, through the Veil. Maybe ... maybe wherever it lives is so different, that our reality is poison to it. Maybe it's poison to us, so just being in the water is affecting people."

"Can we send it back?" Osric asked.

"I don't see how. There doesn't seem to be a rift here, and even if there was, I have no idea how to send something through the Veil."

"So it's just going to starve to death here? If it can't eat anything?"

It seemed the creature could not only hear them, but was listening.

At Osric's words, it wailed, saying, "Pain. The air, the water, they burn. Please, end it. Let me die."

Osric was almost overwhelmed by the emotions it transmitted. Anguish. Desperation.

"We can't just kill it!" Rowan said angrily.

Talia placed a hand on his arm. "We can't send it home, and we can't stop its suffering. Wouldn't it be kinder to grant its wish?"

Rowan shook his head and said, "I can't watch this."

Turning, he walked away, close enough that they could still see him, but his back remained turned.

Osric took another step toward the creature and said, "Is that what you want? Do you really want us to ... kill you?"

"Please. Pain."

"I'll try to make it quick," Osric said.

Osric waded into the shallows, ignoring the acrid burn against his ankles. Raising his sword and gripping the hilt with both hands, he positioned the tip against the creature's skull just above where its eyes were, where the creature's brain seemed to be.

"I'm so sorry," he said and plunged the sword as hard as he could through the creature's skull, piercing scales and bone.

The creature let out a piercing shriek that reverberated across the lake. Its tentacles thrashed violently for a moment, and then it sagged, the light fading from its eyes as it went limp.

Osric pulled his sword free with a sickening squelch, black ichor coating the blade. He stepped back, out of the burning water. He stared at the blade for a moment, his stomach churning, before kneeling at the water's edge. He plunged the sword into the shallows, watching as the dark blood swirled away in lazy tendrils. He wiped the blade off on some nearby grass to remove the remaining poison. He then wiped it clean the rest of the way with a cloth from his bag.

He performed his task almost automatically as he stared at the dead creature, his mind numb.

Talia's hand on his shoulder startled him.

"You did the right thing," she said softly when he looked up at her. "I'm proud of you."

Osric just nodded, not trusting his voice. He stood, sheathing his sword, and looked for the ranger.

"Rowan," he called out.

The ranger, much more grim-faced than normal, came back. He looked from Osric to the creature and back.

"I'm very sorry. If there'd been some other way …"

"I don't blame you," Rowan interrupted him, sounding less angry than he had a few minutes earlier. "Talia was right; it was a kindness, in the end. That creature was suffering. I just … I don't understand how Wyndra could allow something like this to happen. She is the protector of all wild things. How could she let a creature be torn from its home, left to starve and burn in a world not its own?"

"Maybe she isn't," Talia said. "It's not clear to me which gods are part of this Veilguard, but we know there are some who are communicating with us. If the Sage is right, they are trying to point us in the direction of a solution to the tears in the veil. The gods interfere with our world, but can't work directly in it, so maybe this is the best they can do."

"Maybe," Rowan said.

"We need to get it out of the water," Osric said, changing the subject. "If its body was burning just from being here, it's probably still releasing something into the lake. That could be what's tainting the water downstream."

"Yeah," Rowan said, joining Osric by the water's edge.

Together, they waded into the shallows. Osric grabbed a tentacle, suppressing a shudder at the rubbery texture. Rowan took hold of another, and they heaved, dragging the creature's bulk toward the shore. It was heavier than it looked, and they strained with the effort. With a final grunt, they hauled the creature fully onto the muddy bank and a little way from the water's edge, close to the tree line.

"We should burn it," the ranger said, breathing hard. "Make sure nothing else can be tainted by it."

"Rowan ..." Osric began, but the ranger shook his head.

"I'll gather some wood."

He stalked off toward the tree line without another word.

"He'll be alright," Talia said, coming to stand beside him. "He just needs some time."

"I hope so," Osric murmured. "Now that it's out of the water, do you think the water will be able to clean itself?"

"Probably. Ponds like this are usually supplied by underwater springs. With that and a few rains, the remainder of whatever it put in the water should wash downstream. We know the stream was enough to dilute it before it got to the next village, so it should be okay, although it will probably take a few weeks."

Osric just nodded. He didn't doubt she was right. Talia knew things, after all.

When Rowan returned, they built a small pyre around the creature and lit it. Whatever it was made of, or what was on its skin, must have been very volatile, as the flames seemed to burst to life as soon as they contacted the creature's body, burning hot enough to force them back a good distance. They stood and watched as the fire consumed the creature's remains. Smoke billowed into the sky, carrying the acrid stench of burning flesh with it.

"We should go," he said finally, when the fire started to die down. "We're still a long way from finding this cleric, if he even exists, let alone finding the other half of the document the Sage needs."

The other two didn't respond, just gathered their things as Rowan put out what was left of the fire. As they started toward the village the barman had told them about, Osric gave one last look back to what remained of the pyre.

It felt like an eternity since this all started, and he could feel the scars from each battle, inside of him, marking him. He couldn't help but wonder how much more he could carry.

The Thief and the Bandits

It was getting late in the day when the four of them reached the outskirts of another village, this one not nearly as beaten down as the last. It was larger than that village, with no boarded-up shops or empty taverns. They knew they were getting close over an hour before reaching it, thanks to the well-tended fields stretching out on either side of the main road. In the town itself, there were the normal signs of life. People milled around, going about their daily business, shops had signs out, advertising their wares, and the tavern seemed to be doing a brisk business.

It was a welcome sight, and one Osric hoped turned things around for them.

Since they'd left the lake and sacrificed the creature the day before, a somber mood had hung over the group, with very little conversation between them as they trudged west, each lost in their own thoughts. The events weighed on each of them, and while Osric felt he'd done the right thing, he was still struggling with what he'd done.

He'd gone his whole life without taking another life, until a few weeks ago. But that had been different, as he'd been defending himself and others. While he wouldn't say he'd grown accustomed to the fights and the killing, it hadn't pressed on him like this. But then, this had been different. This hadn't been in the heat of battle, and he wasn't defending anyone.

Rowan pointed to a small store near the center of town, its weathered sign proclaiming it to be "Bertram's General Goods."

"We need to resupply," the ranger said, the first words he'd uttered in hours. "Our food stores are running low, and we've still got a long way to go."

"Sure," Osric said, trying to make it sound as normal as possible.

Rowan gave him a pat on the arm and led them into the store; the tinkling of the bell above the door was a cheerful counterpoint to their mood. The interior was dim and musty, the shelves crammed with an eclectic array of goods ranging from foodstuffs to farming tools to bolts of rough-spun cloth. An elderly man was leaning up against the counter, watching another man going through what looked like bags of seed.

"Welcome," he said, turning his attention towards them. "What can I get for you?"

"We need supplies for the road. Dried meat, hardtack, root vegetables, whatever you've got that will keep."

"I think I can scrounge up most of that for you," he said, and then gestured to a shelf next to them where an assortment of dried fruits and nuts sat in baskets. "You might find those useful as well."

Rowan, who had an eye for these things as well as being a bit picky, began to examine the offerings.

"We're also looking for someone," Osric said, while the old man waited for Rowan's decision, trying to sound nonchalant. "A young woman named Grace Thornton. We heard she might be in this village."

It was instantly clear the man had heard of her, as his expression soured, his lips pursing in distaste.

"That little thief? No, I don't deal with her kind. She's not welcome in my store."

"Please, it's important we find her. Do you know where she might be staying?"

"Sorry. I think she left town, but I don't exactly follow her movements. Girl's nothin' but trouble."

The man waiting, looking through the seeds, who'd been surreptitiously watching them the way people in a small village watch newcomers, cleared his throat to speak up.

"She left town a few days ago," he offered.

"Do you know where she went?"

The man hesitated, glancing at the store owner before continuing, "There's a group of ... umm, businessmen who tend to travel from village to village, never staying anywhere long. They were here for a few days, and spent a long night gambling at the tavern. The way I heard it, she was there and doing very well for herself, at least until one of the men accused her of cheating and scamming them. Don't know if she was or not, but ... these are men who don't like to lose."

The store owner snorted, although if it was because he thought she did scam the men or because of the men's dislike of losing, he didn't say. The other man, the farmer, as Osric had started to think of him, gave a knowing nod in return.

"Anyway," the farmer continued, "from what I heard, she packed up real quick and left before the sun came up. A few hours later, the band... businessmen had sobered up or were at least less drunk, realized what happened. They found out she had skipped town and went after her. Last I heard, they were heading southeast."

"Where do these businessmen tend to travel? Are there any known places Grace likes to hole up outside of town?" Rowan asked.

"The ones chasing her? They stay wherever they like; no one can tell them not to. But Grace … there's an old windmill on the edge of the old Whiston farm. Whole area got abandoned when the father died and the rest moved up to Farvale. Rumor has it she's used it as a hideout before when she's in trouble."

"That's where Toman found her, the time she tried to sell his goats when he'd gone to market, I think," the shop owner said.

For someone who claimed not to pay attention to her, they both seemed to know a whole lot about her. That was the way of small towns though. Gossip was currency, so it paid to be up on all of it.

"And you think she would go back there again?" Rowan asked, a little skeptical.

"She's nothing if not a creature of habit. Considering the number of times she's been run out of town, she must be, otherwise she wouldn't keep coming back."

"Do you think you could mark the location down?" Rowan asked, pulling out a small, hand-drawn map of the barony.

"Sure," the storekeeper said. "Maybe if enough of you chase her, she'll run further away and stop bothering people here."

It had taken them only an hour to reach the area the shopkeeper had marked on the map, which was good since the area was only a rough approximation and Rowan needed at least a little light to find their trail.

They'd stopped for the dozenth time since reaching the area, standing back and watching Rowan move slowly, inching along the ground in a half squat. To Osric, it looked like he was just staring at clumps of dirt and tufts of grass, but he'd heard about the ranger's uncanny ability to track people through the lightest scrub or thickest forest. So far, it seemed the legends were true.

He'd actually managed to put them on the trail of a large number of men on horseback very shortly after passing the abandoned windmill. Osric just hoped they'd find them soon because if the light fell completely, they'd have to use Talia's magical light or lanterns to keep the chase going, and either would easily alert the enemy to their presence when they finally got close.

The alternative was to camp and start again at daybreak, but according to Rowan, the men were riding hard, and if he guessed correctly, they had the scent of the girl. If they caught her during the night, there was a good chance she wouldn't survive until morning, and so far, she was their only lead to the cleric from Osric's vision.

The other problem was the number of men, which Rowan estimated to be between fifteen and twenty, all on horseback. Talia and Osric had faced off against only one or two opponents by themselves, and while they had Cinder and Rowan, the odds were still heavily stacked against them.

Not that they had any choice. They had to find her and the cleric. The small vision Osric had been given at Godfrey's house while healing Talia had convinced him of the absolute urgency of accomplishing their mission. The very world was in danger, and if he had to fight fifteen men to do it, then that's what he was going to do.

Rowan started off again, and they began to move, picking up the pace but not quite running, with the ranger looking to the ground most of the time.

Just as the last of the blueish light of dusk began to fade, they heard it. Laughter. Lots of it, followed by shouts and whistles. There were a lot of voices, and it seemed likely they'd found the men they'd been tracking, but they didn't immediately see any sign of them. It wasn't until they crested a small rise that they saw them, nestled in a kind of dell with a thicket of trees blocking the flickering firelight of their camp from being visible farther away.

It was actually a good camping spot for people who didn't want to be easily seen, Osric thought. Or would have been, had they been quieter.

The group dropped to a crawl, letting the darkness hide them as they closed in on the edge of the outcropping of trees that the bandits were using to block their firelight.

Another mistake. Even if they'd had sentries, which they didn't, there would have been enough firelight at their back to make seeing anyone sneaking up on them difficult. The fact that they didn't even post sentries spoke to how freely this group had been operating in the area.

They had no fear of being tracked down as revenge for their extortion.

In the center of the clearing was a campfire, around which sat a rough-looking group of men. They were heavily armed, with swords and daggers on their belts, and several had bows leaning against nearby trees. Tied to a post at the edge of the camp, was a young woman with short, messy blonde hair who Osric assumed to be the thief they were searching for.

"Come on boys, let's not be hasty. I'm sure we can work something out. After all, it was just a bit of fun, playing cards to pass the time. No harm done, right?" she said.

The largest of the men, a burly brute with a thick beard, stood up and walked over to her, crouching down, bringing his face level with hers.

"A bit of fun? You cheated us out of our money and ran. I'd hardly call that a good time."

The girl batted her eyelashes, making herself look small, tilting her head provocatively. "Oh, come now. It was just a little misunderstanding. I'm sure a bunch of big, strong, handsome men like you can afford to let a little thing like that slide. I mean, I thought you lost on purpose, to be sweet. You're all so smart, I was sure you saw right through me. How could I cheat brave, experienced men like you?"

For a moment, the man seemed to hesitate, until one of his companions called out from the fireside.

"Don't fall for it, Garn! She's just trying to trick you again!"

Garn's face hardened as he wheeled back and back-handed her across the face, snapping her head to the side, making a sickening wet sound when it impact-ed.

"You think you can bat your eyes and wag your tongue, and I'll just melt like butter? I'm not falling for your tricks again, wench."

The girl's demeanor changed in an instant. Her eyes narrowed, the smile still there, but no longer coy. Now it was cocky and arrogant.

"Fine. You want to play rough? Untie me, and let's see which of us is still standing at the end."

"I'm done with your games. You're going to tell us where our money is, or things are going to get very unpleasant for you."

The girl spat blood onto the ground. "Do your worst. I'm not afraid of you."

Garn turned to his men. "You heard her, boys. Looks like we're doing this the hard way."

The men jeered and shouted their approval, some of them rising to their feet. Osric looked at Talia and Rowan, seeing his own tension mirrored in their faces.

"We have to do something," Talia whispered.

Rowan nodded grimly. "There's too many for a direct fight. We need a distraction."

As if on cue, the girl stood up, her wrists suddenly freed, a knife appearing in her hand. Garn looked at her, his hand going to his belt where an empty dagger sheath sat. Osric hadn't seen her free herself, let alone manage to pull the man's knife from him. It was impressive. It also eliminated any other options they'd had.

Moving so fast Osric could barely see her hands, she lunged at Garn, the blade finding its mark in his flesh. The burly man roared in pain and surprise, staggering back from the unexpected attack.

Osric and his friends didn't wait, taking her sudden attack as the distraction they needed. Talia stood and stepped through the trees that had been obscuring them, weaving her hands in a complex pattern until she finally pressed her hands forward, thrusting her palms toward the campfire.

A powerful blast of air surged from her hands, scattering the flames and sending embers flying. The bandits around the fire were caught in the gale, several of them knocked off their feet by the magical wind.

As the bandits struggled to regain their footing, Rowan nocked an arrow to his bowstring, drew it, and let it fly, burying itself in the bandit leader's shoulder. Already off-balance from the pain of the dagger cutting into his stomach, the arrow sent the bandit leader spinning, crashing into the ground.

Seeing the bandit leader wounded, Osric and Cinder charged forward, the pair flanking one of the closest bandits who had been knocked over by Talia's spell. Cinder got there first, leaping at the man, his powerful jaws clamping down on the bandit's arm. The man screamed as the wolf's teeth tore into his flesh.

The rest of the bandits, caught completely by surprise, struggled to regain their footing and draw their weapons. Some fumbled with their swords, others reached for their bows, each looking confused, probably wondering where these sudden attackers had come from.

Osric, following on Cinder's heels, lifted his sword with two hands gripping the hilt, bringing the blade plunging down into the man's chest, easily piercing through his simple leather armor, cutting off the man's screams as he went limp.

Grace, now standing above the prone bandit leader, dropped to her knees and plunged the blade into his exposed throat, causing Garn to emit a gurgling sound.

"I told you I'd be the last one standing," she hissed, looking into his eyes as he choked and died.

Talia, seeing the bandits who hadn't been knocked down coming for her, slammed the butt of her staff into the ground, causing a shimmering translucent blue field to surround her before disappearing just as the blades of the bandits found her, the metal skidding off the invisible force.

Across from her, Rowan loosed two more arrows, each one finding its mark in a different bandit. The men staggered back, an arrow protruding from the thigh of one man with another tearing through the other's side before continuing off into the darkness.

Seeing the danger Talia was in, Osric moved to position himself in front of her, Cinder taking the other side, seeming to understand what he was doing. As one bandit tried to maneuver around him to get at Talia, Osric's blade lashed out, catching the man in the side. The bandit stumbled, blood seeping from the wound, but he pressed on, bringing his sword down towards Talia.

At the last moment, Osric threw himself in the path of the blow, the bandit's blade glancing off his armor. He grunted at the impact but held his ground, refusing to let the man past.

Another bandit, seeing an opening, lunged at Talia from the other side. But Cinder was there, leaping at the man, his powerful jaws clamping down on the bandit's sword arm. The man screamed as the wolf's teeth tore into his flesh, pulling his blade off target.

Despite their initial surprise, the bandits quickly rallied, their greater numbers allowing them to surround Osric and his companions. Steel clashed against steel as the fight turned into a chaotic melee. A bandit slipped past Osric's guard, his blade cutting a shallow gash across Osric's thigh. It burned like fire, but Osric saw an opportunity; the man had exposed himself in the attack, and Osric managed to catch his attacker across a shoulder, slicing through the outer edge of it, leaving a large gash behind.

Two more closed in on Rowan, seeking to overwhelm the archer in close quarters. But Rowan was far from helpless. Ducking, he weaved away from an attacker, backing up several more steps to give himself room to fight.

It was surprising how fast the little thief moved, grabbing Garn's dropped sword and darting through the chaos of the battle to engage another bandit, stabbing the former leader's blade into the man's chest before he even realized she was there. A surprised look locked onto his face as he collapsed to the ground dead.

Talia, seeing more bandits closing in, raised her staff and began weaving her hands in a complex pattern, even while one grasped the staff. Left hand raised, fingers splayed, her right hand traced glowing circles before thrusting forward sharply. Three shimmering bolts of arcane energy shot forth from her palm, streaking through the air. They struck another bandit squarely in the chest, searing into his flesh. He staggered back, grasping at the charred wounds before collapsing.

Rowan took aim at the two men who'd closed in on him, firing off two more arrows in rapid succession. The first caught one of the bandits in the shoulder, the steel head punching through leather armor. The man staggered, grasping at the shaft protruding from his flesh. The second arrow found its mark in the other bandit's thigh, sinking deep into the muscle. He let loose a howl of pain, his leg buckling under him, sending him crashing to the ground.

Osric and Cinder, working in tandem, focused their assault on a single foe. Osric's sword cleaved into the bandit's side, the blade biting deep. As the man reeled from the blow, Cinder lunged, his jaws clamping down on the bandit's leg. With a sharp twist of his head, the wolf sent the man sprawling to the ground. Osric followed up with a thrust of his blade, ending the man's life.

The remaining bandits, though still outnumbering Osric's group, were clearly shaken by losing so many of their friends so quickly. Their attack faltered for a moment, but then continued as anger and pain won out over surprise and fear.

One charged at Osric, his sword arcing down in a vicious overhead strike. Osric raised his own blade, managing to deflect the attack slightly. The bandit's sword skittered off Osric's, but not before the tip grazed Osric's upper arm.

Two more bandits descended upon Cinder. One managed to land a glancing blow, his sword cutting a shallow gash along Cinder's flank, causing the wolf to yelp in pain and lunge at the closest enemy to him. The second bandit managed to jump back just in time, narrowly evading the snapping jaws.

Rowan, now the target of three bandits, found himself hard-pressed to keep his foes at bay. He ducked and weaved, as one blade caught him across the ribs, drawing a grunt of pain from the ranger. Rowan retaliated with a swift kick, his boot connected with the bandit's knee with a sickening crunch. The man howled, stumbling back, but his companions pressed forward, seeking to capitalize on their momentary advantage.

Grace never stopped moving, stepping behind another man who was focused on the arrows and spells coming at them, she plunged her stolen sword up through the man's ribs, killing him without the man ever knowing she was there.

Talia ignored the ring of bandits trying to close around her and targeted the group that was threatening to overwhelm Rowan. With a flick of her wrist and a complex series of hand movements, she unleashed a large greenish projectile which streaked through the air, splashing against one of his attackers. The man cried out in pain as the corrosive magic ate away at his flesh, smoke rising from a sizzling wound.

Rowan continued to retreat as the enemy pressed on him, firing off two arrows into one of his attackers, plunging both shafts into the man's chest, knocking him off his feet and into the dirt.

Some of the pressure had been relieved for the ranger, whose opponents had been reduced to two, the others either dead or squirming in pain in the dirt. Talia, for all of her confidence in Osric and Cinder to protect her, wasn't out of danger yet, however.

Multiple bandits pressed in on her, recognizing the danger she posed for them.

Osric had gone entirely on the defensive, blocking stabs and slashes, trying to keep the blades away from Talia and Cinder, relying on the wolf to reduce the number facing them. Cinder did his best, fangs sinking into the thigh of another attacker as he ripped out a chunk of flesh, sending the man bleeding into the dust, grasping at the gaping wound.

"Talia," Osric warned as he and Cinder were pushed back, becoming overwhelmed by the mass of men.

Talia turned her attention from the men assaulting Rowan and lifted her staff, moving it in a dancing pattern before thrusting it out, past Osric, toward the massed bandits in front of them. Flames erupted from the tip of the staff in a wide cone, engulfing five of the attackers. Their screams pierced the night as the fire seared their flesh. When the flames dissipated, one lay unmoving, the others staggering, their clothes and skin charred.

The roar of the flame caused the other attackers to pause, turning their attention toward the sound. Rowan, who had already seen Talia use similar magic, used the distraction to his advantage, firing off two more arrows, each of which sank into the chest of an attacker, sending both stumbling backward from the impact before crashing to the ground.

Osric and Cinder fell on the burned and injured men in front of them, tearing through them as they tried to put out the fire and fought through the pain, leaving all five dead in a matter of moments.

Only a handful of men remained, but the sudden, brutal deaths of seven of their number in a matter of moments was enough to knock sense into them. The survivors turned and ran, not wanting to follow their friends into the afterlife.

But there was no escape. Rowan's arrows found the runners, dropping them one by one. The one man lucky enough to evade the shafts was chased down by Cinder, who pulled him to the ground, mauling him.

Osric didn't have any sympathy for them. He'd seen bandits like this before, even helped Master Ironhand and a group of other residents of Eldham defend their village against their ilk. Men like this murdered anyone they pleased, took anything they wanted, and were a scourge to all of the good people of Peridia. They would not be missed.

"Are you alright?" Talia asked Osric, indicating the numerous cuts and slashes on his arms and legs.

"I'll be fine. Nothing a little time and your magic can't fix."

Rowan and Cinder joined them, both looking equally rough for wear. It was a victory, to be sure, but not one without cost. It would take time for their injuries to heal, and Osric wasn't sure how much of the healing magic the Veilguard had gifted him with he would be able to use.

They all turned to the messy-haired blonde girl wiping her acquired blade on the dead bandit leader's
shirt.

At least they'd found who they'd come for.

The Cleric

"Well, that was a bit of fun, wasn't it? Lucky you all showed up when you did. I mean, I would have handled it, but still, much obliged," Grace said, and then knelt beside the nearest body and began rummaging through the man's pockets.

Osric cleared his throat. "Actually, we were looking for you."

Grace froze in place for a moment before standing back up, sword suddenly in her hand, as she backed away from them.

"Is that so? And who exactly sent you?"

"It's not like that," Osric said, holding up his hands in what he hoped was a placating gesture. "We came looking for your help."

Grace's eyes narrowed and the sword tip dipped a bit. "My help?"

"We're trying to find someone who is supposed to live in this area. We were told if anyone knew where this man was, it would be you," Talia added.

For a long moment, Grace didn't move, her gaze flicking between the three of them, assessing. Then, slowly, she lowered her sword.

"Oh, in that case ..." a sly grin spread across her face. "How much are you paying?"

Osric blinked. "Paying?"

"Well, I don't work for free, do I? Information, like anything else, has a price."

"I'm afraid we don't have much in the way of coin," Osric admitted. "But this is important. We're seeking an old cleric named Jasper who lives somewhere on the edge of the forest. His knowledge could be vital."

Her expression changed instantly.

Shaking her head, the thief said, "No. No way. I'm not going anywhere near that grumpy old codger."

"This is important," Rowan said. "What we're doing could mean all of our lives, the lives of everyone in Aeloria, and the fate of the world."

"Then you should all get busy dealing with whatever that is and leave me alone. Besides, what do you need me for anyway? I thought you Rangers could find whoever you wanted."

"It's not the same thing. Look, I'm certain you have, or will, run into problems with the Rangers. It would be helpful to have one who owes you a favor when that happens."

Her dismissive expression dropped a bit, and Osric thought she might actually be considering helping them. Of course, from what they'd heard about her, Rowan was probably right. She had probably already run into trouble with the Rangers ... and anyone else tasked with maintaining the peace.

She didn't immediately agree, though.

"We just rescued you. Surely that counts for something," Osric said, trying a different track.

"I didn't need rescuing," she snapped. "I had everything under control."

Talia snorted. "Really? Because from where I was standing, it looked like you were outnumbered and outmatched."

"Listen here, Red," Grace said, agitated.

"Alright, alright," Osric said, interrupting them before the insults could actually start. "Perhaps 'rescue' was the wrong word. But we did help you out of a tight spot. All we're asking is for a little help in return."

"Look, we tracked you down once, and I'm guessing there are plenty of others out there who'd love to do the same. Maybe we should just go find them and see how much they'd be willing to pay for a little help locating an annoying little thief."

"You wouldn't."

"He just told you that what we're doing could mean the fate of the entire world. If you don't think that's worth a few threats, you're out of your mind. Besides, it's not like you've made us feel very charitable, have you?"

"Alright, alright, no need to get nasty," she said, reaching down and grabbing a sword sheath from Garn's body and putting her newly acquired weapon in it. "I'll make you a deal. Let me keep whatever valuables we find on these sorry sods, and I'll take you to see the old man. But I'm warning you, he's not exactly the friendly type."

Rowan looked across the scattered bodies, his expression clearly displeased, but the notion didn't actually bother Osric. Anything these guys had, they'd probably have stolen from someone else, anyway. So what did it matter if the thief took it for herself? It was better than stealing from people who'd worked for what they earned.

Besides, they needed her cooperation.

"Agreed. You can have whatever they're carrying. All we want is your help finding Jasper."

"Fan-bloody-tastic," Grace said, the words coming out dry and sarcastic, as she knelt back down and resumed her riffling of the corpses.

"So, how far is it to where Jasper is?" Osric finally asked after watching her meticulously check each man for anything valuable.

"About a day's walk, give or take. I've had a long day, so maybe we can do that tomorrow, after a good night's sleep," she said, straightening up and tucking a small pouch into her belt, before eyeing the bodies all around them. "But maybe we should find somewhere to camp that doesn't have quite so many corpses lying around, yeah?"

"Agreed. Lead the way."

The thief finished her pillaging, pocketing a few more trinkets before gesturing for them to follow. Osric fell into step beside Talia as they headed east, toward the forest, Rowan and Cinder bringing up the rear. After about thirty minutes of walking, they found a small clearing that seemed suitable for a camp. As Rowan started a fire, Talia pulled Osric aside.

"Maybe we should keep watches, just in case she decides to kill us in our sleep and steal everything we have. Or run off," she said in a low voice.

That had occurred to Osric as well. The thief had been in good spirits for their short walk, but considering her behavior since they'd met, there was a good chance she'd take the first opportunity to ditch them.

They rejoined the others, and Talia announced that she would take the first watch, claiming she needed to study her spell books. Rowan promptly volunteered to watch with her, leaving Osric and Cinder to take the second half of the night. Grace, for her part, seemed utterly unconcerned by the watch arrangements.

"I don't care what you lot do, but I'm not losing sleep over it," she declared, throwing down her bedroll.

Without further ceremony, she flopped onto it and seemed to fall asleep almost instantly. Osric shook his head, marveling at the thief's ability to rest so easily after the battle they'd just been through. He supposed when you lived a life like hers, you learned to take your rest where you could get it.

Rowan left to do a once-around the area, just to make sure there wasn't anything to be worried about, and Talia promptly pulled out one of Elder Miriam's books, losing herself in it as she did, which meant there wasn't much need for him to stay awake, since he'd be basically talking to himself.

Settling down in his bedroll, with Cinder curling up next to him, Osric closed his eyes and tried to fall asleep.

He was still wide awake when Rowan returned. The Ranger moved as quietly as he normally did and didn't say anything, so it shouldn't have caught Osric's attention, but it did. He could hear him stir the fire, shuffle, and just breathe. Osric couldn't get his mind to turn off. After Farvale and the search for Grace, they were now, finally, close to the cleric from his vision, and thoughts of where that would lead them, and what the next step in this journey would be, plagued him.

He'd just begun another loop through possibilities when he realized the low murmur that had started in the background, pushing into his spiraling thoughts, was actually Talia speaking.

"So, Rowan, where are you from originally?" she asked.

"I grew up near Beartooth Ridge, at the bottom of it in the forest. I don't really think of it as home, though. My family was poor and had many kids, so there were too many mouths to feed. When I was thirteen, I set out on my own."

"And that led you to become a Ranger?"

"In a manner. I always had a knack for tracking and navigating the forest. Started working at one of their outposts, doing odd jobs like cleaning and repairs. In exchange, they taught me the trade. Eventually, I became a Ranger myself."

"You're the first Ranger I've ever known personally, so I'm not really sure how you all work. Won't they be upset that you just up and disappeared?"

"No, it's not like that with the Rangers. We're not as structured as knights or city guards. We go where we're needed, keep our own schedules. Sure, we were originally organized to defend Greenwood and the forest, but it's not a strict hierarchy."

"Are they why you worship Wyndra? I didn't realize those who weren't clerics could call on her assistance, but you did when we faced that ... lake creature."

"Most Rangers worship her, yes. I think it's because her principles really resonate with us. The balance between nature and civilization, the importance of preserving the wilderness and its creatures. It makes sense for us. As for calling on her assistance, that ... I won't say it's unusual, but is fairly new. There are other Rangers who have had success asking for assistance from her, and have shared that information with the rest of us, which is why I thought to do it. I think it's rather new. For a while, I thought it was maybe because we were becoming more devout or maybe she was pleased with the work we were doing, but now I realize it's because the Veil you and Osric talk about is making it easier for her to work through us directly."

"Then I'm sorry."

"About what?"

"If we're successful in repairing the Veil, it will cut you off from her just as you've found that more direct connection."

"I ... I hadn't really thought of that. I guess that's true, but if what you say is true, it will also save our reality and all the creatures living in it, so in that, I am more fully doing my duty to her. Following her teachings."

"That makes sense. I guess ... I'm not very devout. I know most practitioners follow Lorelei, or at least most of those at the Conclave do, but ... I don't know, I just never felt the call."

"I don't think you have to worry about that. From the sounds of it, magic, or at least how you wield the power of the Veil, is separate from the gods. I'm just amazed by what I've seen you do. To have that kind of power ... it's amazing."

"I'm still learning. You saw what Godfrey did. I can only do a fraction of what he managed. But, maybe one day I'll be that good, if I study hard enough. Although, as scary as this has all been, I've done more magic in the last month than I did the entire rest of my life, so in that, at least, it's been good.

"And we're glad you're along to do that. It's saved us enough times," Rowan said. "Although I know that's not why you're doing it. It's good that Osric has someone special in his life, who supports him like you do."

"Oh, Osric and I aren't together," Talia said quickly. "We're just friends. We both grew up in Eldham as apprentices, in the care of someone else, so we kind of latched onto each other."

While she wasn't wrong, hearing her say that out loud made the bottom of Osric's stomach fall. Suddenly, he felt a little sick.

"Well, I'm glad you have each other. It's important to have people you can rely on. I need to add more wood to the fire. Do you want to help me grab some, maybe stretch your legs?"

"Sure," she said, and Osric listened as they walked away.

They didn't go far, and he could still hear the murmur of their voices as they walked away. Enough that he thought he could hear a change in the tone of both of them, a lighter lilt in Talia's laughter, and a little less somber in Rowan's baritone.

"Stop," Talia said, giggling, as they came back into earshot. "That's so funny. You must have been so embarrassed."

Osric could imagine her gently putting her hand on Rowan's arm, caressing it as she laughed. He could picture Rowan stepping closer to her, their sides touching. An irrational surge of annoyance flooded through him.

"Could you two keep it down? I have to be up to watch in a few hours," he snapped, his voice harsher than he intended.

He didn't get up or turn to look at them. He didn't want to confirm to himself how close they were sitting to each other or if her hand was on him. He wanted to be able to pretend it was all in his mind.

"Oh, sorry," Talia said. "I thought you were asleep."

"Yeah, well, it's a bit hard with you two chattering away. Weren't you supposed to be studying your spells?"

Before Talia could say anything, there was a rustling as Rowan stood up and said, "It's alright. My apologies for disturbing you. I think I'll do a perimeter check, make sure everything's secure."

"Thank you," Osric muttered, closing his eyes and trying to pretend to fall back asleep.

He could feel Talia's eyes boring into him, cutting holes in his back, but he ignored her. He didn't want to turn and face her. After a few minutes, he heard her book open and the rustling of pages as she returned to her studying.

Even with the quiet, Osric found falling asleep very difficult.

It took just over half a day to reach the forest where the cleric lived, all of it spent in silence. Osric tried to make a few passes at conversation with Talia, but she was tight-lipped, answering everything with limited grunts and nods. For his part, Rowan made himself scarce, ranging far ahead of them, saying he was keeping an eye out for more bandits. Osric was pretty sure the Ranger could feel the discomfort in the air and chose not to be a part of it.

For her part, Grace ignored it completely. For someone who had to be threatened to go along with them, she acted like this was a fun jaunt, and continued a near stream-of-consciousness monologue the whole way. It might have been charming had Osric not been so concerned about the damage he'd managed to do between himself and Talia.

Once they reached the forest, the rest of the way only took a few hours, with Grace announcing they'd arrived after they entered a fairly large clearing.

Off to one side of the clearing, nestled against a particularly large tree on the east side of the clearing, was a humble wooden hut, weathered planks gray with age. A rickety fence encircled the dwelling, more of a token gesture than a true barrier. Osric had seen countless such cabins like this in the forest. Although he lived in one of the scattered forest villages, the majority of the people who lived in the Great Forest lived like this; by themselves or with only their immediate family, in their own world away from the rest of humanity.

Grace didn't even pause to open the fence, choosing to hop over it instead.

Marching up to the door, she banged on it with a closed fist, yelling, "Jasper, open up you old goat."

She kept banging until the door was flung open, revealing the man from Osric's vision. Osric imagined he was normally kindly looking with his graying hair and weathered face, but at the moment it was twisted into a scowl as he looked down at the diminutive thief.

"I thought I told you not to come back," he started to say, when he looked past Grace to the people who were with her, his eyes locking on Osric. "You. The gods gave me a vision of you."

"They showed me you, as well," Osric said. "It's why we're here. We've come to talk to you."

Jasper looked past him to Talia, Cinder, and Rowan, before saying, "You'd better come inside. All of you."

Entering the now fairly cramped hut, with the four of them plus Cinder, Osric found himself in the same space he'd seen in his vision. A lived-in, cozy one-room cottage. Every available surface was covered in books and scrolls, stacked precariously in towering piles, and the entire place smelled of old paper and aging leather.

"I can't believe we finally found you," Osric said, excited and relieved that they'd found him and he was real, not just a lie Godfrey had told him while he tried to get more information. "We've been such a long way. The gods led us to you, I think, so you can help us repair the Veil before our reality is destroyed. We've come from Avendell, sent by the Sage, a druid there, to find the other half of an ancient document, one written before the founding of Aeloria. These tears in reality are, we think, ruptures in the Veil and a sign it is weakening, allowing all kinds of beasts from other realities into ours. We think the gods have been leading us to this document because ..."

Osric was practically babbling, the words tumbling out of him as fast as he could say them.

"Whoa, whoa, slow down," Jasper said, holding his hands up.

"Perhaps you should start from the beginning, Osric," Talia said, resting her hand gently on his arm. "And do it slower."

Osric looked at her hand and then up to her. It was the first thing she'd said to him since he'd snapped at her and Rowan the night before. Her expression was passive, giving him no clue what was in her head. She only nodded at the old cleric, silently telling Osric to get on with it.

"You're right, sorry," he said. "It's just that we've been through so much trying to find you. I got a little carried away."

"It's quite alright, my boy. You all look like you've had quite the time of it. Please, make yourselves comfortable. You're safe here."

He gestured to the few pieces of furniture around the room. To his credit, everything looked worn-in and comfortable.

As they settled in, Jasper said, "Now, why don't we take your friend's advice and start from the beginning? I'm curious why the gods showed us to one another, and what this is all about."

"It all started when I found this strange ring in the forest near our home village of Eldham," he said, pulling the chain holding the ancient jewelry from under his shirt and holding it out for the cleric to examine. "Even I could see that it was very old, so I showed it to a wise woman in our village, Talia's mentor, because she knows about these kinds of things. She told me it was filled with some kind of magic, which we later found out was just a byproduct of being thrown through a tear in the Veil from long ago, or something like that. The magic's gone now, but at the time you could almost feel it."

Jasper took the ring and turned it over in his hands, nodding but not saying anything.

When he handed it back, Osric continued, "Soon after I found it, a man showed up in our village. I learned later he was part of a secret group called the Brethren, and he tried to kill me and take the ring. I ... I got lucky and was able to escape, with the help of my friend Talia here. We fled into the forest, which is where we met Cinder, who, we think, was tasked by the gods to show us to the ancient ruins of a keep deep in the forest, up toward the Wyndemer. Inside, we found a recently repaired secret door, leading to an area guarded by more of these Brethren. We fought them and, after that, discovered half of a document written in a language we couldn't read. Since the Brethren were both guarding it and trying to kill me, and because we were led there by Cinder, who at the time we thought was reacting to the ring, we realized it was important and took it. We managed to escape with the document, but the Brethren pursued us relentlessly. That's when we stumbled into Avendell and met the Sage, a powerful druid who is in charge there."

Osric paused, reaching down to scratch Cinder behind the ears as the wolf looked up to him, reacting to its name.

"You went inside the barrier?" Jasper asked, a little in awe, at least proving that the cleric knew a lot more about what was happening in the forest than Osric had.

"Yes. We were told the gods let us through, as they're the ones who put the barrier in place. There, the Sage told us about a veil of energy, or magic, or whatever, that surrounds our world, protecting our reality. He also told us that, on the other side, are other realities, some very different and hostile to our own, and that the Veil keeps our worlds separate. He said the Veil was breaking down because of people using magic incorrectly, and that there was a collection of gods, those who'd been watching over Avendell, who he called the Veilguard, that wanted to repair the damage and protect the Veil. He told us that it was actually the gods that had been directing Cinder to guide us and that the ring had come through one of these tears in reality, thrown through time by a member of an ancient group called the Calaphium who ruled Peridia before the Age of Chaos and the rise of the first kings of Aeloria. The Sage told us that he believes the Veilguard led us to this document, which was written way back then, by the same person who sent the ring, in order to guide us in repairing the Veil. Unfortunately, in the thousands of years since their fall, the document, which is protected by powerful magic, was torn in two, and we need both halves of it to be able to understand it, since their language is very complex and impossible to translate without the full thing. He sent us out to find the other half, starting with a place where the Veil was the weakest and we could more easily communicate with the gods who'd been guiding us thus far. Which is when I saw the vision of you."

"It wasn't just a vision," Jasper said. "While you were looking at me, I was seeing you through a tear that suddenly appeared above me. I don't think that was a vision, but some kind of opening that spanned the distance between us, connecting us."

"I think so, too," Osric said. "I know this is a lot to take in, and I wish I had better explanations for all of it, about the Veil and everything, but …"

"Actually, you've explained enough. I know about the Veil and the Calaphium, and the Brethren," he said, pausing for a moment to look at his hands before raising his eyes to meet Osric's levelly. "I actually used to be one of them."

Osric sat back, distancing himself from the old cleric, and could feel Talia and Rowan doing the same. As Osric's hand dropped to the hilt of his sword, Jasper raised his hand in a placating gesture.

"It's alright. I said I used to be. I left them a long time ago when I realized they were selling nothing but lies."

Osric let out the breath he'd been holding and asked, "What kind of lies? Can you tell us more about the

Brethren? We've been running from them since I found this thing, and they've tried to kill us more times than I can count."

"About the organization, some … but not a lot. I was never very high in their ranks, never made it past the second order. They're obsessed with secrecy, even keeping information from those in the lower orders. It's how they get people to commit, to become more entrenched and loyal. They dangle the promise of learning more secrets if you climb higher in their ranks. What I do know is that they're a large organization, very powerful, with members spread across Peridia. But I never knew anyone outside the chapter I was in. Only the leaders of the local chapters knew who the regional leaders were, and only they knew where the other chapters were located. I know it's broken up regionally, usually based out of a major city. I did learn, after I left, that Greenwood has three chapters - one in Wolfridge, one in Farvale, and a very small one in Meareham, although I'm less sure of that last one."

"But why are they chasing me? What about this," Osric asked, holding the ring at the end of the chain up again, "makes them ready to kill me?"

"Its mere existence is enough. Anything connected to the Calaphium is guarded incredibly closely. You know enough to know they're dangerous. When I first joined as a young man, they told me we were protecting magic and the world from those trying to destroy it, which they said were the remnants of the Calaphium. They told me the Calaphium were ruthless in their control of magic. That they made sure they were the only ones who got to use it and removed anyone who tried to stop them. They taught that the Brethren was formed in secret by those who wanted to use magic to help their communities, and slowly rebelled against the control of the Calaphium. When the dictator's regime began to break, and the Brethren launched an attack on them, the Calaphium chose to tear open the Veil in an attempt to end the world rather than lose control of it."

"That isn't what the Sage told us. He said that the Calaphium did control magic, but they did so because they understood that its use could damage the Veil and weaken the boundaries between realities. When the Veil was ruptured, it was a last group of Calaphium leaders who helped close the damage. They then hid away in Avendell with help from the gods. The fact that the same gods who helped them are directing me to fix the Veil makes me believe that story more."

"I'm not doubting he was telling the truth. I studied with the Brethren for years, did their bidding, only to realize much later that they didn't give a damn about the world or protecting magic. They only cared about amassing power for themselves and relied on the same tactics they claimed were used by the Calaphium they were fighting against. So you really went into Avendell?"

"Yes," Osric said. "It's unlike anything I've ever seen before."

"You know, the Brethren have been trying to gain access to it for years, centuries maybe, but the boundary around it has never let them in. We'd heard about the Sages, the line of druids who control Avendell, although we were told the Sage was an ancestor of the Calaphium and the leader of their remnants still trying to destroy the world. I guess that was rooted in some truth, that he's somehow related to the last Calaphium, from what you said."

"I think so, but I don't think he's trying to destroy the world."

"I've always wanted to see it," Jasper said, looking off a little before he seemed to snap his attention back to Osric. "Why did the gods send you to me? I don't know anything about a document or how to repair the Veil. I knew about the Veil and that it was weakening. I was taught that by the Brethren, but considering how much of that was lies, it makes me far from an expert."

"Before I saw you, the gods showed me something else. A great battle, fought around an ancient temple. In the midst of the chaos, a powerful mage cast a spell that tore the earth apart, swallowing the temple whole, sending it vanishing into the depths. When I first saw you, before you turned, I saw you had a book open, and there was an illustration of that very battle."

Jasper turned and reached, his hands tracing along the spines of several books, before pulling one out and setting it on the table he'd pushed to one side, opening it.

"This?"

"Yes," Osric said, recognizing it as the same image he'd seen in his vision.

"This is a rendition of one of the few battles the Brethren actually discuss from the Reckoning, which is what they call the simultaneous assaults on the Calaphium strongholds, the only other one being their great citadel, which was located where Shadowfell is located today. It is remembered by them as their great victory, more so than the battle of the Calaphium Citadel, probably because it didn't wipe out hundreds of miles of fertile land in an instant."

"So you do know of it?" Talia asked.

"I do. The Calaphium called the temple the Sanctum of the Gods, but the Brethren referred to it, then and still to this day, as the Hall of Whispers. It was one of the Calaphium's most sacred places, where their practitioners sought to communicate directly with the gods themselves. According to Brethren lore, many of those who used magic without permission were taken there for torture, to give up accomplices, before ultimately being sacrificed to gain favor from the gods. Although how much of that is true is unknown."

"But there was a battle there?" Osric asked.

"There was. As far as I'm aware, the temple was swallowed up and is gone forever."

"But there's a chance it's still there, or at least parts of it. Why else would the gods send us there?"

"It makes sense. The Brethren revere that battle. It could be a place they'd keep something like that. As I said, they were not big on sharing their secrets, so I don't really know. If you're going, I'd like to go with you."

"Are you sure?" Osric asked.

Although Jasper wasn't up to the same age as Elder Miriam, he was still much older than the rest of them, and it would surely be an arduous journey.

"For years, I've been praying to Heathus, asking for a way to undo some of the pain and suffering I caused in my years with the Brethren. You have been sent to me, quite literally, by the gods. I don't think I could have a clearer answer than that."

"Well, I'm glad I could introduce all of you," Grace, who'd been sitting quietly off to the side, said, slapping her knees and standing up. "I guess my good deed is done for now, so I'll be on my way."

"Not so fast," Jasper said, surprisingly fast for his age, his hand snaking out and snatching her by her collar. "I know you well enough to know you'll sell whatever information you heard here today the moment you reach a big enough town. I'm sorry, my little friend, but you're going to have to come with us."

"With you? Are you nuts? I'm not going to any creepy buried temple," she said, proving that she had, in fact, been paying attention.

"I'd prefer not to have to turn you into something unpleasant, but if that is my only other option ..." Jasper said, his face completely serious.

Grace clearly believed him, too; because she blanched a little at the threat.

"I'm sure there's going to be some good stuff in there. You seemed pretty keen on taking money off the bandits we defeated, so maybe you'll come out of this a rich woman," Osric offered, hopefully to counterbalance the threat.

"Rich?" Grace said, clearly thinking about it.

"Rich and not a frog, or whatever," Talia said. "Seems like a good deal to me.

"Well, why didn't you say so," Grace said, smiling in a way that made Osric check his own coin pouch. "Count me in.

"Okay. So where are we headed?" Osric asked, turning back to Jasper.

"I'm afraid I don't know the exact location of the Hall of Whispers. The Brethren kept that information closely guarded, even from most of their own members.

"So we're at a dead end?" Osric said, deflating.

After all they'd been through, all the danger and miles traveled, to be stopped now felt like a cruel joke.

"No, I don't know where it is myself, but I do know who would."

"Who?"

"The leader of the Brethren in Farvale and the surrounding area. I know the hall is somewhere in this region and he controls this area and had access to ancient tomes and scrolls with all of the Brethren's knowledge of this part of the world. If anyone knows how to find the Hall of Whispers, it would be Godfrey."

Osric froze and looked over to Talia, who had an equally shocked look on her face.

"Damn," Osric said.

Return to Farvale

The walk back to Farvale was going to take them at least two full days. They spent the first night at Jasper's cabin, or at least camped near it, and the next day walking north, through the forest. They'd at least made good time, and Rowan thought they'd make it to the city just after dark the following day.

Osric thought that was probably a good thing. Considering how they'd left the city, the fewer people noticing them, the better.

The long walk did give Osric more time to think. Even though their quest was going well, and it looked like they were getting close to at least knowing where the other half of the document was, things between himself and Talia had not improved. If anything, the longer they walked without addressing it, the icier the space between them became.

When Rowan called a halt to camp that night, Osric stopped Talia short, so they could talk outside the earshot of the others, who'd begun to set up for the night.

"Talia, can we talk?"

"About what?" Talia asked coldly, folding her arms across her chest.

"I hate how things have been between us the past few days. I wanted to apologize for snapping at you the other night. It was uncalled for."

"You're right; it was uncalled for. There was no reason for you to act like that, no matter how tired you were."

"It wasn't actually because I was tired," Osric admitted, looking away from her, to the ground near their feet. "I was upset because of how you were talking to Rowan, the way you were laughing and joking with him. And then when you said you and I were just friends …"

"We are just friends," she said matter-of-factly.

"I know, but … after everything we've been through together, I realized that I like you. Well, I think I've always liked you, but these last few weeks it's … I don't know, more."

"Osric, I like you, too," she said, her expression finally thawing a little.

"I don't mean like that, I mean …"

"I know what you mean," she said, laying a hand on his arm. "And I mean it the same way."

"You do?" he said, honestly shocked.

"Yes," she said softly, before quickly shifting her tone back to more direct and no-nonsense. "That doesn't mean what you did was right. We've never talked about being … anything, and you have no claim over me. To be mad because I was talking to someone else, when you and I have never even discussed being anything more than friends, was unfair to me. Now, I admit we've been a bit busy lately, what with all the life-threatening situations we've found ourselves in, but that isn't an excuse either. I'm sorry if you thought I was flirting with Rowan, which I wasn't. I was only being friendly. Even if I was, though, I'm allowed to talk to or flirt with anyone I want. If we'd discussed things or done … anything that indicated we were more than friends, that would be different, but we haven't. Which is why, when he asked, I said we were just friends. It was the truth. I'm not saying we'll always be just friends, but you can't start acting like we're something we're not. Do you understand?"

She put particular emphasis on that last statement, sounding frighteningly like Master Ironhand when he was lecturing Osric on some mistake or error he'd made. Not that she was wrong. He'd overreacted and been unfair to her and then been mad at her for being upset at his unfairness, which was also unfair.

"You're right. I apologize. It won't happen again."

"Good, 'cause I hated being mad at you," she said.

"Maybe, sometime, we could talk about being more than just friends?"

"Maybe," she said, a smile playing at the corner of her mouth. "But I think maybe it will have to wait until we aren't constantly fighting for our lives."

"That's fair. When this is all over, then?"

"When this is over," she agreed, leaning in and placing a soft kiss on Osric's cheek, her wild red curls brushing against his skin. "Until then, let's just go back to being best friends, okay?"

"Deal," Osric said, his chest feeling lighter than it had in days.

With a final smile, Talia turned and walked back towards the others and began to unroll her bedroll for the night. Osric watched her go, admiring the sway of her hips as she set about her task, thinking about the future they might have together.

The group timed their arrival in Farvale so they could slip into the city under the cover of darkness, taking a roundabout path Grace said she knew that would keep them off the main thoroughfare, hopefully to avoid much attention. While they'd made it out of town successfully the last time, after fighting Godfrey, it seemed likely that someone had noticed the group when they'd first arrived, especially considering the presence of Cinder, who would have stood out in a major city even more than he did in small villages.

The streets were quiet, far different from the bustling markets they'd gone through the last time. Even with that, Osric couldn't help but worry that eyes were following them as they went, watching them.

His concern that the death of Godfrey would have been taken seriously by the town authorities was confirmed when they finally reached the outskirts of the main square and saw a pair of city guardsmen standing at the bottom of the steps leading up to the front of the mansion.

"That's a problem," Osric said.

"Could we go around?" Jasper asked.

"We can try, but I'm not sure how much good it will do us. I didn't really put it together before, but I think he built that place to be hard to enter. We had to walk up those huge steps to get to the front door, and it looks like the bottom floor is all foundation. Look at the windows on this side of the building. They're a little higher than even the second-story windows of the buildings on either side. We'd heard the man living here had set himself up in high style, so at the time I'd just written it off as wanting to be seen as important, above everyone else. Looking at it now, though ... I don't know."

"Look at how the foundation slopes outward slightly as it goes up. Maybe to make it harder to climb?" Rowan said, pointing at the base of the structure.

"So we're stuck," Osric said, disheartened.

"You all give up so easily. I can get us in. Follow me around back," Grace said.

She darted down a side street, motioning for them to keep up.

Osric still wasn't completely sold on the little thief, but she certainly was confident all the time. He and the rest hurried to catch up to her as they made their way around the rear of the structure. Thankfully, there weren't any guards there, but there wouldn't be, considering how the building was constructed. The closest entry point, a darkened window, sat well above their heads, out of any of their reach.

"Wait here," she said, disappearing down another narrow alley.

While it was a big building, and they were well on the other side from the two guardsmen, Osric and the rest remained silent. If getting noticed was a bad idea, getting found lurking behind the house of the man they killed was certainly worse. As the minutes ticked by, Osric became more and more worried. Grace had made enough comments about not wanting to be on this adventure with them that there was every possibility she'd decided this was her moment to run. With what she knew about them, she could cause big trouble if she decided to try and sell that information, or even if someone like the Brethren found out she'd been with them and forced the information out of her.

"Did she just ditch us?" he finally asked, breaking the silence in frustration.

Jasper opened his mouth to respond, but stopped as Talia gasped, pointing upward. "Look!"

Above them, a lithe figure leaped from a nearby rooftop, landing on the mansion's roof in a crouch.

He could just make out the thief's short, messy blond hair before she disappeared from sight again.

"Impressive," Rowan said.

She wasn't done yet. A few minutes later, the window directly above them swung open, a rope dropping down out of it.

"Guess that's our cue," Osric said, and then knelt down next to Cinder, who definitely wouldn't be making the climb with them. "We'll be back in a little bit. Find a place to wait for us."

Cinder gave a soft whine and licked Osric's face, but obeyed, slinking off into the shadows. Osric wasn't concerned about the wolf. He'd shown a good instinct for being able to stay hidden and had found them before, even when they'd run in separate directions.

Osric grasped the rope, testing its tautness, and then started to climb, hoisting himself up hand over hand.

Grace's face appeared above him, smiling mischievously.

"Nice work," he said, pulling himself through the window.

"I told you I could get us in," she said, rolling her eyes.

As the others followed up behind him, Osric let his eyes adjust to the darkened room. With its massive four-poster bed, this was obviously a bedroom. The nicest one Osric had ever been in. Calling it opulent would have been an understatement. If he had to guess, he'd say the contents of this room must have been worth more than his entire village.

"Which way?" Grace said as she pulled up the rope and put it back in her pack, closing the window to remove any sign of their entry.

"This way," Osric said, leading them in the direction of the study on the first floor.

They moved quietly, just in case there were any guardsmen stationed inside, but the entire place was silent. Someone had closed the double doors leading into Godfrey's study but, thankfully, hadn't locked them.

"Looks like quite the fight," Grace said, giving a low whistle as Osric ushered them inside.

"You have no idea," Osric said.

The room was much as they had left it, in utter disarray with papers scattered across the floor and furniture overturned. The piles of sticks and wire, the remains of the animated statues, were where they'd been left, along with a large dark spot on the rug where Godfrey had fallen.

Other than the removed body, it didn't look like anything had been touched.

"Help me look through these books," Jasper said, heading to one of the large bookcases against one wall, while pointing at another one. "It's in one of these two. It didn't have a name on it, and the text is in multiple hands. I think it said something about the 'true and just history of the world,' or something to that effect."

Rowan and Talia moved to follow his instructions, pulling books down one at a time, flipping through pages. Grace didn't even bother pretending to help them. Instead, she started opening drawers and containers on shelves, occasionally pocketing something she found inside, as she began to thoroughly loot the place. Osric shook his head but didn't say anything. They had promised her access to treasures they found, and considering that Godfrey had tried very hard to kill them in this very room, he couldn't bring himself to care about the man's house being ransacked.

Besides, Osric's attention turned to the desk. It had been covered with various letters and documents, most of which had been scattered on the floor by Godfrey's magic. Osric began scooping up as many as he could, looking through them. Godfrey was not only the leader of the Brethren in this area, he'd known about Osric, either by description or because of their mention of Eldham. That had all happened far from here, deep in the forest, and Osric had gotten the impression from Jasper that the leaders of these sub-groups of Brethren had a limited geographical jurisdiction. Which meant someone had been keeping Godfrey up to date on Osric and his actions, and Osric wanted to see what they were saying about him.

The first few documents were innocuous, detailing mundane matters of estate management and requests from the Farvale city council for his assistance. There were letters to the Conclave, requesting access to a few tomes of instruction, and even a response to a letter that suggested Godfrey had been trying to pawn off his student, the young girl they'd sent to Elder Miriam, on another instructor, going so far as saying he would be happy to 'be rid of the pest.'

While this all painted Godfrey as a thoroughly un-
friendly but educated and important man, it wasn't
what Osric was looking for. Then he finally found
what he was looking for in one of the last letters
he grabbed. The bottom of the letter had partially
burned, wiping out some of the last paragraph and
the signature, although Osric could still make out
the first name Ranulf.

It detailed the loss of junior members of the
Brethren, sent to scout for 'the artifact,' focusing on
small villages near the Wyndemer and describing
a 'boy from the village of Eldham, possibly accompanied by a girl from the same village,' as having
the ring. It instructed Godfrey to send notice to the
Brethren in his area of operation to be on the lookout
for the pair, as they lost them near the borders of
Avendell, and had not been able to find them again.
It said he was sending most of the men from near
the Wyndemer toward Avendell, in hopes of finding
them, but that it was possible the boy had slipped
through. The last paragraph, which was partially de-

stroyed by fire, made mention of the other half of something, although the part of the sentence with the specifics was burned away. The next sentence, and only other partial sentence Osric could see, said 'send more men to guard,' and then disappeared again.

It sounded like they did not know who Osric was, at least not his name. They knew he was traveling with Talia, but hopefully that would be harder to work out now that there were five of them instead of just the two. Something finally in their favor.

Osric was distracted from looking through any of the other papers when Jasper suddenly explained, "I think I've found it."

"You did?" Osric said excitedly, joining them at the bookshelf.

"Well, not it exactly, but a reference," Jasper said, pointing to a page in the large book opened in his arms. "There are references to the battles, including several landmarks. Ones that I recognize. I'm pretty sure I can get us at least close to it. The section also indicates that the ground is still scarred with the remnants, and something about an obstacle surrounding it to discourage any from stumbling into the site unknowingly. I don't know what that's about, but it means we should know it when we find it."

"That's good enough. We can figure out the rest when we get there."

"Good, the sooner we get out of here, the better," Grace said. "This room gives me the creeps."

"Not enough to keep you from stealing anything not nailed down, though," Rowan said.

It was clear the ranger wasn't a fan of her less-than-honest living. For her part, Grace didn't seem to care, just giving a disinterested shrug in response.

Before they could discuss it anymore, or leave, the doors to the room slammed back open, revealing a

woman in ornate armor, flanked by a dozen guardsmen, all bearing the insignia of the Farvale Guard.

"In the name of the Farvale Guard, you are all under arrest."

Chapter 18

I Fought the Law …

"Stop," Osric called out, more to his friends, whose hands were going instinctively to their weapons, than to the guards. "We surrender. There's no need for violence."

"A wise choice," the woman, who was clearly their leader, said. "Disarm them."

The latter was said to the men with her, who quickly removed everyone in his group's weapons, finding a surprising number of knives and other small implements on Grace, suggesting the thief was more dangerous than she let on. They even took Talia's staff, although Osric didn't know whether it was out of precaution or because they recognized that it was, in some way, magical.

"This isn't what it looks like," Osric said as he handed over his sword. "Please, let us speak to your superior and we can work this out."

Osric wasn't sure who he'd need to talk to, but considering Godfrey was the highest member of the Brethren in the city, Osric hoped that someone in a position of authority might be safe to deal with, and not be a member of the Brethren.

"I'm Captain Lockewood, and I'm in charge of the guard. So if you need to talk to someone, you talk to me. Not that it will do you any good."

Everyone was jumpy, and all it would take was one person overreacting for things to go wrong very quickly.

Holding up a hand in a pacifying gesture, Osric said, "Captain Lockewood, I understand how this must look, but I assure you, we are not criminals. We were merely searching for information vital to the safety of the world."

"The safety of the world?" Lockewood asked, an eyebrow raised, her tone dripping with skepticism. "The world hinges on two children, an old man, a thief, and a Ranger? We should be so lucky. And I suppose breaking into a nobleman's home and rifling through his possessions is just part of your noble quest?"

"Godfrey was not the man you think he was. He's the leader of a secret group that has spread itself throughout the barony, attacking people in the forest."

Not exactly true, but also not untrue, and it saved trying to explain about the Veil and messages sent through time and space.

"Which explains why you murdered him, left, and returned to the scene of the crime, does it? Witnesses saw you. Several witnesses reported seeing you two, along with a Ranger and his pet wolf, leaving in quite a hurry."

"We didn't murder Godfrey," Osric said firmly. "He attacked us, and we defended ourselves."

"A likely story," Lockewood scoffed. "I'm sure the magistrates will take it under advisement."

"Captain, I am Rowan Wycliff, a duly sworn Greenwood Ranger," Rowan said, pushing his way in front of Osric. "I am tasked with the defense of the realm. The defense against Godfrey was done under my authority, in protection of these people who are under my protection."

"Is that so? Well, Ranger, let me make something very clear. You hold no authority here. In Farvale, the law is upheld by the guard, not by self-appointed vigilantes who think they can play judge, jury, and executioner. Your kind has always seen themselves as above everyone else, a law unto yourselves. But not in my city."

The Ranger looked to the guards, who seemed to stiffen at that proclamation, then back to Lockewood, and said nothing in response. She eyed him for another hard moment, and then turned to Osric.

"Your story might hold more weight if you weren't gallivanting about with a known thief and nuisance. This one," she said, gesturing toward Grace, "has been a thorn in Farvale's side for a long time. Breaking into homes, stealing from honest citizens, and now, apparently, graduating to murder to get what she wants."

"Please," Grace said, scoffing and crossing her arms. "Like I need to murder someone to get what I want. I'm not an amateur."

"Grace," Jasper said. "Shut up."

Grace opened her mouth to retort, but a sharp kick against her heel from Jasper silenced her. She settled for a disgruntled huff instead.

"You'll have your chance to plead your case before the magistrates in the morning," Lockewood said, watching the interchange. "Though I wouldn't get your hopes up. The penalty for murder is clear. You'll be taken to the block come dawn."

"Captain, please," Osric said, seeing everything they'd worked for coming to a screeching halt. "Godfrey tried to kill us. He was a dangerous man, involved in dark things. We were only defending ourselves."

"Which naturally explains why you came to his home, knocked on his door, and were seen being ushered inside. Because that's what one does when defending oneself from a dangerous man."

Osric opened his mouth to defend himself further, but Captain Lockewood cut him off with a sharp gesture.

"Save it for the magistrates. I'm sure they'll be fascinated by your tales of secret societies and noble quests. Personally, I'm just glad you were foolish enough to come back and try to loot Godfrey's house. Makes my job that much easier," she said, waving a hand to her men. "Get them out of here. I want them in cells before the sun rises."

Osric sat on the hard wooden bench in the dimly lit cell, his head in his hands. This had all gone so wrong, and exactly at the moment they found out where the temple was. What if they couldn't talk their way out of this? He'd heard that prisoners who weren't sent to the block were shipped off to the mines on the far west side of the kingdom, to work the outer ranges of the Cragshire Mountains, digging into the ground until either they died in an accident or from sheer exhaustion.

Or maybe the Veil would break and the world would end before that.

The rest of his companions looked about as dejected as he felt. Well, except for Grace. She acted like this was some kind of fun excursion. Of course, she'd been in this position many more times than he had, so maybe for her, it was.

He was finally pulled out of his wallowing by the clang of a key in the thick metal door. For a moment, he hoped it might be Captain Lockewood, here to tell them she'd examined their story and they were free to go, but when the door opened, it was just some junior guard officer. Osric thought maybe he was here to bring them food or interrogate them some more until he saw the cold look in the man's eyes.

He ignored everyone else and looked directly at Osric. "You, come with me."

Something about the way he said that, and the look in his eyes, told Osric not to trust him. That there was more going on here than just normal guard business.

"Why?" Osric said.

"Because I told you to. Or do you want me to come in there and make you follow me?"

"Tell me what you want, first," Osric said, standing up and backing away.

The rest of his friends, minus Grace, had started to close in on Osric, blocking him with their bodies. The guard, whoever he was, looked at each of them contemptuously for a moment before looking past them, focusing on Osric.

"I want you to come with me and stop giving me lip. If you listen to me now, your friends can live. But you're coming out here one way or another."

"He's not going anywhere with you," Talia said, standing in front of Osric.

"Have it your way," the guardsman said and waved to the side, beckoning in six men who were definitely not part of the city guard.

They were, however, armed.

"Kill his friends and bring me ..."

"What is the meaning of this?" a voice called out from just outside of the door, interrupting him.

A moment later, Captain Lockewood appeared behind them.

"Captain ..." the guard said, whirling and staring at her open-mouthed, his calm demeanor gone. "You aren't supposed to be here."

"Clearly," she said, laying a hand on the pommel of her sword. "Who are these men, and why are you in here with the prisoners?"

"Leave now, Captain, and we can discuss this later."

"I will not."

"Fine," the man said, his surprise going back to confidence as he looked over his men and then back at Lockewood, clearly reasoning out the odds. "Kill all of them."

Chaos erupted as the men all drew weapons and attacked. Lockewood reacted instantly, charging toward the traitorous guard, her longsword glowing faintly blue as she pulled it from its sheath, the blade just catching under the man's shoulder pauldron, drawing first blood, causing him to stumble back in surprise at how quickly she acted.

She wasn't the only one who acted quickly. Grace darted in between two of their attackers, pulling a pair of daggers that the men searching her had somehow missed. The man nearest her barely had time to register her as she came around him, one arm dropping low, slashing behind his knee, and the other swinging down as he toppled backward, puncturing the side of his neck with her knife. He didn't even have a chance to look surprised as he fell, dead before he'd even taken a step.

The guardsman Lockewood was fighting was no amateur and brought up his own weapon as he staggered back, slashing out wildly at her. Lockewood ducked back and brought up the rear of her blade, catching his at the hilt and deflecting it before her sword whipped around in a lightning-fast riposte. She was at a full arm's length away from him, so the weapon did little more than cut a gouge out of his cheek, but if he survived this, he would have a scar to remember it by.

Several of the men turned to see their friend falling from the seemingly unarmed Grace, an opportunity Rowan didn't waste. Grabbing a nearby man's wrist, Rowan tucked it in his own and twisted, his hands holding the wrist in place as the hand turned, causing the enemy to cry out and drop his sword.

Osric saw him moving and thought it the best chance for him as well, since he was equally unarmed. Unable to reproduce whatever maneuver Rowan had made, Osric instead went to grapple a distracted man, closer to him. Wrapping his arms around him, Osric pulled him close, putting the muscles developed over the years at the forge to work as he crushed the man's body against his own, pinning his arms.

Talia brought up her hands and, as she'd done before, weaved them in a pattern, pulling at the parts of the Veil none of them could see, until the shards of magical energy appeared out of her palms, slamming into one of the men, sending him staggering back, multiple burn marks evident where they punched through his armor.

Another of the attackers, seeing Talia as a threat, slashed out at her. She managed to jump back just in time, but the blade came much too close to her.

"Heathus, aid us now," Jasper said, his hand going into the air, a small symbol of his god in his palm.

While Osric knew the gods had the ability to work their magic here in their world, and had had them do it through him several times, he'd never actually seen their power invoked before. The medallion in Jasper's hand shone a bright white that caused Osric and everyone else to have to look away, the light washing over everyone.

Osric felt something, as it did. Some kind of ... energy, or feeling maybe, surging through him. He suddenly felt surer, more steady, more confident. He didn't know exactly what Jasper's god had done, but Osric could definitely feel ... something.

Grace never stopped moving, darting behind the man Rowan had disarmed. He made a grab for her as she passed, but she easily ducked under it, bringing one of her daggers up underneath the leather front piece of his armor, whipping her blade across as she did, opening his stomach up. The man screamed, falling to the ground making an effort to hold himself together, the color quickly draining from him. Grace kept moving, ignoring the very soon-to-be-dead man.

Behind her, the traitorous guard, blood pouring down his cheek, pressed his attack against the captain, who managed to bring a metal bracer up, deflecting the blade.

Rowan scooped up the dead man's sword and charged forward toward another attacker, who brought his sword up in time to block the attack.

Talia, seeing men pressing toward her, took a small step back and weaved her hands in a pattern around herself, until the shimmering field of energy Osric had seen before materialized around her just in time to stop one of the blades that would have otherwise certainly cost her her life.

Jasper brought his outstretched hand down, still grasping the amulet, as he pointed to the man who had just attacked Talia. In a voice that was his, but was also not his, almost as if a higher pitched voice mirrored his own, speaking simultaneously, he commanded, "Defend us!"

Osric wasn't sure, but it seemed as if, for a moment, the man stiffened, before whirling around and bringing his sword down into the shoulder of one of his comrades, who looked from the blade to his comrade in horror.

Osric couldn't think about that too much, as he was still tightly gripping the struggling attacker. Lifting him off the ground, Osric slammed him down into the hard stone floor with all of his might, causing his weapon to skid out of his hands. Osric released him immediately and scooped the blade off the floor, bringing it up in a defensive stance.

After seeing her kill another of their friends, more men went for Grace, who slid under and around every attack, never stopping long enough to be anything other than a blur of movement.

Next to Osric, Rowan cried out as he moved left instead of right at the wrong moment, a blade slashing across his upper arm, leaving a red trail behind.

Lockewood continued to press her attack. Maybe she'd been fighting slower at first, as she tried to take in the whole scene and work out what was really going on, but now that the battle was in full swing, she showed what she was really about, moving faster than Osric had ever seen someone move with a sword.

After pushing away the guardsman's blow with her brace, she swung in hard, slicing just under the man's breastplate and then continuing to slide the blade sideways until it cleared the bottom of his chest piece, leaving a trail of red behind, and then coming back up, punching into his unprotected underarm. Finally, she pulled the blade back and up, so that it was reversed with the pommel at head height and the blade pointing to the ground, just in time to block the guardsman's counter swing.

She wasn't done yet. As soon as she deflected his counter swing, she smashed the pommel into his face, which emitted a sickening crunch as his nose shattered, leaving his face a bloody mess. In just a few seconds, she'd defended herself while injuring the turncoat three times.

It was an impressive display that sent the man staggering backward.

Grace was equally as impressive. After stabbing one and eviscerating another, she dodged under an attack, her hand shooting out, sending one of her daggers sailing across the room into the eye of a man heading toward Talia, dropping him where he stood.

That left just one attacker coming at Talia as she backpedaled, her hands weaving furiously. Just as the man lifted his sword to strike, she stopped her retreat and reached forward, pressing her palm into his chest just as electricity exploded from it, wrapping around and through the man.

Osric could smell the unpleasant odor of something cooking as the man dropped to the ground.

Half their attackers were dead, but they were still in danger. As the guard Jasper had bewildered attacked another of his friends, making successful contact as another friend didn't expect the sudden attack, Jasper charged forward and tangled himself up with one of the men who'd been coming for him. His hold was tenuous, but it made it impossible for his attacker to swing at him until he untangled himself from the old priest.

The man Osric had slammed to the floor was back on his feet, eyes going to the fallen sword of one of the dead men. Osric wasn't going to let that happen and lunged forward as the man went to grab it, piercing him through the side. The man managed to roll away from the blade, keeping it from going in enough to cut anything vital, but he was bleeding profusely out of the wound as he got back to his feet.

The guardsman, enraged at this point, hefted his longsword with both hands, sweeping a wild arc at the captain, who ducked low under the attack, the blade whistling over her head, and then sprang up, slicing across his chest. The sword bit deep, parting armor and flesh.

Before she could make another attack, Grace seemed to appear out of nowhere, leaping onto the guardsman's back and plunging her remaining dagger deep into his exposed neck. It was like watching a marionette with its strings cut, the man going limp as he fell to the floor.

Grace, in a bit of exuberant excess, pushed off the man as he fell, performing a flying somersault before landing lightly on her feet.

As Rowan dispatched another attacker, Talia backed away, trying to separate herself from the fight. It occurred to Osric that, far too often, she was exposed, even with or often in front of himself and Rowan. It wasn't hard for their enemy to identify her as the largest threat they faced, putting her in far too much danger.

Jasper still valiantly held onto his foe, relatching on every time an arm or leg was pried loose. He then surprised everyone by headbutting the assailant hard in the face. The damage seemed minimal, but it was surprising to see such ferocity from someone like him.

The man who'd been under Jasper's control seemed to finally snap out of it, stopping cold in the middle of the room, his sword dropping to his side as he tried to figure out what was happening. Unfortunately for him, he had done enough to convince his friends that he was a danger and one of them slashed him across the chest, sending the man reeling.

"Have you lost your mind?" he bellowed. "We're on the same side, you fool!"

The guardsman gone, Lockewood pressed forward into the melee, catching one of the men facing Rowan unaware, gripping his shoulder and pulling him back onto her blade as she skewered him.

The few remaining men fell swiftly as the tide turned against them, until only the one Jasper was grappling remained. The cleric let him go and jumped back as the man went for his sword. It wasn't until after he grabbed the weapon that he realized he was now all by himself. Blood trickled down his nose from where Jasper had headbutted him and he had a desperate, crazed look in his eyes.

"Drop the sword and surrender," Lockewood said, leveling her sword at him.

For a moment, it looked like he might consider it, as he looked around at the bodies of his friends, when suddenly he leaped forward with a wild cry. Lockewood pulled her weapon back into a ready stance, prepared for the man's attack ... an attack that never came as Osric lashed out with his own sword, intercepting the man and cutting him down before he could get close to her.

Osric pulled his borrowed sword out of the man and looked around the room. The would-be assassins were all dead at their feet, and the immediate danger was gone. But a shocked-looking Lockewood was still between them and the door, and it was unclear what would happen next.

"Are you alright, Captain?" he asked.

"I'll live," she said, shaking herself out of her stupor and sheathing her sword, which amazingly remained free of blood in spite of the damage it had done. "Will someone explain to me what the hell is going on? Who were those men, and why did our own guardsman just try to kill me?"

"It's as we told you. There's a group, working in secret, towards some agenda we don't fully understand yet. This is not the first time they've tried to kill us."

"Why? Why are they trying to kill you?"

"It's ... hard to explain. Or at least it's a very long story."

"The gods have given Osric a mission that will hopefully save the world," Jasper said. "They have spoken to him, and myself, in visions, and have set him on a task of the utmost importance."

"What kind of mission?" Lockewood asked, the skepticism in her voice impossible to miss.

"Have you seen, or at least heard about, the strange creatures that have begun to show up in the forest, and maybe other places, over the last twenty or thirty years? The sudden attacks by monstrous creatures like Webscuttlers and the like?" Rowan asked.

"I know of them."

"These aren't beings of our reality, but creatures that have escaped from other places of existence through gaps in the world. The gods want to close these gaps and have quested Osric here to do that."

Osric wasn't sure it was completely true that the gods had quested him to do anything. They'd nudged him in a direction, to be sure, but the Sage, who, by his own admission, had limited contact with the gods, had been the one to send him. And only for a document, not to actually close the gaps in the Veil itself. That would have required a whole lot more explanation, so Osric went with it, since as hard as the story was to believe, the truth would be a lot harder to convince her of.

"And they want to stop you? Why?"

"We don't know," Osric said. "We only know they have been trying since we first learned of the problem and started trying to solve it. We came to Farvale originally because I was given a vision of Jasper, and Jasper a vision of me, but we didn't know how to find each other. We'd heard of Godfrey and thought he might know where we could find Jasper. Had we known he was involved in this organization, we wouldn't have gone to him."

"Godfrey was almost gleeful that we delivered ourselves to him," Talia said. "He attacked us and tried
to kill us, as we said. He was just a part of the organization, though, and clearly, they aren't ready to stop.
They don't want Osric completing his quest and are
willing to kill anyone to stop him."

"And what is this quest? Where are you supposed to
go from here?"

"We're going southwest, to the hills between here
and Eldamar, looking for an ancient battle site,"
Jasper said. "It's why we returned to Godfrey's house.
After they found me and we talked, I realized that
Godfrey was the only one who might know the location of the place Osric is looking for. We'd just found
it when you and your men arrested us."

For a moment, Lockewood just stared at them. Osric
could see her working through everything they'd just
laid at her feet and hoped she would believe them.
It was a lot to ask. He knew that. Missions from the
gods, a secret organization spread across the king-

dom, and holes in reality. Asking anyone to believe all of that was a stretch, and yet it was their only hope.

In custody, eventually, the Brethren would be able to get to them and kill them. And just when they were so close to their goal.

He needed the captain to believe them, at least enough to let them go. He held his breath as he watched her working it out, deciding if they were telling the truth or not.

"This is ... a lot to take in," she finally said.

"I know it sounds far-fetched, Captain. But you've seen the evidence with your own eyes. You have to have wondered about the escalation of creatures in the forest. We all have. You saw your own man try to kill you. I don't know if you heard everything he said to us, but he led these men in here. Armed. Why else would he do that?"

She looked at the bodies spread across the room, still considering, before finally saying, "You're right. I can't deny what's right in front of me."

She fell silent again, wrestling with something in her own mind. Osric didn't say anything; he tried not to breathe. He knew what she was deciding, and he didn't want to do anything that might interrupt her from the obvious conclusion, to make her lock them back in the cell.

"I'm going to let you go," she finally said.

"Really?" Talia asked, hopefully.

"Yes. I don't fully understand what's going on here, but clearly, there's some element of truth to your story. Enough, at least, that if it is true, then the part about the gods and a danger to the world might also be true. I swore to protect the people of my city, and I can't very well do anything myself about holes in the world, or whatever you said. The only thing I can do is let you go and hope you stop whatever is happening, so that my people don't have to face it."

"Thank you, Captain," Osric said. "We appreciate your trust in us. If we can stop this and keep your people and everyone else safe, we will."

"I'm not sure how I'm going to explain all of this. A dead guard, armed strangers, escaped prisoners …"

"Tell them the truth," Rowan suggested. "Or at least, a version of it."

Lockewood raised an eyebrow. "Which is?"

"That your man tried to have us killed," Osric said. "Hired thugs to do his dirty work. You arrived just in time to prevent a slaughter, and in doing so, proved our innocence."

"I suppose that could work. He never was very popular anyway. I can't exactly tell them about secret assassins and ancient quests, can I?"

Grace chuckled. "Not unless you want to end up in a cell next to ours."

"You should be careful," Osric said. "Between God-frey and your guardsman, they've managed to get men into fairly highly placed positions. They are almost certainly not the only members of their group in Farvale."

"Is there a way to identify them?" Lockewood asked. "Know who they are?"

Osric shook his head. "I wish I knew. We're still trying to figure that out ourselves."

"Alright. I suppose that's a problem for another day." She gestured towards the door. "You should go. Get out of town, now, while you still can."

"We will," Osric said, stepping over the bodies, before pausing and turning back to Lockewood. "Thank you again, Captain."

"Just ... be safe out there. And if you find out anything more about these bastards infiltrating my city, you let me know."

"We will," Osric said.

Chapter 19

The Temple

They'd been walking for the better part of two days. Once Captain Lockewood let them go, they'd managed to make it out of Farvale with no additional issues. Cinder had even managed to find them, although where he'd been hiding, Osric didn't know. They hadn't seen the wolf even as they made their way out of the city, but as soon as they were out of sight of it and there were no people around, the animal appeared out of the underbrush, nearly scaring Grace to death.

Osric wondered if he'd been in the city watching them the whole time but staying out of sight as ordered, or if he'd left the city and been waiting outside of it for them. Not that he'd ever get an answer from the animal, but he once again wondered just how smart Cinder was.

Although Jasper hadn't been able to bring any of Godfrey's books with him, and had only looked at them for a few minutes, he still seemed fairly confident that he knew where they needed to go and could get them fairly close to the location of the temple.

They were heading into the backcountry, off any roads or even most trails, eventually ending on a cart path that roughly went in the direction they were headed. They weren't far from the forest, but this corner of the barony, away from Great Road, didn't have a lot of people. Rowan had said he'd heard the land wasn't great for crops, which is why most farmers stuck to the northern side of the Great Road or further to the west, outside of the barony.

Osric was just happy they had some kind of path, rather than just trekking blindly cross country. A few hours earlier, Jasper had said they were around the area the book had suggested, but to Osric, it all looked the same. There were definitely no signs that an ancient battle had been fought anywhere around there, let alone the remnants of a temple. Heck, there weren't even any people.

Or there hadn't been.

As they crested a small rise, a weathered farmhouse came into view, up against a field that looked more like dry dirt and rocks than it did a proper field. The farmhouse was still in good order and looked to be lived in, though. That was confirmed a moment later when a man in a wide-brimmed hat came around a corner, pushing a rickety wheelbarrow full of what looked to Osric to be weeds.

"Ho there, travelers," he called out as they drew near. "What brings you out this way?"

"Just passing through," Rowan said.

"Nothing but rough ground south all the way to the border, and no people that I know of," the farmer said, setting down his wheelbarrow. "You've come from the direction of the village and I don't think you're here to see me, so I have to ask, what are you looking for? You seem out of place, if you don't mind me saying."

"We are looking for the site of some old ruins. They'd be ancient, maybe just a stone or two, since way back from the founding of the kingdom," Jasper said.

"You don't want to go there," the farmer said, suddenly serious.

"So you do know of them?" Osric asked, suddenly hopeful.

"I know there are some ruins to the west of here, not that I've ever seen them. Can't be what you're looking for, though. That area's cursed. Most people who go there come back mad. Or don't come back at all."

"But someone went there once, right?" Osric asked. "For you to know there are ruins there. Is this curse new? Something that happened recently?"

As soon as the man mentioned a curse, Osric's mind instantly went to the creature in the lake. The villagers there had talked of a curse, too, and it made sense that if this was where a great battle was fought at the fall of the Calaphium, there might be a weak point in the Veil near it, where something could have come through and caused a similar disruption to the area.

"No, no," the farmer said, waving a hand. "Been that way for generations. My grandfather warned me about it, and his grandfather before him. Nobody goes out there, not if they value their life."

"But you know there are ruins?" Jasper asked.

"I know some of those who've gotten lost and gone that way have come back, talking of ruins. But they spoke through madness, forgot their own names, and weren't good for much else beside sitting on a stool, watching the sky all day. So who knows what's really out there other than death or madness."

"It sounds like that's exactly what we're looking for then," Jasper said.

"Suit yourselves," the farmer said with a shrug. "But don't say I didn't warn you."

Writing them off as dead men, apparently, the farmer picked up his wheelbarrow and began pushing it to the corner of his plot, dumping out the weeds and who knew what else into a pile with a collection of other vegetation and scrap.

"Well, we thank you for the warning," Osric said, turning west.

Grace looked back after a few minutes, as the farmhouse had already started to disappear in the distance. "If it's cursed, maybe that's exactly where we shouldn't go."

"No, Jasper was right," Talia said. "If it's cursed, it's almost certainly just where we want to go. We've encountered curses like this before."

"That began recently, though," Osric pointed out. "Something escaped through the Veil a few months before and became trapped there. The Veil is failing but, based on what the Sage said, it's only started tearing again in the last fifty or a hundred years. The farmer said his grandfather and his grandfather's grandfather knew this place was cursed. If this has always been like this, maybe it's different."

"This isn't the first time the Veil has been broken," Talia reminded him. "The Sage said that, too. When the Calaphium fell, there were holes torn open in the Veil then too. So there's a chance whatever this is has been stuck here for thousands of years."

"If that's true, and if it's some kind of animal like the last one, don't expect such a reasonable response," Rowan said. "That other thing, it was nearly mad, and it had only come through recently. Imagine what it would have been like after hundreds of years."

"Then we'll deal with it," Osric said. "We don't exactly have a choice."

They continued west for several more hours. It was still early afternoon, and they had a lot of light ahead of them, but Osric hoped they'd find the area they were looking for soon. If this place was cursed, he'd rather not have to camp here.

He didn't have to wait much longer. He knew Talia well enough to tell when something was off, and for the past ten minutes, she had not been her normal self. She'd been agitated and twitchy, like she'd rolled in a bed of ants and had a few she couldn't get off.

"There's something off about this place," Talia finally said. "Can you feel it? It's like the very air is … tainted."

"I don't feel anything."

"I do," Jasper said. "There's an … unnatural stillness."

"The animals do, too," Rowan said. "Have you noticed, no birds, no small animals in the underbrush? We've seen those for the last several days, but they've all disappeared as we've headed further this way."

"That just means we're still going the right way, doesn't it?" Osric said.

"I guess," Talia said, but she didn't sound as confident as he did.

Even as she said that the sky darkened, turning a deep shade of red and orange. These were not the reds and oranges of sunset, which should still be hours away, though. These were deeper. More sickly looking.

It didn't happen all at once or slowly. It was more like it had been that way for a while, but Osric just noticed.

"What's that?" Grace said, ranging a little ahead of them.

It took a moment for Osric to make out what she was pointing at. The grass and foliage had taken it over so completely, it was hard to see anything but a lump of vegetation. At least not without looking at where Grace was pointing.

He did see it, eventually. Old, weathered stone, pitted and crumbling with age. As old as the keep he and Talia had found. Maybe older.

"These are ancient. Older than any settlement I've seen," Rowan said.

"Creepy is what it is. Let's just find what we're looking for and get out of here. This place gives me the shivers," Grace said, kicking a part of the stone loose.

Osric barely heard their words, his attention drawn to a strange shimmer in the air above him. It was like a heat haze, but directly over his head. Close enough he felt he could grab it if he jumped up. He wanted to reach out and try to touch it.

As he started to raise his hand, Talia hissed, "Osric, what are you doing?"

"There's something ..."

Before he could finish the sentence, the shimmer pulsed, expanding outwards and dropping to the ground in front of him. The air grew cold as it shifted, becoming more translucent than transparent, its shape slowly coalescing into that of a man. A specter.

"You will die for coming to this place," it said, its voice both hollow and echoing.

Not angrily. Not threatening. More matter-of-factly. It floated towards them, its feet not touching the ground, as it raised a hand, reaching for Osric. Behind him, Osric heard the creak of Rowan's bowstring as the ranger pulled it taut.

"Wait!" Osric stepped back, away from it, his hands raised. "We know why you're here. You came through the Veil, didn't you?"

The specter halted. Its placid face shifting for the first time. It was hard to tell, but Osric would say it almost looked … curious.

"What do you know of the Veil?"

"I know it's tearing, that it's in danger. Things are coming through from other realities. That's how you got trapped here, isn't it?"

The specter's form flickered.

"No, I wasn't trapped here. I died here."

"Were you here when the temple was attacked?" Jasper asked.

The specter's face turned, looking to the cleric, "Yes. There was so much destruction. Fire rained down. Burning my family. My city. Everything."

"You were trapped here?" Talia asked.

"I fell," it said in its echoing voice, as if a dozen people were speaking at once. "My soul reached for the heavens, to rejoin the Veil. There was … a flash of energy as a great tear opened above the temple. Things came through. Horrible things. I could see the Veil. So close. So close."

"The energies kept you from it?"

"Yes. So close, but I couldn't move. Couldn't rise. The tear closed, in time, but even still, I couldn't leave. Locked here. In this place. In this damnable place."

It was becoming agitated. Angry. The pulsing of its form quickening.

"We're trying to repair that damage," Osric said, hoping to calm it down, unsure of what it would do if it got angry. "We've closed the Veil elsewhere, I think. I think there's something in that temple keeping the Veil unrepaired. Otherwise, it would have fixed itself when the Veil was fixed elsewhere. The tear is gone, but it isn't repaired. I think that's why you can't go through."

"This should allow me to finally pass on?"

"I don't know for certain, but I think so. I can try, at any rate."

The specter nodded, its form beginning to fade. "Then you may pass. I hope you succeed. I am tired of this place."

"I'll come back and make sure. I promise."

The specter only looked at him. Stared through him, before it vanished, the oppressive atmosphere lifted slightly. Grace let out a low whistle.

"Well, that was spooky. You sure you know what you're doing, Osric?"

"No," he admitted. "But I have to try. We have to try."

The walk to the site of the temple was not long, but it was disquieting. Most of the way, they could make out the outline of the city where the specter had lived, now little more than faint outlines of stone buildings etched into the earth. People had lived, and ultimately, died here, caught in a fight that wasn't theirs.

Even Cinder, who normally trotted happily next to Osric or ran off searching for game, was on edge, every now and then letting out a soft, mournful whimper.

"We're here," Jasper said, almost reverently.

They hadn't needed the cleric's help to know they had arrived at their destination. Directly in front of them was a massive rend in the ground, torn open across a mile or more and hundreds of feet wide, as if the gods themselves had cut the land open. The edges had been worn and dulled over time, but here and there, jagged rocks still protruded, speaking to just how violent the event had been.

Walking to the edge and looking in was like looking into a deep, endless void.

"If they are guarding this, how do they even get down there?" Osric said. "I guess they've had time to figure out a way to get past the specter, since it's been here since the temple vanished into the ground, but they'd have to get down to it, right? I mean, they were guarding the other one, and I saw a note in Godfrey's office from someone named Ranulf talking about the hall, I think, and asking him to send more men. If they guard it, they'd have a way to get up and down from it, right?"

"You saw a letter about this?" Jasper asked.

"It was a partial note, damaged in the fight, and it just said to send more guards. We already assumed they were holding onto the other half, so it didn't seem important. Besides, a moment later you found your clue and then the guards showed up. After that, it slipped my mind."

"Reasonable," Jasper said. "And you're right; it does mean they must have a way down. Let's spread out. Look for it."

The group spread out, some going one direction along the chasm and the rest going the other direction. Osric hoped it wasn't on the other side, requiring them to go all the way around the massive hole in the ground.

Thankfully, it wasn't.

"Over here!" Rowan called out after only a few minutes of searching.

They all hurried over to him. There, hidden behind a large boulder, was a set of rough stairs carved into the rock face, leading down. They were narrow and irregular, and seemed like a very dangerous way down. If someone slipped, there would be nothing to grab onto before they plummeted into the darkness.

"Well, I'll be damned," Grace said. "They must have spent years carving these out. And now we have to go down them."

"Hold on," Talia said, handing Rowan her staff.

A few quick motions later, a globe of bluish light appeared above her hand.

"Good thinking," Osric said. "Lead the way. Just watch your step. These don't seem very stable."

With the globe floating slightly above them, Talia led them down, Osric right behind her.

As they made their way down, an excited Jasper said, "I've spent the last fifteen years researching the Veil and the Calaphium, trying to understand what happened all those years ago and how far the Brethren's lies went. There were so many references to this place. To think that I am going to see it is just ... I don't have the words."

"Did you learn anything about it that we might find useful?" Osric asked.

"Not a lot. Most of what I found were references to earlier writings that don't exist, so it's a little like trying to piece together a story from little notes where each generation has to remove a word until you're left with a few scattered sentences. That is to say, what I know is very much conjecture."

"Noted," Osric said.

"I believe this place was used by the Calaphium to have some effect on the Veil, although whether that was to manipulate it, repair it, or limit it was never really clear. I just know that it was somehow important to their understanding of the Veil and the way magic worked, which is maybe why the Brethren attacked it.

Before he could explain anything else, Talia let out a yelp as a part of the stair she stepped on cracked and broke away. In almost slow motion, she began to flail sideways as her foot dropped and the rest of her body began to follow after it.

Osric leaped forward, his hand darting out to grab her outstretched hand that was pawing at the air, his hand locking around hers just before she would have fallen beyond his reach. He leaned back until the rear plate of his armor clanged against the rocky side of the chasm wall, trying not to go over after her. He managed to keep both of them from going over ... but just barely.

She wrapped both arms around him, clutching onto him on the narrow steps, her whole body trembling as she lay her head on his shoulder and steadied herself.

"It's alright," he said softly in her ear. "I've got you."

"Thank you," she said, pulling herself together. "You should probably put me back on my own two feet."

Osric realized he was holding onto her as much as she was holding onto him, her feet dangling in the air. He twisted and set her down on the steps, in the lead again.

"Just be careful this time," he said, which got a smile out of her, although a half-hearted one.

"I'll try."

Thankfully, the rest of their trip down was uneventful, if long and slow. When they finally found the bottom, they might as well have transcended into another world. The sky was not visible from that far down, and they could only see as far as the light of Talia's orb could illuminate.

What they could see, though, was impressive. It was also hard to work out what they were looking at, or even standing on. It was clearly man-made, created out of stone and fired clay, but it wasn't paving stones or any other kind of flooring Osric could think of.

"We're on the roof," Jasper said, figuring out what they were puzzling over. "Look, I think this used to be railing, part of a top deck, separating it from ... I think these are some kind of roofing tile, maybe."

He was right. They were worn and chipped and had settled into a flat rather than slanted design, making them look like strange paving stones at first. But the larger parts did look like clay roofing tiles. He could also see what the cleric meant about a top deck. There were holes, evenly spaced in some kind of marble or granite that could have once held a wooden railing, although the wood would have rotted away long ago. There was, however, a clear delineation between the marble and the roofing tiles, so some kind of deck or top section for people on the roof made sense.

"I believe I saw something about part of the temple's function being to observe the heavens," Jasper said. "This must have been where they did that from."

"If that's the case, and this is the roof, then there has to be a way down. Inside. Right?" Osric asked.

"Yes. There would have been stairs. I imagine the Brethren have hidden them, even this far down. They're paranoid like that. Look around for them."

The group spread out, but it was Cinder who found the stairwell first, scratching against what looked like a rocky side of the cliff with vegetation growing out of it. It wasn't that at all. It was well camou-flaged, though. Part of the side of the ravine had been pulled down around it, making it look like an extension of rock and dirt. What Cinder had found, seemingly sniffing out the smells of the people who'd passed through there, was a cloth stretched over the entrance painstakingly designed to look like rock, with vegetation artfully applied to it, extending the effect and making it more three-dimensional.

They pulled the sheet aside, but before anyone said anything, a sound echoed from down below. A metallic clank. Osric froze, holding up a hand, directing everyone else to hold their positions.

Talia's hand whipped around and the orb blinked out in an instant, blanketing them in darkness. Not complete darkness, though. There was a flicker of faint light coming from the stairwell.

Osric pulled his sword and started down, with Rowan following after him. They descended the stairs as silently as possible. It was a short stairwell, which opened up into a large chamber. In the center stood a man, his back to them, digging through a satchel of some kind.

Rowan drew his bow, the string creaking as he pulled it back. The sound made the man whirl around, his eyes widening as he saw them. He moved fast, lunging for a lever, but Rowan was faster. His arrow shot out and caught the man in the chest, sending him staggering back. He crashed to the ground with the arrow protruding from his chest, and lay still.

They all held in place for a moment, looking around, but nothing stirred. Jasper pushed past them, approaching the lever and kneeling down to examine it, as well as looking over the side of the sharp drop-off next to it.

"There are tracks. I'm betting this lever brings whatever carries people down back up, or maybe alerts the people below to send it up. He was probably trying to alert someone below. I'm betting these tracks are a part of an elevator system of some kind."

"We can't use that to go down," Osric said. "It would alert them that we're here. There's no way of telling how many Brethren are down there. You said this level was for worship. Do you think it had this big drop-off? I can't imagine this elevator goes all the way back to the destruction of the temple."

"No, this was a second floor, and I think it had stairs that lead down to the bottom floor, although that looks much further down than the second floor would have been from the first. Maybe it separated as it landed down here. This," Jasper said, waving his hand, indicating the room. "Is much too small for what should have been the second floor. I wonder if it's all that remains, and the rest of the second floor collapsed into the first, the roof getting caught up here."

"What about this?" Talia said. "This looks like a doorway, or a door frame. Someone bricked over it. These bricks don't look nearly as old as everything else."

"We can probably break through," Osric said.

"Maybe we should consider not going into an area these guys were so scared of that they bricked it off and made an elevator get down."

"Just because they bricked it off doesn't mean there's something dangerous through there," Jasper said.

"You're so naive, Jasper."

"We don't have a choice," Osric said. "There should be another way down, and we can't throw ourselves down there, into who knows what. We've got to be careful about this. Let's break through."

Rings and Guardians

"There are glyphs above it, like the ones in the keep," Talia said as they began looking at the wall, to figure out the best way to take it down. "I can feel the energy from it. I think they're active."

"It has to be to help reinforce the wall and keep it up," Jasper said. "If they were scared enough to brick this up, then they'd want to make sure the wall stayed up."

"Can we remove them?" Osric asked.

"Yes. That's the downside of glyphs and why they're not used much. If you alter the symbol, it loses its magic. While powerful, it's one of the weaker enchantments artificers can make, mostly because any change in the glyph renders it worthless. Remember the cuts down the one we saw in the keep? That is why they were depowered. They're really only good when you can place them so the people they need to affect can't get to the glyph itself."

"Like here," Grace said.

"Like here."

"So, go ahead and do whatever you have to do to depower it, then," Osric said.

"Should I point out again how this door is not only bricked up but has magical protection over it on this side of the wall, meaning it's targeted at keeping something in there in, not keep us out?"

Talia ignored her and, with a hand up from Osric, scraped some notches out of the glyph with her dagger.

"That should do it," she said as Osric set her down.

Osric hadn't felt anything, but if she said it was gone, then he'd believe her. The magic must have been doing the heavy lifting, because together, he and Rowan managed to knock the wall down fairly easily.

The air on the other side was stale and musty, opening into a long hallway with rooms on either side all the way down. They carefully entered this section of the second floor, peering into the rooms which were small and completely unadorned.

"Meditation rooms. This close to the observation deck, this would have been for the priests here to meditate on their findings, or maybe work on their research. The writings weren't clear," Jasper said.

"Do you know what's beyond this area?" Talia asked.

"No. There weren't a lot of good descriptions. There was something about meditation rooms close to the platform where rituals to the gods would be held, or so I assumed. Most of what I know is about the first floor, and that is still very limited."

There was a doorway at the end of the hall that opened into a T-intersection, where they could either continue straight, along what Osric thought was the front of the temple, or turn right, continuing deeper into the temple. Or they could have turned right if the second floor was complete. The hallway turned into a sheer drop-off about a hundred or so feet down, which roughly corresponded to the drop-off in the antechamber. It appeared like the entire second floor, aside from the section close to the front supports, had collapsed in on itself, which didn't bode well for them finding an alternate way down.

Rowan held up a hand, signaling for silence. "Did you hear that?"

They all strained to hear. At first, all Osric could hear was an occasional creaking. Then he heard it. A faint clicking sound, almost like an echoing skittering. It only lasted for a second, but as they started forward again, they could hear it. It was hard to pin down where it was coming from exactly, just that it was getting louder.

Suddenly, a flicker of movement caught Osric's eye. A small creature had darted out of one of the meditation rooms and into the next, too quickly for him to clearly make out what it was.

"Did you see that?" Grace said from the back of their group.

Talia gasped. "Is that … it can't be."

"I think it was," Jasper said.

"What was?" Osric asked.

"A skivver. I've read about them, but I thought they were all extinct."

"What's a skivver?"

"They used to be everywhere, at least in Aeloria, back in the early days of the kingdom. Most writings from that time mention them as a pest, and they were common enough that they get referenced a lot, but they were hunted to extinction because they would steal things from people's homes. They were nocturnal and lived in burrows, caves, and under buildings. People hated them. Unfortunately for the skivver, they breed slower than mice or other creatures, so once the hunt started, it didn't take long for the population to dwindle. It's been nearly a thousand years since the last sighting."

A head popped out of the meditation room. It was bigger than Osric first thought, maybe the size of a cat. He might have accidentally mistaken it for one if it wasn't for the elongated snout and very large ears and eyes. It didn't seem afraid. More ... curious. Just staring at them, its little nose twitching.

Osric took a cautious step forward.

"Careful," Rowan warned. "We don't know if it's dangerous."

"Yes, it seems deadly," Grace said sarcastically.

Osric bent down, extending his hand. "Hey there, little one. It's alright, we won't hurt you."

The skivver cocked its head, long ears wiggling back and forth. For a moment, it almost seemed tempted to approach. But as Osric took another step, it quickly scurried away, disappearing into a narrow crevice in the wall.

"Guess it's pretty skittish around humans," Jasper mused. "Can't say I blame it, given the history."

"As fascinating as this is, we need to stay focused," Rowan said. "I doubt that glyph was installed to protect them from that."

"Probably not," Osric said, straightening.

They continued on down the hallway, past the next junction, moving beyond the meditation rooms. Beyond the junction, the hallway opened up into an immense room, easily three hundred feet long and almost as wide. Lining each side of the chamber were six stone pedestals with stone steps to walk up, each bearing a large, upright stone ring.

"By the gods ..." Talia said.

"We've seen these before," Osric told the others. "In the keep where we found the first part of the document, there was a room like this. Smaller, although not a lot smaller, but with the same pedestals and rings."

"I believe these are teleportation stones," Jasper said, moving forward to examine one of the rings more closely. "There are references to chambers like this that were in the major Calaphium outposts. The magic taken to create these was incredible, although the arts needed for it are long lost. Even the Conclave hasn't managed to reproduce it."

"You could travel from place to place using these?" Grace asked, showing a rare moment of honest awe.

"Yes. I never really understood how they worked, although after hearing Osric's stories, I think they might have created some kind of controlled rupture in the Veil, connecting two physical points. It would have been similar to the magic used to send your ring through time."

"They created ruptures on purpose?" Osric asked.

"That's a guess, but it makes sense. We know they did it at least once, with your ring, right? We've seen that these ruptures aren't just between realities, but in our own world as well. You saw me through one, and we're in the same reality, and you saw this temple."

"But they're dead, right? The ones we saw before didn't work either. Talia said the magic had all faded from them."

"They appear to be," Jasper said, running a hand along one of the rings.

"We found another room," Osric said. "It wasn't like this, long with a bunch of these stones. It was smaller, with workbenches and a single stone on a much smaller pedestal, but that ring was half melted. The ring, my ring, not the stone one, still had magic in it and, when I got close to the melted stone ring, a rupture appeared right before us. We could see through it, and I'm pretty sure now that we were looking through time. We saw the same room, but cleaner, not ruined, and there were men inside it. The men were wearing black robes and working on something around the ring. Other men stormed in, shouting about them being 'under arrest in the name of the council,' and then a fight started and the rupture closed suddenly."

"If I had to guess, the council probably meant the Council of Elders, the ruling body of the Calaphium. It's strange though. It sounds like the people in that room were working on learning the secrets of teleportation, but I hadn't heard of anyone learning that magic outside of the Calaphium themselves."

"So the Calaphium wanted to put a stop to those experiments?" Rowan asked.

"It's possible. In the latter portion of Calaphium rule, they tightened their grip on magic use. All but the most basic spells were outlawed, with no explanation given to the populace. It was the whole reason the Brethren came into being, through resentment that the powers people once used were outlawed. It was what made their other stories about the Calaphium believable but ... with what you've told me about the damage to the Veil caused by magic use, and the claims that the Calaphium were caretakers of magic ... perhaps they had good reasons for their strict control."

"So that keep was run by someone in the Brethren?" Talia asked.

"Maybe. I'm not sure if they're the only ones who were fighting against the Calaphium at that time, as I found a few references to others, but not enough to actually know if that's accurate. Either way, they would have put a stop to any research like what you described."

"That is where we saw the glyphs before," Talia said. "They were protecting, or at least blocking access from the teleportation room there, much like the one here."

"Maybe they were worried about something coming through, using their own stones against them. A door works both ways, right?" Osric said.

"Maybe," Jasper said, sounding unconvinced.

"No, that's not right," Grace said. "The one here wasn't blocking this room, it was blocking this entire section. You said it was put in by the Brethren guys, and it probably happened after the temple fell down here, which probably means these teleportation things were already dead, too, right? That wasn't for protecting from teleporting; it had to be for something else."

"She has a point," Rowan said.

"Keep your eyes open ... in case Grace is right."

The next chamber was nearly as long as the one they'd just left. Instead of a line of stone rings along each wall, however, there was a line of statues, three on each side, each maybe nine feet tall.

They were intricately carved, and Osric wondered who they had been based on. They were wearing armor, or carved to look like they were wearing armor, all bearing the same sigil, although not one Osric had seen before. Unlike most of the rest of this place, these statues did not bear the mark of time. It seemed as if they had just been created, their edges and lines still crisp and visible.

A stark contrast with the rest of the ruins.

"Can you feel that?" Talia asked.

"Yes. The magic here is still alive. It's practically … crackling."

"That's good, right?" Grace asked. "Because everything else, aside from that glyph put in by the Brethren guys, has been dead."

"Maybe," Jasper said.

Osric wished he'd sounded more convincing.

"What's that on their chest?"

"It's the sigil of the Calaphium."

"Ohh, it's different than the one on my ring."

"Yes. Your ring bears the mark for a small group inside the Calaphium known as the Seers of Tomorrow. It was their job to use magic to look forward and see problems that might threaten the Calaphium. I've only seen a few references to them, and I never understood how that magic could have worked, but ... knowing what I know now, I'm guessing they opened the Veil into the future, to look through. I'd always wondered how the Calaphium had a whole order of diviners and missed their demise, but ... apparently, some didn't. It would be interesting to learn what these Seers knew about the end, before it happened, and why the rest didn't heed their warnings."

"Maybe they ..." Talia started, and then stopped as an audible cracking sound could be heard clearly through the room.

Osric listened as it happened again. It was as if two stones were rubbing against each other. He'd just had that thought when the statue nearest him moved.

Osric paused, looking hard at the statue. He was about to decide he'd imagined it when it moved again, turning its head to face him. Its large, soulless granite eyes narrowed as it stepped a massive foot off the pedestal, bringing up the large stone blade it carried in its hand.

"The statues!" Osric shouted, drawing his sword.

The other two statues in front of them stepped off their pedestals while the three behind them came to life and stepped down, blocking their retreat in that direction.

"We can't fight them all! Run!" Rowan said, nocking an arrow and letting it fly at the nearest statue.

The arrow shattered against the stone, leaving hardly a scratch.

"Heathus protect us!" Jasper called out, grasping his amulet and stretching out his other hand.

A shimmering barrier sprang up in front of Grace just as a statue's massive fist swung towards her. The blow glanced off the divine shield, sending Grace stumbling but unharmed.

Osric charged forward to meet the lead statue, his sword ringing as it struck stone, the force of the impact sending shockwaves up his arm. A stone fist impacted against his chest plate in return, sending him stumbling backward.

"Osric!" Talia cried out, her hands weaving a spell.

A glob of acid shot from her fingers, striking the statue square in the chest. The stone hissed and bubbled, but the construct kept coming.

Everyone finally started moving, running for the far door, ducking and weaving, trying to avoid the swinging stone swords and the statues' grasping hands. Osric deflected another blow with his shield, the statue's fist slamming into the metal with enough force to lift Osric off his feet and send him flying backward, hitting the ground hard.

Jasper, who was behind the others, running slower, grabbed Osric and pulled him to his feet, "On your feet, lad."

Another green bolt shot past them, splashing against the knee joint of the nearest statue, causing it to stumble as some of the stone melted away. Osric didn't need to be told twice, pulling Jasper along as he ran all out for the exit.

Osric could hear the massive footsteps close behind him and pulled Jasper with all his might, throwing the cleric ahead of him through the doorway just as a stone fist slammed into the ground where the older man had been a moment before.

The tremor sent Osric stumbling after the cleric as a section of the floor crumbled and dropped away. Talia was standing just on the other side, and her hands were weaving even before Osric made it through the doorway. Almost as soon as he was clear, she thrust her palms upward, unleashing a crackling wave of electricity that struck the top of the doorframe. The stone exploded, raining down chunks of rock and debris. The doorway collapsed, sealing the gap between them and the charging statues.

The thunderous footsteps halted, replaced by the sound of shifting rubble as the animate guardians tried to break through the impromptu barricade.

Osric bent over, hands on his knees, gulping in lungfuls of air, his chest stinging from the impact of the statue's fist, glancing as the blow was.

"We can't get out that way now."

"It was that or let ourselves be pulverized," Talia said defensively.

"I'm not blaming you." Osric straightened up. "It was the right call. But now we have to figure out how to get out of here another way."

"If we can find a way down to the ground floor, we could use that elevator to get back up to the antechamber off the roof access," Rowan said.

"What even was that?" Grace asked.

"Constructs of some sort. This close to the teleportation room, between it and the rest of the temple, perhaps it was meant to protect them from anything unwanted that might get through. If so, then we must be getting close to the stairs leading down to the first level."

"If they're intact," Rowan said. "Otherwise, we're stuck up here with no way out."

"Why don't we check first, before the doom and gloom," Osric said. "Is anyone injured?"

They looked at themselves and each other, but miraculously, they had made it through intact. They gathered themselves up and continued on. Osric had to imagine they were almost out of places to look, unless there was some part of the second floor that hadn't collapsed along the other side.

He just hoped Rowan was wrong.

Chapter 21

New Friends

They didn't continue for long after exiting through the doorway. In fact, it looked like everything outside of the statue room was a big, open landing, and the statue room might have been the entrance to the second floor, opening into the rest of it through the hallways beyond the room with the teleportation rings. Osric hadn't seen it at first because a good part of the roof had collapsed in this section, making it look like it was another hallway at first.

As they made their way around the collapsed column of roofing, they found what looked to be the remains of a stairway.

Calling it a stairway didn't do it justice. It was wide enough for four people to walk abreast and looked to have finely carved banisters on either side. While one was broken off halfway down, so all he could see was the stone support, the other remained in place. At the top of the stone pillar was a finely carved creature of some kind that Osric had never seen before. It still had some kind of jewel in one of its eyes.

Unfortunately, that was almost all that remained of the stairs. Two steps down, the stairway had broken away, giving way to a gaping void that plunged down hundreds of feet to where the main floor of the temple had settled.

"Damn," Rowan said.

Grace was reaching around the carved banister top, trying to pop the jewel from the statue's eye using a knife, but the creature's head stuck forward, its long neck making it hard to reach its eye while she kept both feet firmly on the ground. Especially for someone of Grace's short stature.

Her foot slipped on some loose rock at the edge, sending a shower of small stones skittering over the side. Rowan's hand snaked out and caught the thief by the back of her shirt, hauling her in right before she followed the stones over the edge.

"Watch it," Rowan said.

"I just wanted to look at it."

"We have bigger problems than that, Grace," Osric said. "Look around. This platform, or whatever, has this broken stairway on one side and the blocked doorway to the statue room on the other. Unless we can figure out how to get all the way down there, we're stuck."

"We have rope," Grace offered.

"We have, what, maybe a hundred feet? And we'd have to tie several together. Besides, the only thing to anchor it to is this banister, and the whole thing wobbled when you leaned on it. I don't trust it to hold our weight while we try to climb down a spliced-together rope. Even if we went one at a time."

"There are spells that will let us float down," Talia said excitedly, before deflating. "I don't know them though."

They all fell into silence, looking over the edge. Even Cinder seemed depressed by the sudden realization that they were trapped there.

"So that's it?" Grace said, kicking a bigger rock over the side. "We come all this way, fight our way in, almost get smushed by statues, to get stuck on this platform where we'll all starve to death?"

"We'll probably die of thirst first," Rowan said.

"You're not helping. Either of you," Osric said. "Come on, there has to be a way down. We can't just hit one obstacle and give up."

"Like what, Osric?" Grace said. "Where do you want us to go? Through that stone wall? Dig out that doorway and get killed by the statues? Jump and hope the bottom floor is made of feathers? What do you want us to do?"

"Like maybe act like this is important and give a damn about it. Some of us are trying to do something to stop the world from ripping itself apart, not just steal anything that isn't …" Osric started to shout at Grace before stopping, holding up a hand for them all to be silent.

A faint scrabbling noise came from the other side of the room. For a moment, Osric thought it might be the statues digging their way out, but it wasn't coming from the doorway, it was coming from a corner of the room where there was a gap in the wall of the cliff itself, where the building had wedged against it, almost like a dark recess or alcove.

Osric stared in that direction, listening hard, trying to figure out what the sound was when a small furry head poked out of the opening, its large eyes blinking at them. It was the skivver they had seen earlier, or perhaps another of its kind, it was impossible to tell. The creature made eye contact with him and then pulled its head back in, disappearing into the darkness, maybe realizing it had been spotted.

"I think it's the same one from before. It might have been following us," Osric said, taking a few steps toward the opening and kneeling down.

The creature poked its head out again, whiskers twitching in the air. Osric remained perfectly still, hardly daring to breathe. At first, the skivver just looked at him, its little head cocked to the side, as it seemed to consider him. Then, surprisingly, it crept out of the hole in the wall, cautiously, its nose wiggling back and forth.

Osric shifted slightly, almost unconsciously, and the creature skittered back a few steps, but then stopped, and looked at him again.

"It's okay. We're not going to hurt you," Osric said in as gentle a voice as he could manage.

To Osric's surprise, the little creature made a series of chirping, squeak-like sounds, almost as if it was answering him. Osric was no woodsman, but he'd spent his life in The Great Forest, and that meant being surrounded by animals of all types. Yet he'd never seen behavior like this, except from Cinder, who was unnaturally intelligent, maybe through a gift from the gods.

"Friends," Osric said, testing it again.

The creature let out a single squeak that, to Osric's ear, had the pitch and intonation of the word he'd said. Osric glanced back at Talia.

"You did that spell, at the lake, so we could speak to the thing that got trapped there. Does that work on animals?"

"No. The spell lets us understand languages, but it's very specific that it only does that for actual languages and not things like animals or plants. There are references to other spells that will let you talk to animals, but ... I don't know any of them."

"But … is it possible he's using a language? It sounds like one, kind of. At least, the rhythm of it is like language."

"I don't know. Maybe. I can try."

"Please," Osric said.

He wasn't sure what he hoped to accomplish through this, but he didn't have any other ideas and it wasn't like they were doing anything else. Talia's hand began to weave. It was quick and short, like at the lake, and like then, the air seemed to shimmer between him and the creature for a moment.

"Can you understand me?"

The creature froze, its head turned to the side, its large eyes opened as big as they could get.

"You can. Can't you?"

"You speak <squeak>?"

As with the spell at the lake, he could hear the skivver making the squeaking sounds, but in Osric's mind,

they came out as words. Except the last one. Whatever it said, even the spell couldn't translate it.

"No. My friend, she has ... magic. An ability that lets
us understand each other."

"Ohhhh ... What's magic?"

"I, umm, it's a special thing she can do," Osric said,
not sure how to explain magic to the creature. "My
name is Osric. We mean you no harm. We're just
trying to find a way down to the lower levels of this
temple."

The skivver's nose twitched rapidly as it took another tentative step forward.

"You ... not like others. Not like who come before."

"Others? You've seen the Brethren? Men who come
down, take the elevator ... umm, moving cage down
the side of the wall, to the bottom?"

The creature let out a series of agitated chirps. "Yes,
yes! Bad <squeak>. Hurt us. Trap us. You not them?"

"No, we're not with the Brethren," Osric assured the skivver. "We're trying to stop them, actually. They're, um, very bad and hurting the whole world. There's something at the bottom of the temple we hope will stop them."

The skivver's head cocked to the side, considering Osric's words. It took another step forward, its nose twitching as it caught a new scent. Suddenly, Cinder emerged from behind Osric, curious about the small creature. The skivver let out a terrified squeak and darted back toward its hole.

"Wait, wait!" Osric called out, holding up a hand to stop Cinder. "It's okay. This is Cinder. He's a friend. He won't hurt you."

The skivver paused, halfway to its hole, trembling slightly as it eyed the large wolf. Cinder, for his part, sat down, his head tilted curiously.

"Cinder, no eating the skivver, okay?" Osric said firmly.

The wolf let out a soft whine but didn't move. Slowly, the skivver crept back out, its eyes darting between Osric and Cinder.

"Friend?" it asked hesitantly.

"Yes, friend," Osric confirmed with a smile. "Do you have a name?"

"Blip."

"It's nice to meet you, Blip," Osric said. "Do you think you could help us? We really need to get to the lower levels."

"I don't ..."

The skivver seemed hesitant, looking back at the hole. Osric had an idea and reached into his coin purse, pulling out a small silver coin. Blip let out an excited series of chirps, its eyes fixated on the shiny object.

"Would you like this? As a gift for helping us?"

Blip's eyes widened to an almost comical size. It darted forward, snatching the coin from Osric's hand and cradling it to its chest like a precious treasure. It let out a series of happy chirps and squeaks.

"Blip, is there a way for us to get to the lower levels?" Osric asked.

Blip nodded vigorously. "Yes, yes! Blip show. But ... must ask <squeak> first."

"Must what?"

"Come. Come," Blip said, and dashed into the hole.

Osric crouched down, peering into the hole Blip had disappeared through. The skivver's bushy tail flicked once before vanishing into the darkness.

"You can't be serious," Rowan said. "We'll never fit through there."

"Do you have a better idea?" Talia asked, already shrugging off her pack. "Unless you want to try your luck with those statues again."

Rowan made a face but didn't argue further.

Osric took a deep breath and started squeezing into the tunnel. The rough stone scraped against his armor as he wriggled forward, feeling like he was going to get wedged in and stuck at any moment.

Ahead, he could hear Blip's claws skittering across the rock.

"Why'd we let the big guy with armor go through first?" Grace said from somewhere behind him. "He's going to get us stuck."

"Less talking, more crawling," Jasper grunted.

They inched along in near darkness, the tunnel twisting and turning with no end in sight. Osric thought it felt like they were going down, the tunnel feeling like it was carved on an incline. Several times, his armor got caught on a jagged protrusion and he felt like he might get stuck. It occurred to him that there was no way he would be able to turn around,

and on an incline, it would be very hard to go backward, especially with the turns.

Just as he was beginning to think this might have
been a trap, and they were going to die down there,
the tunnel opened up and Osric found himself tumbling into a massive cavern, lit by some kind of moss
or plant along the wall and at the end of poles, much
like a torch.

This wasn't part of the temple. The walls were rock
and stone. The skivvers, or maybe something else
before them, had dug away from the temple, into the
earth. Maybe under the dead village, if he had his
directions right.

The cavern stretched farther than he could see, the
ceiling lost in shadows high above. But it was far
from empty. Intricate structures rose from the stone,
built from bits of scavenged wood, metal, and cloth.
Ramps and bridges crisscrossed between the towers,
creating a multilevel city.

And everywhere, there were skivvers. Hundreds of them. They swarmed over the structures, gathering in small groups, or darting across rope bridges. Their squeaks and chirps became excited at the appearance of humans.

One by one, Osric's friends came out of the tunnel behind him, stopping in awe at the unexpected sight.

"Gods," Jasper breathed. "An entire civilization, hidden away. This is so unexpected."

Blip reappeared, bouncing eagerly in front of them. It gestured for them to follow, scampering off across one of the bridges. Osric glanced at the others and shrugged before setting off after the diminutive creature.

As they made their way deeper into the skivver city, Osric couldn't help but marvel at the ingenuity of it all. Scavenged parts, probably all from the temple, had been repurposed into all manner of contraptions, including clever pulley systems.

Talia had said she couldn't communicate with animals, that that was a different spell, and the one she used was for understanding languages. When the spell worked, Osric thought maybe Talia had misunderstood the book she'd learned the spell from. Now he saw that she had not. It took intelligence to do this level of work.

Skivvers ran and hid as they passed, their large eyes peering out of the doorways of the buildings made of discarded bits and pieces. Blip led them to the base of the largest structure, that looked almost like a pyramid, atop of which was an ancient-looking skivver perched on a throne of polished stone, metal, and glass.

Tufts of gray fur stuck out around its ears and its whiskers drooped with age, but its eyes seemed bright and sharp.

Blip scurried up to the throne, his tail twitching with excitement.

"Skitter! Skitter! Look what I found! New friends from the upper place!"

The old skivver, apparently called Skitter, looked down at Blip with an expression Osric read as annoyed or angry.

"Blip, what have you done? Why have you brought these dullsnouts into our home?"

Blip's ears drooped. "They're not like the others, Skitter. They're good dullsnouts. They want to help us get rid of the bad ones who've been hurting us."

"After all the harm their kind has caused? Did you hit your head?"

"No. I watched them. They killed one of the dullsnouts near the metal cage. They gave me a trinket. See!" Blip said, holding up the coin Osric had given him.

Skitter's eyes went wide and there were chitters and squeaks all around them, from the closest hiding skivvers.

"Ohh," Skitter said, almost in spite of himself, before regaining composure. "And what do these … friends of yours want in return?"

"They need to get to the lower place. They're looking for something, something important. They said it was important. They promised to get rid of all of the dullsnouts who hunt us if we show them."

"He tells the truth," Osric said. "We apologize for intruding into your home, but we are desperately searching for something at the bottom of this place, and we need help getting there."

"It would be protected by a group of … uhh, dull-snouts who have been hiding in this place. People we call the Brethren."

Skitter's ears went back and his nose twitched. "Yes, we know of them. They kill us if they see us. The dullsnouts have been coming here since the time of my father's father. They stay mostly in the lower place, so we rarely go there."

"But do you know how to get to the lower place?" Osric asked.

"Yes, there is a path. But it may not be safe. Not long ago, something changed. There was a great sound and screams. My people did not get close enough to see what was there, too afraid to find out what made dullsnouts scream. More and more dullsnouts came, trying to get to where the others were, but few left that place. They've been trying to get back in ever since, but something stops them. Something dangerous."

"In Godfrey's office, a letter talked about sending more men to deal with ... something, I don't know what," Osric said, turning to his friends. "The same letter mentioned that I'd escaped Eldham with the ring. Could whatever happened here have been at the same time that the ring came through?"

"Could they have lost control of something?"

"Maybe," Jasper said. "Although I think it's more likely that if someone used a rift to send the ring through, it could have caused other rifts. Especially if it was tied to the parts of this paper you're looking for. You said the ring took you to one half, tied to a piece of the Veil. But it didn't take you to this one. Maybe in coming through, this part broke, ripping a tear here and letting something through."

"Or maybe it was only tied to that part. The Sage said there was a protective enchantment on it."

"It doesn't matter either way. It all but confirms this is the place the letter to Godfrey was talking about, and the timing suggests it's connected. That's all that matters," Osric said, and then turned back to Skitter. "Can you show us this place?"

"We stay away from there. Too many of us have been lost already."

"We understand, and you wouldn't have to go there yourselves. We don't want to put your people in danger, but we have to get down there. It's the only way to stop the Brethren and protect everyone, including your people."

Skitter was silent for a long moment, his tail swishing back and forth.

"And what do we get in return?"

Osric turned back to his friends. "They like bright things, right? Trinkets. What does everyone have?"

"You, too," Jasper said, pulling Grace into the small huddle as she tried to back away. "You, too. Unless you want to live with the skivvers, give it up. I know you have something."

Grace looked sullen but said, "Fine."

They each had small bits of things. Pieces of metal, a piece of glass, a few particularly shiny coins. Grace, however, had the most, including small pieces of jewelry she was reluctant to part with, only giving them up after Jasper scolded her a second time.

"We offer these gifts, to you and your people," Osric said, turning back to Skitter and laying the collection of objects in front of the skivver.

Skitter chittered excitedly, bouncing up and down on his throne.

"Yes, yes! This is good. Very good. Blip! Show the dullsnouts to the lower place."

"Thank you, Skitter," Osric said. "We won't forget this kindness."

"Just remember your promise. Get rid of the bad dullsnouts."

"We will. You have my word."

The Heart of the Temple

They left the skivver city with Blip, who led them down another tight tunnel almost too small for them to fit through. This one sloped downward slightly, as did the last one, but it didn't go nearly as far. After crawling for just a few minutes they came back out into the ravine.

They were not at the bottom level, however. This tunnel had dropped them out onto a small ledge, barely big enough for two of them at a time. They were still fifty feet up from the bottom. Below them, a crumbling stone pillar stood maybe four feet away and ten feet lower. Below that, wedged into the ravine, was a piece of what might have been part of the floor, maybe another ten feet down.

"You can't be serious," Grace, who came out of the tunnel behind Osric, muttered. "We'll break our necks."

"The safest way. Trust Blip," the skivver said before leaping down to the pillar with ease, his tiny claws finding purchase on the weathered stone. He looked back expectantly, waiting for them to follow.

Osric exchanged a glance with Grace and leaned down to look into the tunnel, coming face to face with Talia, who was waiting for them to clear out of the way before she came out.

"We're going to have to jump down. There's ... you'll see when you get out here. We'll go one at a time. Just follow the person ahead of you. And be careful," Osric said to her, before straightening up and turning to Grace. "Wait until Talia is out to follow me, so the people behind us know what to do."

"Sure," Grace said, for once not sounding sarcastic.

Seeing that Osric was ready, Blip jumped down to the next piece, making room for him to jump down. Osric took a deep breath and leaped. His feet hit the pillar with a jarring impact, nearly sending him stumbling off the edge. He windmilled his arms, steadying himself. Blip looked back up to him again, and then jumped to the next perch.

Osric followed him down, each landing feeling like he was going to go careening over the edge. Above him he heard exclamations and curses as each of his friends followed after him.

The final jump was the worst. It was by far the farthest, and it was dark enough at the bottom that Osric couldn't be sure where the floor was. To make it worse, Talia's light was high above him, causing shadows to dance around, obscuring the floor even more.

Not that he had any choice now. He'd already committed this far. With one last leap, he hit the ground hard, pain radiating up his legs. Nothing broken, though. He was able to stand and shake it off in time to see a much more nimble Grace touch down next to him, easy as could be.

There was one tense moment when Jasper almost went over the side of the third landing, sending a shower of pebbles down. Osric still wasn't sure how the old man managed to regain his footing, but he did. Thankfully.

"Let's not do that again," Talia said when she landed, her elbow bleeding from when she hit the ground and fell forward, smashing down on her arms.

"Agreed," Osric said, helping her up.

Once they were all on the ground, Blip said, "Come on, not far now."

Blip scurried ahead, leading them through the ruins of the temple's once-grand entrance. The rooms that once sat there were now mostly crumbled stones, faded remnants of a lost civilization. Blip led them toward the center of the building, stopping just before a half-standing doorway.

"Usually here," he said, indicating the door.

Osric edged toward it, listening and hearing nothing. Peeking inside, he saw what looked like a makeshift camp, complete with tents and crates that looked much newer than the temple ruins around them.

"They're gone," Osric said.

"But where?" Jasper asked, coming up behind him.

"Grace, keep an eye out," Osric said, as they went in to look through the supplies.

Everything was in good order, as if they'd walked away from it expecting to come back. The remains of a fire were cold, so it had been some time since they'd been there, but the food stored in a sack near one of the tents was still fresh and good. It had been brought down maybe a week ago at most, which matched with what the skivver said about when the

new Brethren arrived and the timeline of when Godfrey would have dispatched additional men.

"Gone to the center place," Blip said as they dug
through everything. "They come, then go to the center place. They never come back."

Osric didn't like the sound of that, but it was almost
certainly where they needed to go.

"Show us," Osric said.

Blip chittered anxiously but led them deeper into the
complex. They followed him to a large open area,
possibly a courtyard, in front of a massive set of
double doors that stood cracked open. It wasn't clear
what this area was used for, as it was in the center of
an open-air building and was mostly surrounded by
debris, some of which looked like it had been pushed
aside to clear the area out more.

What was more shocking by far, however, was the
carnage in its center. The bodies of half a dozen men,
likely Brethren, lay strewn about, their bodies twist-

ed and lying where they fell. There were still two men standing, fighting some grotesque beetle-like creature that stood about waist-high. It had cuts and slashes on its body and a sword stuck out of its side.

One of the two men was swinging a sword desperately, backpedaling, trying to get away from the creature that was lunging forward, its mandibles closing around the mid-section of his friend.

That man's eyes went wide in shock as the monster lifted him off the ground, letting out a raw, primal scream as the pincers clamped down with an audible crunch that Osric could hear from where he stood. The scream was cut short when the powerful jaws closed all the way, severing the man into two pieces.

His friend, with a bellow, reversed his grip and stabbed forward, his sword sinking deep into the beetle's head. The beetle let out a screech and skittered back a step, wavering before ripping the sword that was still stuck in its head out of the man's hands. It shook its head, trying to dislodge the weapon, but it was stuck fast. Opening its jaws again, it hissed and a stream of some kind of green, viscous ichor shot out, splattering across the man's face and armor.

The beetle then took a sideways step, fell over, and spasmed. The man didn't even notice his victory, screaming himself, trying to simultaneously wipe the green liquid from his face and pull his armor off, as everywhere it had splashed began to smoke. Osric watched in horror as the skin on the man's face began to blacken and peel, spreading wider and wider, revealing the skull and sinew beneath as the substance ate through him. He managed one last scream before falling dead.

And then it was quiet.

"Did that one creature do all this?" Rowan asked, looking at the bodies.

"There are two more beetle things over here," Jasper pointed to a side of the courtyard, where two more bodies lay, covered in cuts and slashes.

After seeing the effect of the acid, no one wanted to get closer.

Blip, hiding behind Osric, let out a whimper.

Osric knelt down, placing a gentle hand on the skivver's head, and said, "You should go back to your people. It's not safe here. Thank you for all your help."

"You should leave. Run away," Blip said, clearly afraid for them.

"I can't. I wish I could, but I have to do this. It's important."

Blip looked at him with its big eyes, and then reached under itself, almost like it was rummaging around in its own fur, before coming up with a small, very old-looking pendant that was missing its chain. For a moment, Osric wondered if the skivver had pouches of some kind, like some surface animals had. It would be convenient, given their predilection for shiny trinkets.

"A gift. For remember Blip," the skivver said, pressing the pendant into Osric's hand.

He took the small piece of metal and said, "Thank you, Blip. I'll treasure it always. Now, go, quickly. Stay safe."

Blip looked at him for another moment, and then scampered off, disappearing into the darkness.

"You don't have to do this with me," Osric said, standing. "It'll be dangerous."

"Don't have to tell me twice," Grace said, before Jasper grabbed the back of her collar, holding her tight.

"We're with you, Osric," Jasper said.

Everyone pulled weapons as they approached the large doors. They weren't open wide enough for them to get all the way through, and from the position of two of the bodies, it looked like they might have been trying to push them closed and were stopped in the process.

Osric took one look back at his friends before gripping the massive door and heaving it open. The metal groaned as it was pulled back, scraping against the tile, ruining any chance of them sneaking in quietly.

The chamber inside was poorly lit, mostly illuminated by the floating ball next to Talia and the torches put in place by the Brethren in the courtyard outside, creating shadows that danced and moved inside the chamber. Shadows that did not do enough to hide the monstrous creature inside as it turned towards them.

It was a grotesque amalgamation of insect and nightmare, a massive beetle-like abomination with a jagged patchwork of mottled brown and black chitin plates, scarred with deep grooves and fissures. Between the segments, bulbous sacs of grayish flesh pulsated, covered in some kind of slimy substance that reflected the light.

Where pincers should have been, a gaping maw split its face, a ragged hole lined with needle-like teeth, some kind of dark green viscous fluid dripping from it.

As Osric watched, one of these sacs pulsated more than the others, and a beetle-like creature burst from it, leaping to the ground, snapping its small pincers at them.

"By the gods," Rowan breathed. "What is that thing?"

As if in response, the creature let out a bone-shaking roar, a sound that was part insectoid chitter, part agonized howl. It reared up on its hind legs, towering over them, its bulk filling the chamber.

Rowan reacted instantly, notching an arrow and re-leasing it at the monstrous creature, managing to sink the shaft into softer skin between two of the hard plates protecting the beast.

A putrid odor filled the room as its dark, black blood began seeping from the wound, eliciting another roar from the creature.

Cinder darted forward, leaping at the smaller beetle, the two bowling over as their jaws snapped at each other. Grace was not far behind the wolf, dodging past the spindly legs of the creature and stabbing as they rolled around, her blade managing to find the beetle while avoiding Cinder.

Talia and Jasper stayed back, each performing magic in their own way. Talia slammed her staff down, again bringing up the magical barrier to protect her. Jasper called for his god's favor, once again filling Osric with a warmth and confidence.

Osric gave a roar, almost out of reflex, as he charged forward, longsword held in a high grip, swinging at the creature as soon as he got close. The blade skidded along one of the hard pieces of carapace before sinking into flesh. The creature wrenched back, nearly pulling the blade out of Osric's hand, but he managed to pull the weapon out just in time before he would have been disarmed.

As the behemoth landed, another of the pulsating sacs on its abdomen began quivering before, with a sickening sound, bursting open, sending another of the small beetle creatures to the ground.

The creature Cinder and Grace were fighting, managed to dislodge Cinder, throwing the wolf free. Its mandibles snapped out at Grace, clamping down on her leg, eliciting a cry of pain.

Cinder rebounded from being thrown off and charged again, snapping down on the edge of the smaller creature's mandible, forcing it to release Grace, who stumbled back, a nasty gash across her thigh.

"There are more of them!" Rowan warned, releasing another arrow, which sank into the creature a hand span from the first.

Grace started to move back into the fight when the second small beetle the creature had released charged at her. Dancing aside, although not as effectively as before, her leg giving a little as she put weight on it, she raked her sword across the new beetle's side before pushing hard, managing to pierce its exoskeleton and pierce the creature itself, which screeched and leaped back, abandoning its charge.

Talia, who had been looking up at the ceiling, began weaving her hands, casting a spell. Except this one didn't emit electricity or acid or glowing bolts. Instead, high above them, a piece of the still-intact roof of the temple pulled free, floating on its own for a moment as it spun in mid-air until the most pointed of its edges faced down toward the creature. And then gravity took over, the large piece of masonry and tile plummeted into the huge creature, the weight of it cracking the carapace along its back and causing it to stagger sideways slightly.

Osric followed it, his sword stabbing up into its unarmored underbelly before dashing back out, just in case the beast tried to drop its weight on him. One of its large legs kicked out, only to be blocked by a golden, shimmering barrier that formed around Osric.

Confused, Osric looked back to see Jasper holding his hand out toward him, clutching the symbol of his god in the other. Osric gave the cleric a nod of thanks before returning his attention to the giant creature, which was focusing on him now.

The creature's massive jaws clamped down on him, hooked fangs sinking into his flesh as it lifted him from the ground. He cried out in pain. The beast shook him violently.

In spite of the pain and disorientation, Osric managed to bring up his sword, thrusting the point forward as hard as he could into the creature's mouth. It screeched and tossed its head hard to the side, releasing him and sending him flying across the room. He crashed against the far wall and then fell onto the ground, the wind knocked out of him.

Below the massive creature, one of the smaller beetles tried charging Grace, but the nimble thief leaped over it, placing a hand on its hard back and using its own body to help her clear the danger. As she did, she stabbed downward with her short sword, piercing the center line of its carapace and deep into its body.

Jasper tried to help, using the heavy mace he hadn't employed until now, but the blow glanced off the creature's hard exoskeleton, and it barely seemed to notice.

Only Rowan continued to have success, sinking yet another arrow into the massive creature. Not that any of them seemed to be slowing it down. At least not until Talia's hands stopped weaving and thrust forward, a gout of flame erupted from her out-stretched hands, engulfing the beast and its spawn. A sickly burning smell filled the room as the beasts burned, the one Cinder had been fighting shriveled up as it cooked inside its own carapace.

It was a good blow, but they were not done. The creature shuddered once more, sending another of its spawn bursting out, poised to skitter across the floor at them.

The beast immediately lunged at Grace, who danced aside before countering, plunging her sword straight into the beast's open jaws, the hilt of her weapon the only thing keeping its jaws from closing on her arm as it convulsed in death throes.

Across the room, Osric struggled to his feet. He could feel pain, both from the rough impacts and the numerous wounds from where the creatures' fangs had pierced his skin. Part of him wanted to stop, to sit for a moment, but he couldn't. His friends were still fighting for their lives. Gripping his sword, he pushed away the pain and dashed back into the fray.

The large central creature turned its head back to the humans in front of it as well, looking directly at Jasper. Opening its maw again, Osric could see a sickly green liquid bubbling up in its throat. He had seen what that vile liquid could do and pushed harder to get to his new friend, knowing he wouldn't reach him in time.

Thankfully, Talia was faster. Even as it looked at Jasper, Talia had begun weaving a spell. As a stream of the acidic substance shot toward the cleric, Talia's hands extended, creating a shimmering barrier around him. The acid splashed against it and then deflected to land on the ground several feet away, hissing and steaming as it ate holes in the floor.

Grace's luck finally ran out as one of the smaller creatures also spat acid, and without any shield to block the stream of noxious sludge it landed against her chest and she screamed, ripping at her clothing trying to stop the pain. Thankfully, Jasper was near her. Placing a hand on her head, a white light shone around her as he called out to his gods for help in protecting and healing her. As soon as the light started, the pain on Grace's face went away.

Osric was almost back to the beast when he felt his feet lifting off the ground. For a moment, he was in shock, unbelieving that this beast continued to have new, amazing powers at its disposal, until he looked down and saw Talia concentrating, her hands outstretched.

It took him a moment to understand what was happening as he rose higher and higher. She was moving him toward the creature, above it. He made eye contact with his friend, who gave him a slight nod. Readying himself, he felt the invisible force holding him aloft dissipate and gravity take hold. As he fell toward the creature, he stabbed down, his sword pierced into its back. He then used the sword as an anchor to hold him in place and keep him from sliding off.

It was a good thing he did, because the beast chose that moment to roar and rock back on two legs, before crashing back down and charging forward, its weight shaking the room. There was nothing he could do as Rowan, Grace, Jasper, and Talia were sent flying in all directions as it stormed through them. Wedging his shield between the carapaces, to continue having a hold on the creature, Osric withdrew his sword and stabbed down again and again, a pool of ichor forming at his feet.

Below him, Cinder, who had managed to avoid the charging beast, snarled and clamped his jaws down on the upper face of one of the smaller creatures, fangs piercing through the unprotected flesh, then shaking it hard, whipping the creature's head back and forth. It shrieked and went limp as Cinder released it, dropping its body to the floor.

Osric held on tight as the beast realized there was something on its back, hurting it. It began shaking violently, trying to dislodge him. Osric sank his sword into its back, barely managing to stay on the creature as it shook violently.

Across the room, his friends were struggling to their feet, battered and dazed from the creature's charge, but they headed back into the fray. All except Talia, who struggled to get up. Jasper rushed to her and knelt beside her, placing both hands on her, praying, his eyes closed tight. The white light came again, concealing both of them for a moment. When it receded, Talia looked better, more conscious, and she got to her feet.

Grace ignored the two smaller creatures still fighting Cinder and ran at the large beast, apparently coming to the same conclusion as Osric. They needed to stop this thing before it killed them. Leaping, she kicked off one of its legs, grabbed the side of a carapace, flipped up, and then used her sword like Osric had his - as a climbing tool - pulling herself up to join him.

There were now two of them on its back, hurting it, cutting into it. The beast thrashed harder, trying to dislodge them as they both held on desperately.

Meanwhile, Rowan had found his dropped bow and began shooting again, this time at one of the smaller creatures that was scuttling rapidly toward him. He kept firing, but it was a much smaller target, and only one of the four arrows he shot at it connected. The rest bounced off its exoskeleton. Reaching him, its mandibles snapped onto his leg. Only the fact that he got the shaft of his bow in the way kept it from severing the limb entirely. It still cut into him deeply, crushing down on his leg and starting to splinter the bow, causing him to scream in pain.

They needed to end this. Osric pulled his sword free and took two, long leaps, thinking that if he was in the air the thing couldn't knock him around, and finally landed near the beast's head. As he landed he brought his sword down with all of his might, just beyond the end of its hard protective plates, pushing his sword all the way down, putting every bit of his strength and weight behind it as it punctured through sinew and bone, until it was buried to the hilt.

The creature staggered twice, shuddered, and collapsed. Osric pulled his sword free as he was flung off the beast, landing much harder than Grace, who managed to end up on her feet after being flung free.

Across from them, he could see Cinder, cut and bloody, wrestling the second to last smaller beetle to the ground, tearing at its neck and head. The final beetle was being dealt with by Talia and Jasper, who were hitting it over and over with their staff and mace, respectively, while Rowan used a knife to stab into the beetle's eyes, trying to get it to let him go.

It finally did, releasing him as it convulsed and died.

And just like that, the battle was over. They were far from unscathed, with most of the group cut, bruised, punctured, or burned by acid. Grace and Rowan were limping badly, Rowan using half of his broken bow as a cane to stay upright, fighting the pain of his severely injured leg. Osric could feel blood pooling inside his armor.

He and Jasper did what they could to heal the group, praying to the gods for their assistance, but Osric was finding that each time he used the power the

Veilguard gave him, it took a little from him. He could not do that indefinitely, and it seemed Jasper was much the same.

They were able to stabilize everyone, and repair the worst of the damage, so that none of them were in danger of perishing, but that was as much as they could manage. They would all be walking wounded for some time.

"Osric, look," Talia said, pointing past where the beast had been standing.

Osric looked where Talia was pointing and saw a small altar at the back of the room, still mostly obscured by the monstrous creature's bulk. Atop it sat a piece of parchment, the edges ragged and torn, as if it had been ripped from a larger document.

He walked toward it, almost holding his breath. He couldn't believe it. After all their searching, the pain, the multiple times they'd been on the brink of death, they'd found it.

As he reached the pedestal, he saw that the parchment was indeed covered in the same strange script as the one they had found in the keep ... what seemed like a lifetime ago.

"Is that it?" Rowan asked, limping over to join him.

"I think so. I think this is what we've been looking for."

"Great. Can we get out of here now?" Grace said, limping to his other side. "This place gives me the creeps."

"We should be able to take the Brethren's elevator back up to the surface. Just ... be careful."

Thankfully, although the trip back to the long drop-off and the cage that led back to the surface was painful and slow, it was uneventful.

"Do you feel that?" Jasper asked as they neared the exit.

Talia nodded. "Whatever I felt before is gone. The air feels ... lighter."

"I think killing that creature did more than just clear our path to the document," Jasper said. "I think that thing was somehow affecting the Veil, like a stain on reality. Now that it's gone, the Veil is returning to its natural state."

Osric considered this as they piled into the elevator, the mechanism groaning as it carried them back up to the temple's main level. Was it that easy? Probably not. There seemed to be multiple things causing harm to the Veil, each interconnected and affecting the others.

Still, they'd fixed this one. It had to matter, in some small way, each time they lessened the damage done to their world.

As they emerged into the antechamber to the temple's roof, Osric thought he caught a glimpse of movement in the shadows. Small, furry shapes darting between the rubble. Skivvers perhaps? But when he looked again, they were gone.

They made their way out of the temple, each step a little easier than the last as the promise of fresh air and open sky drew them onward. And when they finally emerged, blinking, into the sunlight, Osric couldn't help but gasp. The sky, which had been a sickly color when they entered, was now a clear, vibrant blue.

"Would you look at that?!" Rowan said, a grin spreading across his face. "Seems like the world's looking a bit brighter."

Osric looked around at his companions, battered and weary, but alive and victorious. They had faced unimaginable horrors and come out the other side. They had found what they were looking for.

"Come on," he said. "Let's get back to Avendell. We still have work to do."

Return to Avendell

The walk back to Avendell was, thankfully, uneventful. They managed to make it to the barrier without encountering any more of the Brethren. Osric hoped that might have meant they were in disarray after the death of Godfrey, and would no longer be a problem, but he knew that was wishful thinking. Jasper had made it clear that Farvale was just a small outpost for the Brethren, and Godfrey would only have been in charge of that one area, not their entire network.

Once they were through the Veil the stag-folk, who Rowan found fascinating, led them back to the heart of the forest. The entire way, Jasper couldn't stop talking about the barrier and what it was like to pass through it. Even Grace, who seemed to not be shocked by anything, was amazed at the experience.

The walk through the forest didn't disappoint them either as they kept catching glimpses of shimmerlings, grovewalkers and briarwolves.

The real wonder started, however, when they reached the Concordant Grove. Jasper nearly fell to his knees when he walked into the cleared circle flanked by carved symbols of the gods that made up the Veilguard.

"I can feel Heathus's presence here, filling me. It's like he's standing right beside me. It's ... miraculous."

"Strange," Rowan said from next to him, frowning. "I see the symbol of Wyndra carved there, but I do not feel her presence."

"Not all experience the grove in the same way," the Sage said, walking out of the forest to join them. "You are welcome to meditate here and reach out to her."

"I might," Rowan said, clutching the pendant he wore around his neck, proclaiming his service.

"I'm sorry for my rudeness," the Sage said, smiling. "Welcome to the forest. I was so happy to hear of your return I rushed here to greet you. I do not know how you fared out there; but we could feel some kind of change, a lightening of the Veil, even here, from what you did."

"There was a creature in an old Calaphium temple that was ... damaging the Veil somehow. We defeated it and found the missing part of the document," Osric said, stepping forward and holding out the torn piece of parchment they had recovered from the ancient temple.

The Sage took the parchment reverently. "Well done. Very well done. This will take some time to translate and decipher, weeks ... perhaps longer. The Calaphium language is complex and layered with meaning. This, above all the other pieces of their language we have seen, is critical that we get the translation completely accurate. We can take no chances that we might mistake a word here or a phrase there and cause harm instead of repairing the Veil."

"I have some experience with Calaphium texts," Jasper said. "Could I assist you in the translation?"

The Sage's smile widened. "A fellow scholar of the Calaphium. I would be delighted to have your help. As for the rest of you, you have all earned a rest. Please, take this time to relax and recover from your trials. Also know that any who wish to leave are free to do so."

All eyes turned to Grace, who'd made more than a few comments about doing the quest under duress, even after leaving the temple.

She gave an uncharacteristically shy shrug and said, "Nah, I think I'll stick around. This has been fun. Besides, I got some good stuff off those dead cult guys."

Osric hadn't even seen her search the dead Brethrens' bodies, but he didn't doubt she was telling the truth. And yet, he almost felt like there was more there. Like she wanted to be here but didn't want to tell them that.

"Last time we were here, you told me that you could teach me more about magic, about how to use it without damaging the Veil," Talia said. "Since we have time, are there people here who could guide me to that understanding?"

"Of course. Of course. We would be glad to train you."

Talia beamed. She loved knowledge more than almost anything else, and Osric knew she'd always dreamed of traveling to the Conclave of Magic to get real, formal training. This would be the next best thing, maybe even better, since she would learn how to do it without damaging the Veil, which she was now very concerned about.

"I could use some help learning to fight better. I've gotten by on luck so far, but I don't really have any formal training. If there is anyone here who can teach me to be a better ..."

"I'd be happy to train you, Osric," Rowan said, clapping a hand on his shoulder.

"There are also some among the stag-folk who are skilled warriors," the Sage added. "I'm sure they would be willing to share their knowledge with you as well."

As the group dispersed, each to their own pursuits, Osric stood there, watching them. It was odd. Other than Talia, he'd only met them within the last week or two, and yet they'd become friends so quickly. Especially Rowan. Osric wondered what would happen to them now, once the document was deciphered and the Sage knew what needed to be done.

Would they all go their own ways? Would he go back to Eldham? Back to the forge? Something on his face must have given away what he was thinking because Talia came to him, instead of finding some of the gathered druids who'd agreed to teach her more about magic and its effects on the Veil.

"You okay?" she asked softly, putting a hand on his shoulder.

"I don't know, really. I was always dreaming of adventure, of a more exciting life, you know? Ever since we were kids, I wanted to be out here, exploring the world, being a hero. But now that I've had a taste of the world ... it's not like what I thought it would be."

"What do you mean?"

"I was scared to death all the time, Talia. Not just for myself, but for you, for all of us. The things we had to do, like that creature by the lake, putting it out of its misery. And the things we saw, like that spirit before the temple. It's opened my eyes to how terrible the world can be sometimes."

Talia reached down and took his hand, pressing it between hers. Her touch was warm. Comforting.

"But you did good, too, Osric. So much good."

"Yeah, I found the document like the Sage asked me to, but ..."

"It's so much more than that, Osric. You helped a village that was dying, its people starving. You made friends with creatures we thought were extinct, who now have a home free of danger. You exposed corruption in Farvale. You freed trapped spirits and removed a dark stain from the world. You've done so much. There are people out there who are better off now than they were before you met them."

She squeezed his hand, looking deep into his eyes, "I'm very proud of you, Osric."

They stood there, hands clasped, eyes locked. Osric felt a warm sensation, deep in his chest. For a moment, the weight of everything they'd done and the things they'd still have to do, lifted ever so slightly.

"Thanks," he said, turning back to look at the grove, still holding Talia's hand, watching his friends.

They had a long way to go, but he realized that with Talia next to him, he was confident they could manage it.

To Be Continued ...

About the author

Travis writes science fiction, fantasy, and thriller novels (and the occasional coming-of-age story), with the hope of transporting and enthralling readers. Publishing novels since 2015, Travis's passion is creating worlds and characters that live and breathe, and experiencing the joy of those stories with his readers.

When not writing, Travis enjoys connecting with readers and other writers, managing the popular Complete Marvel Reading Order website, where he works on his other passion for comics and graphic novels, and spending time with his family.

If you have enjoyed this book, please consider taking a moment to rate or review it wherever you found your copy, as it helps new readers find my works and ensures I can continue writing book into the future.

Find out more at:

amazon.com/TravisStarnes/e/B072YBDC3S/

Or visit

https://tstarnes.com

Maps available at

https://tstarnes.com/book-series/imperium/

Signup to get free previews and notifications of up-coming books at

<u>http://tstarnes.com/preview-notification-newsletter/</u>

Also by

Fanfare

Dissonance

Elegy

From the Top

Imperium Series

The Sword of Jupiter

The Trumpets of Mars

The Sands of Saturn

The Depths of Neptune

The Fires of Vulcan

The Triumph of Venus

Shattered Lands Series

In the Shadow of Lions

The Veilguard Saga

Threads of Destiny

Stand Alone

Going Home

Ingram Brothers
Series

ROZ LEE

DEDICATION

To my wonderful, devoted readers.
You inspire me every day.

TABLE OF CONTENTS

Ingram Brothers #1
WILL
USA TODAY BESTSELLING AUTHOR
ROZLEE

Thank you so much for purchasing *Will – The Ingram Brothers #1*. If the town of Willowbrook, Texas and some of the characters seem familiar, then I'll assume you've also read *Lost Melody* by my alter ego, Dolores W. Maroney. If you haven't, then Melody, Hank, and a few other characters will be new to you. No worries. I loved the town of Willowbrook and its residents so much I had to go back there to see what they were up to. I hope you'll love them as much as I do, and if you haven't read *Lost Melody*, will choose do so when you've finished reading Will's story.

Thanks again. I hope you enjoy the read.

Roz

CHAPTER ONE

William Ingram stared at the drink he held loosely between his thumb and middle finger. Was this going to be his only drink today or the first of many? In the last six months, he'd gone from mildly successful to virtually broke. So, the decision was a no-brainer. It would be the first of many—or at least the first of as many as he could afford.

The boarding pass in his jacket pocket and the drink in front of him represented the majority of the funds he had left to his name. The few art supplies he hadn't sold at rock-bottom prices to fund his return home had been checked as luggage which, an airline employee by the name of Brandy had assured him, would be transferred to the new plane as soon it arrived to take him and the rest of the passengers aboard their aborted flight on to their destination.

Just his luck. He'd admitted defeat and then his flight from New York made an emergency landing in Philadelphia. It seemed the universe wasn't done with him.

The airline had booked as many of the stranded passengers onto existing flights as possible, starting with the ones who were making a connection in Dallas. He wished he was one of them, but the truth was, once he got to Texas, he was there to stay. He'd ventured out into the world, had followed his dream until it had turned into a nightmare. When things had gone to shit, he'd raged and fought back, convinced the police would eventually find the people responsible and return his property to him. After several

4

months with no break in the case, his confidence had eroded until he'd lost hope and slid down the slippery slope into despair. His girlfriend/agent had stolen more than his livelihood, she'd stolen his will to create, leaving him one option—cut his losses and return home to Willowbrook, Texas.

What he'd do once he got there was anyone's guess. Maybe he could get a job painting houses. It was honest work and required the one thing he still had—an able body. He'd never been one to do much physical labor, avoiding it at all costs, but in New York, he'd seen the necessity of keeping in shape and had been a regular at the local gym until he'd had to cancel his membership due to lack of funds. He'd never painted a structure before, but he knew how to hold a paintbrush. It wasn't like anyone would be asking his opinion on the color or anything else. He'd be hired muscle to get the mindless job done.

He gave himself two, maybe three weeks before the mind-numbing physical exertion pushed him to the edge of his sanity.

Great. Just fucking great.

He took a healthy sip, closing his eyes as the cheap bourbon ate away at the lining of his throat and nibbled at the ragged edges of his mood.

A knee to his hip almost knocked him off his seat and caused the liquor in his glass to slosh over the side onto the back of his hand. Grabbing the bar to steady himself, he groaned at the waste of alcohol he'd been counting on. "Shit! Watch what you're doing!"

"Sorry."

The feminine voice slid through him like fifty-year-old whiskey, setting fire to parts of him that had suffered Jessica's betrayal perhaps more than any other. It was good to know the physical damage wasn't permanent even if he had no intention of taking any part of himself out for a test run. Determined not to engage, he sucked the liquid from his skin. The bartender hustled over with a rag, drawing Will's attention upward. His gaze locked on the reflection in the mirror behind the bar, and he damn near bit his hand as he recognized the woman sitting next to him.

He didn't know her name, but he'd seen her before. More importantly, he'd seen her type before. Beautiful, sexy, and high maintenance. Everything from her clothes to her hairstyle to the perfect application of makeup on her clear complexion screamed *rich girl*.

She'd been on his flight—in first class while he'd been lucky to be in the cheap seats. If not for the cute flight attendant who'd taken pity on him and offered to let him change seats, free of charge, to an open bulkhead seat, he never would have seen this woman. She'd come breezing in at the last minute like she owned the plane, and taken her seat next to the aisle in the last row. Just feet from where he sat trying not to notice anything about her. Of course he'd noticed everything, from the color of her hair—auburn—to the shape of her body—a perfect hourglass—to the slight sheen of perspiration on her forehead as she shoved her Louis Vuitton carry-on into the overhead bin. He'd looked her over as a man then and liked what he saw, but now, with only her face visible in the mirror, the artist in him took over.

She wore makeup, but it was artfully applied, so, at first glance, it appeared she wore none at all. Strategically placed streaks of—whatever-the-hell-women-called-it—highlighted already distinct cheekbones. Some sort of dark magic applied to her eyelids showcased the most beautiful blue irises he'd ever seen. Shades of blue paint swirled through his mind as his brain automatically tried to replicate the color in his preferred medium—oils.

Coupling what he'd already seen of her body with what he now knew about her face, he realized he had to paint her. Only he didn't paint anymore. The sharpness of the realization had him reaching for the glass the bartender had so kindly refilled at no cost. Forcing his gaze from the mirror, Will gulped the last of his whiskey. Placing the cheap highball glass on the bar, he contemplated his next move. He couldn't paint her, but there was something else he could do to her, and he wanted to do the *something else* even more than he wanted to commit her likeness to canvas. Just because he'd sworn off relationships didn't register in his thinking. This was a one-time deal. Nothing more. They were two passengers on a one-way trip to Hell. Well, that was *his* story, but they were passengers on the same cursed flight. What would a little fuck between strangers hurt?

The barkeep arrived with the woman's order, and Will signaled for a refill of his own. He'd expected to see something pink with an umbrella or maybe a cutesy martini glass rimmed with sugar and swirled with chocolate sauce. Instead, her drink looked suspiciously like his. No-nonsense. No ice. Just two fingers of amber liquid—probably the good stuff. She surprised him by knocking the contents back with one swallow. She didn't even gasp for air afterward, confirming his suspicions about the quality of the whiskey. It was either good whiskey or there was more to her than he'd thought.

He couldn't wait to find out. He turned to face her. "Hi. Looks like we're going to be here for a while. Know someplace we can go to kill some time?"

"That's the worst pickup line I've ever heard." And MacKenzie had heard plenty. However, none had tempted her the way this one had from the Hot Guy she'd spied earlier in the boarding area at JFK. Tall, dark, and handsome despite his grim countenance. And despite her recent vow to abstain from anything with a Y chromosome, his voice ignited something inside her she'd almost hoped was dead for good. Men were trouble. It was a lesson well learned from her latest failed relationship. Men thought with their little head more often than not, and it tended to lead them astray.

Like the guy on the barstool next to her.

Yes, after determining she wasn't going anywhere anytime soon, she'd made a quick stop at the ladies' room then gone in search of him. He'd been easy to find. Their gate was at the far end of the terminal, and he'd stopped at the first bar he'd run across.

She couldn't blame him. She needed a drink in the worst way possible, as clearly did he. Travel could tempt a person to drink, especially when things went awry, as they had today. She didn't know anything about how planes worked, but she figured if the pilot decided he needed to set the thing down as quickly as possible, then whatever had gone wrong must have been major. The way she saw it, she was lucky to be alive, even if her life was a shitstorm.

If today's events didn't call for a couple of fingers of Macallan and a good fuck to celebrate surviving a near-death experience, then nothing did. She'd save the recriminations for later—like when she got to Texas and started her new job. From what she'd heard of the small town where she'd be living, she'd have plenty of time to visit past regrets and beat herself up over her poor decisions in regard to men. It didn't appear there was anything else to do there.

Her savings were dwindling fast. Thankfully, her new employer had sprung for the plane ticket—first class—much to her surprise, leaving the remains of her nest egg untouched. She'd need most of it to get settled. She had no idea what a place rented for in off-the-grid Texas, but she assumed it was considerably less than what it would have cost her to rent a place of her own in Manhattan. After her boyfriend/boss had gone missing, she'd had no choice but to move out of his modern high-rise and into a friend's closet. It hadn't actually been a closet, but Bethany had been using it as one and probably was again since MacKenzie had cleared out.

She'd calculated and recalculated her financial situation enough times the grim figures were etched on her brain. Pocket change was short, but she still had room on her American Express card. With a bit of luck, she'd be able to pay it down once she was receiving regular paychecks again.

The guy sitting next to her didn't need to know her hard-luck story. Today was about celebrating life and maybe just a little about celebrating her *new* life, and that was on her. Today, she wasn't the loser who'd been duped and dumped. Today, she was a strong woman with a future. A woman who saw what she wanted and went after it.

And she wanted…him.

She dug the well-worn card from her wallet and waved it at the bartender. He hustled over. Making a sweeping motion with her hand to indicate Hot Guy's drink and hers, she said, "Close out our tabs, please."

Hot Guy's head jerked up. "I can pay my own way."

"I'm sure you can but allow me." Before he could argue further, she thrust her card at the bartender who snatched it like it was platinum instead of green plastic, smirked at Hot Guy then took off to process the sale.

"No, really," Hot Guy protested.

MacKenzie signaled him to stop. Fantasy was about all she had left and she'd be damned if he was going to ruin this one. "I've got it." She slid off the stool, deliberately letting her breasts brush his arm. The bartender returned with the charge slip which she signed and slid back to him. Grabbing the extended handle on her carry-on, she made eye contact with Hot Guy. "You coming? Or not?"

It was all she could do not to look over her shoulder to see if he followed her. Once she'd made it out to the crowded concourse, he caught up to her. "Where are we going?"

"Someplace private."

He said nothing, just matched his stride to hers and used his broad shoulders to clear a path for her. If she hadn't been as nervous as a cat in a room full of rocking chairs, she would have admired the little bit of chivalry from a man who didn't have a clue where they were headed. Now, if she could only remember where the article she'd read in the magazine she'd found in the seat-back pocket had said the micro suites were located. She hadn't paid much attention since she'd never in a million years envisioned being in a situation where she'd actually use one. She'd been impressed at the number of airports where the mini-hotels had been installed and wondered if they'd been selected because they had the highest number of stranded passengers, or if there'd been another reason. What did it matter? She was horny and they had one here—somewhere. She scanned the directional signs posted overhead for a hint then, there it was! On the wall, sandwiched between the ladies' room and an automated candy dispenser hung a giant illuminated advertisement for the fancy no-tell motel. Noting the location, she made a quick assessment of their whereabouts then pointed. "That way. It isn't far now." She hoped.

A right turn sent them down another wide concourse lined with stores selling souvenirs and survival gear for weary travelers. Nestled in their midst was an oasis of calm. MacKenzie stopped. The check-in desk reminded her of a mid-range hotel chain with its faux wood counter and cheap artwork.

"Whoa. Wait a minute."

She whipped her head around to glare at Hot Guy. "What? You've changed your mind?"

His head swiveled from side to side. "No. I haven't changed my mind, but I was thinking of something a little less expensive—like a janitor's closet or something."

"I'm going to pretend you didn't just say that and get us a room. Will an hour be enough?"

"Sure."

"Wait here. I'll be right back." The disinterested employee behind the counter walked her through the check-in process with all the enthusiasm of a turnip. Under other circumstances, she'd be annoyed, but none of it mattered in this instance. She held the key up for Hot Guy to see then, heart pounding, she strode past the desk to the short hall, dragging her carry-on behind.

She waved the keycard in front of the electronic lock mechanism and clasped the telescopic handle on her suitcase. "Allow me." Hot Guy's body pressed against her from behind. A long arm reached around her to push and hold the door open for her. It wasn't much, another one of those chivalrous acts she'd grown unaccustomed to in New York, but it did unexpected things to her insides.

"Thank…thank you," she said as she stumbled over the threshold, the sight of his hand, purely masculine, with long fingers and strong knuckles making her clumsy, and for the first time since she'd decided to take him up on his offer, nervous. *What the hell am I doing?* She didn't know this guy from Adam. He could be a serial killer or…or…something. But damn, he smelled good—like the Catskills on a warm summer day. If he'd been a tree, she'd hug the shit out of him.

The door swooshed shut, the sound of a dead bolt sliding into place sounding like the final nail in her coffin. Whirling around, she gasped at the sight of him leaning against the door, his arms behind his back and his ankles crossed. His eyes blazed with a heat she'd only read about in romance novels as he slowly undressed her with his gaze. The tiniest hint of a smile as he completed his inspection told her how much he liked what he'd seen. Turnabout was fair play. She released her tight grip on her luggage then kicked off her shoes before returning the favor.

Her first impression of him at JFK was that he was a man who took care of himself, and, at closer inspection, she'd been right. She'd bet the available balance on her last credit card there was a sculpted body beneath his expensively cut suit coat and tailored dress shirt. His tight-fitting jeans, worn nearly white in all the right places, left little to the imagination. She checked him out all the way down to the Italian leather loafers on his feet before letting her gaze slide up again to caress what promised to be a very generous package barely contained behind a button fly. Whoever he was, he had style. In fact, he reminded her of a guy she'd seen on the cover of a magazine once. She'd gotten herself off to the cover, and, after the magazine had gone missing, to the memory of it, more times than she dared recall.

Finished with her perusal, she dragged her eyes back up to his. "Thanks for getting us a room, but you don't have to do this."

And he's too fucking nice. She didn't want nice. She wanted wild-monkey sex. The kind where words weren't necessary. Where both parties took what they wanted without regard to the needs of the other. There was only one thing she wanted to know. "Do you have protection?"

"I do." The timbre of his voice nearly melted her panties off.

MacKenzie dipped her chin once to acknowledge his answer then reached for the top button on her blouse.

CHAPTER TWO

Holy, fuckin' shit.
Will could hardly believe his eyes. Maybe his luck was changing. How else could he explain the goddess doing a striptease before him?

Maybe she was a siren sent by the Fates to finish him off. If so, she was doing an excellent job of incinerating him. Fists clenched behind him, he forced himself to remain glued to the door as she slowly revealed herself to him, one inch of creamy skin at a time.

Like any piece of exquisite art, she deserved to be admired, to be studied, and knowing this would be his one and only chance to do so, he took in the sight before him with both his artist's vision and the appreciation of a human male who had seen his fair share of nude females.

He'd recognized her beauty from the beginning, but even his artist's eye couldn't have imagined the gentle swell of her breasts or the sweet curve of her hips or, god help him, the enticing pillow of a belly that drove him insane with lust. That part of the female anatomy seemed so womanly to him. He was glad to see she hadn't tried to diet it away like most women did these days.

As a teenager, he'd fallen in love with the paintings of voluptuous nudes by the old masters. While his brothers and friends had studied purloined centerfolds, he'd studied Rubens and Bouguereau. A woman's body was a thing of beauty to be admired and, in this instance, coveted. Any man would be fortunate if they could claim her as theirs, but it wasn't in the cards for him. He had this one opportunity, and, as much as his fingers itched for a piece of charcoal and a pad of paper, he needed the physical release more — needed this reminder he was still alive.

Mustering as much restraint as he could, he lifted his right hand and, with his index finger, signaled for her to turn around. Her lips curved into a seductive smile then she did a graceful about-face, peeking over her shoulder to gauge his reaction which was immediate. Will pushed away from the door with one thing on his mind, taking what she so freely offered.

Fully clothed, he pressed his front to her back. The need to touch her, to commit every inch of her body to tactile memory was almost more than he could bear, but to touch her the way he wanted to would make this encounter too personal. There was nothing personal about it. She wanted to be fucked, and by god, he wanted to oblige her. No names. No more physical contact than was absolutely necessary to get the job done. An anonymous encounter they'd both, hopefully, recall fondly years from now. Hell, if it went no further, he'd be eternally grateful to this woman, though she'd never know what she'd done for him. He hadn't looked forward to anything in months.

Hoping he didn't need words to get his message across, he nestled the hard ridge of his erection in the cleft of her cheeks and, with a subtle nudge of his hips, silently demanded she move closer to the sofa. God bless her, she took the hint and shuffled her feet in the right direction.

"Stop," he growled in her ear. "Bend over."

She bent at the waist and braced herself on the edge of the pleather sleeper/sofa. A tap with his foot against hers and she spread her legs, offering her priceless treasure for him to plunder.

Will removed his wallet, extracted his in-case-of-an-emergency condom, clenched the packet between his teeth then returned his wallet to his pocket. There was precious little in the billfold, but he couldn't afford to leave it behind, and god knew if he'd have any brain cells left when he was done. Better to pack it away now.

Valuables stowed, he slipped the top button on his fly through the well-worn buttonhole with ease. Then he did the next one and the next. He didn't bother with the last one. Hooking his thumbs in the waistband, he shoved the denim until it bunched at his hips.

From there, it was a simple thing to maneuver the front of his briefs out of the way.

Shit. He nearly came at the sight of his dick, engorged and throbbing, laying heavy on the curve of her creamy smooth backside. He was fucking ready, but was she? He'd always been careful to make sure his partner was prepared, and had just enough courtesy left in him to do the same for her. A two-finger swipe between her legs brought a groan to both their lips. He'd never donned a raincoat as fast as he did then.

Positioning the head of his cock at her entrance, with the last vestiges of his control, he growled out, "Tell me to stop now or hold the fuck on."

Spontaneous. Human. Combustion. The words crystallized in her brain. Pseudo-scientific bullshit—or so she'd thought up until this moment. Naked and spread wide, waiting for this stranger to fuck her senseless, she was perilously close to going up in flames. He hadn't removed a stitch of clothing, and god, wasn't that hot? No sweet talk unless she considered his warning to *hold the fuck on* sweet, but damn if her insides hadn't turned to liquid at his gruff command. She'd never done anything like this in her life and had to wonder why the fuck not as she gave him the consent he demanded. With a shift of her weight, she pushed her hips back and drove herself onto his cock.

Sweet mother of god.

He was thick and hard, and as he flexed his hips and filled her the rest of the way, her toes curled into the industrial-grade carpet, and her fingers instinctively dug into the upholstery. A groan of pure pleasure escaped her lips. He gripped her hips with hands so hot she was certain he'd branded her with his touch. He pulled all the way out of her then slammed back in. If not for him holding her, she would have collapsed from the force of his thrust.

This is what it feels like to be taken.

This wasn't love. It was pure lust unleashed without restraint, and she loved it.

She'd been desired before, but it had always been tempered with civility and/or consideration, but there had *always* been caution. There was no caution here. Hot Guy took her as if he owned her. Like it was his right, and only his, to fuck her. And as he rode her like a cowboy on the run from the law, she thought for a moment, it wasn't an illusion. He was running from something and he was taking her with him.

I'm his. No one will ever do it for me the way he does. It was a crazy thought, driven from her mind as his balls slapped an age-old rhythm against her clit, and the delicious pain of tender tissues stretching to take all of him coalesced into a dizzying need to come.

As if he'd read her body, he tightened his hold on her hips and said the magic words. "Take it, baby. Suck me dry."

Dear. God.

His words were filthy and raunchy and the sexiest thing she'd ever heard. The image they created in her brain, of bringing this powerful man to his knees, was all it took. The tremors began in her thighs and spread upward where they detonated charges in her womb. Her clit throbbed; her nipples tingled. When her pussy spasmed around the steel pole reaming her, Hot Guy let out a primal groan and lost control. His thrusts became short. His groin ground against her as if he was trying to burrow deep inside her and never come out, and, in some way, he had. With a string of profanities directed at a supreme being, he came, filling the tip of the condom with scalding cum.

The moment he let go of her, MacKenzie's knees gave out and she tumbled face-first onto the sofa bed. Breathless and feeling like a rag doll, she must look a sight, but she couldn't find it within herself to care. She'd move—eventually—then she'd thank Hot Guy. Maybe offer to buy him another drink. It was the least she could do for his stellar performance. She hadn't been with many men, but she'd been with enough to know what she'd felt, what she'd experienced today was beyond compare. Hot Guy was a sex god, and he had the equipment to match his status. It was a shame they'd never see each other again. She could get used to his style of sex on a regular basis.

The sound of the door opening spurred MacKenzie to action. Bolting upright, she crossed her arms over her breasts and winced as the pleather upholstery snagged her bare ass as she tried to scoot into a sitting position. By the time she peeled her abused flesh off the sofa and resettled, she opened her mouth. "Wait!" hovered in the air, a second too late as the door closed. Hot Guy was gone.

"Asshole." MacKenzie tucked an errant strand of hair behind her ear. Maybe he'd just gone out to get something from the vending machine. She could use a snack herself. Glancing around the room, her gaze fell on the small desk on the opposite wall. The keycard she'd used to open the door lay right where she'd dropped it when they first entered. Her lungs deflated as she spied the used condom lying like a testament to her folly in the bottom of the waste basket. Hot Guy, aka Asshole, wasn't coming back.

Gathering her clothes, she dressed then curled her legs beneath her on the sofa. She'd paid for an hour, might as well take advantage of the privacy to get her head on straight. She didn't think her lady parts were going to stop humming a satisfied tune anytime soon, but she could hope. There was a good chance she'd see Hot Guy again at the gate and she didn't want him to see how his abrupt departure had affected her. Would it have killed him to hang around another minute, perhaps inquire as to her well-being?

He's a love 'em and leave 'em — no — a fuck 'em and flee type.

"What did you expect?" she mumbled to herself. "You picked him up in an airport bar for cryin' out loud." If the situation didn't have pathetic loser written all over it, she didn't know what did. The biggest problem was, she didn't know which of them the label applied to. Her for encouraging Hot Guy or him for taking her up on the offer. It could go either way, but no doubt about it, he was an asshole. If she never saw him again, it would be too soon.

CHAPTER THREE

"Thanks for coming to get me." Will embraced his older brother, Jake, in the baggage claim area.

"We couldn't let you hitchhike to Willowbrook," his younger brother, Rick, said as he engulfed William in a tight hug. His brother felt solid, more like the soldier he'd been, up until the war on terrorism had chewed him up and spit him out nearly a year ago. Over Rick's shoulder, Will's gaze locked with Jake's. The brothers shared a meaningful look. Now was not the time for them to discuss Rick's recovery or his future. There'd be plenty of time to dissect each other's lives once they were all home. "Glad you're back, bro."

"Thanks." He just wished his homecoming was under different circumstances, but like Rick, only a catastrophe could have convinced him to return to Willowbrook for anything more than a visit. Unless pigs sprouted wings, he was here to stay. He wasn't so sure about Rick. Something else they needed to talk about.

"Would you look at that," Jake murmured. William turned to see what had caught his brother's attention.

After he left her, he'd tucked his balled fists into his pockets and walked until he'd found what was possibly the only deserted place in the terminal and leaned against the wall to catch his breath. Only then did he bring the fingers he'd swiped through her juices up to his nose. Inhaling deep, he let her scent take him back to their rented room, to the woman he'd never forget.

It had taken some work on his part, but he'd managed to avoid seeing her in the Philadelphia airport until they'd called his flight. He'd boarded earlier than most and been satisfied with his seat as far from first class as possible. Heck, he didn't know for certain they'd been on the same plane. She could have been waiting on a connecting flight to anywhere for all he knew. They'd exchanged orgasms, not itineraries. But there she was, on the other side of the baggage carousel, a shit-ton of expensive luggage piled on a cart being pushed by a man in the livery of a chauffeur. He hated the way his body responded to her presence. He'd taken what she offered, thinking it would be more than enough, but as the plane had made its way across the country, he'd been surprised to find out it hadn't been nearly enough. Her orgasm had done something to him he couldn't name then she'd collapsed onto the sofa, and he'd had visions of her sprawled across a velvet chaise, looking like she'd just been fucked. He'd wanted to put a just-fucked expression on her face then paint her more than he'd wanted his next breath. He'd had no choice but to leave.

"Seeing *her* is worth the trip, Billy boy."

Will cringed at Jake's use of the nickname he hated with a passion.

"Hey, is that yours?" Rick pointed to a beat-up cardboard box coming around the bend in the carousel. It appeared a band of gorillas had ripped it apart then patched it back together with tape bearing the TSA logo.

"Yeah." Will stepped toward the luggage conveyor, but Rick's hand on his shoulder stopped him.

"I'll get it."

He opened his mouth to protest, but Jake's elbow dug into his ribs. "Let him. He seems to feel a need to be useful these days."

A lump the size of Texas formed in Will's throat. He nodded, silently acknowledging what his brother was saying. Of the three of them, Rick had always been the one to offer a helping hand—thus his desire to enter the military. When he'd first come home, he wouldn't even help himself, much less someone else. He was glad to see this small indication his younger brother still lived inside the shell of a man who had returned to them. Maybe there was hope for Rick after all.

Rick joined them a few minutes later with the battered box tucked under one arm and the strap of Will's giant duffel slung over the opposite shoulder. "Is this everything?"

"Yeah." Not much to show for nearly a decade of life. He reached for the duffel.

Rick shrugged him off. "I've got it."

Jake fell into step beside Will as they followed their younger brother out into the Texas heat. As they crossed the busy roadway to the parking garage, Will caught himself scanning the people loading luggage into cars at the curb, wanting one last look at her — for posterity's sake, he told himself. It wasn't like he was ever going to see her again. He knew for a fact he didn't frequent the kinds of places she did. Everything about her screamed money and class — two things he most certainly didn't have and wouldn't find where he was going. The only thing they had in common was a shared air-travel experience and good sex. Hell, maybe the best sex he'd ever had, if he was being honest with himself. Best to put her out of his mind and get on with his life — whatever that was going to entail.

MacKenzie smiled at the driver who'd been sent to pick her up. She'd expected someone in a pickup truck, not a limo. From what she'd heard about her new employer, he didn't flaunt his wealth or celebrity status. By all accounts, he was a humble, yet incredibly talented man. She appreciated the first-class treatment while reminding herself not to get used to it. He was just trying to make her transition from New York to Texas easier. She couldn't expect to be pampered once she was settled. She doubted the small town where she'd be living had cab service, much less limo service. Besides, a car came with the job — something she'd need since her employer lived outside of town. He'd converted an old barn on his property into state-of-the-art workspace. She'd have an office there, but live in town.

She forced her brain to focus on reining in her expectations of the place instead of obsessing over Hot Guy. She'd managed to avoid him in the Philly airport, wasn't even certain they would be on the same flight to Dallas. He could have been waiting in the bar for a completely different flight. She hadn't asked, and he hadn't offered. What he had offered, she'd accepted way too easily. He'd given her what she wanted then sprinted out of there like the TSA was after him for a strip search.

She couldn't blame him. She'd been two seconds away from breaking her own hastily adopted airport hookup rules. Rule number one being—under no circumstances exchange personal information, i.e. name, phone number, destination—and god forbid—relationship status. Rule number two—under no circumstances beg him for a repeat. One and done. It was the only way.

Then she'd spied him at baggage claim. If not for Bernie? Bennie? *Her driver,* she might have hurdled the carousel like a crazed fan at a rock concert and broken all of her rules for the chance at one more time with him.

He'd seemed more relaxed than he'd been in Philly. Maybe it was the warm greeting from the sexy as hell guys who met him, or maybe he was happy to see his friends? Family? It was difficult to tell from across the carousel. They were all tall with dark hair. If they were related, they each had a distinctive style. The tallest one wore work boots, jeans, and a ragged T-shirt. She wouldn't be surprised to find out he could bench-press a horse. The idea gained momentum when he gathered Hot Guy's baggage, lifting the tattered box and duffel as if they weighed nothing. The other one was the polar opposite of Buff Guy. His suit branded him a professional of some kind—banker, lawyer, corporate exec. His attire fit him well, but she preferred the sexy, sophisticated style Hot Guy sported. There was something about a guy in jeans topped with a smart blazer that did it for her. Especially when she knew what those jeans held.

Perfection.

Yeah, it was a good thing the chauffeur found her when he did. He'd saved her from making a complete fool of herself. It was time to look forward, not back. Her mistakes were behind her, her future a blank slate waiting for her to write a new chapter. Pulling her attention away from the trio of sexy men, she counted the bags stacked on her cart, came up with the correct number, and waved the driver on. It took every bit of self-control she could muster to raise her chin and follow him out the door, without glancing over her shoulder.

"It's about an hour's drive, ma'am." The car pulled away from the curb and accelerated into traffic. "There's water in the mini-fridge on your left."

"Thanks—"

His gaze caught hers in the rearview mirror. There was a smile in his voice when he said, "Bernie, ma'am. No problem. You just relax. Leave the traffic worries to me."

It had been a long time since she'd met with such kindness. Courtesy wasn't a required trait for drivers in Manhattan. Mad driving skills were. If they got you there in one piece, they were good. If you also arrived on time, they were fabulous.

She thanked him again before he raised the glass partition sealing her into a cocoon of silence. God, it felt good to close her eyes and let the rhythm of the road lull her to sleep. She'd done nothing but run at full blast since she'd accepted the job offer in Texas. She'd pared her belongings down to the bare necessities, packed her bags, said goodbye to her friends and colleagues, promising to keep in touch. Her client had an apartment in New York City he co-owned with his partners. She'd been given the go-ahead to use it as needed whenever her new job dictated a trip to the Big Apple, which it occasionally would. He'd also mentioned his agent lived in the city. She'd be expected to work with him on certain projects, too. But her main job would be here, managing publicity for her new boss—Hank Travis.

How in heaven's name she'd ended up working for a rock star—scratch that—a superstar rock band, she'd never understand. She'd been a fan of BlackWing for as long as she could remember. Now, she was going to work for them! She'd been even more surprised to find out her friend Sunny Sheldon knew Hank and his wife, Melody. She'd called on her friends to get MacKenzie this job. The jury was still out on whether she could live in a small Texas town without losing her mind, but what choice did she have? After things had gone south with her previous job, she'd tapped everyone in the PR industry she knew and had come up with zip. Sunny had come through for her. She owed it to her friend to give this her best effort, even if it felt like she was being shipped off to another planet.

They'd left civilization behind almost the minute they departed the airport. MacKenzie gazed out the window at the passing scenery. Trees. Fields of…were those crops? God, she was in over her head. Visions of scruffy men in overalls and women in dowdy paisley dresses down to their ankles flashed across her brain. She was going to die out here in the wilderness. These…farmers probably ate people like her for lunch.

Maybe she could talk Hank into letting her work from home. She could rent a place in Dallas. Video conferencing was practically as good as talking in person. She could do her job remotely. She was certain of it.

The car slowed as they passed through a town. MacKenzie prayed it wasn't her destination. This was worse than she'd imagined. Empty storefronts. Weed-infested sidewalks. Pickup trucks with gun racks in the back window. She'd never survive in a place like this. She didn't relax until the driver turned a corner and she saw a sign indicating her new home was another twenty miles down the road.

Please. Please don't let it be the same. Please.

She remained on edge, surveying the vast empty spaces punctuated by the occasional house, some with barns, some without. When she spied the city limit sign declaring the population of her new home to just over two thousand, she had to hold back her tears. This was going to be awful. Two thousand people? That was…nothing!

"Welcome to Willowbrook, miss." The driver's voice made her sit up and take a deep breath. "Mr. Travis suggested I give you a short tour of the town before heading out to his place."

She couldn't imagine what Hank's reasoning was, but the more information she had about her situation, the better she'd be able to negotiate a move to Dallas. "Thank you, Bernie."

"My pleasure, miss. My mother grew up here. It's a nice place."

The affection in his voice eased the tightness in her shoulders just a little bit. Bernie drove slowly, stopping where it was convenient to give her a better look at a particular location. He pointed out several churches, the schools, the post office and municipal building then circled the park at one end of town. MacKenzie gasped at the heart of the town. Disney's Main Street had nothing on this one. The buildings were quaint and well maintained. The storefronts vibrant with sparkling glass to display their wares.

"Most people around here don't have much, but they take care of what they do have," Bernie said, taking a left off the busy downtown street. "This is my favorite part of town. All the streets are named for trees. Oak. Maple. Pecan. You get the idea. My grandmother lived on Walnut." He made another turn, and MacKenzie powered the window down to get a better view.

Air fragrant with the scent of fresh-cut grass rushed in. It was as different from Manhattan as a place could be, but as she filled her lungs, she thought perhaps it wouldn't be the worst place to live. She scanned the street. The houses were mostly post-war bungalows, painted white with various color shutters, but that was where the similarity ended. Yards were lovingly tended, planted with flowers and shrubs to match the owner's personality. And lining the street were the most magnificent old-growth trees she'd ever seen.

"It's beautiful."

"Yes, ma'am. It is. All the streets in this neighborhood are like this. If you're hunting for a place to live, this would be my choice. It's hard to get in though. Most of these people have owned their houses since they were built after World War II. They've been passed down to kids and grandkids. It's rare to see one go on the market."

"Guess I won't be living here, then," she said, powering the window up.

"Do you have a place?"

"My employer said they'd arranged something for me."

"I'm sure you'll like it." Bernie steered them back out onto Main Street then on to the outskirts of town. "We're almost there." He pointed out the window. "See the big barn with the wings painted on it?"

MacKenzie craned her neck to get a glimpse of her new place of employment. The giant barn rose up from the expanse of crops, its black wings making it stand out from the others she'd seen along the road. She swallowed hard, willing the nerves fluttering like a flock of ravens in her stomach to settle. I can do this. I *can* do this. So what if the job was in the middle of nowhere? A job was a job. BlackWing needed a PR guru, so here she was.

~~

"Welcome home," Rick said as they made the last turn and headed into Willowbrook. Will nodded and mentally added one to the tally displayed on the population sign marking the official boundary. "Lot of people gonna be glad to see you."

"Like who?" He'd never been particularly popular in school and hadn't wasted a minute longer than necessary leaving after graduation.

"Hank, for one," Jake offered. "I saw him the other day at the diner. He asked about you, and I told him you were moving back."

Will closed his eyes and took a deep breath, letting his frustration out with it. He'd been so caught up in his misery, he hadn't given much thought to what it would actually be like living here again. In the same graduating class, they'd known each other since they were in diapers. Hank had lived a few blocks down on the same street. They'd played together as toddlers and stuck beside each other as teenagers when their interests went beyond Friday night football. Hank had been into music and opted to lead the drumline in the high school band, while Will had contributed to the gridiron insanity by painting the team mascot on the paper banner the team demolished by running through it at the beginning of every game. To this day, he could draw a wildcat with his eyes closed. He wondered if Hank could still play his solo riff from memory.

Will chuckled to himself and felt a smile tug at his lips.

"Something funny?" Rick asked.

"Nah." Will shook his head. "Just thinking about Hank and me as kids. We did some stupid stuff."

Jake glanced at him then back at the road. "I thought Dad was going to blow a gasket the time the two of you rode your bikes through half the flower beds in the neighborhood."

"He did blow a gasket." He'd never forget how angry his father had been when one neighbor after another called to demand he do something about his unruly kid. "He took my bike away for the rest of the summer and made me replant every flower we'd run over."

"Hank was right beside you, as I recall," Rick said.

"He was. His parents weren't any happier than Dad was."

"That wasn't all Dad did." Jake twisted his hand on the steering wheel.

"No, it wasn't." Will had missed riding his bike the rest of the summer, but he'd missed his art supplies more. If there was one thing his dad knew how to do, it was punishing his kids. He knew their weaknesses and went right for them. Thankfully, he had his brothers. They'd stuck together—a united front against what had sometimes been cruel treatment. A lump formed in his throat as he recalled how he'd made it through those months. Rick and Jake had risked punishment and smuggled their own art supplies to him. They hadn't had much—colored pencils and crayons—but it had been better than nothing, and they'd known it. Here they were, saving his ass once again.

"Did I say thank you?" he asked, knowing it didn't matter if he had or not. His brothers didn't expect thanks, but he couldn't say it enough. No matter what, they had his back just as he had theirs.

"Yeah, you did." Rick who'd taken the rear seat so Will could ride shotgun nudged him in the shoulder. "So, don't mention it again."

He wasn't promising anything.

They pulled into the driveway of their childhood home. His neck muscles tightened. The place looked the same on the outside, but the inside had recently undergone a complete restoration—thanks to Rick's hard work. "Needs paint," he said past the lump in his throat as his crushed dreams pressed heavy on his shoulders.

"I was saving the job for you." Rick opened his door and piled out as soon as the car came to a stop.

Will took a deep breath before joining him. He'd had such big dreams when he left here all those years ago, and those dreams had taken him to places he hadn't known existed until he'd left small-town life behind. "White, as usual, with black shutters."

"Blue shutters, asshole." Jake joined them in front of the house.

"Black," Rick reiterated.

Will studied the familiar sight. "Does it matter? It's a fucking house."

"It matters if we're going to sell it." Jake had been advocating liquidation since they'd inherited the place. "It needs to stand out from the others."

A quick glance at the houses on either side supported Jake's vision. "He's right. Blue or green or something shocking like red will make the house stand out on the street." Will smiled at Rick's stunned expression.

"Standing out is not necessarily a good thing," his younger brother said as he returned to the car for Will's luggage.

Jake caught Will's gaze, and with a shrug, the two parted—Jake to unlock the front door and Will to help with his worldly goods.

Rick was putting on a good face, but something wasn't sitting right with him, and Will thought he knew what it was. Jake wanted to sell the house and Rick didn't. Will didn't give a shit what they did with it. Jake had never returned to live in the house after he'd left for college, opting to buy a place of his own on the other side of town when he'd returned to take over their father's law practice following the old man's death. Will had only spent a handful of nights in the house since he'd gone off to New York to pursue a career in the art world. Of the three of them, Rick was the only one who had any kind of attachment to the place. On the rare occasions Rick had come home to visit, he'd stayed with their dad, sleeping in the room the three brothers had shared growing up. When Rick had returned home for good, a silent and sullen man with no direction and even less ambition, his older brothers had seized on the sorry state of the house Rick insisted on living in as a form of therapy for him. They'd supplied him with paint, tools, and a modest budget to fix the place up. To their surprise, he'd thrown himself wholeheartedly into the project—or so it seemed from the pictures Jake had sent over the last few months.

"I can't wait to see what you've done inside." Will shoulder-nudged Rick out of the way and reached for his duffel.

"It's looking good if I do say so myself." Rick hefted Will's box of art supplies from the trunk then shut the lid. "You can have our old room. I've been sleeping in Dad's old room since I got it fixed up."

"Please tell me you got rid of the bunk beds in our room." He'd had a king-sized bed all to himself for years. Just thinking about folding himself into a small bunk bed for the foreseeable future made his back hurt. Or maybe it was the heavy bag he'd slung over his shoulder.

"Gone. The room wasn't big enough for anything but a full-size though. Sorry."

Will stifled a groan. None of this was Rick's fault so no need griping about his circumstances. He'd take what he could get and be happy about it. "I'm sure it'll be fine."

"*Fine* might be stretching the truth," Rick teased, "but it's better than the bunk beds we used to have." He held the front door open for Will. "It's a miracle I'm still alive. Those beds were cheap to begin with and we weren't gentle on them. I'm surprised you didn't crash down on me at some point and smoosh me."

Will smiled. "It wasn't for lack of trying. There were times I dreamed of ways to end your life."

"Like the time you put paprika on my toast instead of cinnamon?"

"It wouldn't have killed you," Jake said, taking the box from Rick's arms and placing it on the floor of the hall closet.

"You were in on it, too?" Rick placed his fists on his hips and glared at Jake.

"What can I say?" Jake straightened. "You were a brat. Always up in my and Will's business."

"Was not."

"Yes, you were." Will dropped his bag on the floor and slowly took in the new decor. Rick had refinished the hardwood floors, giving them a darker stain to contrast the light wall color. He kicked off his shoes and dug his toes into the soft pile of the new contemporary rug Rick had used to define the seating area. He ran a hand over the back of the mid-century sofa that fit the clean lines of the house better than the old Early American furniture ever had. A trio of his early paintings hung on the far wall above a couple of chairs that matched the sofa. He recalled sending the paintings to Rick for his birthday in lieu of a real present. It had been Will's first year at college in New York. He'd been full of himself and short on cash. He couldn't believe his brother had kept them, much less displayed them in his home, and this was very much Rick's home now. No wonder he didn't want to sell the place. "Wow, little brother. This is awesome. Who would have thought?"

"I know, right?" Rick waved him on. "Come see what I did to the kitchen."

"You aren't going to believe this," Jake said, trailing behind his younger brothers.

Will stopped cold, blocking the door to the kitchen. If he hadn't seen the outside, he wouldn't have believed he was in the same house.

"I thought about knocking the wall out to create an open floor plan, but I didn't want to change the architecture of the house, so I settled for changing the layout. What do you think?"

"This is…incredible." Will took in the Shaker-style cabinets, new appliances, and countertops. "You did good, bro. Real good."

Jake shoved past him. "Want to see the best part of this room?" Before Will could answer, his older brother yanked on a cabinet handle. A large panel opened to reveal a refrigerator stocked with the essentials. "Who wants a beer?" he said, grabbing three bottles.

Will had dreaded returning to this house, dreaded the memories, but as he sat around the sleek new table in the eat-in kitchen, sipping ice-cold brews with his brothers, he was surprised to find they didn't come. Yeah, there were memories, but most of them were good ones. He wondered if his brother had weaved some sort of magic, throwing out the bad along with the old décor. If so, he was a genius. Will hadn't thought there was a chance in hell he'd feel comfortable in this house, but he was. And so was Rick. Only Jake looked like a prisoner eyeing the door, ready to escape any minute.

It was no wonder. Jake had taken the brunt of their father's abuse. No one had called it abuse back then. They'd called it *stern parenting. Making men out of boys.* Everyone knew better nowadays. Somehow, they'd all survived to varying degrees. Jake, if not ecstatically happy, seemed settled even though he was basically living their father's life—carrying on his law practice in the same offices in the same town with the same clients. Then there was Rick. He'd served his country with distinction and come home with wounds no one could see or touch. In rebuilding this house, he'd rebuilt himself. It was good to see him smile and joke again, particularly in this house that hadn't seen much of either since their mother had passed away. As far as Will knew, Rick hadn't dated since he returned home, and he hadn't mentioned anyone special in all the years he'd been serving the country.

"There's something I wanted to talk to you guys about," Rick said, drawing the brother's attention.

Will finished his beer, tossed the empty in the new built-in recycle bin then got them all fresh bottles. "This sounds serious. What's up?"

"As you can tell, I'm almost done here. Unless we add a second floor, there isn't anything left to do."

"Do you want to add a second floor?" Jake asked.

"Hell, no! Are you insane?" Rick glanced at his feet then lifted his eyes to his brothers. "Don't think I'm not grateful for all the two of you have done for me. I didn't know what to do with myself when I came home. This remodel gave me something to do with my hands while my head caught up." He stood and propped his hip against the counter, arms crossed over his chest. "But it's time for me to move on."

Will's heart jumped into his throat. His brother was leaving? What the hell? "To where?"

Rick cocked his head to one side. "Down the street. Henry Travis contracted me to remodel his kitchen."

"He did?" God, he could barely hear himself speak over the blood pounding in his ears. "When did this happen?"

Rick shrugged. "Couple of weeks ago. He's been stopping in a few days a week ever since I started working on the house. He'd talk while I worked. I think he's lonely. Hank got married. The old lady next door to him—"

"Miriam Wallingford," Jake supplied.

"Yeah, she's the one. She married Jonathan Youngblood and is living in England most of the year now. Anyway, Henry's going to travel some. See the world. He's renting the house out, and he asked if I'd be interested in remodeling the kitchen. It won't be anything as elaborate as this, I'll be staying within the existing footprint, but it's a complete remodel."

"Don't you have to have a contractor's license to do remodeling?" Leave it to Jake to ask the practical questions.

Rick's face turned red. "I have one. Been studying in the evenings. I took the exam a couple of weeks ago and passed."

Will couldn't hide his surprise or his happiness. He smiled and lifted his beer in a toast. "Way to go, bro! That's awesome."

"I didn't want to tell you guys—in case I lost my nerve or failed. I'll have to sub the electrical and plumbing work, but I'll do everything else myself. I gave him a really good price, seeing as he's my first customer. You know, see how this goes. If it works out, maybe I'll look for another job."

He was ecstatic about Rick's newfound ambition, but worrying about his little brother had become ingrained in his DNA. "Are you sure you're up to this? A few months ago—"

"I was a mess. I know." He ran his fingers through his overly long hair. "I don't know if I'll ever be the same person I was before, but I'm coping. Taking one day at a time. I know I can do the work. I don't know how I'll handle the stress of being in business for myself, but I managed to get through the contractor's exam without having a meltdown."

Will nodded. He could imagine the guts it had taken for Rick to step out of his comfort zone and take the test. His brother was slowly working his way back to a normal existence. He wished he had some of his brother's fortitude. "Okay, then."

"Wait a second." Jake had a propensity to beat every subject with a hammer until it was dead. "Who's Mr. Travis renting his place to? Are they going to be a problem?"

"She's the new PR person for BlackWing. I haven't met her yet. Gonna live in it during the remodel, too."

"You okay working around a tenant?"

Rick shuffled his feet. "Don't have a choice."

"You could say you changed your mind about doing the job."

"No. I need to do this. Need to see if I can. Besides, it's not like she'll be watching over my shoulder. She'll be at work when I'm at the house."

Will nodded his acceptance. His brother had made up his mind, and who was he to throw a monkey wrench into Rick's plans? Rick making plans was a monumental step in the right direction. "Well, I'm glad you have something to look forward to. When do you start?"

"Couple of weeks. Thought I'd let the new tenant settle in a bit before I start ripping things out."

"Have you drawn up a business plan? Filed for a DBA?" Jake went into full-lawyer mode, peppering Rick with questions. Will expected his younger brother to be upset by the detailed questioning, but he took it all in stride. His little brother was getting his shit together which made his own lack of planning seem worse in comparison.

"MacKenzie, this is my wife, Melody Ravenswood Travis." Hank Travis smiled at the gorgeous brunette who'd just joined them in the recording studio. "Mel, this is our new PR guru, MacKenzie Carlysle."

Melody extended a slim hand. "So nice to finally meet you," she said as Kenzie took her hand. "Please, call me Mel. Sunny has nothing but good things to say about you."

"Thanks. Please, both of you, call me Kenzie, and Sunny filled my ear about the two of you and all the band members. I can't believe she didn't tell me she knew you until I cried on her shoulder about needing a job."

"Sunny was just honoring our wishes. Despite Hank's high-profile career and my not-so-secret background, we're pretty private people—as you can tell by the way we live. The middle of nowhere suits us, and we hope it will suit you, too."

Kenzie wasn't so sure about being suited to this kind of life, but if there was a paycheck involved, she was all for it...for now. Sunny had been right, Hank and Melody were lovely people who just happened to be famous, much like Sunny who was the daughter of one of Hollywood's favorite sons. "I grew up in D.C., moved to Manhattan for college then stayed there to work. I've never lived in a small town before. I'm looking forward to it."

"I speak for the entire band," Hank said. "We're glad to have you on board. Our agent has been filling in since Jason retired. With the new album dropping in a few months, we need someone who knows what they're doing."

"I've never worked in the music industry, but I'll give it all I've got. You won't be disappointed."

"Excellent. We couldn't ask for more. Jason left a ton of files for you." He indicated the file cabinets behind her new desk. "You'll find a lot of answers there, and Jase is only a phone call away. Feel free to ask us anything. Now, if you'll excuse me, I've got a song to write. Melody will bring you up to speed on the rest." With a kiss for his wife and a wave to Kenzie, Hank Travis left the women alone to talk.

"Wow." Kenzie let out a nervous breath as she turned to survey her new office space. It wasn't much, but it had all the necessities, including a window with a view of…crops. What kind, she didn't know or care. "I'm really here."

"Yes, you are." Melody waved Kenzie to her place behind the desk then took one of the visitors' chairs facing the desk. "How does it feel?"

Kenzie frowned.

"The chair?" Mel clarified. "It was Jason's. If it doesn't fit you, we'll get a new one. In fact, make a list of things you need and we'll get them for you. We want you to be comfortable."

"Thanks." The chair squeaked, and Jason's butt print didn't match her own. A new chair would top her list of needs. Other than proper seating, she couldn't think of a single thing she needed.

"Oh, and we ordered a new cell phone for you. It should be here tomorrow. It will have unlimited everything, so feel free to use it for your personal calls, too. The computer system here is state-of-the-art, but if there are any programs you need, put them on your new company credit card. We need to stop by the bank and pick your card up. Your new company car should be delivered to your house today."

"House?" Kenzie's head reeled with all the information coming in.

Mel's smile lit up her face. "I found a place for you to rent. Well, I didn't exactly find it. It sort of dropped in my lap. It's the perfect place. Not too big, not too small."

She had all Kenzie's attention. "I can't wait to see it. Where is it? When can I move in?"

"It's Hank's dad's house. It's in an older neighborhood, but all the houses are so cute and well-kept. You can move in today."

"Wait. What about Mr. Travis?"

"He's decided to do some traveling. He said he wants to see the world while he still can. He's starting out in England. He's going to stay at Ravenswood with Jonathan and Miriam for a little while."

Kenzie had heard all about Ravenswood, the ancient stone monstrosity Melody had inherited from her father. Since Earl Ravenswood's death, his best friend and former band-mate, Sir Jonathan Youngblood, had managed the singer's estate from his ancestral home. The place was high on Kenzie's list of places to visit if she ever got the chance.

"Is he coming back?" Kenzie wasn't sure she was going to stay here long, but she didn't want to bounce around like a rubber ball, either.

"Of course he is. His only child and his granddaughter are here. But don't worry." She waved her hand. "He'll either stay at Miriam's place, which is next door, or he'll stay with us."

"Sunny mentioned Mr. Travis' next-door neighbor married Jonathan Youngblood."

Mel nodded. "Miriam still has her house here. She and Uncle Jonathan split their time between Ravenswood and Willowbrook; otherwise, you could have rented her house."

"What about furniture?"

"Truthfully, it was all pretty old. I don't think he's bought so much as a new chair after his wife died. Hank convinced him to donate most of it and store the few pieces he couldn't part with."

"I doubt I'll have overnight guests, but I will need a bedroom set for myself, a kitchen table, and some living room furniture."

"No worries. Put it all on your company credit card. Pick whatever you like and consider it a signing bonus from the band. We're so glad to have you, Kenzie. You can't imagine what a burden you're lifting from Hank's shoulders."

"That's really generous." She didn't know what else to say. Her last employer had bought her a new blotter for her desk. She'd had to supply her own pens and staples. Cecil's penny-pinching ways should have been her first clue to his character.

"Oh," Melody said, "Henry — Hank's dad — said you could paint the walls. Even said he'd pay to have any work done you want to do. He'd already had plans drawn up to refurbish the kitchen and the bathroom before the travel bug bit him. If you'll supervise the remodel, he'll cut your rent in half until it's completed."

"What's the rent?"

Melody named a figure. "Half during the remodel."

"That's nothing, practically. Are you sure you got the amount right?"

"Positive. Henry doesn't need the money. He just wants someone to take care of the place and be there to keep an eye on the progress. With Miriam's house next door being unoccupied half the year, he's afraid to leave his empty, too."

"Makes sense, though I don't know about living next to an empty house. Does someone keep up with the maintenance?"

"Yep. Uncle Jonathan had a security system installed and hired a local company to take care of the landscaping year-round. Oh, and we have a key in case we need to use the house for overflow."

"Overflow?"

"When BlackWing is recording, there's not enough room at our place for the band, their families, and all the extra musicians and technical people who come in. We used to send them to Henry's house, but with you living there…well, we didn't think you'd appreciate the company."

"Depends on who you send over," Kenzie said, with a grin. Her spirits were lifting higher with each new revelation from her new employer's mouth. "If they're hot and single, I wouldn't mind."

Melody shook her head. "You're going to fit right in with BlackWing, I can tell."

"Thanks. I'm excited about being part of the team." She was. Really. It was the move and getting used to small-town life…and leaving behind everything leading up to her departure from New York. Once she got past it all, she was sure she'd find her footing in Willowbrook. Or maybe Dallas. She still held out hope she could convince Hank to let her work from home.

"Oh, good. Your car's here." Melody pulled to the curb in front of a small white bungalow on Pecan Street.

Kenzie couldn't believe her eyes. This was going to be her home? She'd fallen a little in love with this neighborhood when her limo driver had given her a tour of the town, but never in her wildest dreams had she thought she would live here. A city girl all her life, the tree-lined streets with their quietly unassuming houses were reminiscent of another time, a simpler life she'd never known would appeal to her — until now.

Kenzie stepped from Mel's Jeep to the shaded walkway and stared at her new home.

The house itself appeared much like all the others on the street, white with black shutters on the windows. Pots and hanging baskets filled with flowering plants adorned the wide front porch. An old-fashioned screened door was flanked by rocking chairs on one side and a swing on the other. Flower beds skirted the front of the house, providing vibrant color against the backdrop of the house and the perfect green lawn. Like a movie set — it was almost too good to be true.

She focused on the neatly edged grass. She couldn't wait to take her shoes off and walk barefoot across it. "I've never had a lawn."

"Don't worry. We hired the same landscape company Miriam and Jonathan use to do yours, too. I think they come on Friday, but don't quote me on that. I have their card somewhere. I'll hunt it up for you. If you need to change the date or time they're here or need something specific done, give them a call.

"Thanks." She'd be grateful for the help, but, seeing the neat flower beds, she thought she might like to give gardening a try.

As if she'd read Kenzie's mind, Mel added, "There's a little garden in the back where Hank's mother used to grow a few vegetables. Henry has kept the weeds and grass out, but it's been years since anyone planted anything there. Feel free to try your hand at some flowers or veggies."

She'd fallen down a rabbit hole. It was the only explanation for all of this. The job. The house. The car. A garden for crying out loud! What was happening to her? First, she'd hooked up with a stranger in the airport — something she should regret but couldn't bring herself to — now she was thinking about gardening. Next, she'd be carrying on a conversation with a cat and attending a tea party.

"Come on." Mel started up the walk to the porch. "Let's see what Henry left in the way of kitchen stuff." She paused on the porch and dug around in her giant purse, eventually coming up with a leather-bound notepad and a pen. "We'll make a list then we'll go shopping."

CHAPTER FIVE

"I've got a bed, a sofa, and a TV. What else do I need?" Kenzie never thought she'd complain about shopping, but she couldn't stop the words from spewing past her lips. She and Mel had done nothing but shop for the last three days. Hank insisted there was plenty of time, but Kenzie was dying to dive headfirst into her new job. Apparently, it wasn't happening today. Currently, they were on their way to the local diner to have lunch with Mel and Hank's friend, Cathy, who owned The Donut Hole on Main Street. Mel had been in there every morning so far and was quickly becoming addicted to their chocolate croissants and dark-roast coffee.

"Curtains, for one thing, and we need to choose paint colors for all the rooms." Mel set a brisk pace any New Yorker would be proud of. "You said yourself the wall colors were dingy."

She had commented on the wall paint, but she was beginning to regret opening her mouth. If she'd known Mel was going to drag her all over North Texas, looking for furnishings, and now, paint, she would have kept her mouth shut and lived with the dull interior finishes. A few cheap prints on the walls would brighten the place up enough for now. She'd already ordered a few from an online art catalog and charged them to her personal charge card. She'd admired the artist's work for years, but when she'd just started out on her own in New York, she hadn't been able to afford even a small print. Once she'd had the funds to purchase whatever she wanted, she'd had no place to hang one. She'd lived in her former boyfriend's loft, and, as an art dealer, every available space had been covered with originals from the artists he admired. There'd been no room for her favorites. She should have realized then what a bastard Cecil was, but she'd been in love — stupid blind love. Until his deceit had restored her vision to 20/20.

She could see clearly now. No more relationships. Just sex. Visions of Hot Airport Guy popped into her brain, making her heart trip all over itself. Why, oh why, did he keep coming to mind? It had been quick, hot, and extremely satisfying sex. Nothing more. End of interlude. End of discussion. So why couldn't she move past it? It wasn't like she was ever going to see him again. He'd gone his way. She'd gone hers. Their paths would never cross again.

"Cathy's good with colors. I'd never dream of choosing a paint color without her input." Mel tugged the door to the diner open. Kenzie followed her inside.

Heavenly aromas greeted the women. Mel may have been immune, but Kenzie inhaled deeply, sure she'd gain several pounds just from the smell of deep-fried everything and home-baked desserts. Her stomach growled, reminding her how long it had been since she'd last eaten.

"There she is!" Mel waved at the woman leaning out of one of the window-front booths. "Come on. You'll love Cathy. She's the greatest."

Like everything else in Willowbrook, the place could double as a set for a 1950s era movie. They crossed the black-and-white checkered floor, weaving through a maze of four-top tables with mismatched chairs and tabletop jukeboxes. So far, everyone Kenzie had met in town had been warm and friendly despite her being a Yankee. She didn't doubt Cathy would live up to Mel's hype.

Mel made the introductions then the two of them slid into the opposite side of the booth from the donut shop owner. Kenzie had expected someone as big as a barn, but Cathy was slim and absolutely gorgeous with a smile to put anyone instantly at ease.

"It's nice to officially meet you," Kenzie said. "I've been in your shop nearly every day this week."

"Really?" Cathy's smile grew brighter. "I hope you're addicted." She directed her next comment to Mel. "I hear I've lost one of my best customers."

Melody adjusted her purse on the seat between them. "If you're talking about Henry, it's temporary. He wants to see a little bit of the world while he still can." She passed out menus from the holder next to the window. "Hank's worried about his dad traveling alone, but nothing we said was enough to convince him to stay."

Cathy opened her menu. "I understand where Henry's coming from. If I were in his shoes, I'd do the same thing. I'm sure glad he found me a replacement for the lost business though." She winked at Kenzie.

"I don't know how many donuts Mr. Travis bought, but I'll do my best to keep up." It wouldn't be difficult. Everything she'd tried at The Donut Hole had been to die for. She needed to find a gym soon, or she'd be a dumpling in no time.

"Well, well, well. Would you look at that?"

Kenzie glanced up from her menu to see what Cathy was talking about. A trio of sexy men walked single file past the counter seating complete with a view of the kitchen pass-through to the circular booth in the back corner of the café. Tall, dark, and brooding, they each had a distinctive style, yet they moved as one cohesive unit. Any woman who didn't sit up and take notice of such a fine display of manhood needed hormone supplements. Her lady parts were doing just fine—thank you very much. No assistance needed. Especially where the one in the middle was concerned. *Lord have mercy. It's* him.

Even from this distance, she could see flecks of white paint in his hair. His tattered, paint-splattered T-shirt and equally ratty jeans hugged and defined every muscle of his lean body. Not exactly the urban chic guy she'd hooked up with in the Philly airport—but it *was* him. No doubt about it. Her core melted as the visceral memories of what she'd done with the man incinerated the mental box she'd placed them in, scorching her from the inside out. Heart hammering, Kenzie ducked back behind her menu, hoping against hope he hadn't seen her. *What is he doing here anyway?* The city girl in her immediately wondered if he'd followed her, but she immediately swatted the thought away like she would a pesky fly. A covert peek told her the guys he was with today were the same ones he'd met at the airport. What were the odds they were just passing through Willowbrook today and stopped for a bite to eat? Her gut told her it wasn't the case, and Mel confirmed it.

"It's the brothers Grim."

Kenzie's gaze snapped to her friend. "Grimm? As in the fairy tales?"

"Their real last name is Ingram," Melody clarified.

"Grim as in ghastly, gloomy, and glum," Cathy offered.

"They live here?" *Please don't say yes.*

"'Fraid so." Cathy closed her menu, set it back in the holder then drummed her fingers on the table's red Formica surface. "They haven't always been grim."

"You know them?" Of course Cathy knew them. If there was one thing she'd figured out in the week or so she'd been a resident of Willowbrook, it was that everyone knew everyone else. She didn't know how long she was going to live here, but if it was longer than another seven days, her path was going to cross with his. Best to know what she was up against, so she could avoid running into him as much as possible.

"Do they have names?" She couldn't go on calling him Hot Guy from the airport.

Mel set her menu aside. "Jake, Will, and Rick. Jake's the oldest and Rick's the youngest."

Instinct, or something more, made Kenzie glance toward the brothers. Her breath caught in her throat. The brothers were looking their way. The one on the far left of the semicircle booth clenched his jaw before returning his gaze to the menu he held open in front of him. Opposite him, another Grim brother shook his head slightly then flipped his menu open. Kenzie's gaze fell on the one sandwiched between the other two. His dark gaze met hers, and, instantly, she knew he knew. Just like in the airport, her brain registered danger, but her body responded like she'd stuck her finger in a light socket while standing in a puddle of murky water.

Oh, he was a dangerous one all right. It was there, in those dark orbs that both threatened and promised with a single look. His broad shoulders filled the space allotted him by his brothers. Was his hair longer, or was it her imagination? She clenched her hands into fists as her fingers itched to see if the dark strands were as soft as they appeared. He'd had a bit of scruff on his jaw when she last saw him, but she was beginning to think he didn't own a razor. The style was sexy as hell on him. Damn. She had it bad if she didn't care he'd gone from GQ model to blue-collar heathen. She still wanted him more than she should. More than was prudent. More than was sane.

Mel waved a hand in front of Kenzie's face, forcing her to break contact. "Earth to MacKenzie. Earth to MacKenzie. Come in, Kenzie."

Another quick glance told her the game was over. Hot Guy hid behind his menu. With a silent sigh, she focused on her lunch companions. "What? Can't a girl look?"

Cathy leaned across the table. "You won't get anywhere with those guys. No one ever does."

Kenzie raised one eyebrow. "Do you speak from experience?" *Please don't tell me she's been with him.* Kenzie didn't want him. She really didn't, no matter what her lower body was telling her. But the idea of any woman having him, especially one she'd just met, unleashed something primal and possessive within. What was it about him that made her go cavewoman?

"No," Cathy insisted. "But I know others who have tried to put a smile on one of those faces. Every single one ended in disaster."

Recalling the intensity of her recent Grim stare-down, she thought smiles might be overrated. There was something to be said for determination and commitment to a goal. Hot Guy had both in spades. He'd proved as much in Philly. "How so? Details, please."

Uttering a long sigh, Cathy sat back. "The stories aren't mine to tell, but I can say any attempts to reform Jake and Rick have been unsuccessful. It's as if they don't want to be happy. And from what I hear, since Will returned last week, he fits right into the family mold."

A waitress wearing a pink-polyester dress, complete with a white collar and the pointed tips of a fake handkerchief poking from a breast pocket, stopped at their table, pencil and green order pad at the ready. A white oval name tag said, "Penny."

"Hey, Mel," Penny said.

"Hi, Pen." Mel gestured across the table. "This is the new PR person we hired for BlackWing. MacKenzie Carlysle, Penny Michaels."

Penny's gaze swung to Kenzie. "Nice to meet you." Tossing her head to indicate the brothers Grim, she waggled her eyebrows. "Saw you checking them out. They're our version of Mt. Rushmore. Bigger than life but cold and hard as stone."

She could see the hard-as-stone bit—and personally testify to the accuracy of the statement in regard to one of them—but cold? No way. She recalled the feel of Will gripping her hips as he drove into her over and over again. After he'd left, she'd checked to see if he'd branded her and been somewhat sad to see he hadn't. Not in any physical way, but he'd imprinted on her brain. As much as she'd tried, she hadn't been able to get him out of her mind. She fanned herself with the menu as she smiled up at the waitress. "And not easily accessible?"

"Many have tried. None have succeeded."

"Told you so," Cathy smirked.

Kenzie laughed. There wasn't a thing she could do about her present situation, so it was time to change the subject. "I'll have a cheeseburger, fries, and a diet soda." She placed her menu back in the rack.

"Excellent choice." Penny asked the requisite questions to complete the order then turned to Kenzie's lunch companions. "The usual?"

"Chicken Caesar salad and sweet tea," Mel confirmed.

Cathy took one last look at the menu then, with a sigh, slapped it shut. "Who am I kidding? I'll have the usual—the cheddar bacon burger and sweet potato fries."

"Diet soda?"

"Yep," Cathy said.

Penny scribbled on her pad then tucked her pencil behind her ear before nodding discreetly at the table across the way. "They weren't always grim," she said. "Cathy can tell you. She dated Rick in high school." Penny cruised over to take the brothers' orders as if she hadn't just tossed a flash/bang grenade in the middle of their table.

Once Kenzie picked her jaw up off the floor, she narrowed her eyes at the woman who'd, moments ago, denied any intimate knowledge of the brothers.

"You dated Rick in high school?" She leaned in closer.

"Yes, I dated Rick Ingram," she said, sounding anything but happy about it. "I went out with Hank Travis a couple of times, too." She flashed an apologetic smile in Melody's direction.

Mel patted Cathy's hand. "I thank you for not sleeping with my future husband when you had the chance."

"You're welcome, though if the offer had included better accommodations and/or a ring, I might have made a different decision."

Mel leaned over and half-whispered to Kenzie. "He offered her a romp in the bed of his pickup." She rolled her eyes. "Can't imagine why she passed on the offer. Can you?"

"Nope." Squelching an urge to laugh out loud, Kenzie shook her head. "Sounds like a pretty good offer, knowing the source." Melody's husband, Hank Travis, besides being Kenzie's new boss, was sexy as hell. Not to mention he was the drummer for BlackWing, one of the hottest rock bands in the country.

"You didn't know Hank then," Cathy said. "Who knew he'd turn out to be a rock star?"

Melody relaxed in the booth. "He asks the same question all the time. But it's what he was meant to do."

Kenzie had to agree with Mel's assessment. Hank Travis was crazy talented. "Enough about Hank." She cocked her head toward the table full of single hunks. "Which one of those is Rick?"

"The one on the right," Cathy said without turning to check.

Kenzie could just see him past Penny's polyester-clad hips. Broad shoulders like his brothers. Hair way too long for convention. His clean-shaven jaw resembled the stone monument Penny had referenced. Thanks to the way the waitress held her arms while she wrote on her order pad, Kenzie couldn't see Rick's eyes, but she could see his hand, clenched in a tight fist, sitting atop a tree-trunk thigh. *Damn.*

"You let *him* get away?"

"I didn't *let* him do anything," she said. "It was his dream to go to the Naval Academy. When he got in, he left and never looked back."

Oh, there was a story there, one she fully intended to hear—in great detail—later on. For now, she'd settle for the broader picture.

"So tell me," Kenzie said. "What happened to make the brothers so glum?"

"Don't know, exactly." Cathy slipped her flatware from its napkin cocoon. Smoothing the white embossed paper over her lap, she continued. "Jake is the oldest. He was a few years ahead of me. William graduated a year ahead of me in Hank's class. Rick's my age, and the youngest of the bunch. There's little more than a year between each of them. Stairsteps, as my mom would say.

"Their mom passed away, cancer, I think, when Rick and I were in middle school. No. Wait. It was our last year of elementary school. I remember because he missed a lot of classes and had to go to summer school to make up the time. My mom was the teacher that summer. She'd come home with a story to tell almost every day about something Rick had done or said."

"He was acting out?"

"I don't know. Maybe." Cathy moved the cheap knife and fork from the left of her placemat to the right.

Kenzie and Melody shared a look, reaching an unspoken agreement to pry the rest of the story out of the woman with a bottle of wine and chocolate later on. Right then, Kenzie wanted all the intelligence she could get on the other two brothers, particularly the one in the middle.

Penny arrived with their food, temporarily distracting them from the subject of the Ingram brothers. Kenzie groaned as she chewed and swallowed her first bite. "Oh. My. God. This has got to be the best cheeseburger I've ever eaten," she said, wiping greasy drippings off her chin.

Melody laughed. "Keep it down, girlfriend. People are going to wonder what's going on over here!"

Kenzie swirled a thick French fry in a puddle of ketchup and brought it to her lips, painting them with the sauce before opening her mouth to take the fried spud in. "Mmm. This is good, too. Soooo good," she crooned.

"Stop it." Mel blushed at the same time she kicked Kenzie under the table. "People are staring."

"What people?" Glancing around, her gaze met and locked with eyes belonging to Hot Guy.

Oh god. Staring wasn't even close to the right word for the way he was watching her. Involuntarily licking her lips, she swallowed hard past her heart which had lodged itself in her throat and forced her attention back to the plate of food she no longer wanted. Yes, she was hungry, but not for food. Everything she wanted was on the other side of the restaurant, and if looks could convey a message, he wanted her, too.

Trying her best to appear unaffected by his gaze, Kenzie popped another fry into her mouth and washed it past the now-massive obstruction in her throat with a swig of her soda. She turned to Cathy. "You were telling me about the brothers Grim. Did the other two go into the military as well?"

Cathy took a quick sip from her glass. "Nope. Jake, he's the one on the left, is a lawyer. Took over their dad's practice here in town a couple of years ago after their dad passed away. William—the one in the middle—went to college in New York to study art. He'd always been the quiet one of the bunch, but at least he used to smile. I thought he was doing well, selling paintings left and right." She shrugged. "Don't know what happened, but word on the street is he's back to stay."

Kenzie froze, the straw sticking out of her soda just a few centimeters from her lips. A hodge-podge of memories flashed through her brain. Paintings. Ingram. The sexy guy on the cover of the New Yorker magazine. Her vision clouded, and she forced herself to breathe as the impossible became highly likely. Her hand shook as she placed her beverage back on the table. "Wait just one minute."

She fought for enough breath to voice what she was almost certain was the truth. It defied explanation but was undoubtedly another chapter in the shit-show her life had become. Leaning in, she whispered, "You're telling me, the man sitting over there—William Ingram—is W.H. Ingram? The artist?"

Before either woman could answer, the images flitting around in her brain coalesced into one.

Oh. My. God.

I had airport sex with W. H. Ingram.

Did he know who I was when he accepted my offer? Suddenly, it all made sense. He was way out of her league when it came to sexual partners. She'd known it then and hoped for the best—and been somewhat stunned when he'd agreed to a hookup. *And why wouldn't he? I fucked him over, and he'd returned the favor. Those glorious moments in the Philly airport were a revenge fuck.*

Thanks to the giant lump still in her throat, Kenzie was able to stifle the groan of misery bubbling up from her gut.

Could my life get any more fucked-up?

"I seem to recall he signs his paintings as W. H.," Mel said. "I can ask him if you want?"

Apparently, it could. "No!" Kenzie recoiled at the sound of her voice raised beyond the acceptable level.

"Or, better yet, I'll look at the one in Hank's office."

Kenzie forced wind past her vocal chords. "Hank has a W.H. Ingram painting in his office?"

Mel nodded, her expression one of concern. "Yes," she replied cautiously. "I bought it from Sunny's gallery in New York a few years ago. That's how we met. I saw a painting in the window and bought it for Hank."

"Did you buy it because Will Ingram painted it?"

"I didn't know anything about the artist when I purchased it. I was walking down the sidewalk and saw it in the window of her gallery. It reminded me of Willowbrook, so I bought it for Hank, and a few others for myself. It wasn't until much later we realized it *was* Willowbrook and Will had painted it. Hank was impressed. He's been trying to buy another of Will's paintings but hasn't had any luck."

No. He wouldn't have any luck finding one unless the man had a secret stash of paintings no one knew about. *Like the ones that have gone missing?* She mentally shook her head. He hadn't taken his own paintings. She was 99 percent certain. He'd been a victim of two ruthless people, just as she had been, for reasons she still didn't understand and might never know. She recalled the paint splatters she'd seen on his clothes when he walked in. Had he resumed painting? The art world would be a better place if he had, but she'd heard he'd vowed he'd never lift a brush again. That kind of hurt was something she could relate to. As much as she loved the art world, she didn't want to go back there. She had this opportunity to work in the music industry, and she was going to give it everything she had.

The part she'd played in the demise of Will's career was a small one, but it weighed heavy on her shoulders. She owed him an apology, but, after the revenge fuck, she doubted he'd be interested in anything she had to say.

She could at least explain why Hank couldn't find another W.H. Ingram to purchase. "He quit painting."

"I didn't know. Hank will be disappointed. Will is a talented artist."

"I agree." Cathy ate another of her fries. "I've seen the painting you're talking about. It's absolutely gorgeous. It should be in a museum."

"It probably should be." Sorrow laced Kenzie's words. "He's really good. Hang on to the painting, Mel. It's probably worth a lot more than what you paid for it, and when your daughter is grown, it will be worth a fortune."

"I don't care what its monetary value is. It's special to Hank and to me. We'll never part with it."

Kenzie pushed her plate away. "As delicious as this is, I can't eat another bite."

Cathy gaped at her. "You hardly touched it."

"I know. My eyes were bigger than my stomach, I guess." She took a couple of bills out of her wallet and placed them on the table. "I need to get a few things from the drugstore. Take your time." She scooted out of the booth and stood, grateful her legs held. "Meet me in front of the hardware store when you're through?"

Both women seemed perplexed at the abrupt change in her demeanor, but readily agreed to meet at the prescribed location midway between the diner and the drugstore. Kenzie squared her shoulders and bolted for the door as fast as she could without making a scene. With every step, she felt William H. Ingram's gaze burning a hole through her.

She'd deserved the revenge fuck. She deserved his hatred. She just wished there was some way to make up to him for what she'd done.

CHAPTER SIX

Will sensed *something* from the moment he'd stepped into the diner with his brothers. Once he'd located the source of the feeling, he couldn't take his eyes off the woman. *What the hell is she doing here? Is she following me? Is she a reporter?* The possibility punched him in the chest and stole his breath. But what would she be doing with those two?

He knew the ladies sitting across the booth from her. Cathy owned The Donut Hole a few doors down from here, and had been in Rick's graduating class, a year behind him. He'd known her most of his life. The other woman had moved to Willowbrook a couple of years ago. She'd been Melody Harper then, just a reporter for the local newspaper. The whole town had been stunned to find out she was the only child of Rock and Roll legend Earl Ravenswood. Her father's music as lead guitarist for RavensBlood had been the soundtrack for his youth and inspiration for Hank Travis, the man Melody had married. *Melody used to be a reporter. Is that how she knew the woman from the airport?*

Shit.

He hadn't told anyone except the police where he was going when he left New York. Had they leaked the information to one of the investigative reporters who'd sniffed around the case at the beginning — or worse — to one of the tabloids?

His brain cycled back to the airport bar and the way she'd approached him. Not the other way around. God, she must have thought he was an easy mark, and he had been. Fortunately for him,